The SNOWCAT PRINCE

AN ONI PRESS PUBLICATION

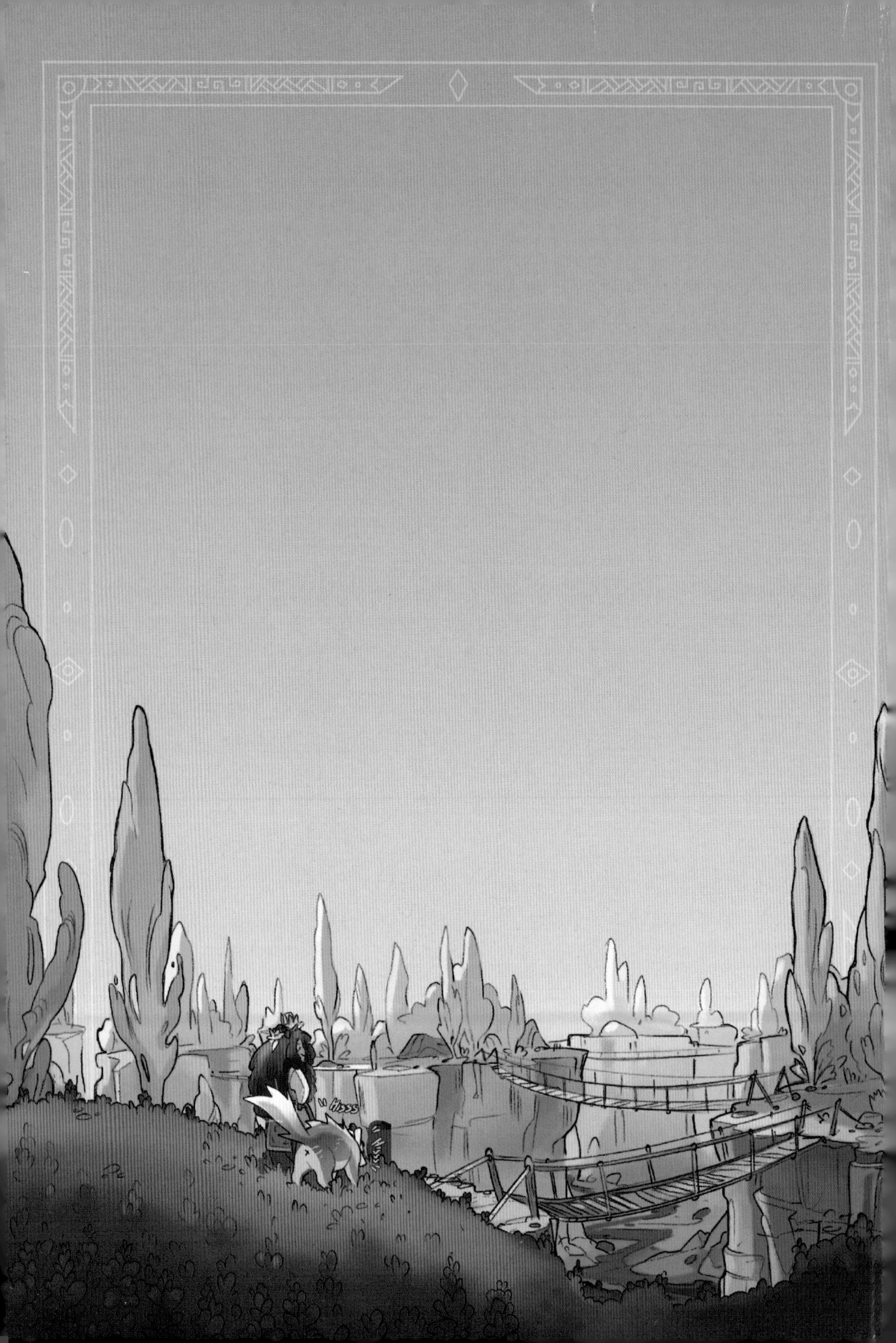
Hisss
Hissss

The SNOWCAT PRINCE

DINA NORLUND

Written and illustrated by Dina Norlund
Lettered by Crank
Oni Press edition edited by Grace Scheipeter
Designed by Hilary Thompson
Original edition edited by Kate Nascimento

Published by Oni-Lion Forge Publishing Group, LLC.

Steve Ellis, e.v.p. of games & operations
Brad Rooks, director of operations
Katie Sainz, director of marketing
Holly Aitchison, consumer marketing manager
Troy Look, director of design & production
Angie Knowles, production manager
Sarah Rockwell, graphic designer
Carey Soucy, graphic designer
Hilary Thompson, graphic designer
Vincent Kukua, digital prepress technician
Chris Cerasi, managing editor
Grace Scheipeter, senior editor
Gabriel Granillo, editor
Bess Pallares, editor
Desiree Rodriguez, editor
Zack Soto, editor
Ben Eisner, game developer
Sara Harding, executive assistant
Jung Lee, logistics coordinator
Kuian Kellum, warehouse assistant

Joe Nozemack, publisher emeritus

1319 SE Martin Luther King Jr. Blvd.
Suite 240
Portland, OR 97214

onipress.com
facebook.com/onipress
twitter.com/onipress
instagram.com/onipress

DINANORLUND.COM | @DINANORLUND

First Edition: March 2023
ISBN: 978-1-63715-198-3
eISBN: 978-1-63715-858-6

Printing numbers:
1 2 3 4 5 6 7 8 9 10

Library of Congress Control Number: 2022946493

Printed in China.

10 YEARS EARLIER...

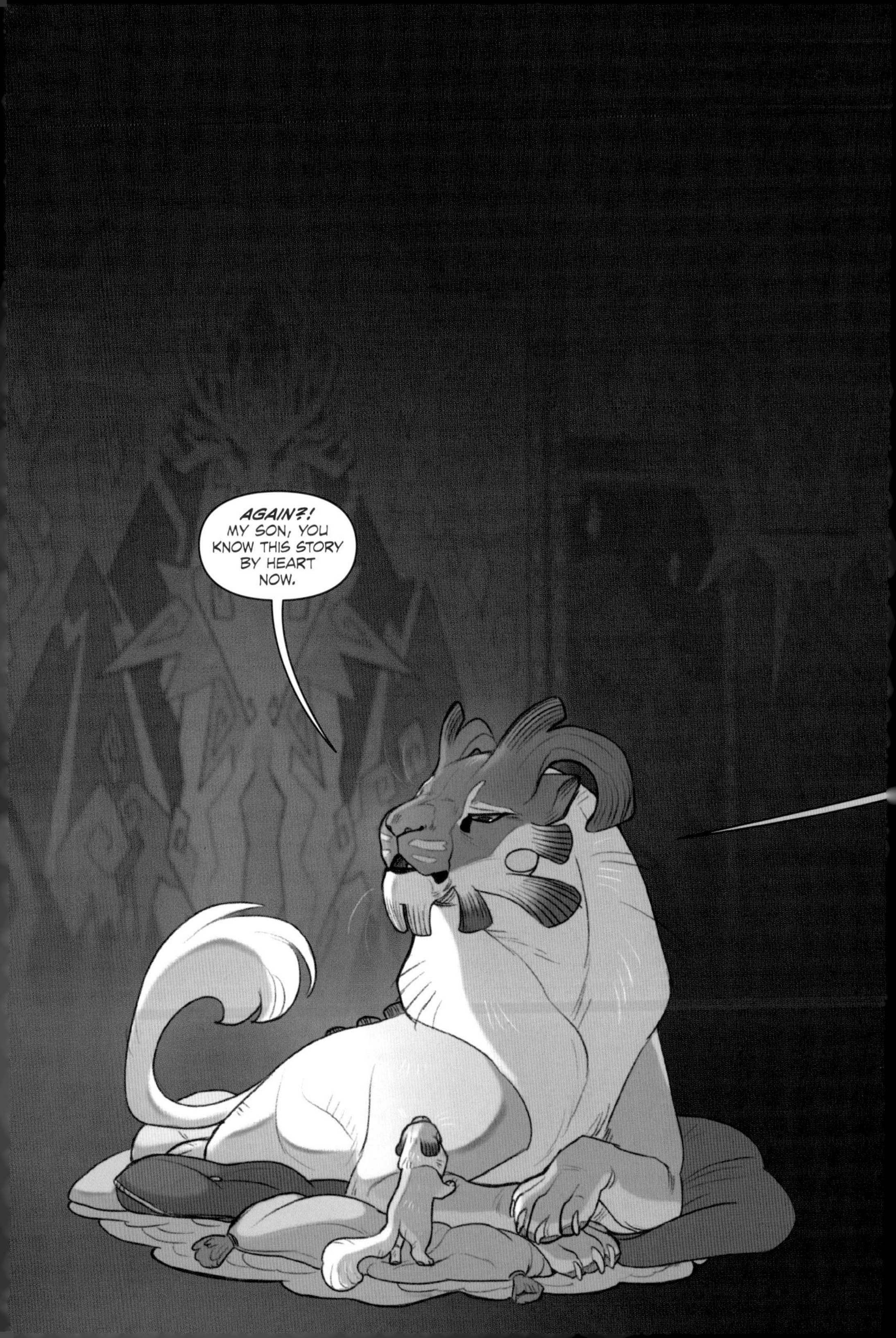
AGAIN?! MY SON, YOU KNOW THIS STORY BY HEART NOW.

OH, WELL... HAVE IT YOUR WAY, LITTLE PRINCE!
I'LL TELL YOU THE STORY AGAIN LIKE I'VE DONE BEFORE, JUST LIKE MY FATHER TOLD ME WHEN I WAS YOUR AGE...

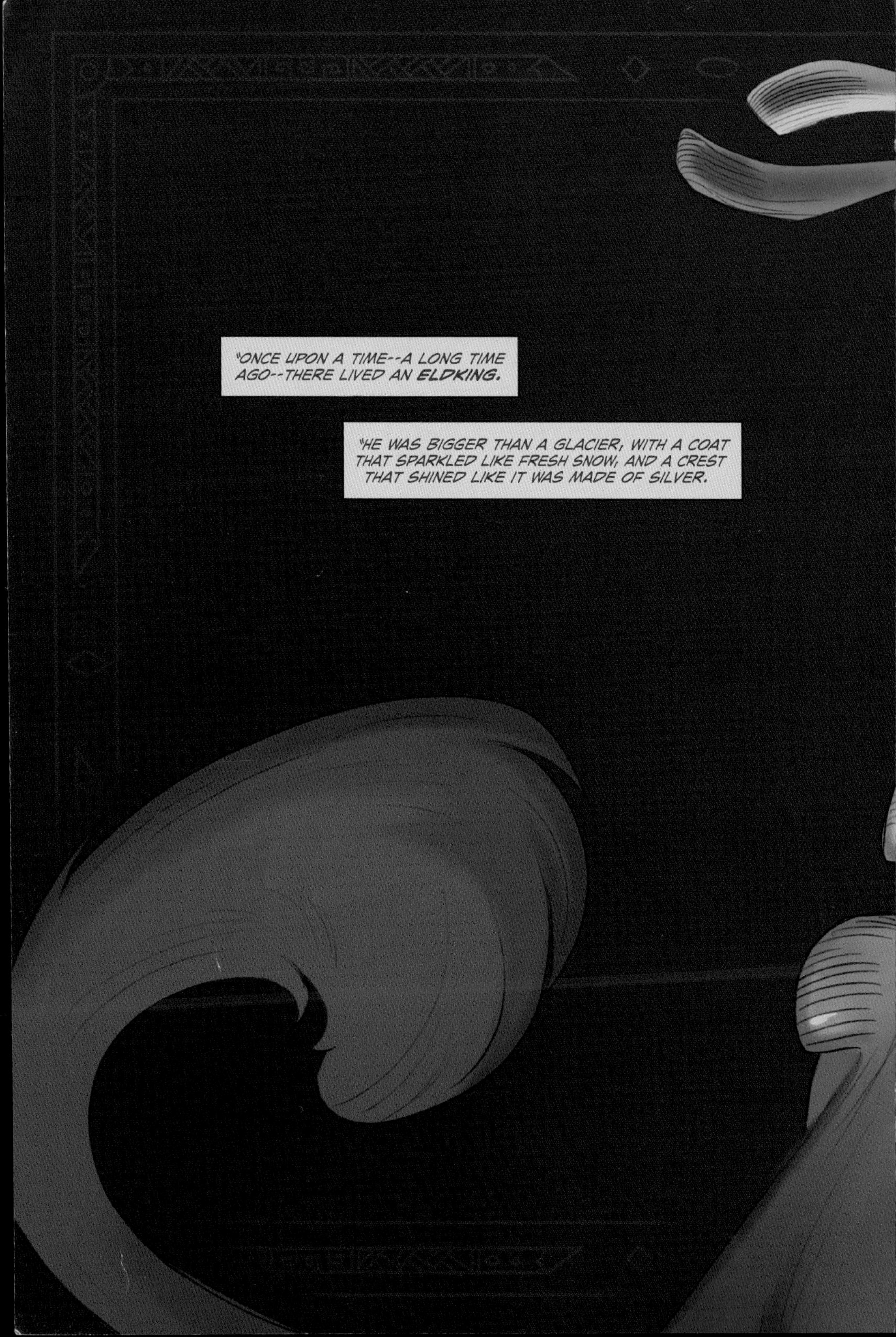
"ONCE UPON A TIME--A LONG TIME AGO--THERE LIVED AN ELDKING.
"HE WAS BIGGER THAN A GLACIER, WITH A COAT THAT SPARKLED LIKE FRESH SNOW, AND A CREST THAT SHINED LIKE IT WAS MADE OF SILVER.

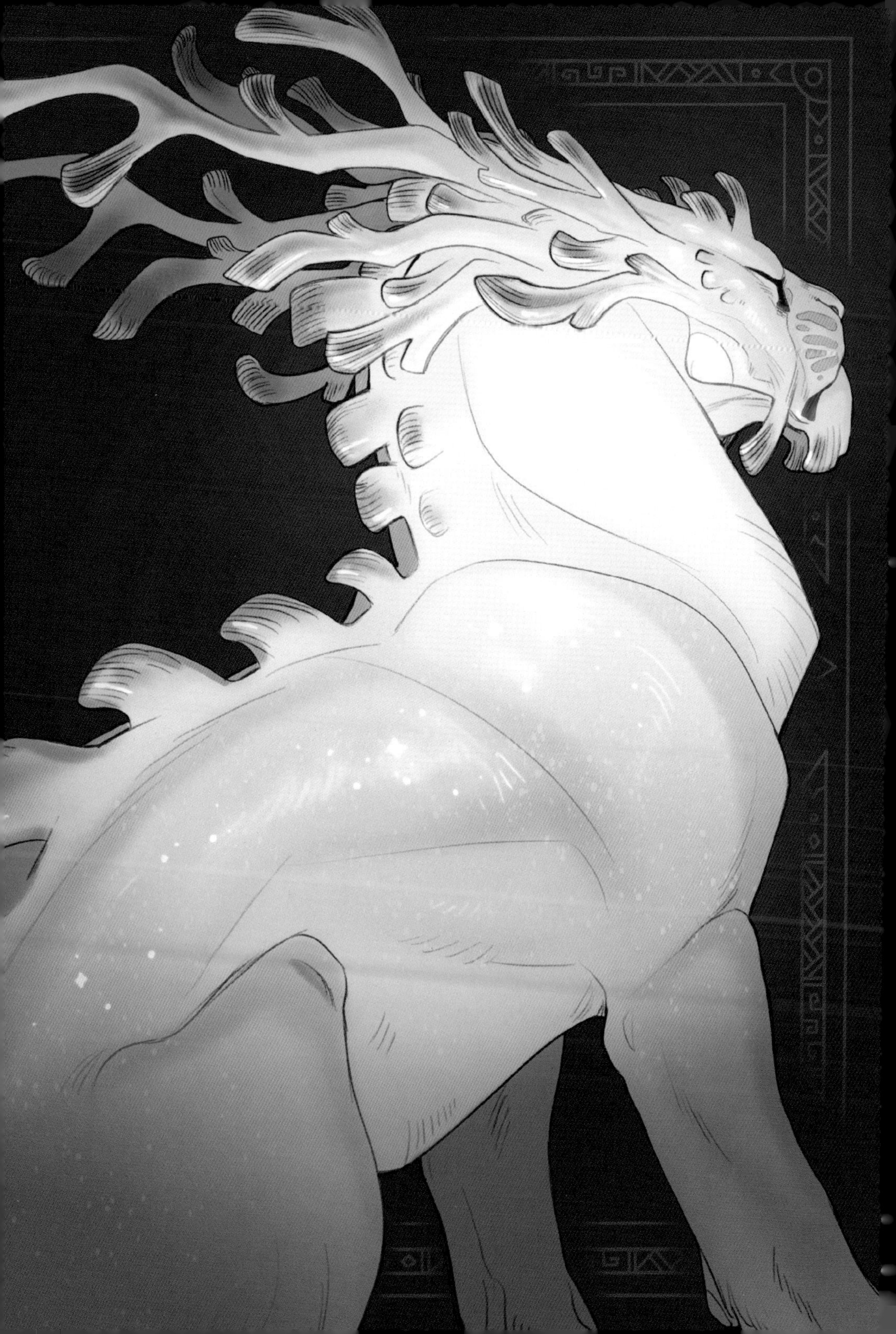

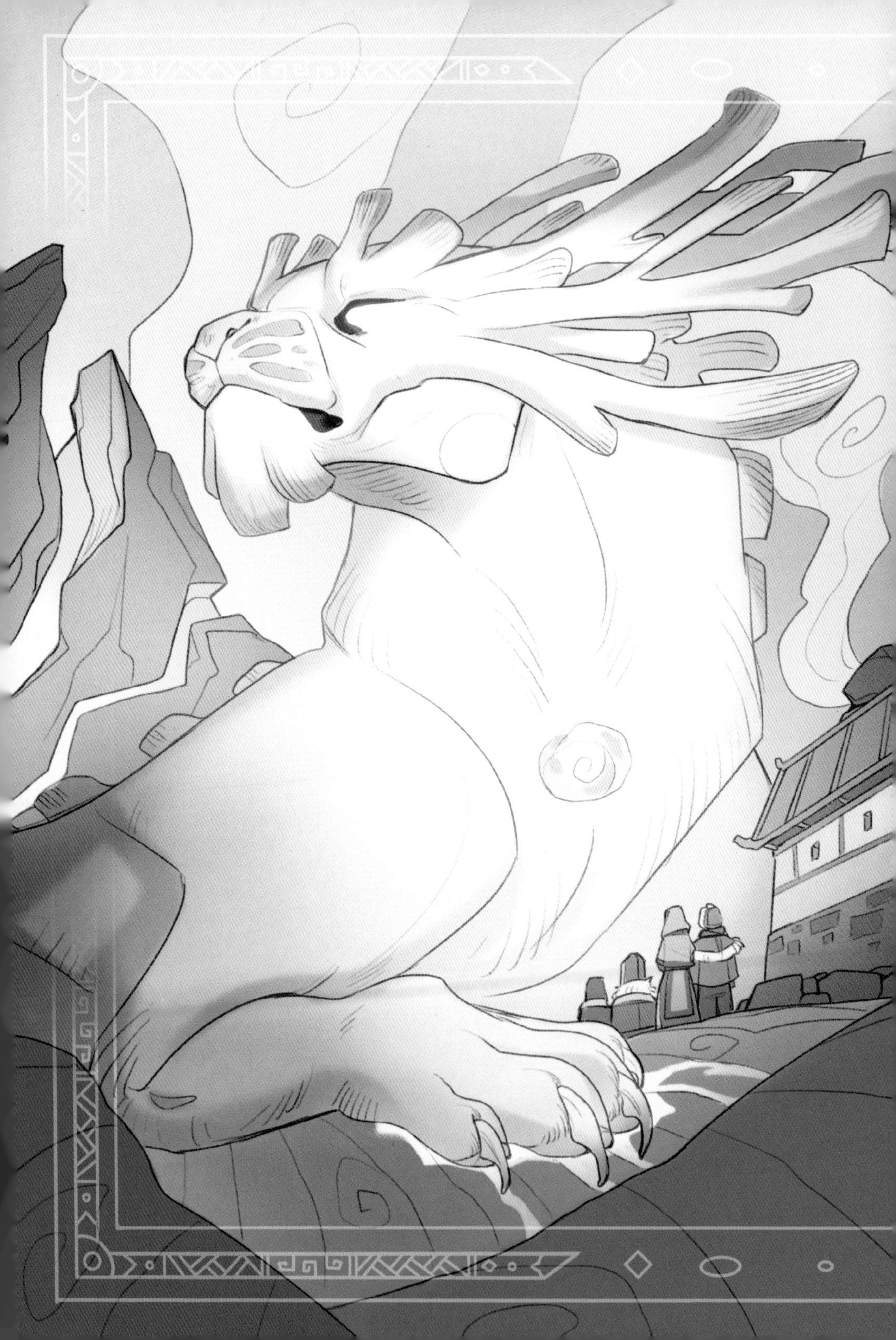

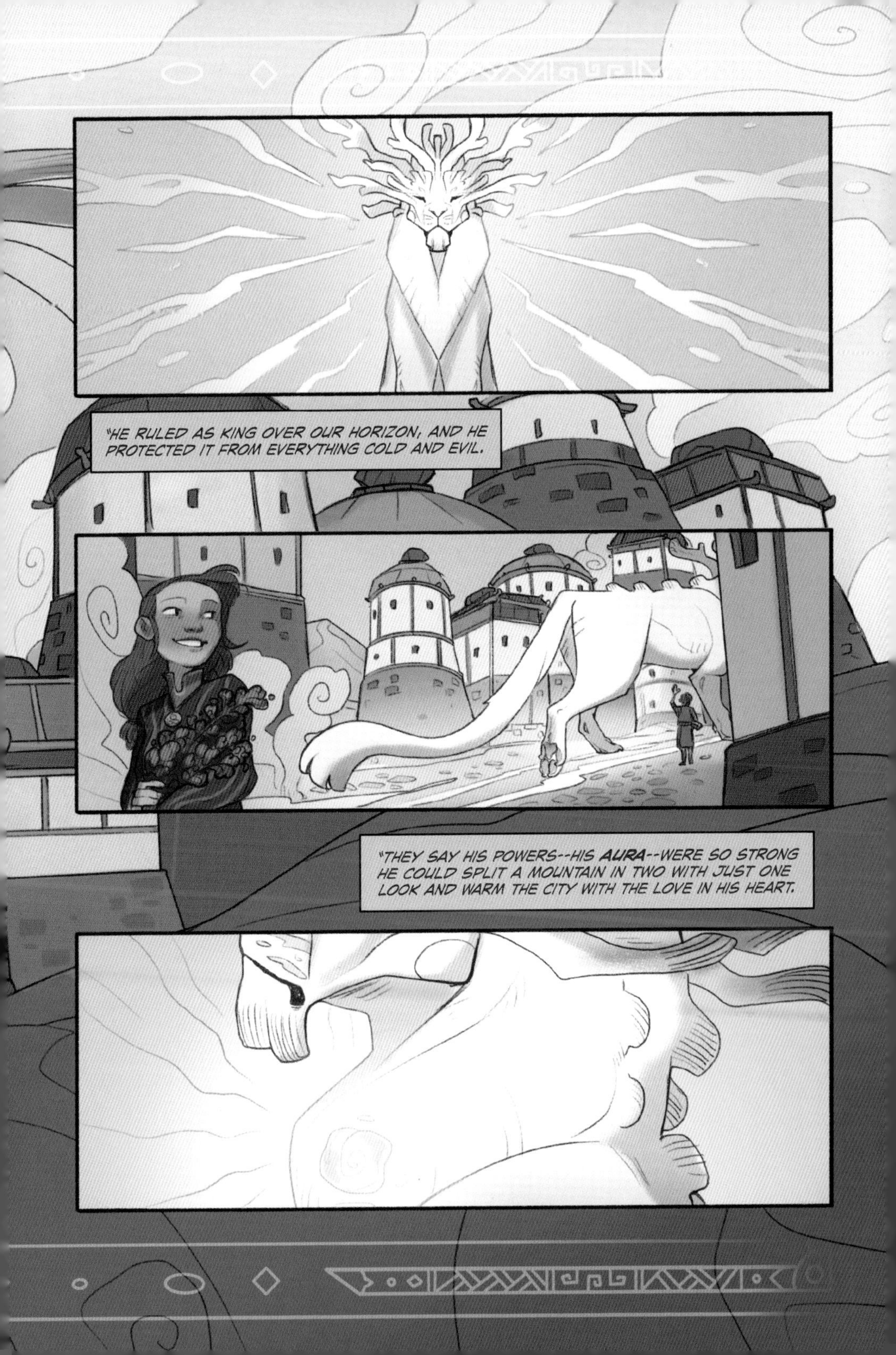
"HE RULED AS KING OVER OUR HORIZON, AND HE PROTECTED IT FROM EVERYTHING COLD AND EVIL.
"THEY SAY HIS POWERS--HIS AURA--WERE SO STRONG HE COULD SPLIT A MOUNTAIN IN TWO WITH JUST ONE LOOK AND WARM THE CITY WITH THE LOVE IN HIS HEART.

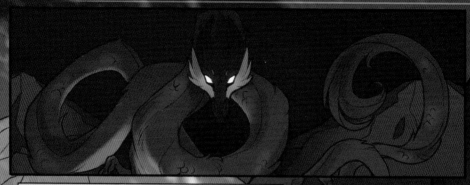

"THE ONLY LIVING CREATURES THAT WERE ALMOST AS POWERFUL AS OUR ELDKING WERE THE **SANDFOXES.** THE EVIL FOXES WANTED OUR KING'S POWERS TO CONTROL ALL THREE HORIZONS.

"SLOWLY, THE FOXES BEGAN TO INVADE OUR HORIZON WITH THEIR **BAD AURA.** THEY MADE THE WINTERS SO COLD AND FROZEN THAT NO PLANTS COULD GROW AND NO ANIMALS COULD THRIVE.

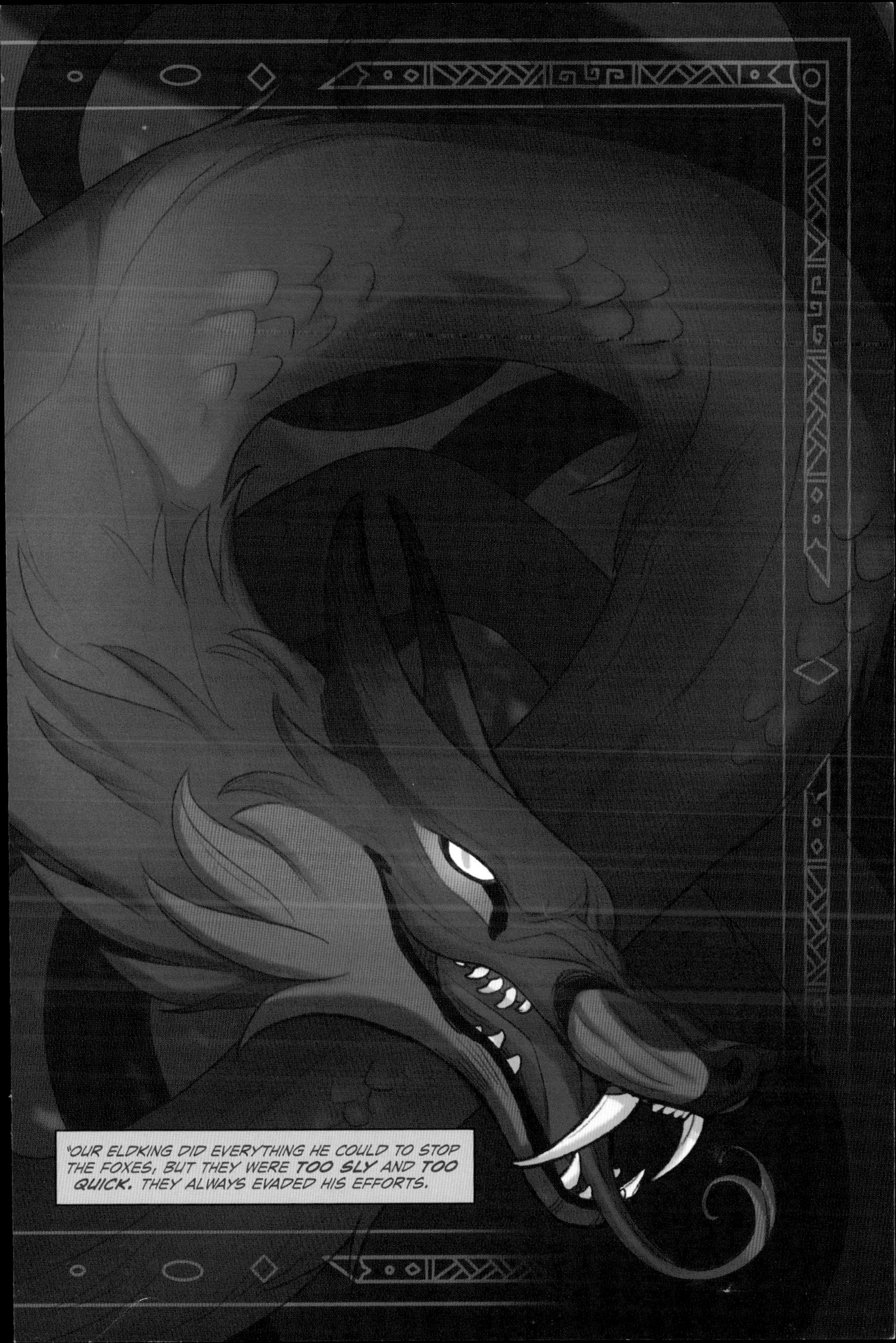
"OUR ELDKING DID EVERYTHING HE COULD TO STOP THE FOXES, BUT THEY WERE **TOO SLY** AND **TOO QUICK.** THEY ALWAYS EVADED HIS EFFORTS.

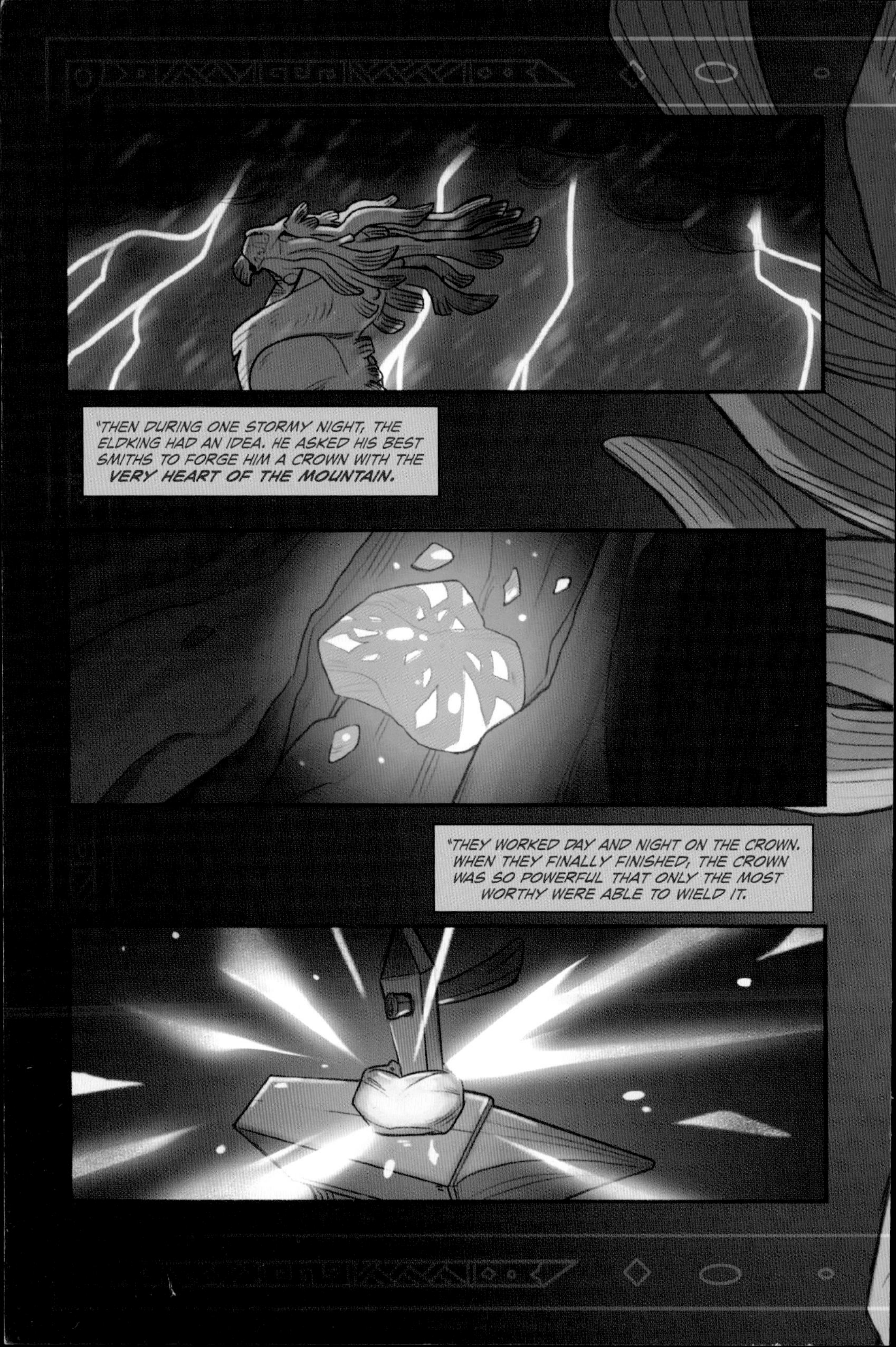
"THEN DURING ONE STORMY NIGHT, THE ELDKING HAD AN IDEA. HE ASKED HIS BEST SMITHS TO FORGE HIM A CROWN WITH THE VERY HEART OF THE MOUNTAIN.
"THEY WORKED DAY AND NIGHT ON THE CROWN. WHEN THEY FINALLY FINISHED, THE CROWN WAS SO POWERFUL THAT ONLY THE MOST WORTHY WERE ABLE TO WIELD IT.

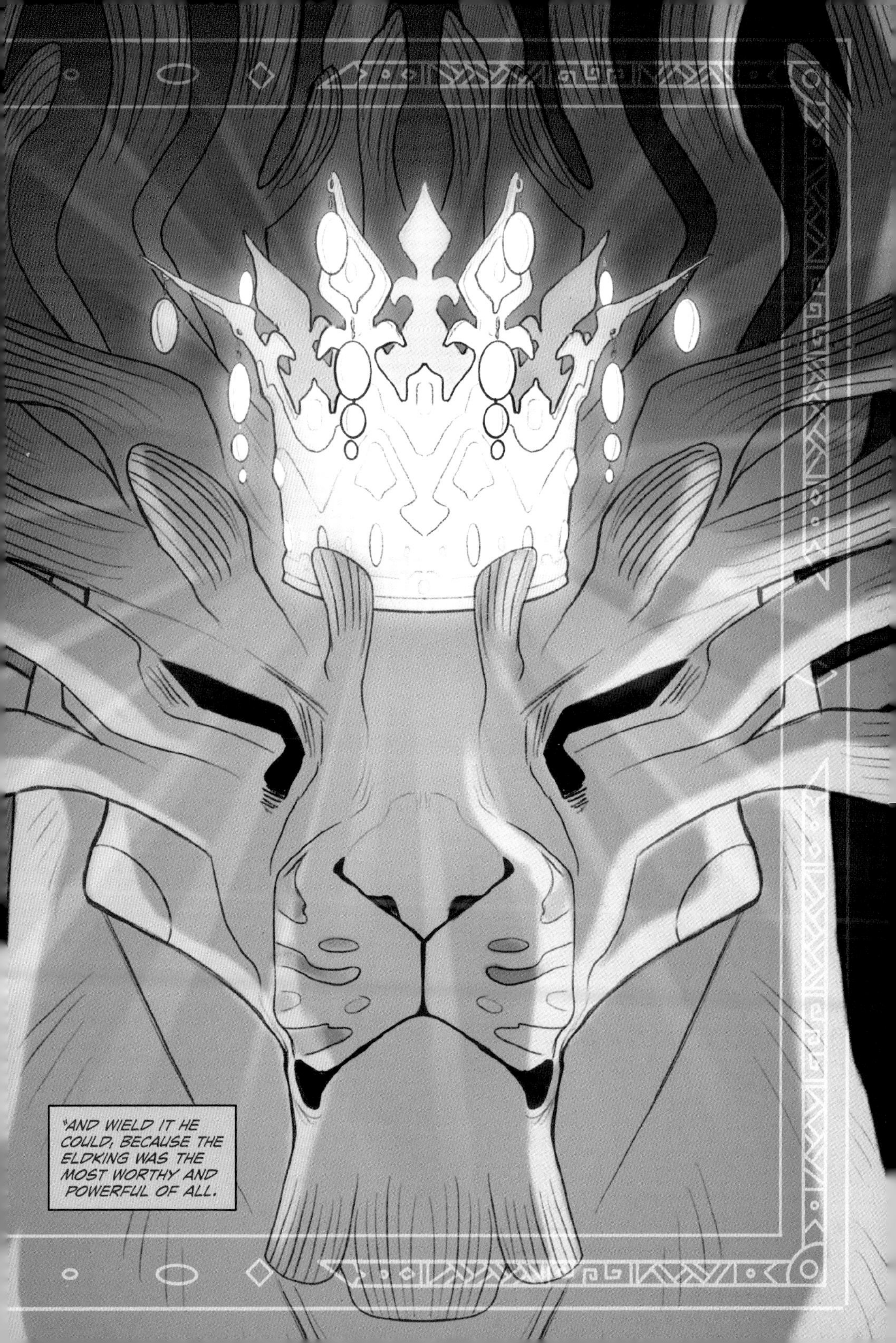
"AND WIELD IT HE COULD, BECAUSE THE ELDKING WAS THE MOST WORTHY AND POWERFUL OF ALL.

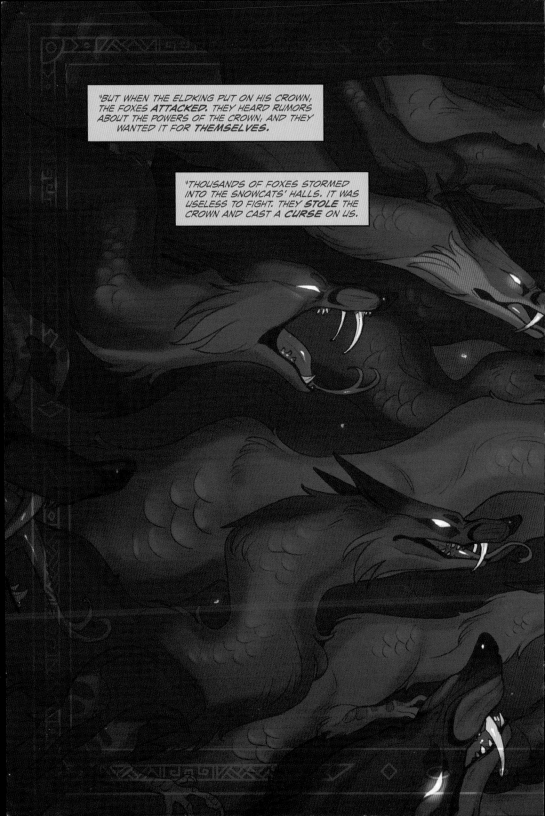

"BUT WHEN THE ELDKING PUT ON HIS CROWN, THE FOXES **ATTACKED.** THEY HEARD RUMORS ABOUT THE POWERS OF THE CROWN, AND THEY WANTED IT FOR **THEMSELVES.**

"THOUSANDS OF FOXES STORMED INTO THE SNOWCATS' HALLS. IT WAS USELESS TO FIGHT. THEY **STOLE** THE CROWN AND CAST A **CURSE** ON US.

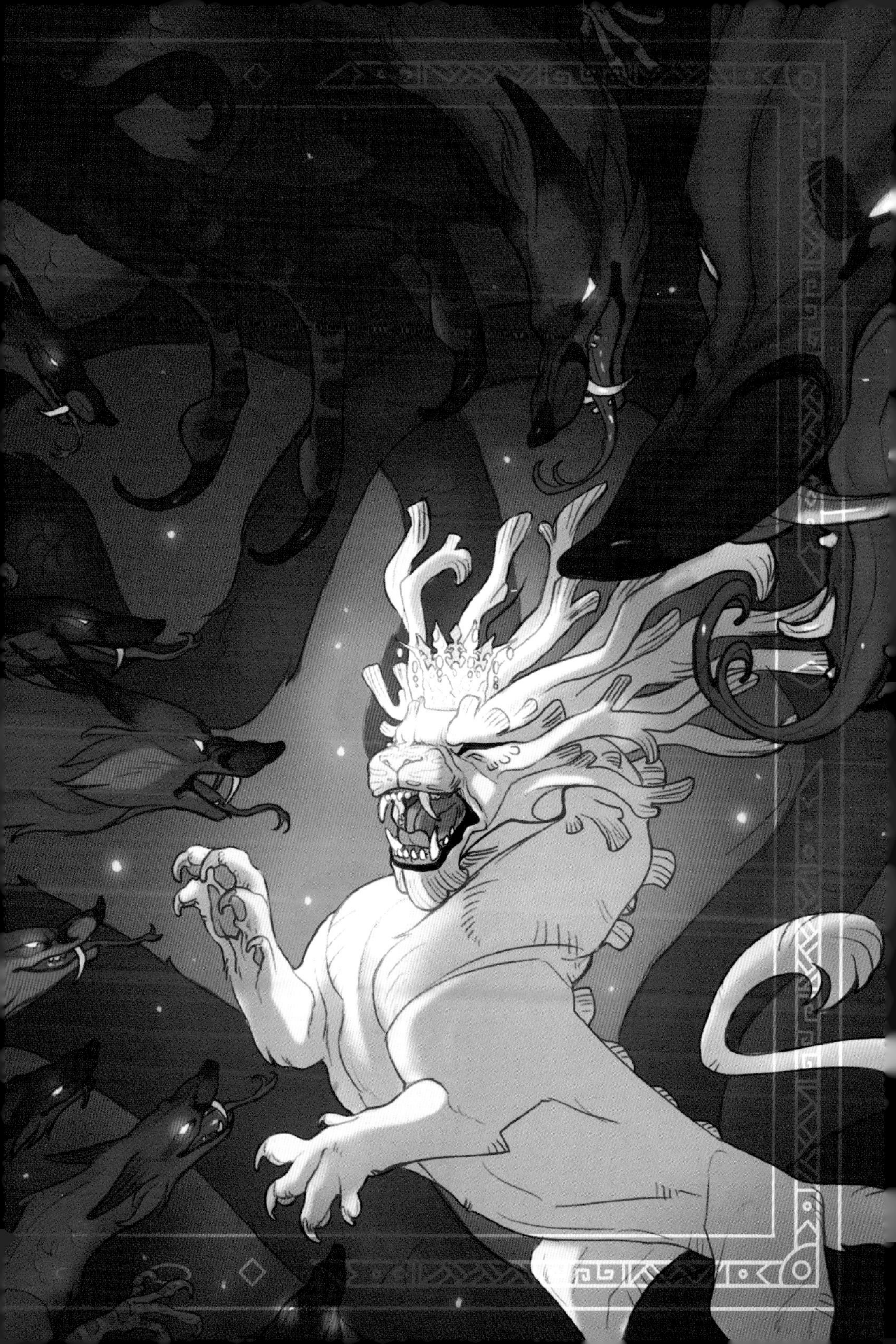

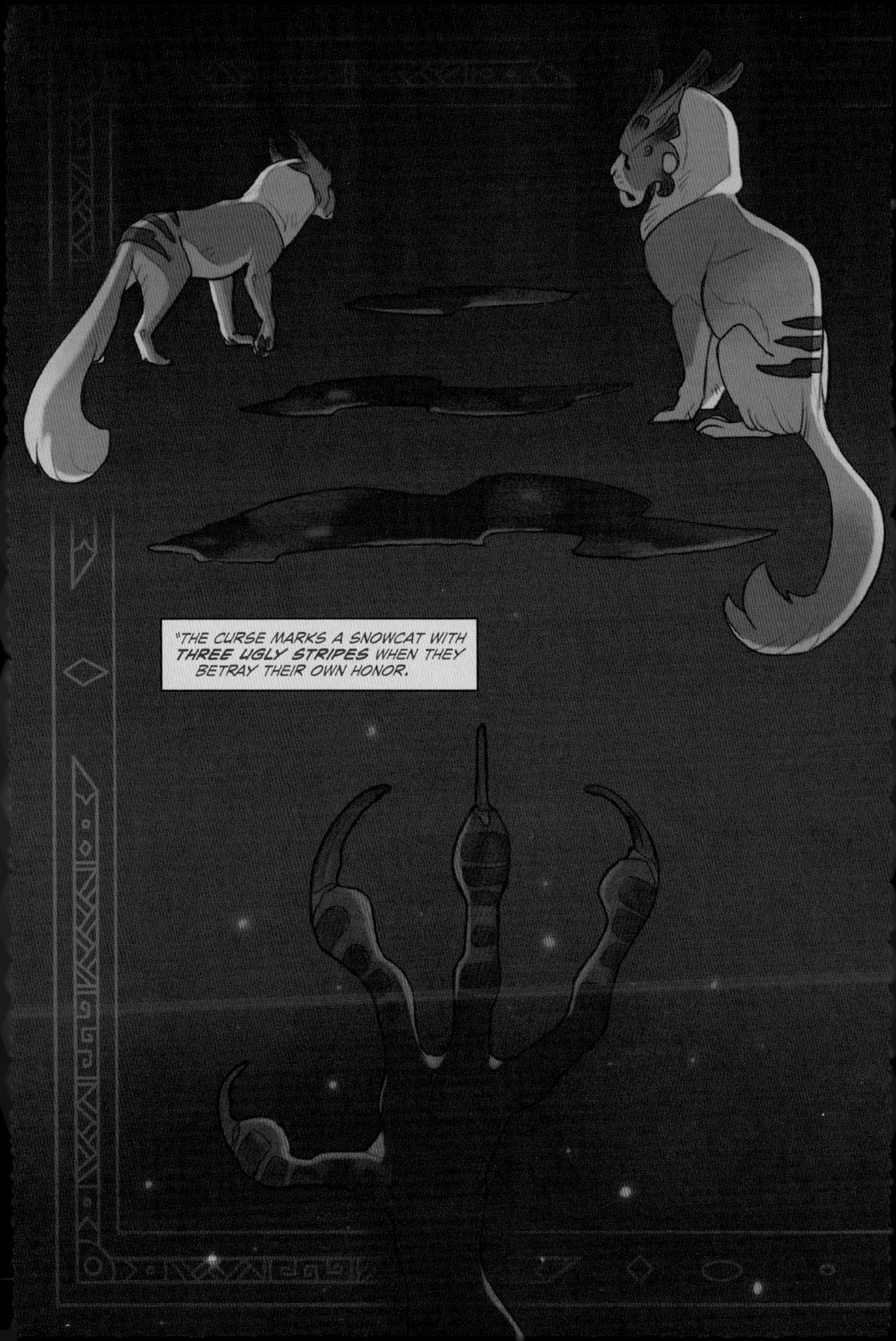
"THE CURSE MARKS A SNOWCAT WITH THREE UGLY STRIPES WHEN THEY BETRAY THEIR OWN HONOR.

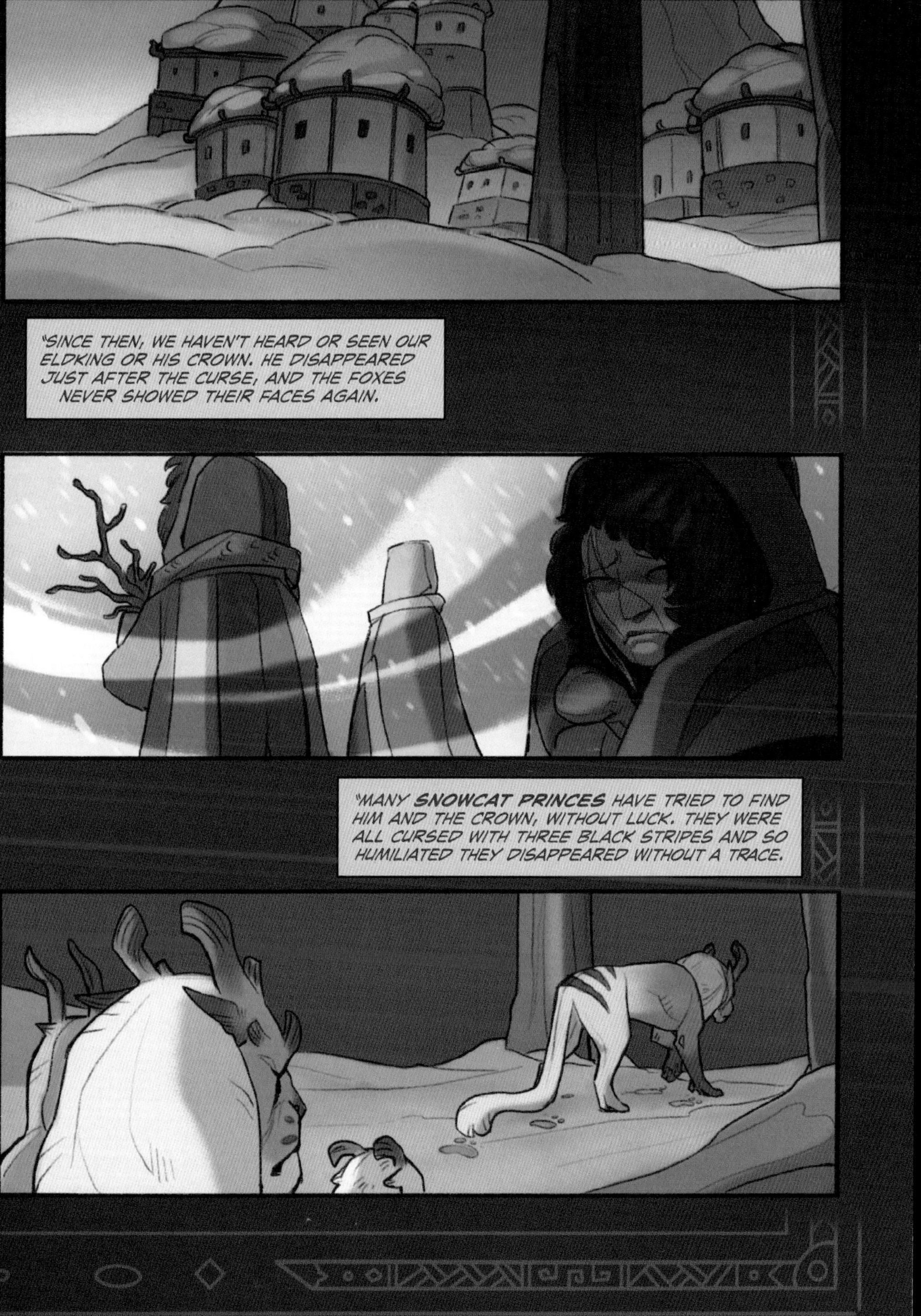
"SINCE THEN, WE HAVEN'T HEARD OR SEEN OUR ELDKING OR HIS CROWN. HE DISAPPEARED JUST AFTER THE CURSE, AND THE FOXES NEVER SHOWED THEIR FACES AGAIN.
"MANY **SNOWCAT PRINCES** HAVE TRIED TO FIND HIM AND THE CROWN, WITHOUT LUCK. THEY WERE ALL CURSED WITH THREE BLACK STRIPES AND SO HUMILIATED THEY DISAPPEARED WITHOUT A TRACE.

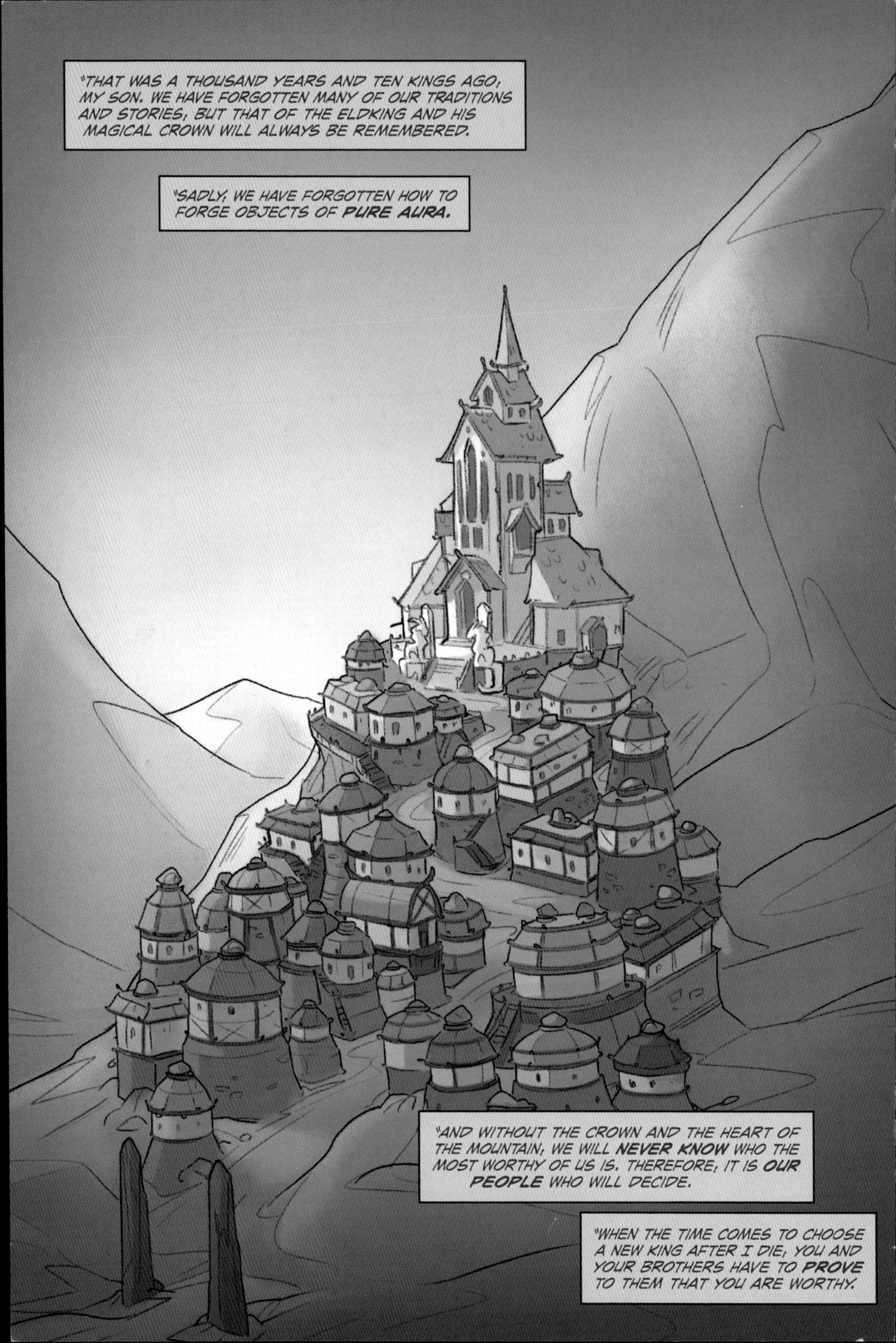
"THAT WAS A THOUSAND YEARS AND TEN KINGS AGO, MY SON. WE HAVE FORGOTTEN MANY OF OUR TRADITIONS AND STORIES, BUT THAT OF THE ELDKING AND HIS MAGICAL CROWN WILL ALWAYS BE REMEMBERED.
"SADLY, WE HAVE FORGOTTEN HOW TO FORGE OBJECTS OF PURE AURA.
"AND WITHOUT THE CROWN AND THE HEART OF THE MOUNTAIN, WE WILL NEVER KNOW WHO THE MOST WORTHY OF US IS. THEREFORE, IT IS OUR PEOPLE WHO WILL DECIDE.
"WHEN THE TIME COMES TO CHOOSE A NEW KING AFTER I DIE, YOU AND YOUR BROTHERS HAVE TO PROVE TO THEM THAT YOU ARE WORTHY.

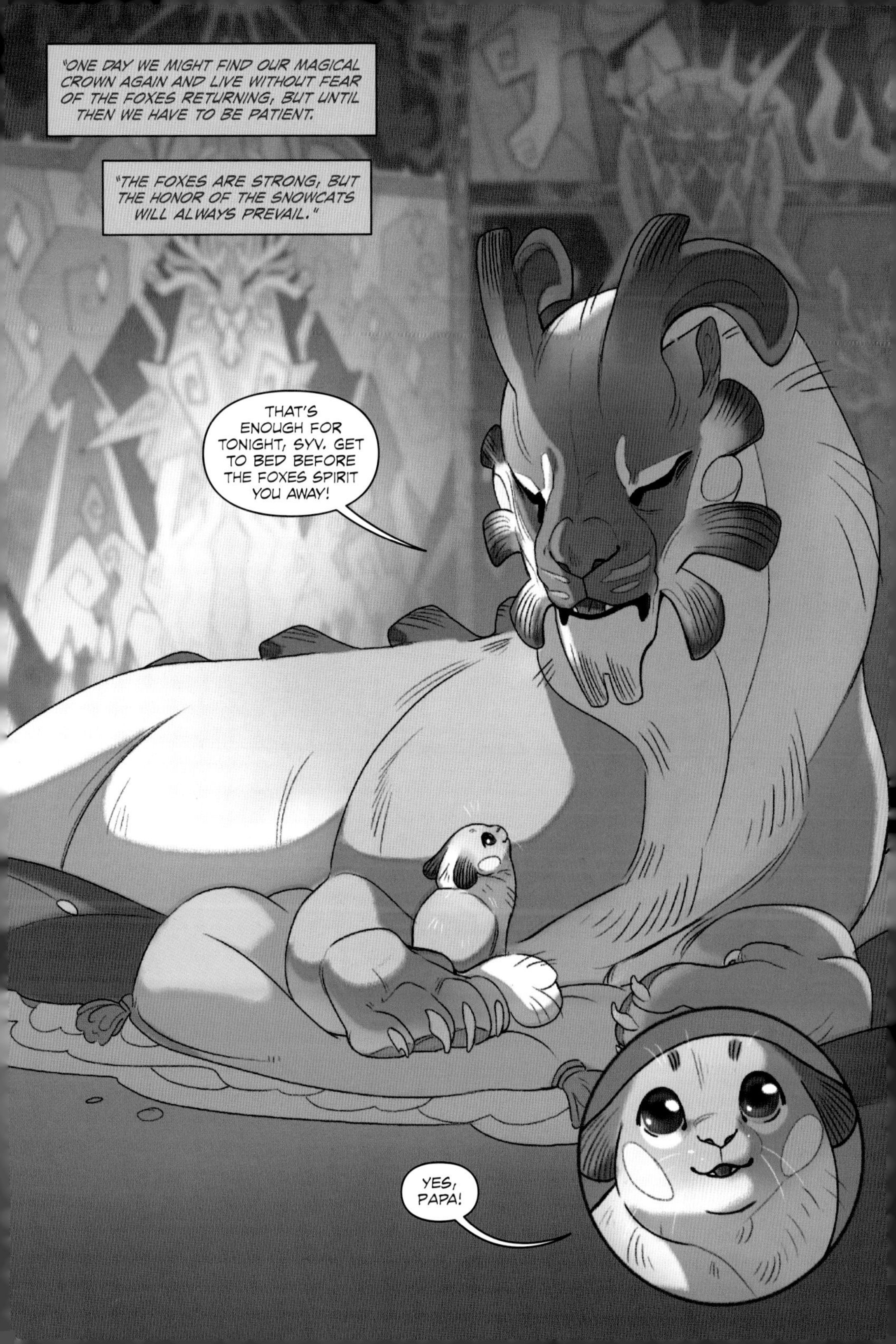
"ONE DAY WE MIGHT FIND OUR MAGICAL CROWN AGAIN AND LIVE WITHOUT FEAR OF THE FOXES RETURNING, BUT UNTIL THEN WE HAVE TO BE PATIENT.
"THE FOXES ARE STRONG, BUT THE HONOR OF THE SNOWCATS WILL ALWAYS PREVAIL."
THAT'S ENOUGH FOR TONIGHT, SYV. GET TO BED BEFORE THE FOXES SPIRIT YOU AWAY!
YES, PAPA!

Chapter 1
THE SEVEN BROTHERS

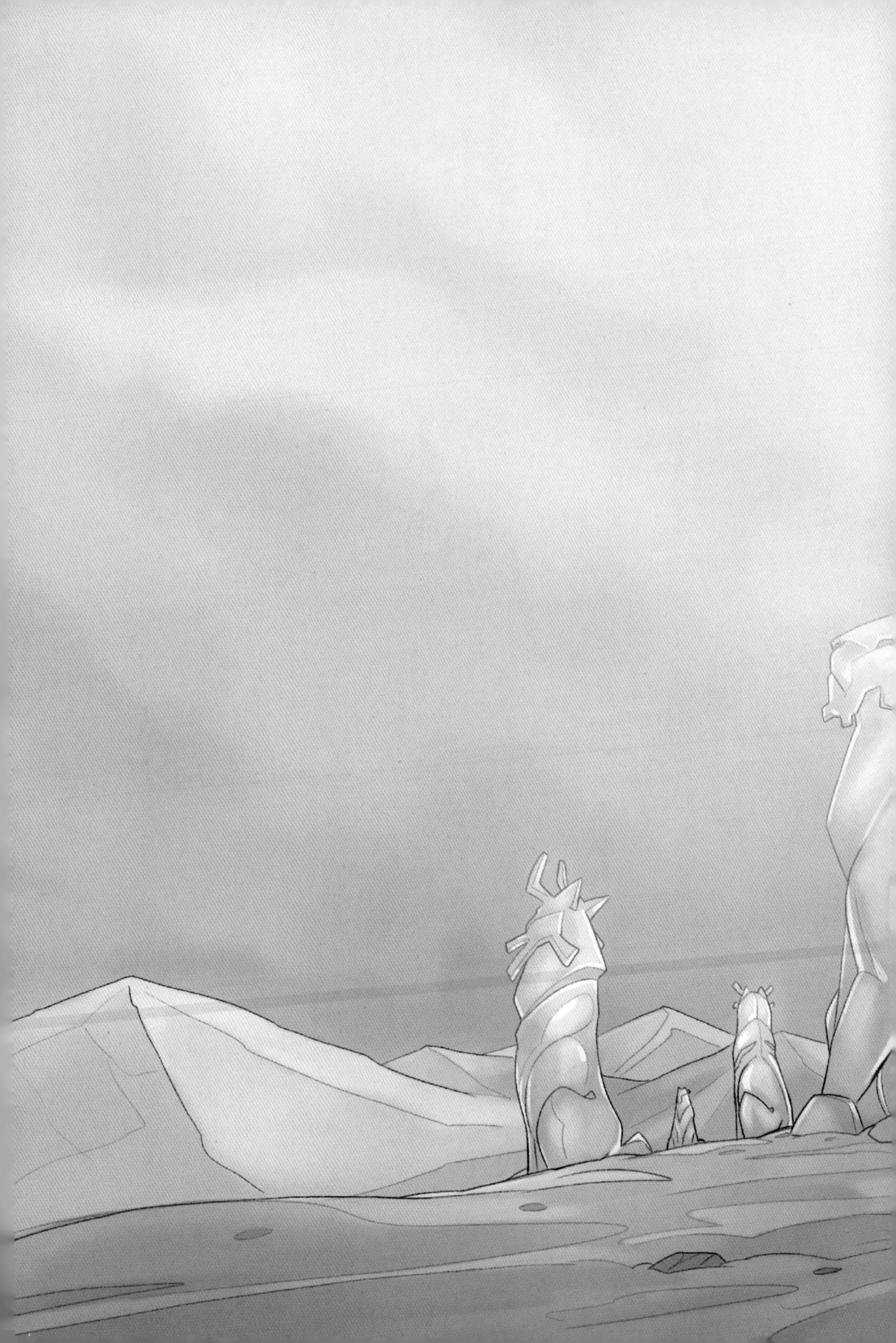

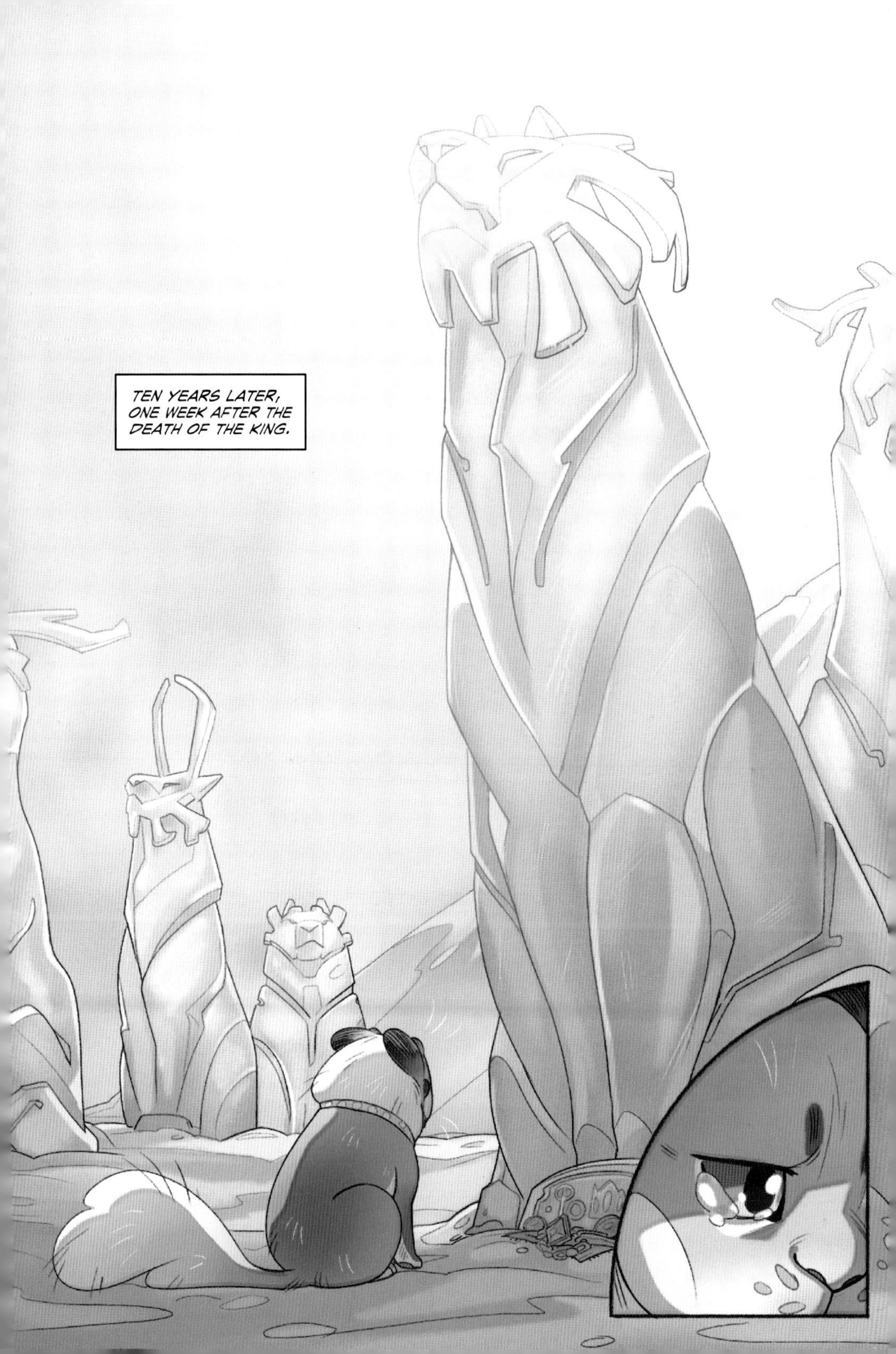
TEN YEARS LATER, ONE WEEK AFTER THE DEATH OF THE KING.

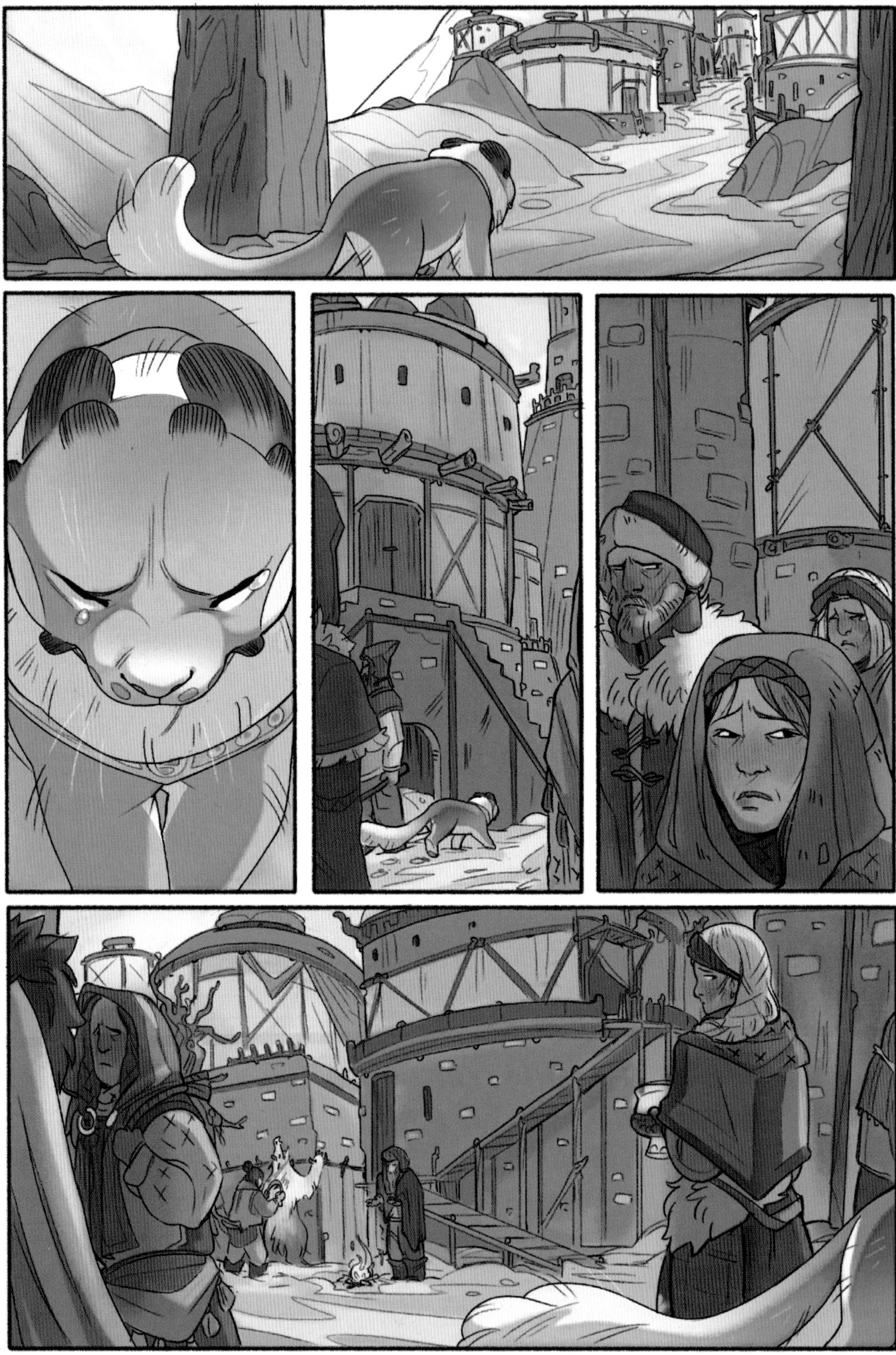

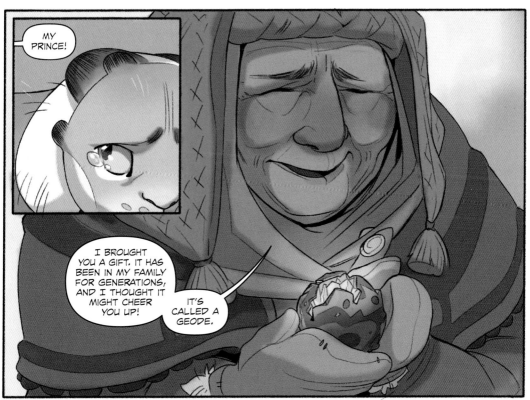

MY PRINCE!

I BROUGHT YOU A GIFT. IT HAS BEEN IN MY FAMILY FOR GENERATIONS, AND I THOUGHT IT MIGHT CHEER YOU UP!

IT'S CALLED A GEODE.

I...

I CAN'T...

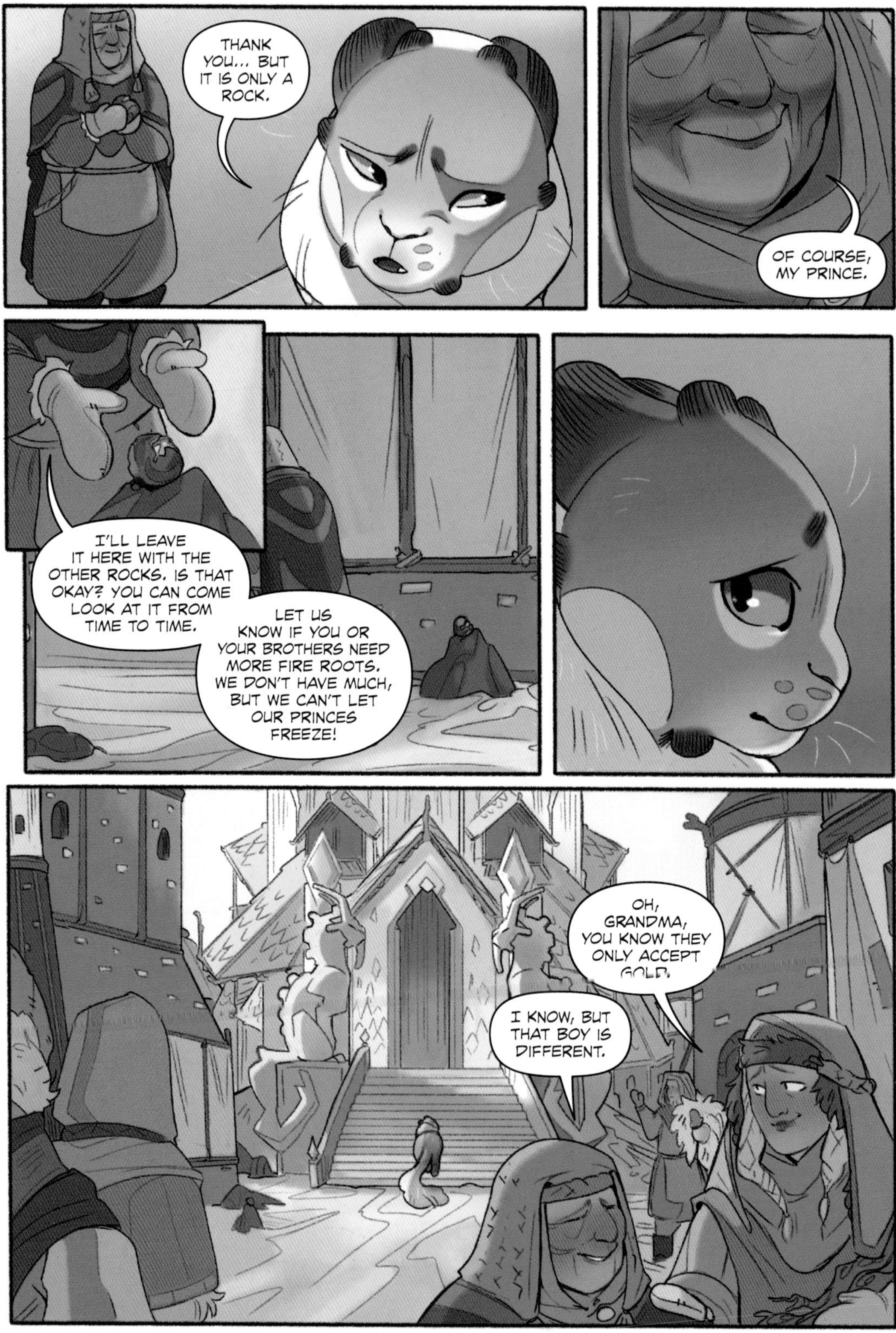
THANK YOU... BUT IT IS ONLY A ROCK.
OF COURSE, MY PRINCE.
I'LL LEAVE IT HERE WITH THE OTHER ROCKS. IS THAT OKAY? YOU CAN COME LOOK AT IT FROM TIME TO TIME.
LET US KNOW IF YOU OR YOUR BROTHERS NEED MORE FIRE ROOTS. WE DON'T HAVE MUCH, BUT WE CAN'T LET OUR PRINCES FREEZE!
OH, GRANDMA, YOU KNOW THEY ONLY ACCEPT GOLD.
I KNOW, BUT THAT BOY IS DIFFERENT.

HSSS...

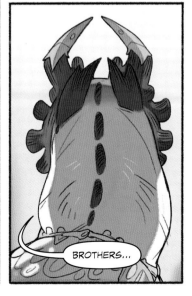

BROTHERS...

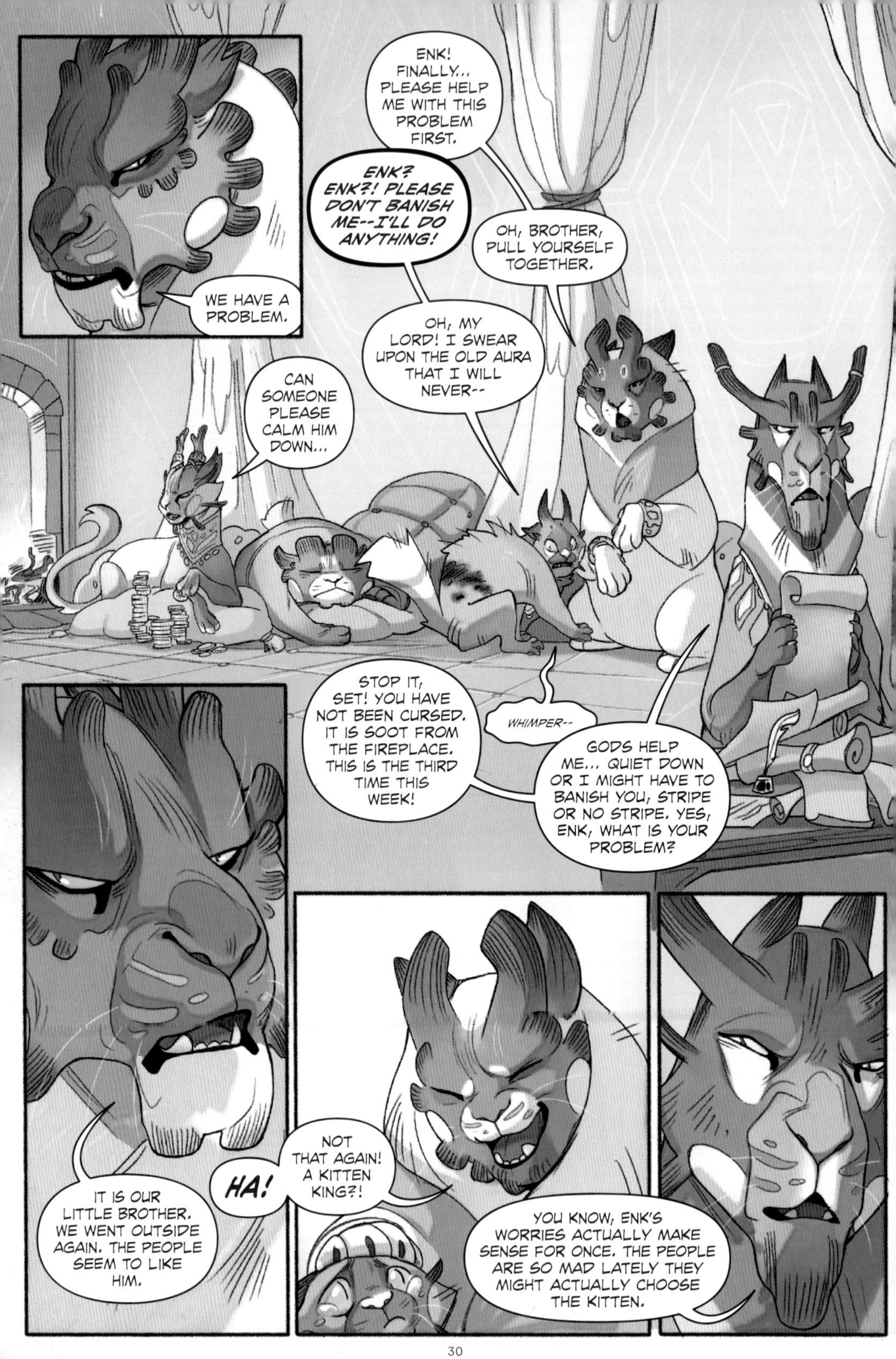

WE HAVE A PROBLEM.
ENK! FINALLY... PLEASE HELP ME WITH THIS PROBLEM FIRST.
ENK? ENK?! PLEASE DON'T BANISH ME--I'LL DO ANYTHING!
OH, BROTHER, PULL YOURSELF TOGETHER.
OH, MY LORD! I SWEAR UPON THE OLD AURA THAT I WILL NEVER--
CAN SOMEONE PLEASE CALM HIM DOWN...
STOP IT, SET! YOU HAVE NOT BEEN CURSED. IT IS SOOT FROM THE FIREPLACE. THIS IS THE THIRD TIME THIS WEEK!
WHIMPER--
GODS HELP ME... QUIET DOWN OR I MIGHT HAVE TO BANISH YOU, STRIPE OR NO STRIPE. YES, ENK, WHAT IS YOUR PROBLEM?
IT IS OUR LITTLE BROTHER. WE WENT OUTSIDE AGAIN. THE PEOPLE SEEM TO LIKE HIM.
HA!
NOT THAT AGAIN! A KITTEN KING?!
YOU KNOW, ENK'S WORRIES ACTUALLY MAKE SENSE FOR ONCE. THE PEOPLE ARE SO MAD LATELY THEY MIGHT ACTUALLY CHOOSE THE KITTEN.

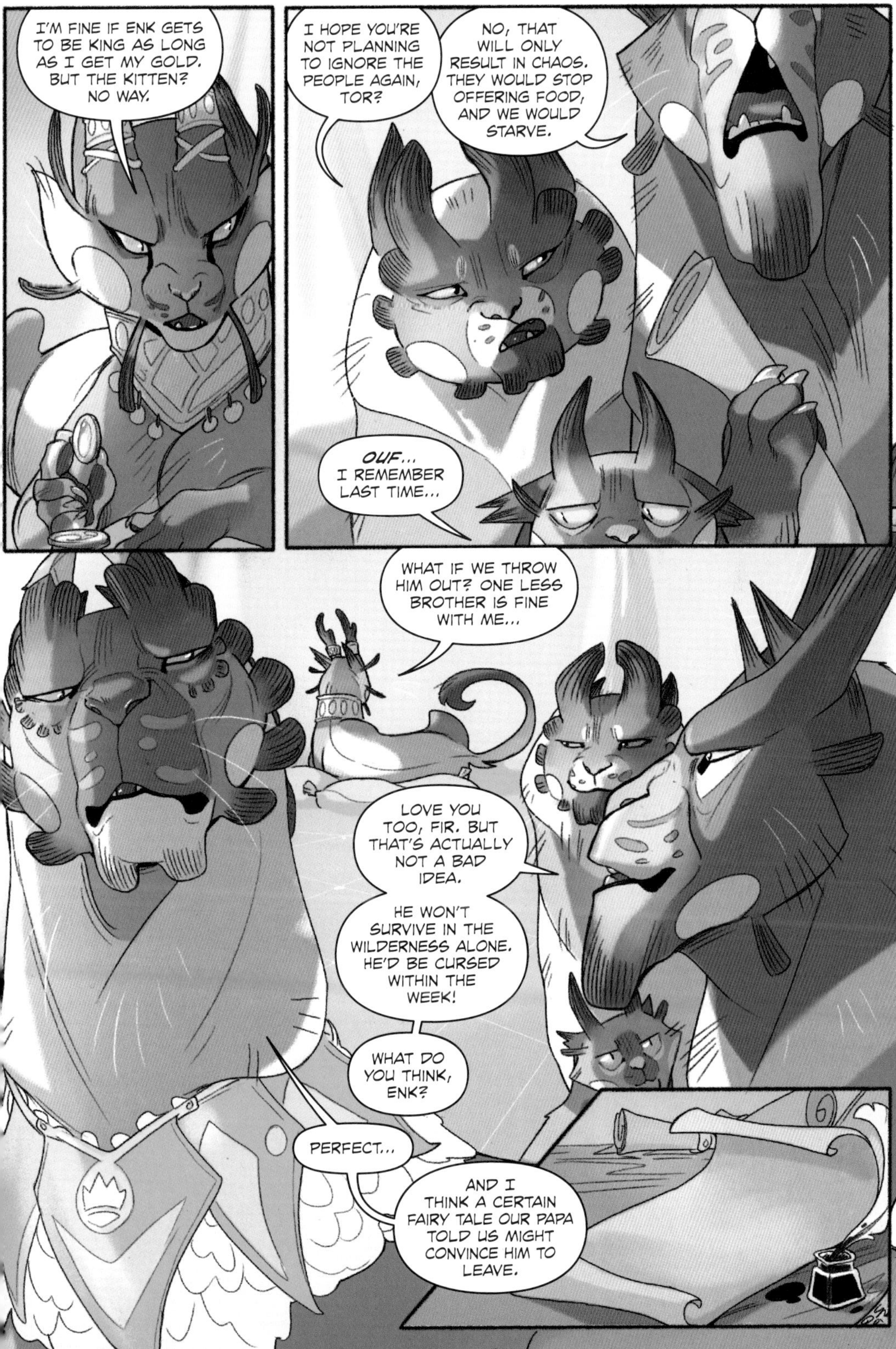
I'M FINE IF ENK GETS TO BE KING AS LONG AS I GET MY GOLD. BUT THE KITTEN? NO WAY.
I HOPE YOU'RE NOT PLANNING TO IGNORE THE PEOPLE AGAIN, TOR?
NO, THAT WILL ONLY RESULT IN CHAOS. THEY WOULD STOP OFFERING FOOD, AND WE WOULD STARVE.
OUF... I REMEMBER LAST TIME...
WHAT IF WE THROW HIM OUT? ONE LESS BROTHER IS FINE WITH ME...
LOVE YOU TOO, FIR. BUT THAT'S ACTUALLY NOT A BAD IDEA.
HE WON'T SURVIVE IN THE WILDERNESS ALONE. HE'D BE CURSED WITHIN THE WEEK!
WHAT DO YOU THINK, ENK?
PERFECT...
AND I THINK A CERTAIN FAIRY TALE OUR PAPA TOLD US MIGHT CONVINCE HIM TO LEAVE.

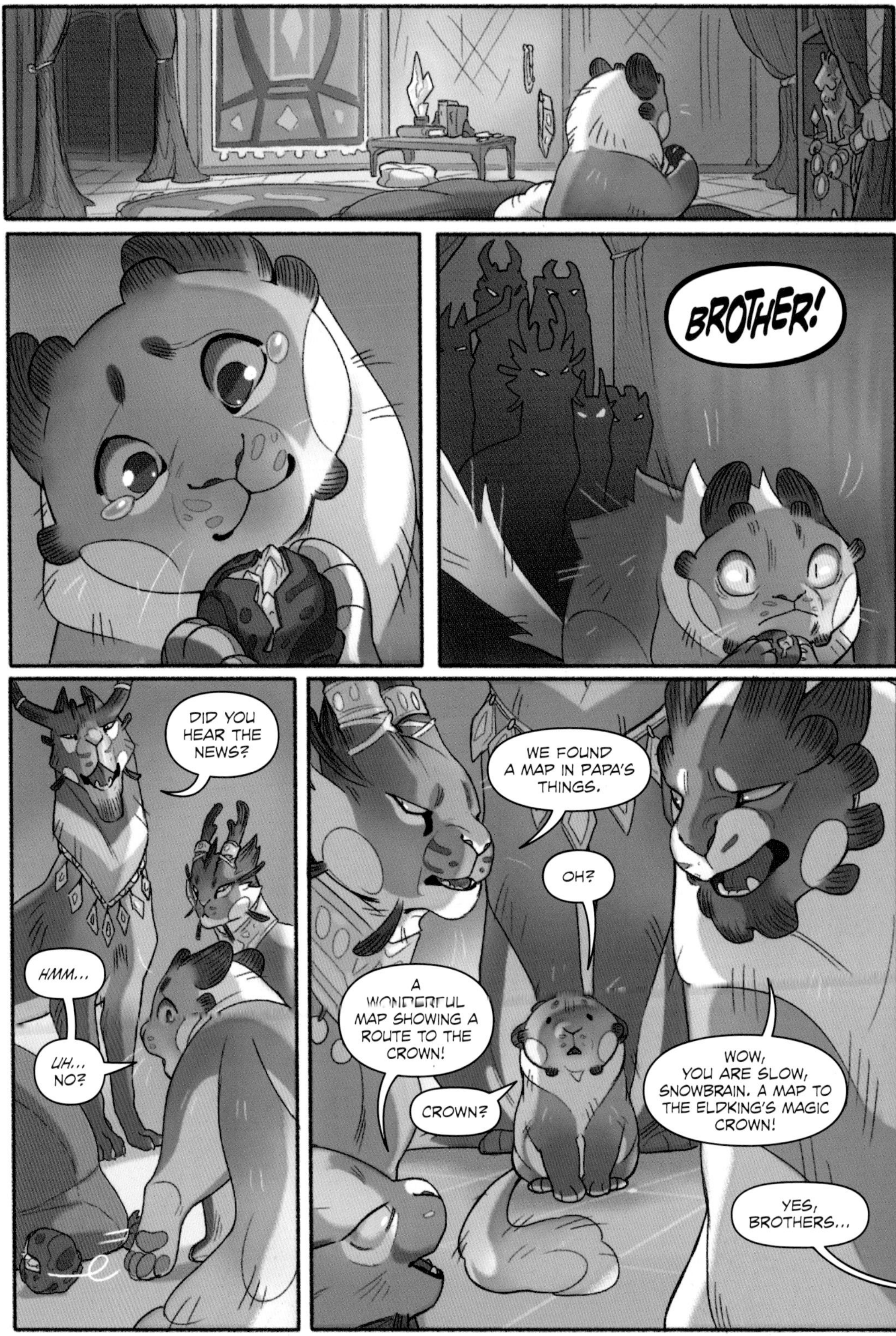
BROTHER!
DID YOU HEAR THE NEWS?
HMM...
UH... NO?
WE FOUND A MAP IN PAPA'S THINGS.
OH?
A WONDERFUL MAP SHOWING A ROUTE TO THE CROWN!
CROWN?
WOW, YOU ARE SLOW, SNOWBRAIN. A MAP TO THE ELDKING'S MAGIC CROWN!
YES, BROTHERS...

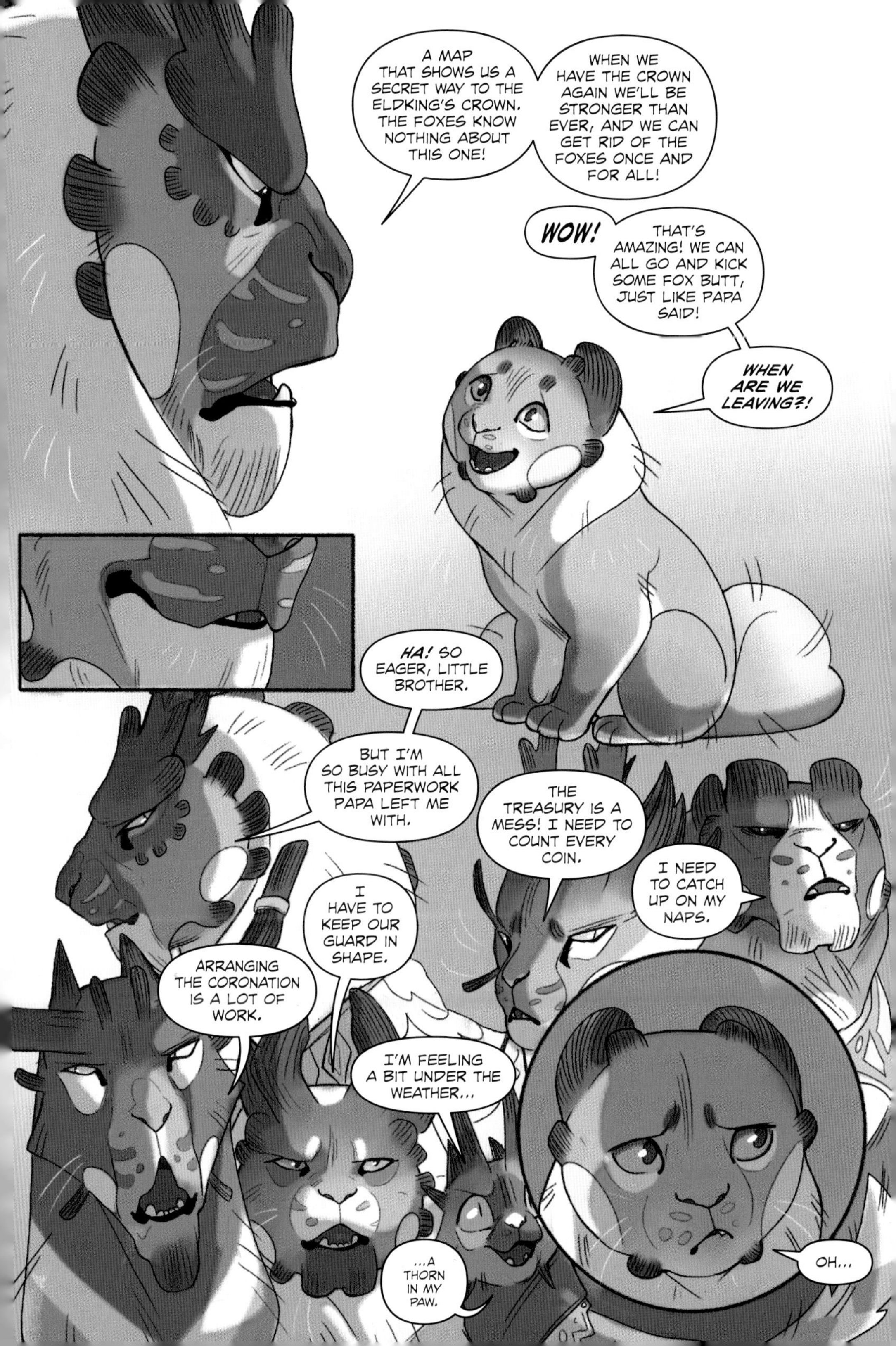

A MAP THAT SHOWS US A SECRET WAY TO THE ELDKING'S CROWN. THE FOXES KNOW NOTHING ABOUT THIS ONE!
WHEN WE HAVE THE CROWN AGAIN WE'LL BE STRONGER THAN EVER, AND WE CAN GET RID OF THE FOXES ONCE AND FOR ALL!
WOW!
THAT'S AMAZING! WE CAN ALL GO AND KICK SOME FOX BUTT, JUST LIKE PAPA SAID!
WHEN ARE WE LEAVING?!
HA! SO EAGER, LITTLE BROTHER.
BUT I'M SO BUSY WITH ALL THIS PAPERWORK PAPA LEFT ME WITH.
THE TREASURY IS A MESS! I NEED TO COUNT EVERY COIN.
I NEED TO CATCH UP ON MY NAPS.
I HAVE TO KEEP OUR GUARD IN SHAPE.
ARRANGING THE CORONATION IS A LOT OF WORK.
I'M FEELING A BIT UNDER THE WEATHER...
...A THORN IN MY PAW.
OH...

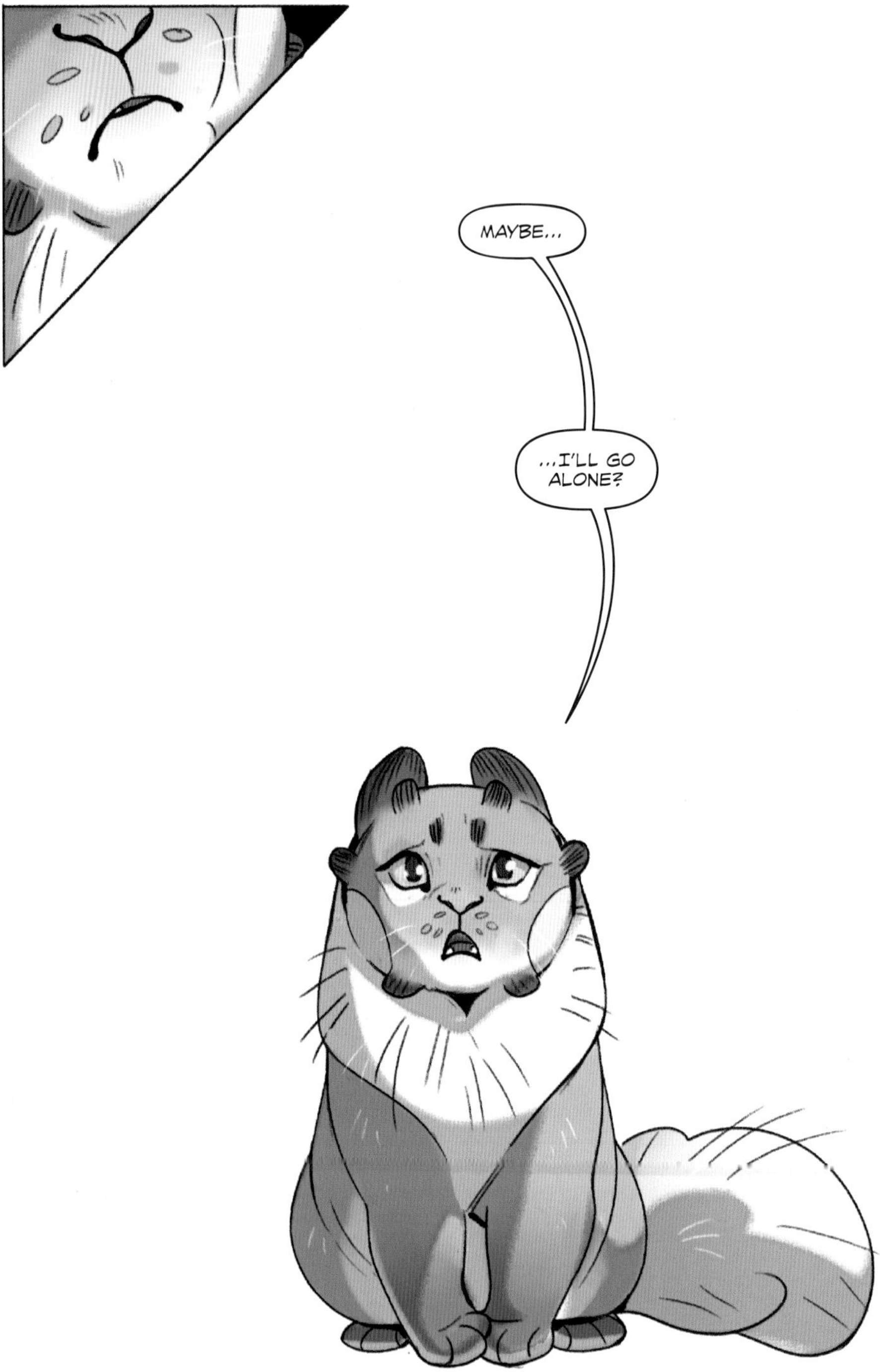
MAYBE...
...I'LL GO ALONE?

Chapter 2
THE BORDER

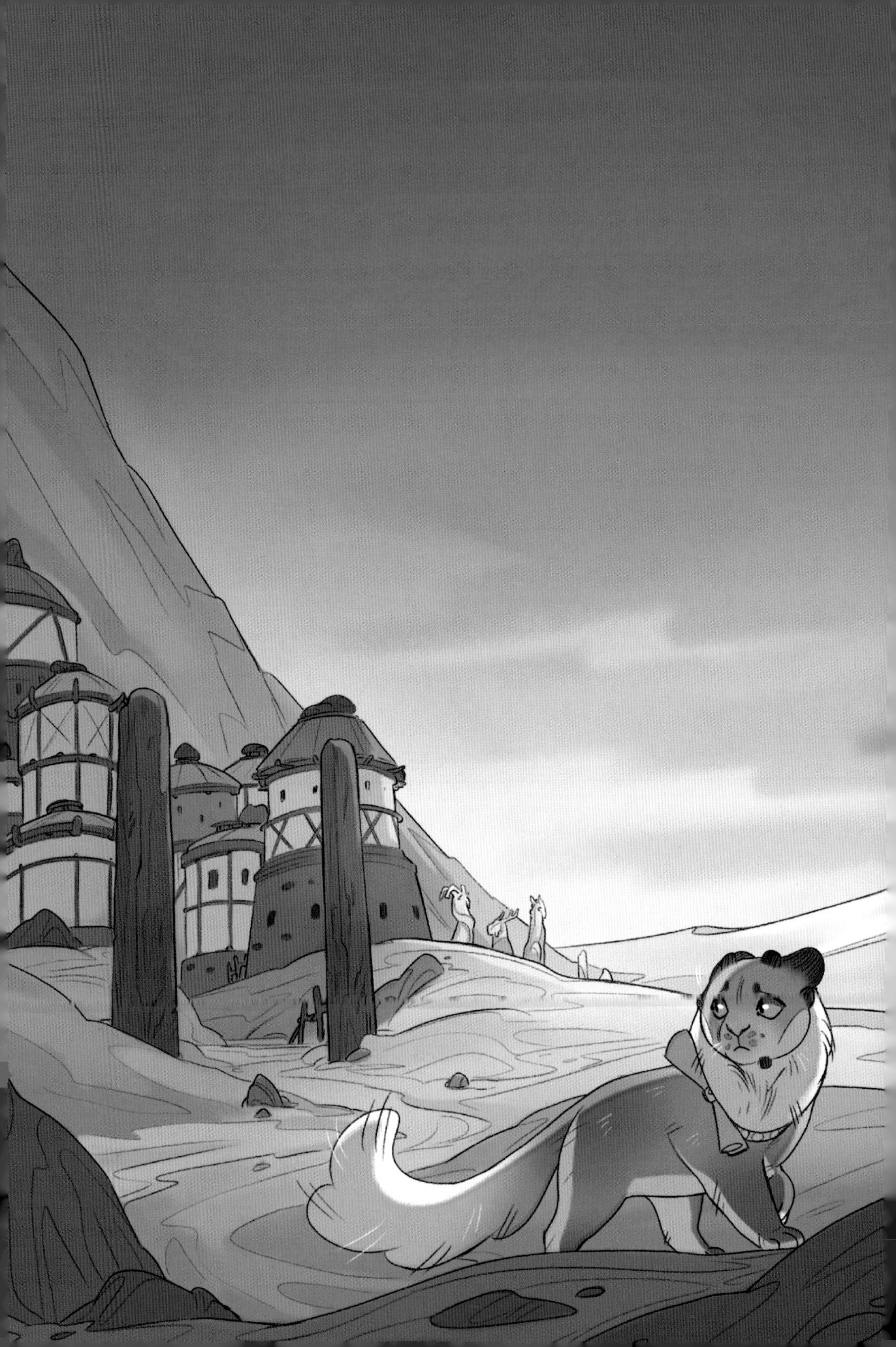

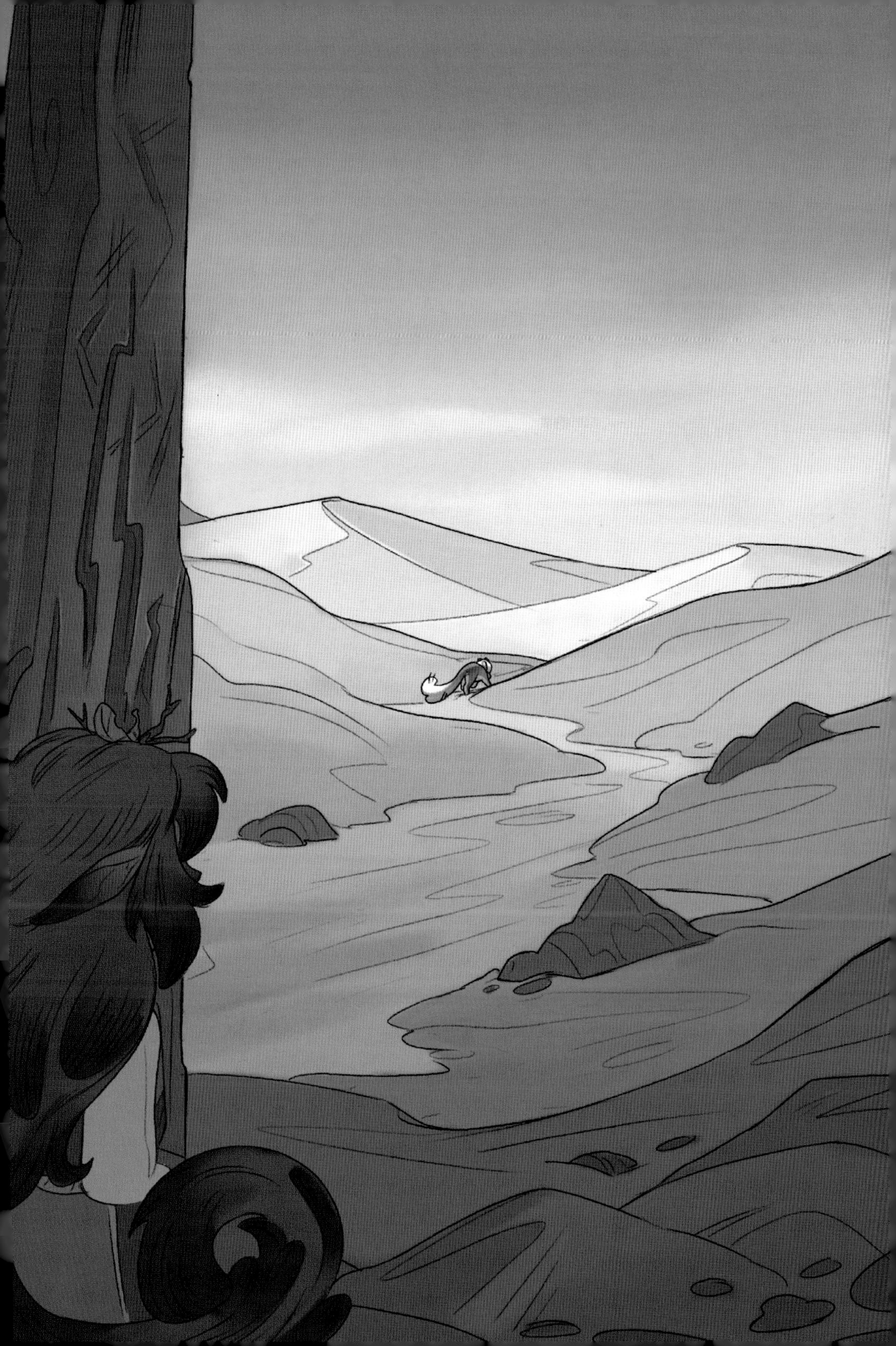

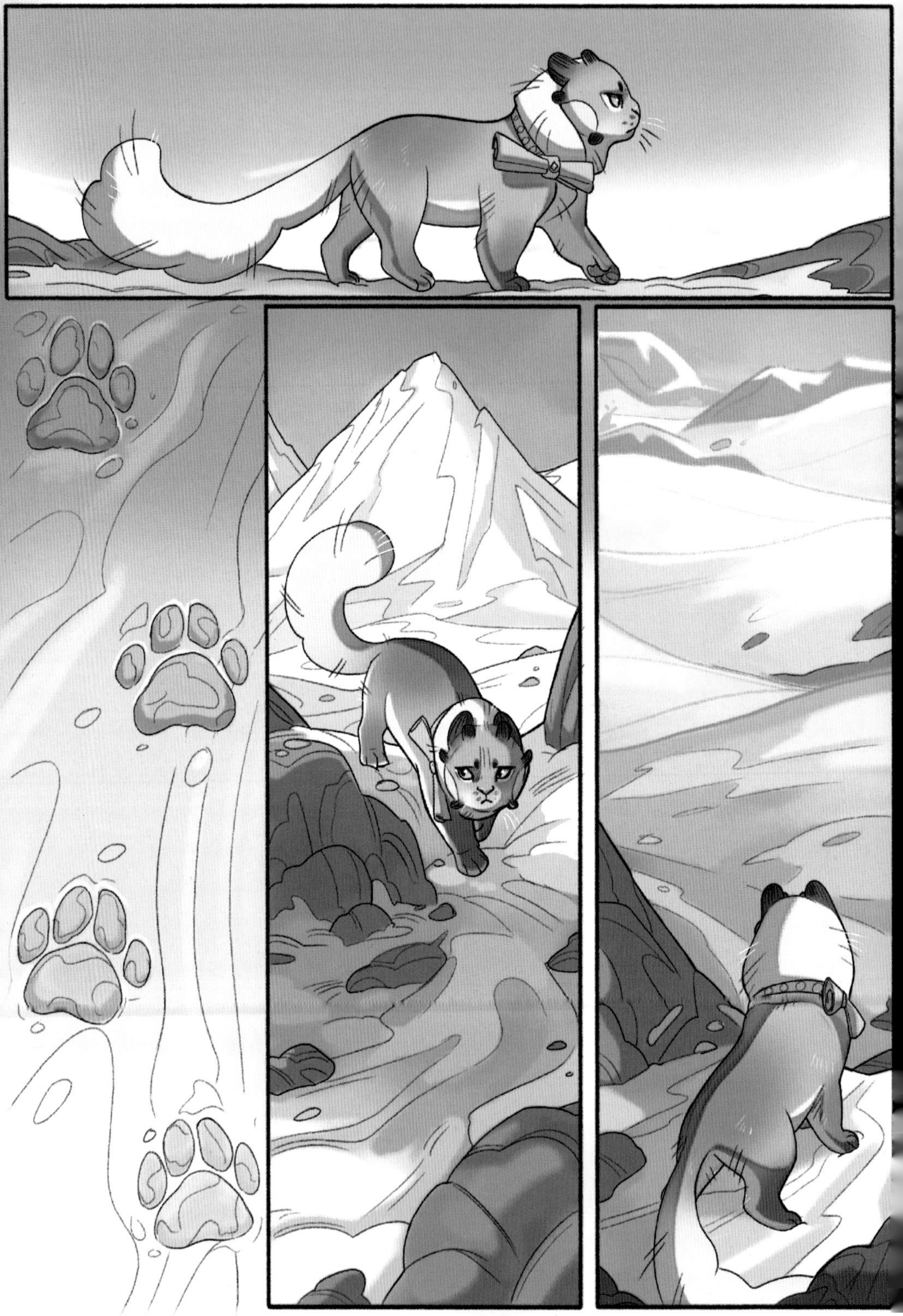

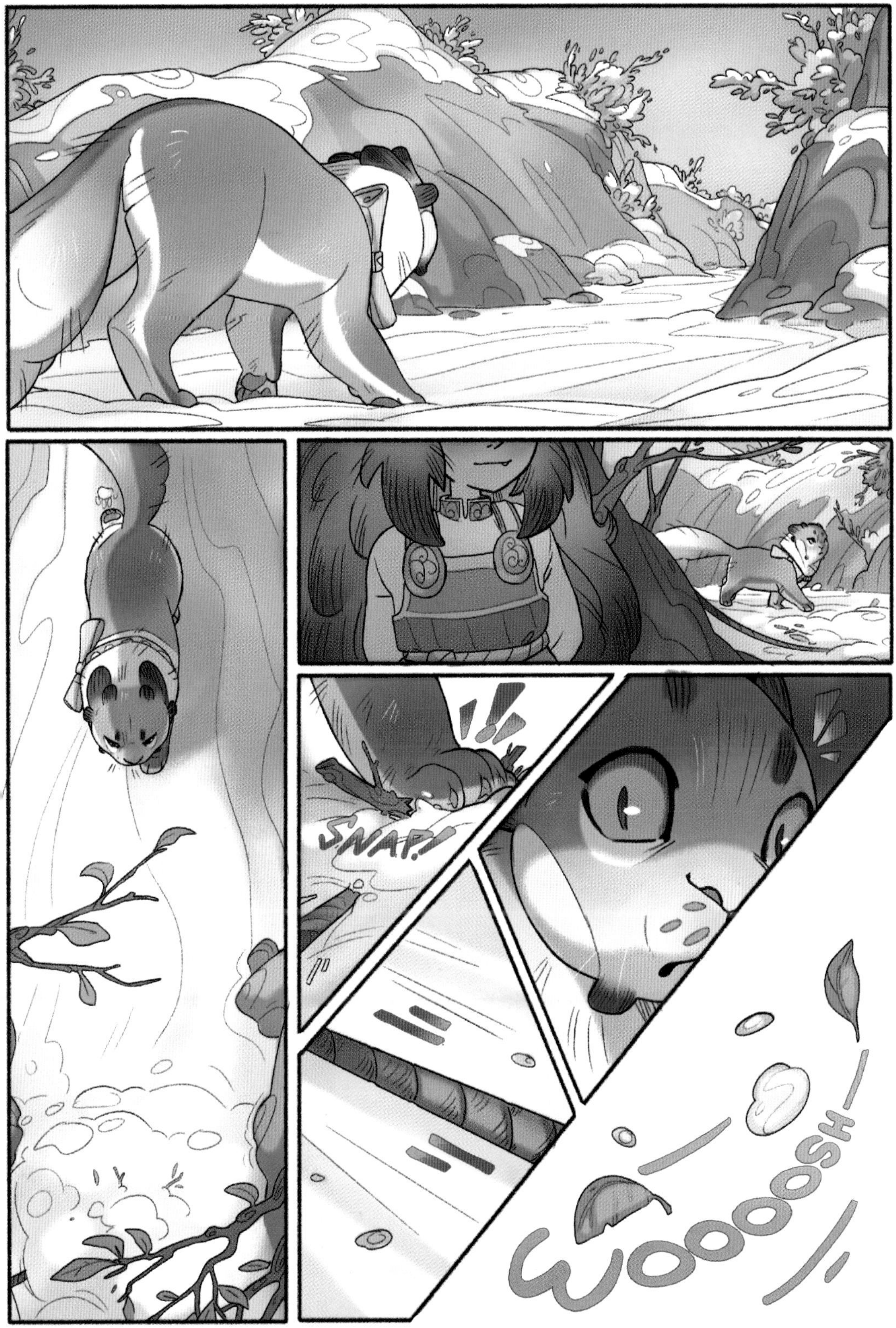
SNAP!
WOOOOOSH

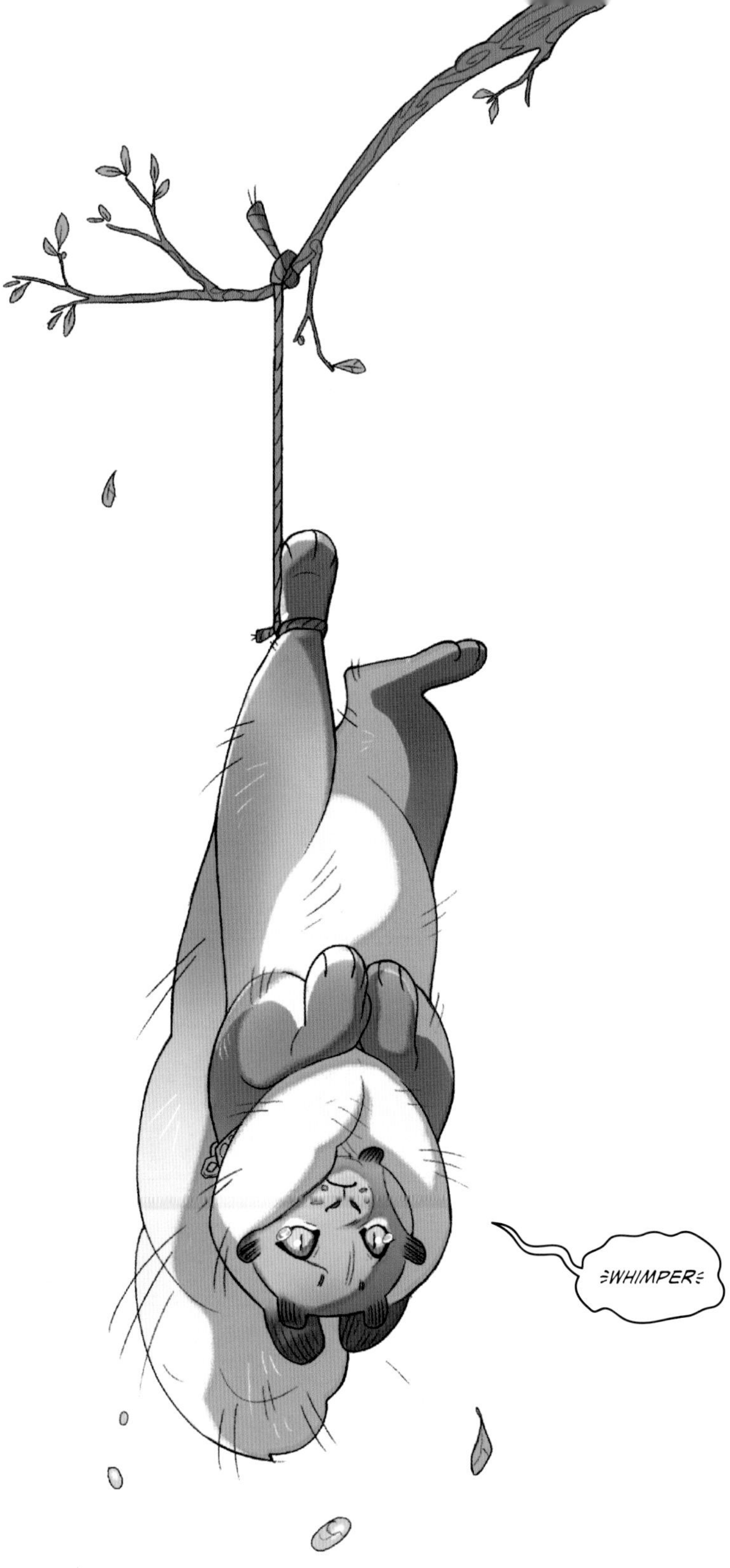
WHIMPER

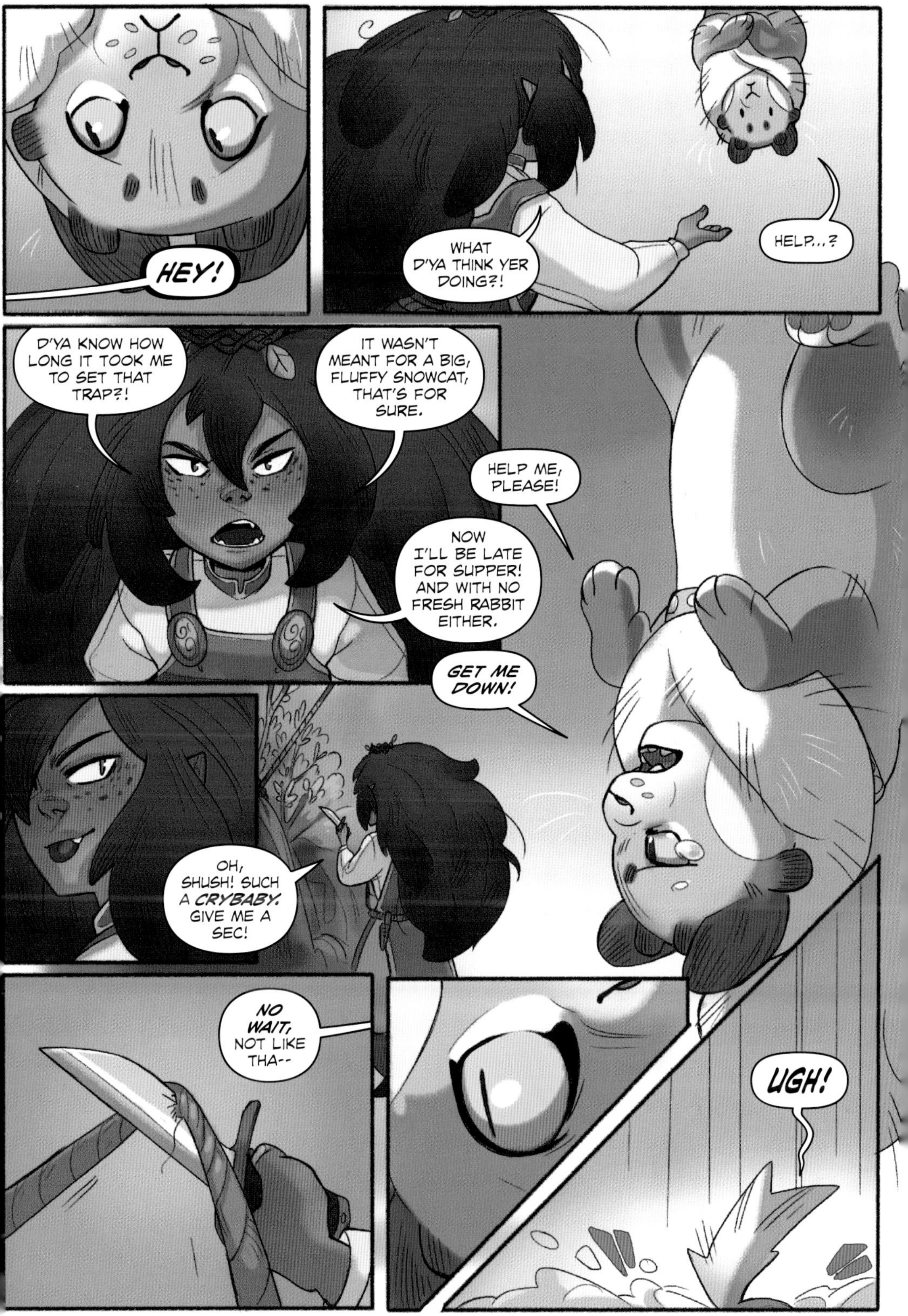
HEY!
WHAT D'YA THINK YER DOING?!
HELP...?
D'YA KNOW HOW LONG IT TOOK ME TO SET THAT TRAP?!
IT WASN'T MEANT FOR A BIG, FLUFFY SNOWCAT, THAT'S FOR SURE.
HELP ME, PLEASE!
NOW I'LL BE LATE FOR SUPPER! AND WITH NO FRESH RABBIT EITHER.
GET ME DOWN!
OH, SHUSH! SUCH A CRYBABY. GIVE ME A SEC!
NO WAIT, NOT LIKE THA--
UGH!

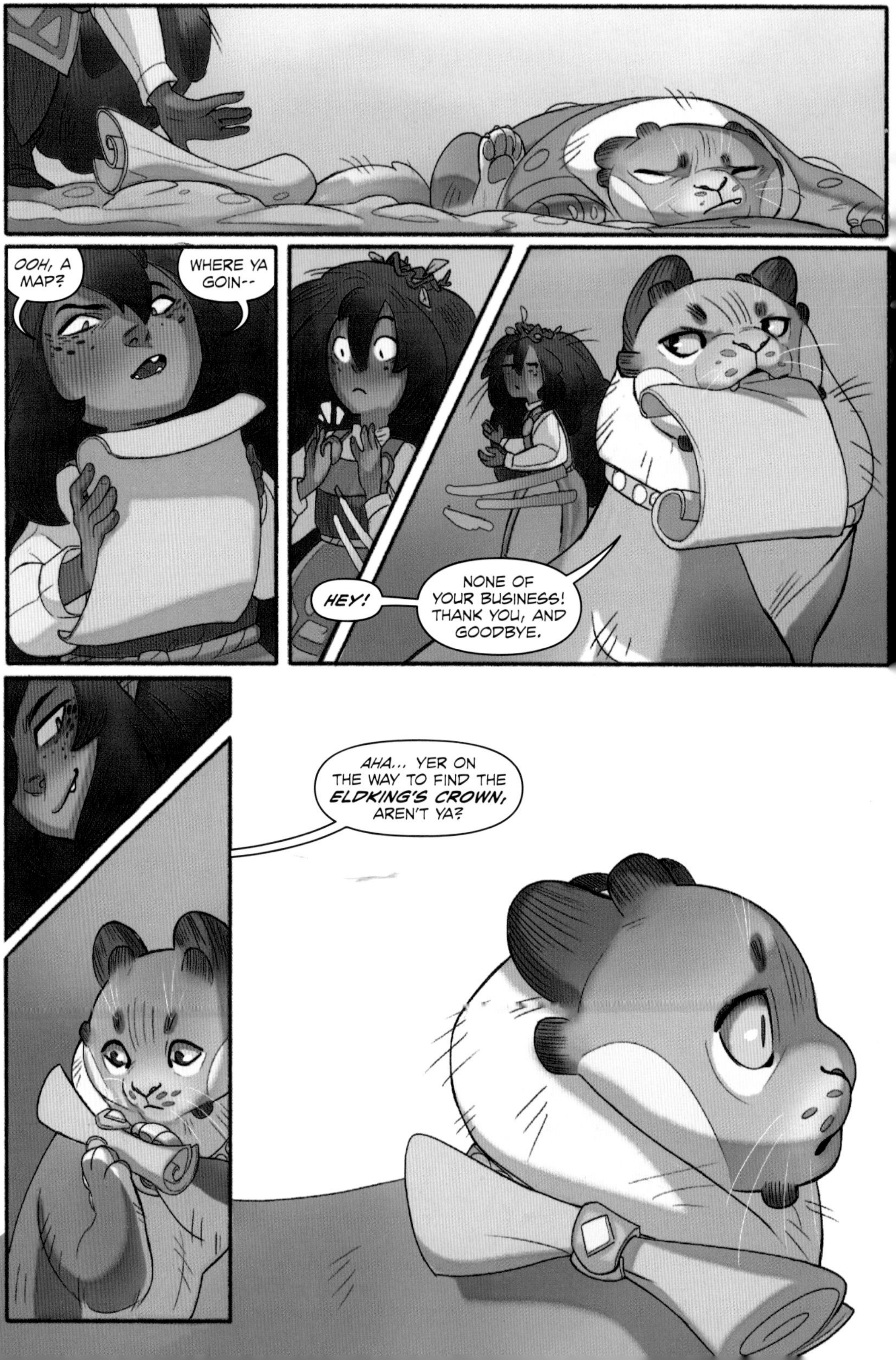
OOH, A MAP?
WHERE YA GOIN--
HEY!
NONE OF YOUR BUSINESS! THANK YOU, AND GOODBYE.
AHA... YER ON THE WAY TO FIND THE ELDKING'S CROWN, AREN'T YA?

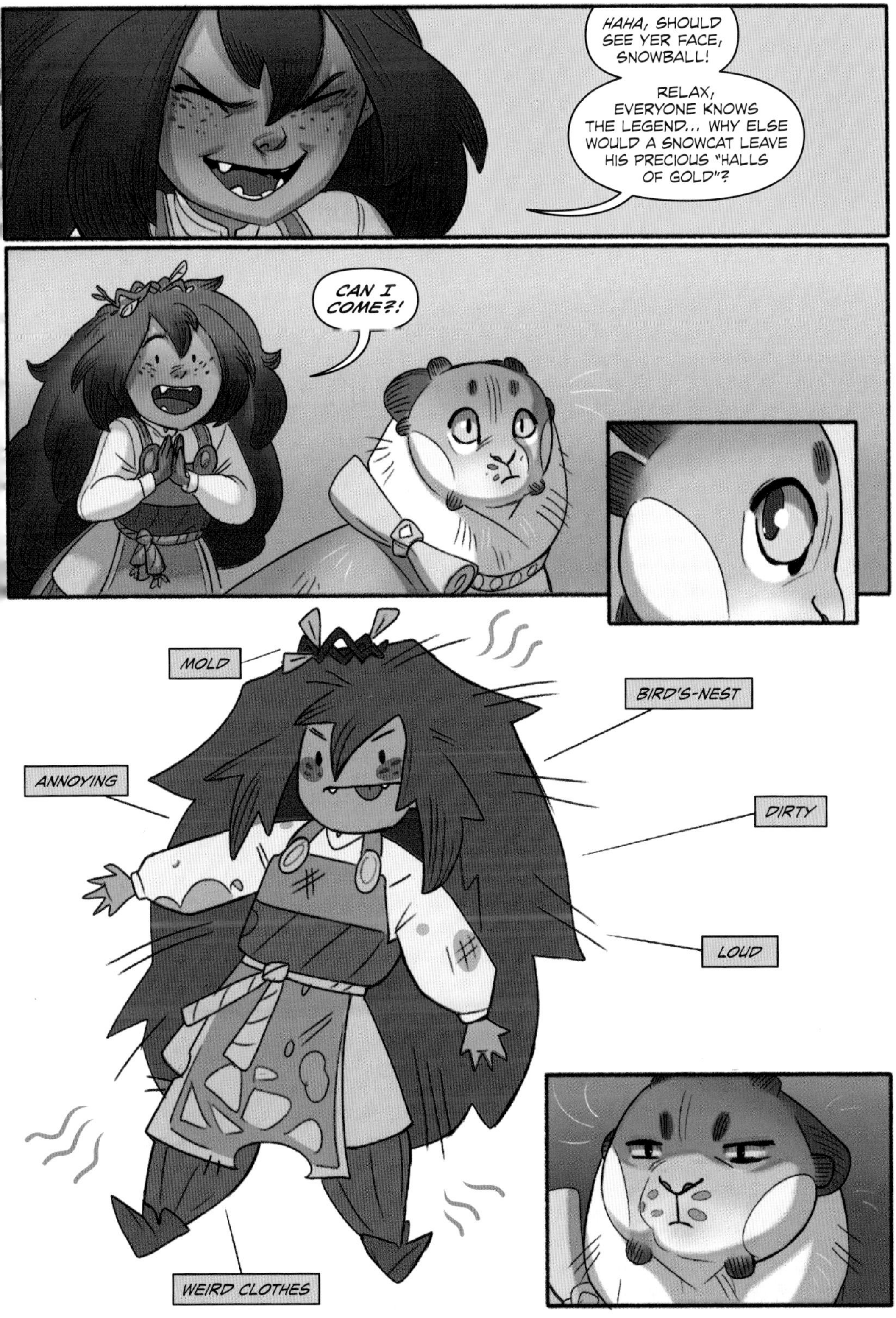
HAHA, SHOULD SEE YER FACE, SNOWBALL!
RELAX, EVERYONE KNOWS THE LEGEND... WHY ELSE WOULD A SNOWCAT LEAVE HIS PRECIOUS "HALLS OF GOLD"?
CAN I COME?!
MOLD
BIRD'S-NEST
ANNOYING
DIRTY
LOUD
WEIRD CLOTHES

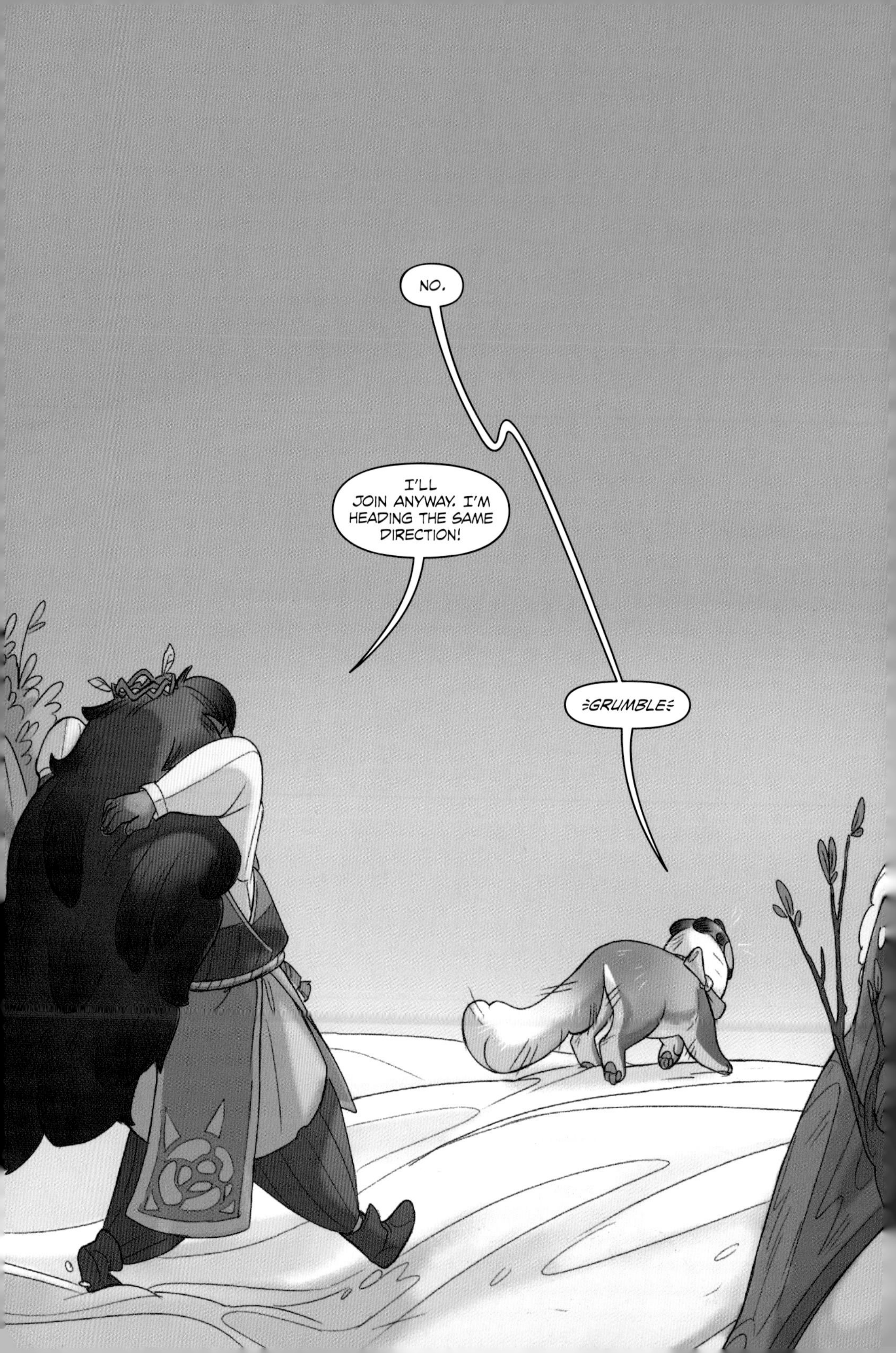
I'LL JOIN ANYWAY. I'M HEADING THE SAME DIRECTION!
NO.
GRUMBLE

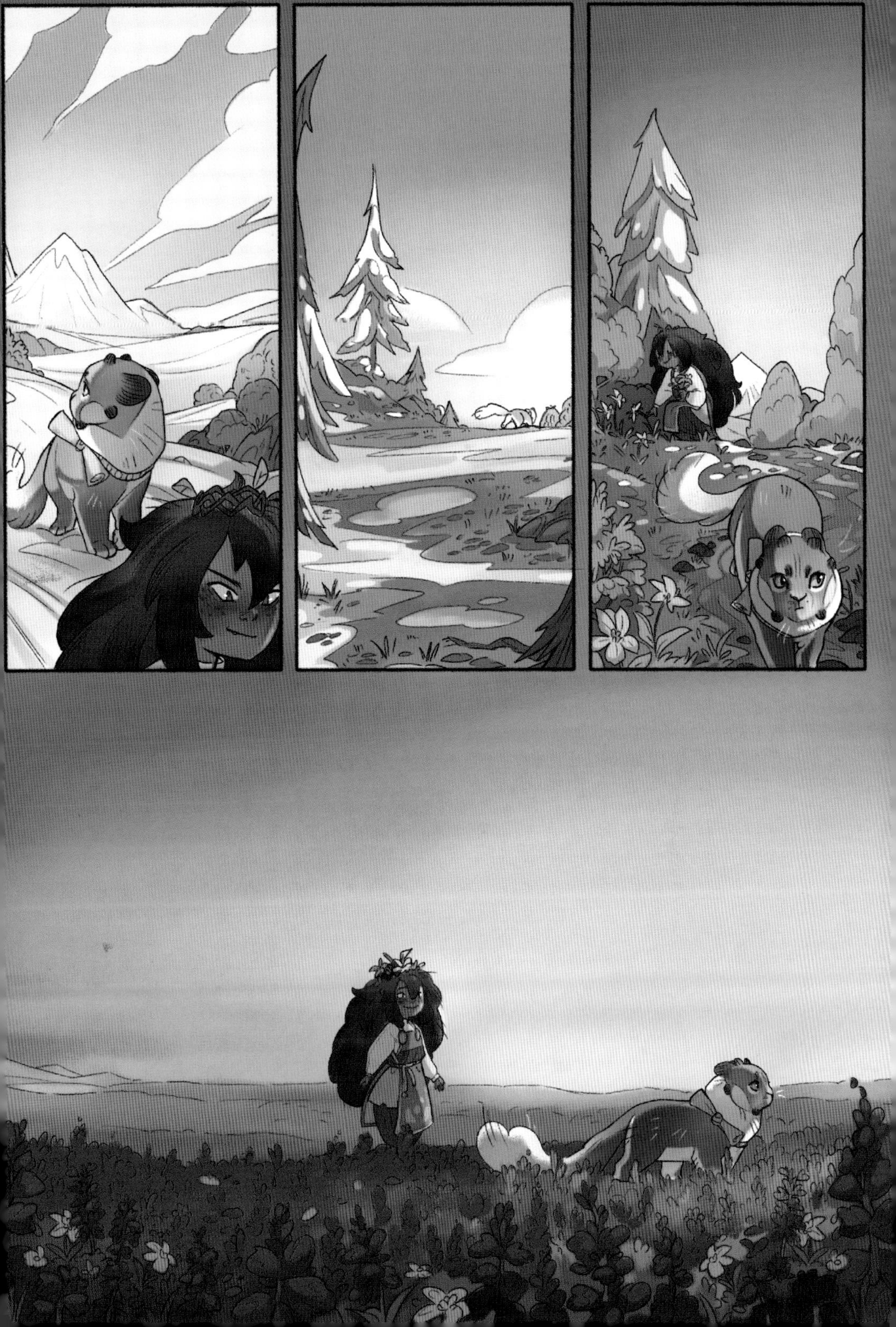

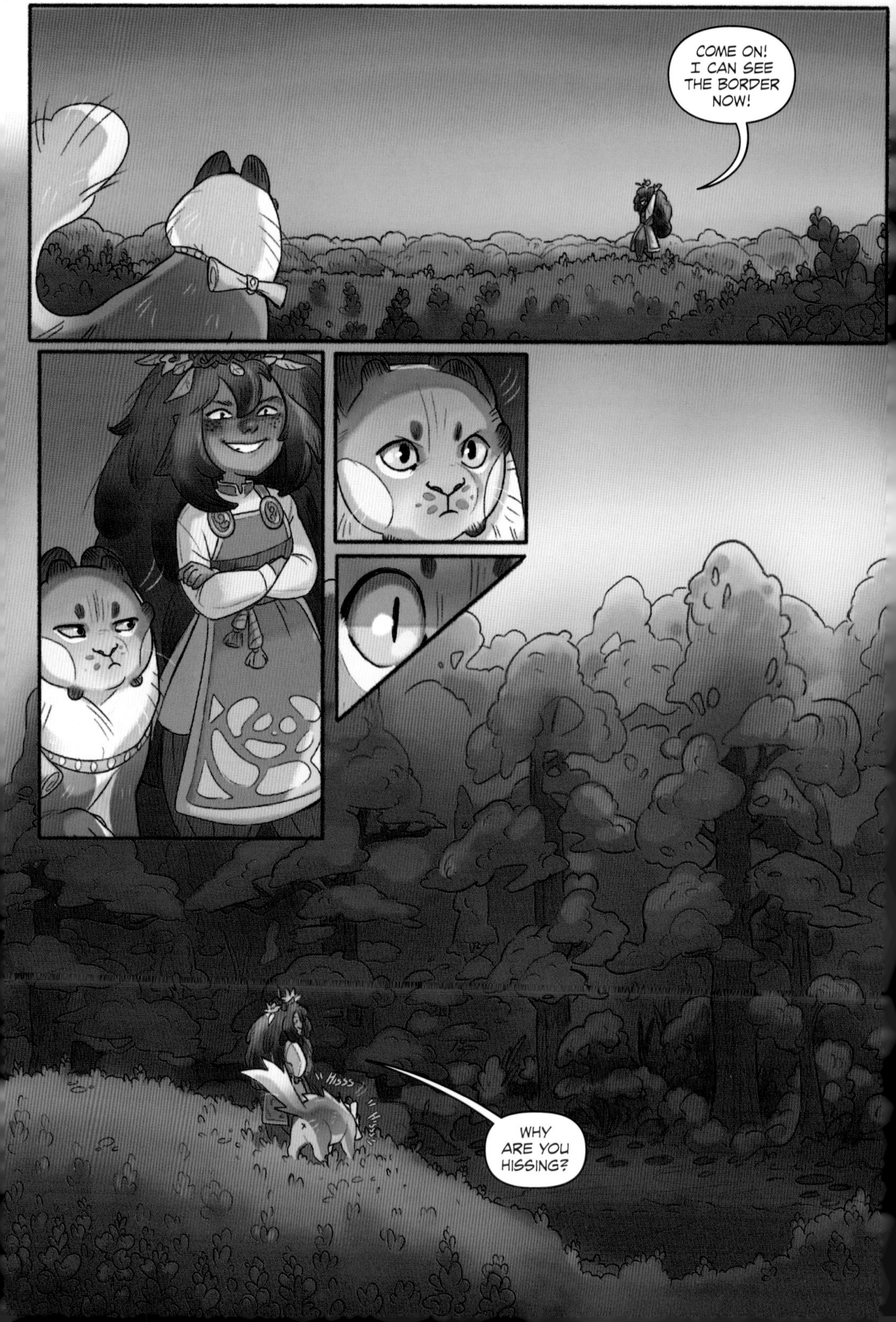
COME ON! I CAN SEE THE BORDER NOW!
HISSS
WHY ARE YOU HISSING?

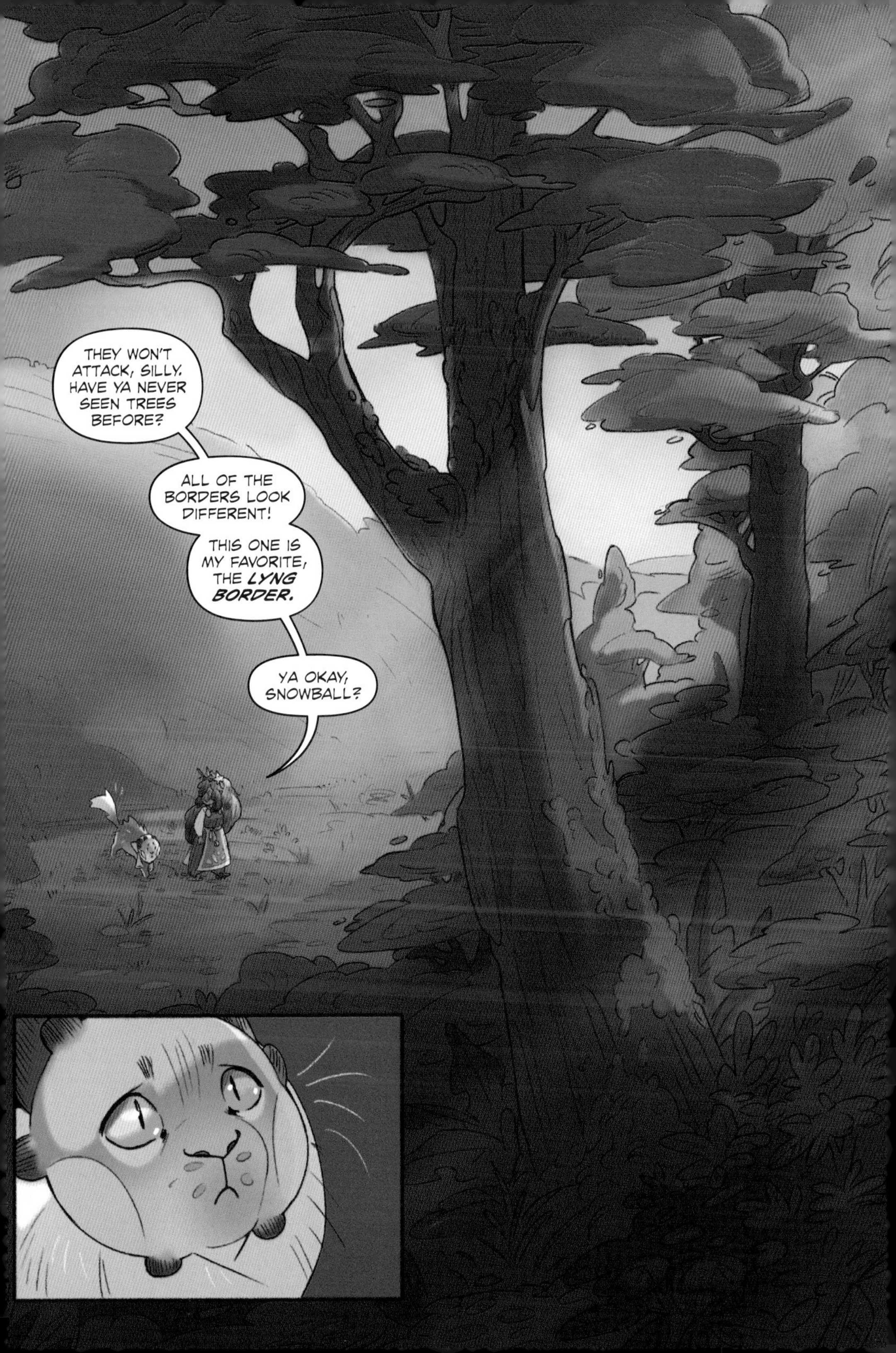
THEY WON'T ATTACK, SILLY. HAVE YA NEVER SEEN TREES BEFORE?
ALL OF THE BORDERS LOOK DIFFERENT!
THIS ONE IS MY FAVORITE, THE *LYNG BORDER.*
YA OKAY, SNOWBALL?

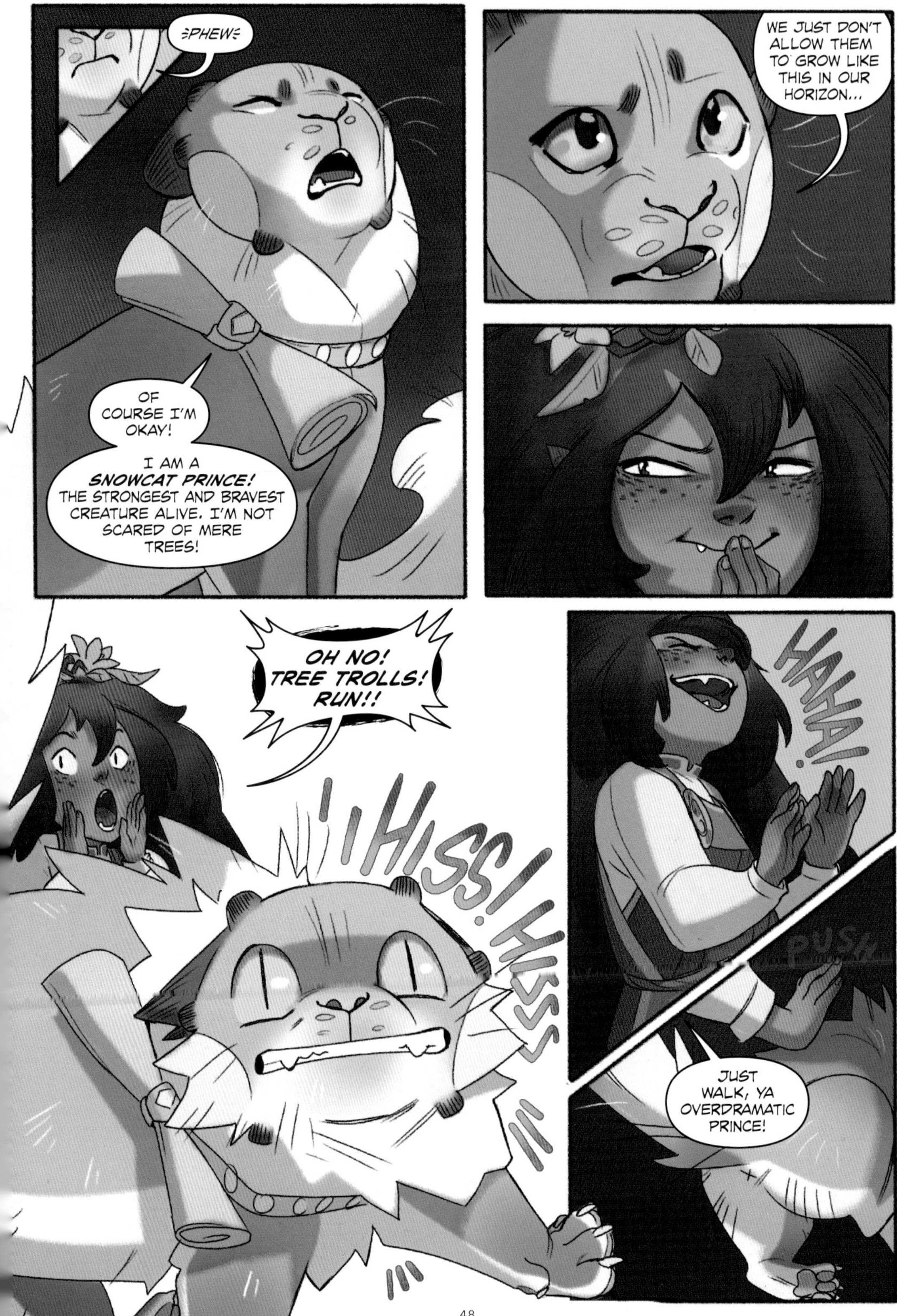

PHEW
WE JUST DON'T ALLOW THEM TO GROW LIKE THIS IN OUR HORIZON...
OF COURSE I'M OKAY!
I AM A *SNOWCAT PRINCE!* THE STRONGEST AND BRAVEST CREATURE ALIVE. I'M NOT SCARED OF MERE TREES!
OH NO! TREE TROLLS! RUN!!
HISS! HISSS
HAHA!
PUSH
JUST WALK, YA OVERDRAMATIC PRINCE!

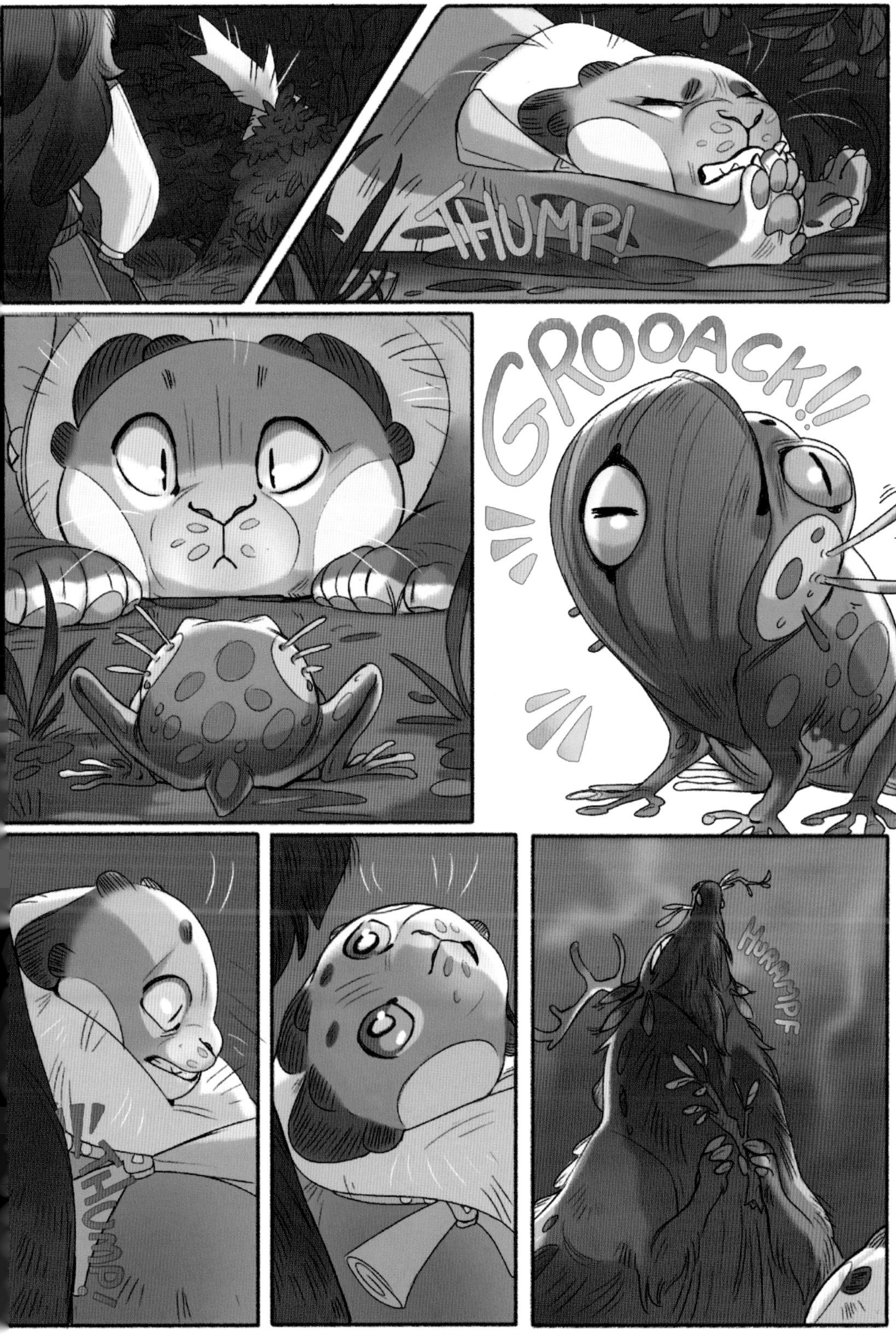
THUMP!
GROOACK!!!
THUMP!
HURRMPF

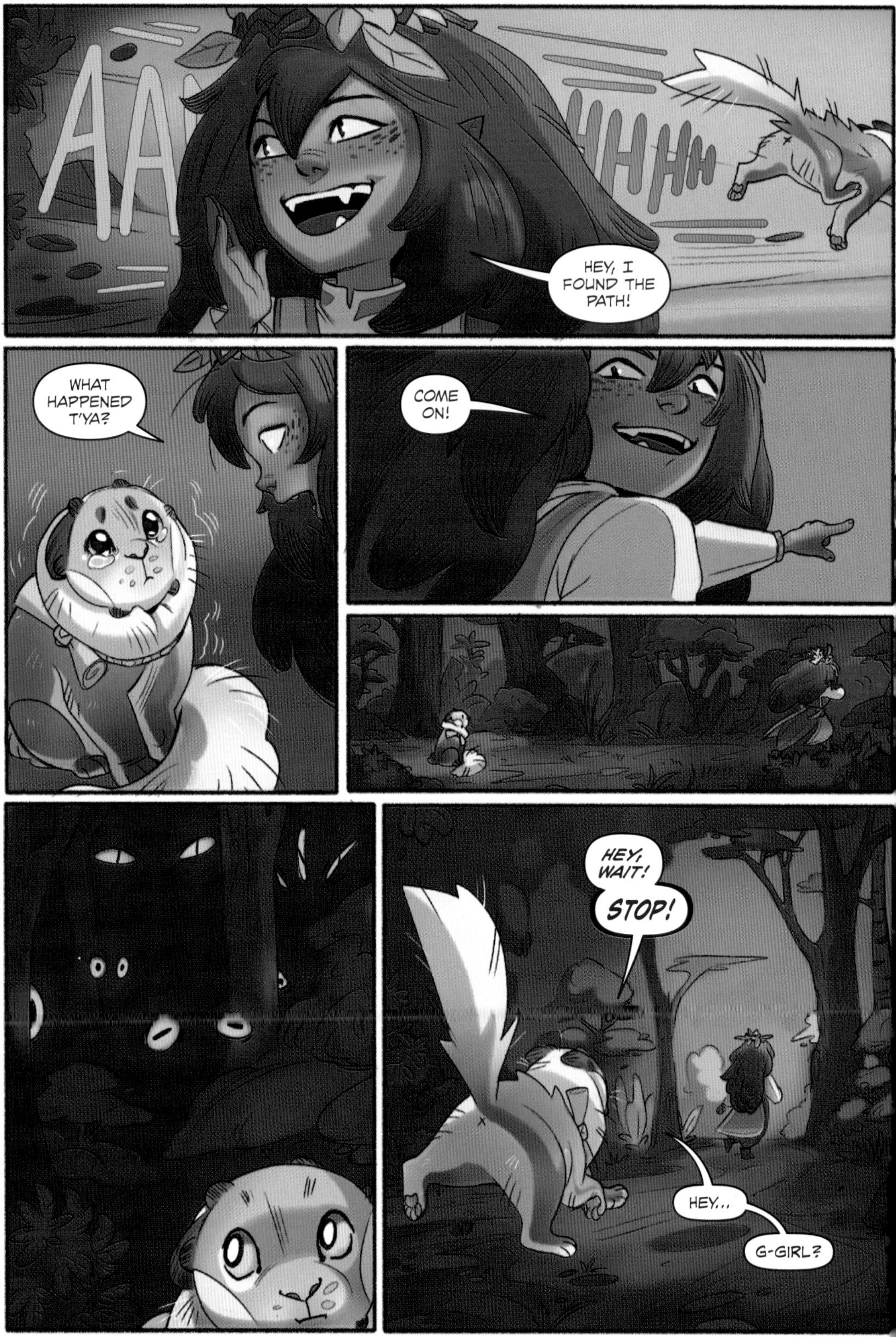
AAHHHHH
HEY, I FOUND THE PATH!
WHAT HAPPENED T'YA?
COME ON!
HEY, WAIT!
STOP!
HEY...
G-GIRL?

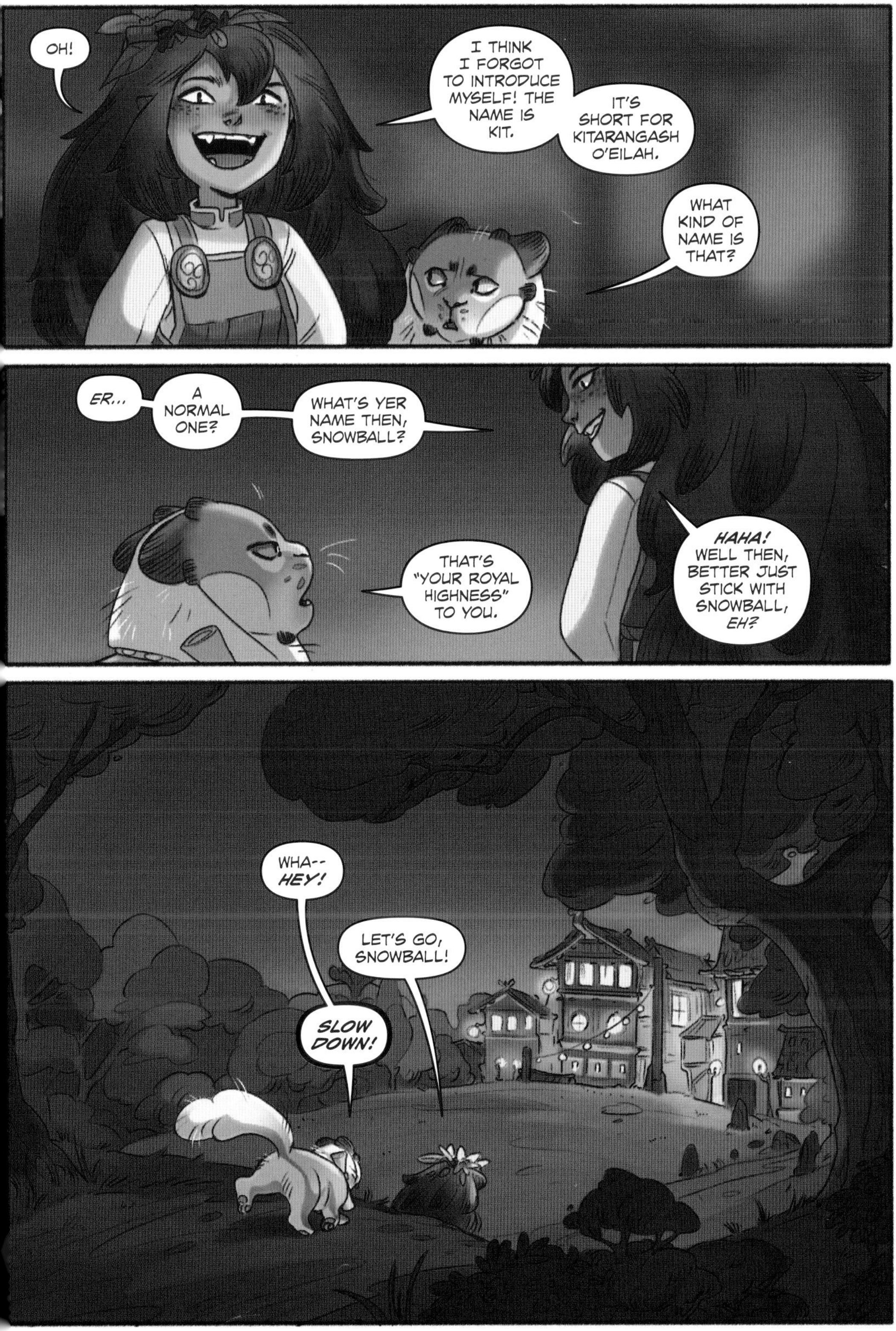
OH!
I THINK I FORGOT TO INTRODUCE MYSELF! THE NAME IS KIT.
IT'S SHORT FOR KITARANGASH O'EILAH.
WHAT KIND OF NAME IS THAT?
ER...
A NORMAL ONE?
WHAT'S YER NAME THEN, SNOWBALL?
THAT'S "YOUR ROYAL HIGHNESS" TO YOU.
HAHA! WELL THEN, BETTER JUST STICK WITH SNOWBALL, EH?
WHA-- HEY!
LET'S GO, SNOWBALL!
SLOW DOWN!

Chapter 3
THE VILLAGE OF OEYE

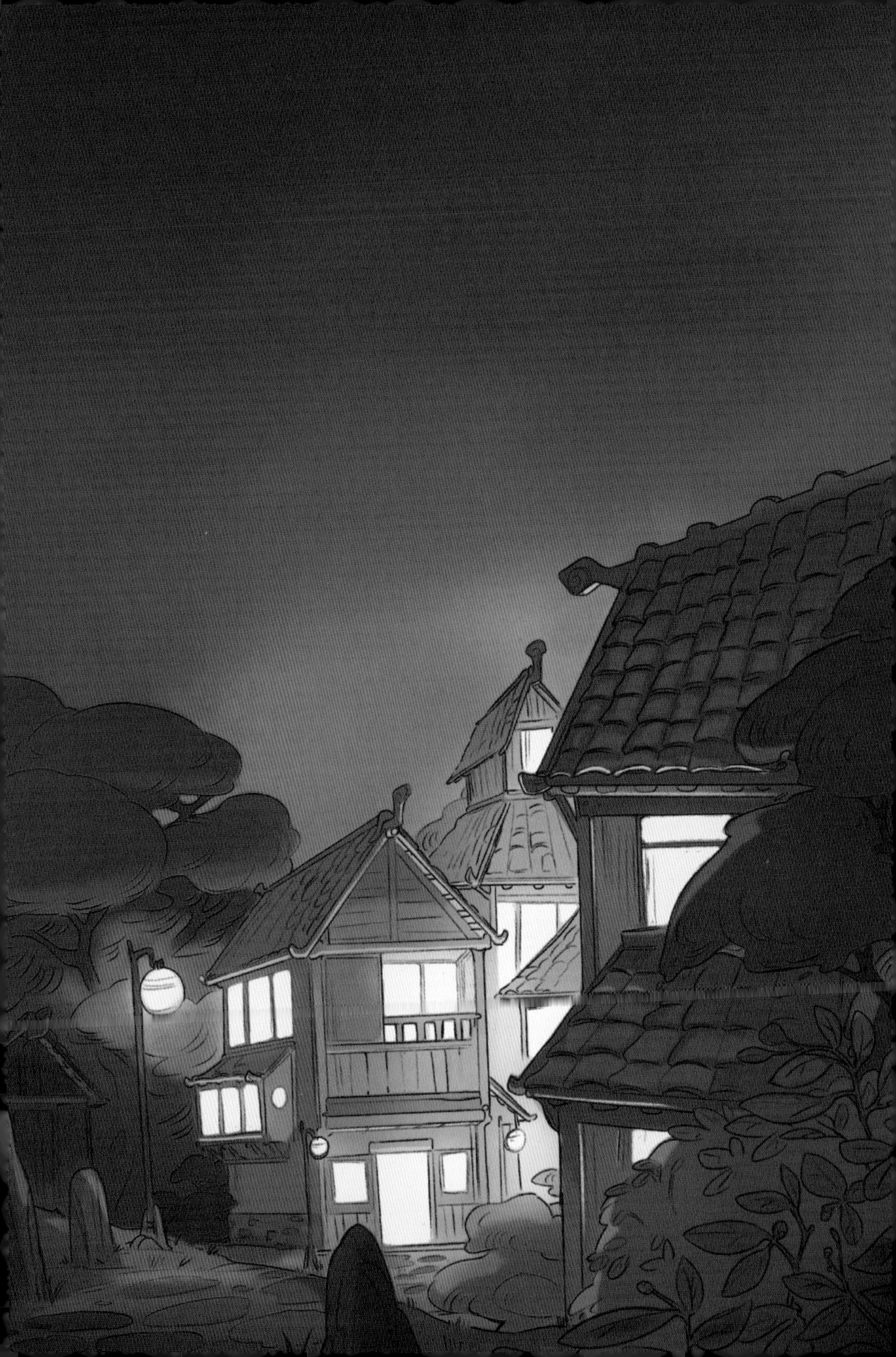

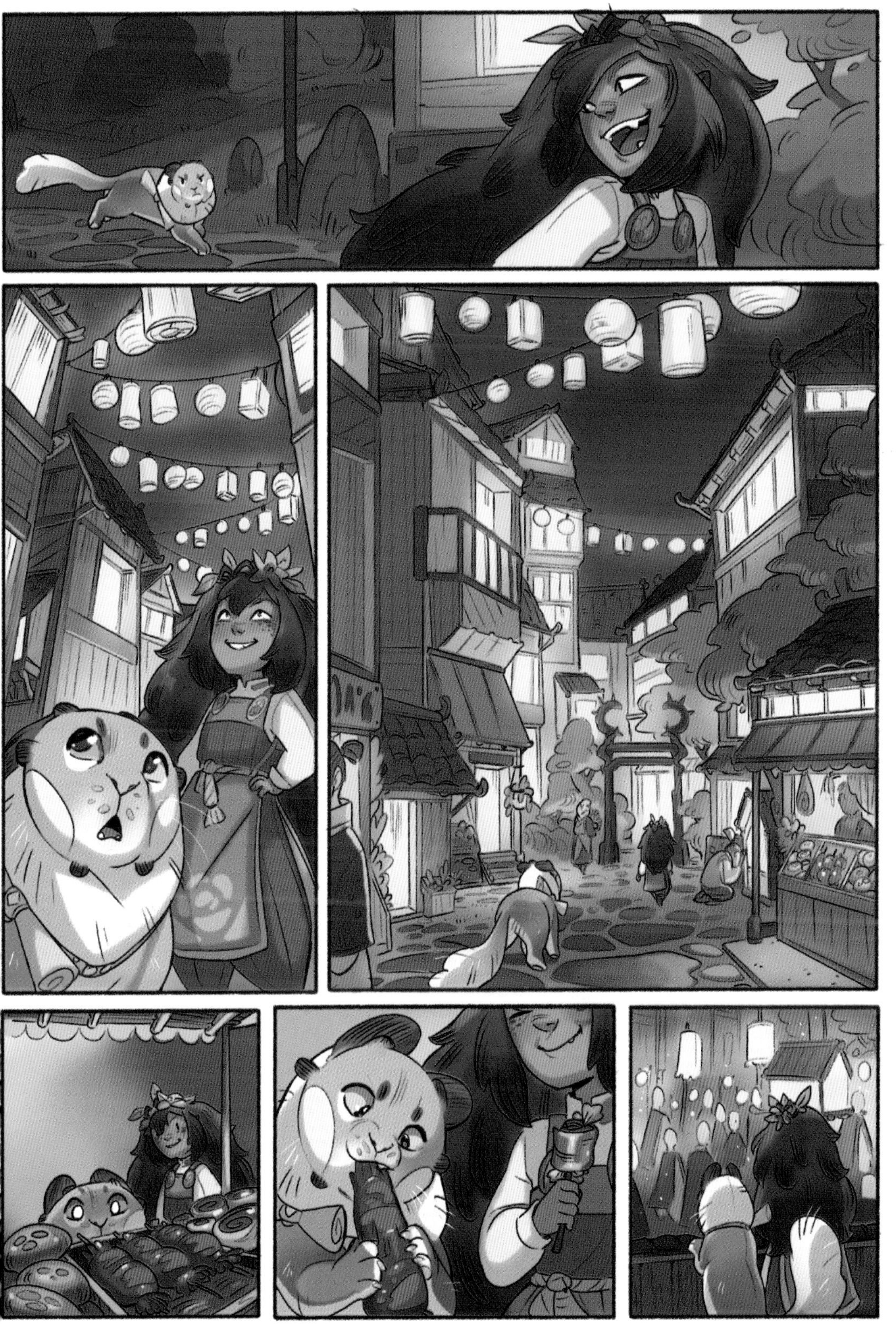

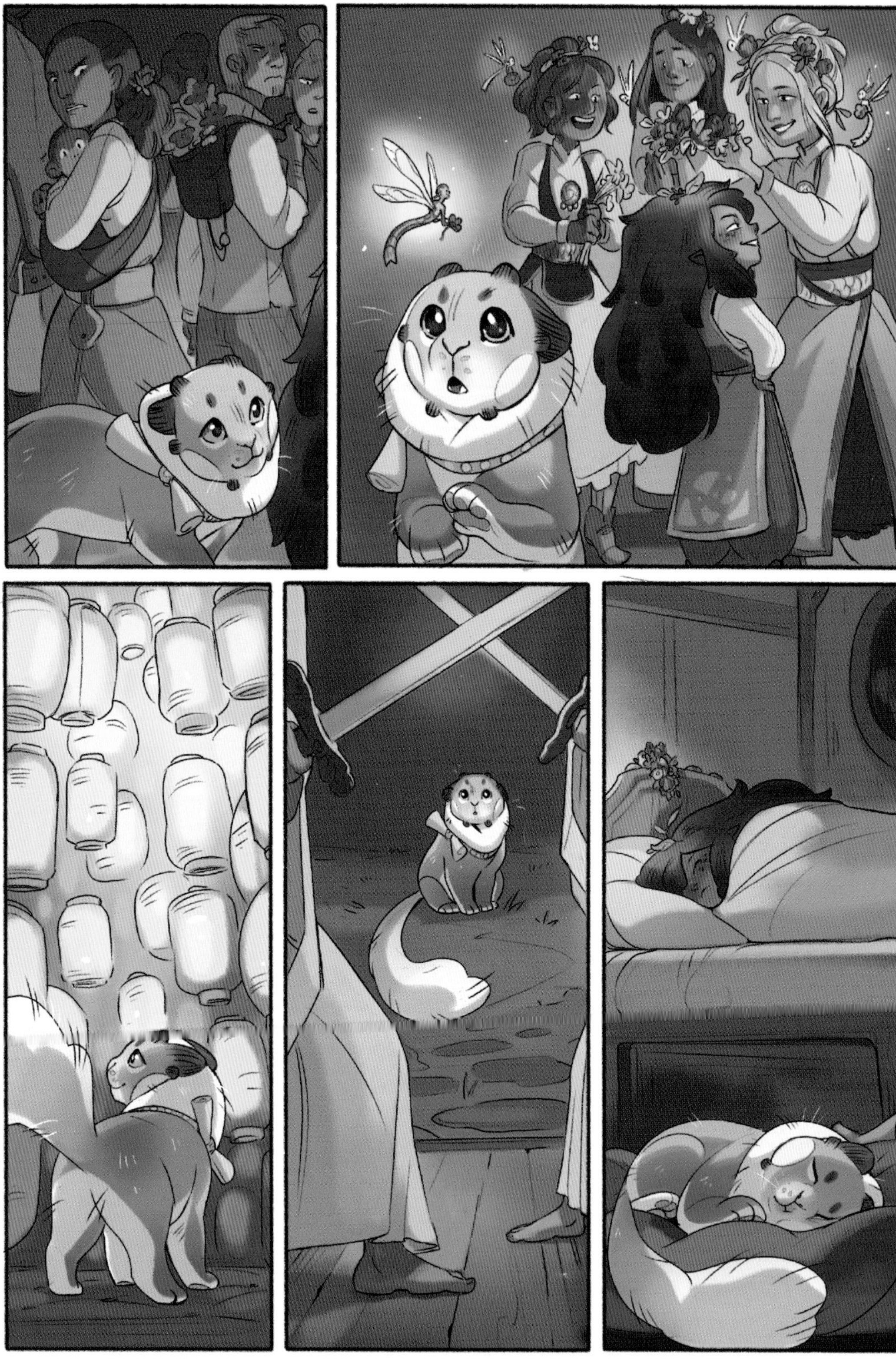

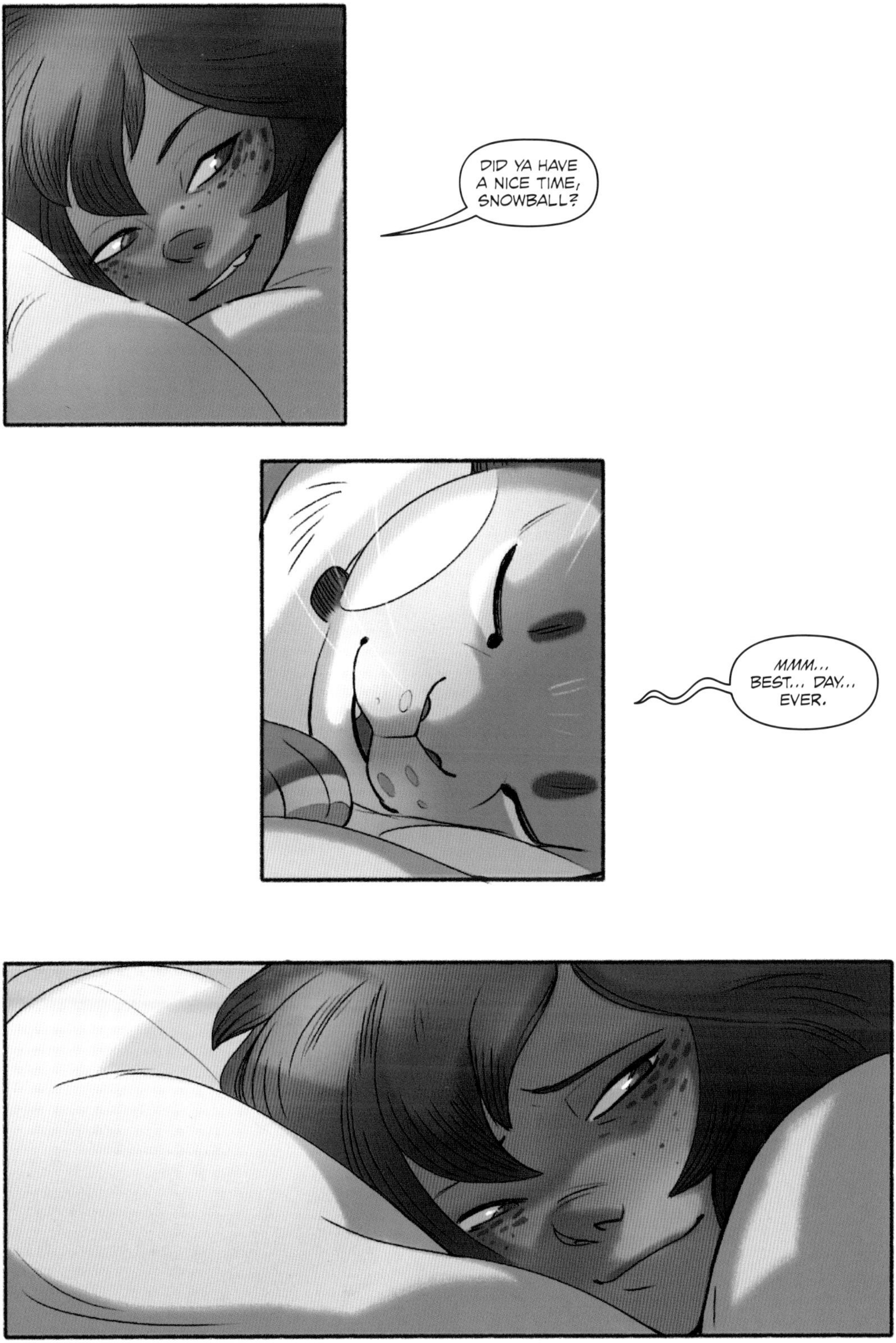
DID YA HAVE A NICE TIME, SNOWBALL?
MMM... BEST... DAY... EVER.

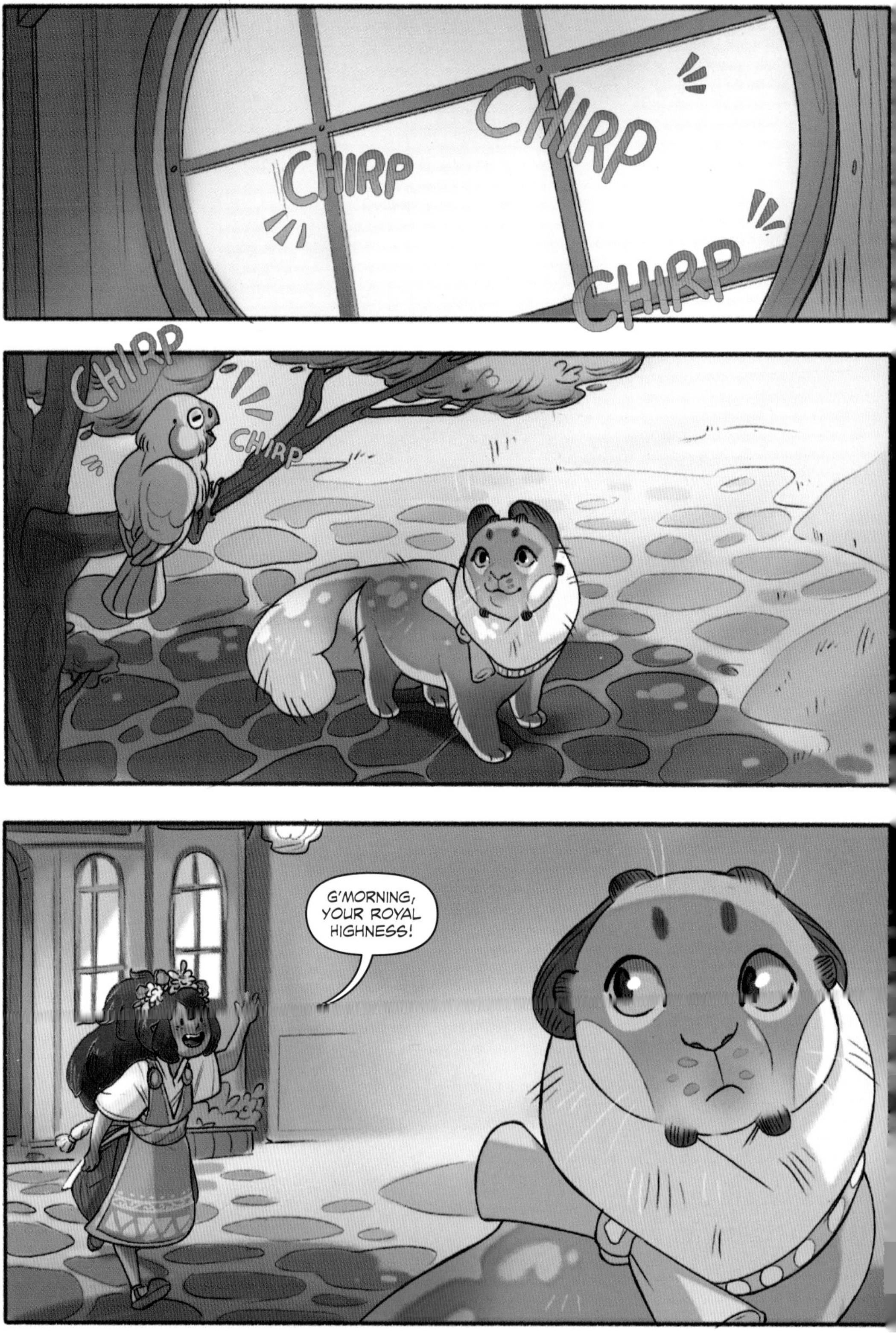
CHIRP
CHIRP
CHIRP
CHIRP
CHIRP
G'MORNING, YOUR ROYAL HIGHNESS!

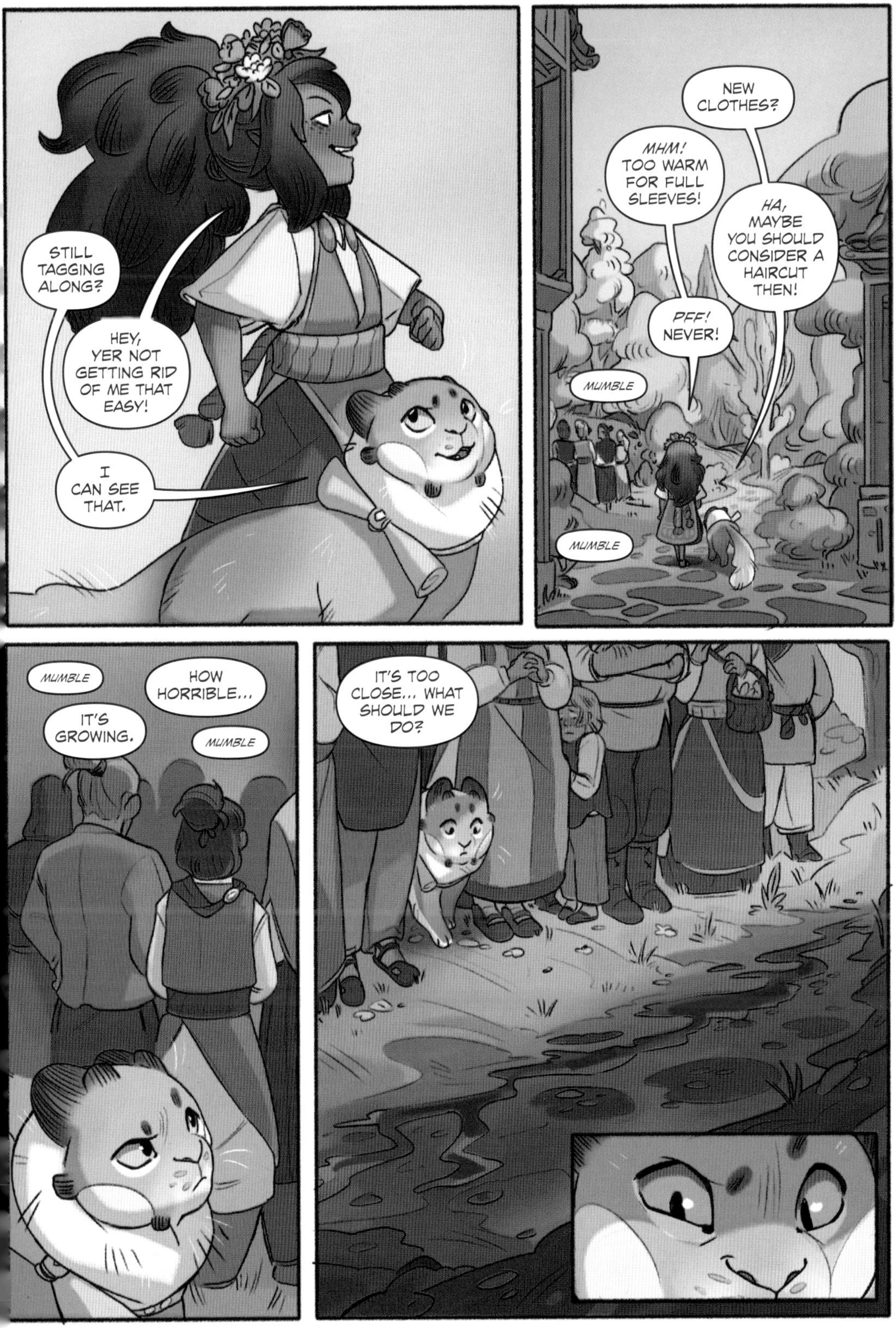
STILL TAGGING ALONG?
HEY, YER NOT GETTING RID OF ME THAT EASY!
I CAN SEE THAT.
NEW CLOTHES?
MHM! TOO WARM FOR FULL SLEEVES!
HA, MAYBE YOU SHOULD CONSIDER A HAIRCUT THEN!
PFF! NEVER!
MUMBLE
MUMBLE
MUMBLE
HOW HORRIBLE...
IT'S GROWING.
MUMBLE
IT'S TOO CLOSE... WHAT SHOULD WE DO?

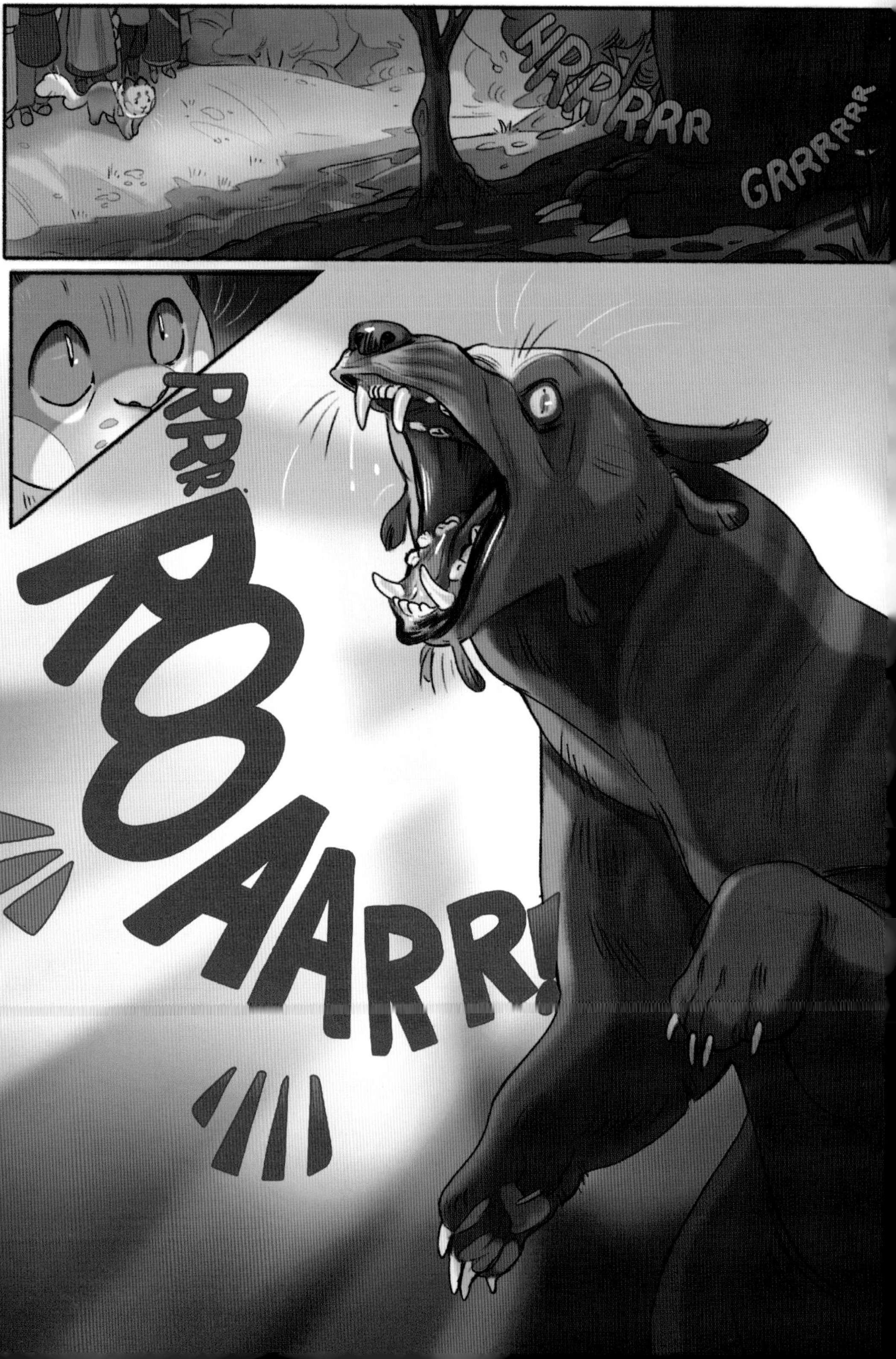
HRRRRRR
GRRRRRR
RRR
ROOAARR!

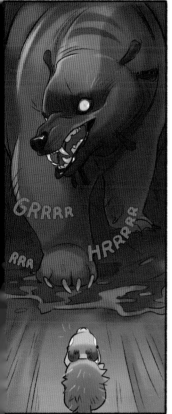

AAAAHH

I NEED TO HELP, SOMEHOW...

PRINCE?

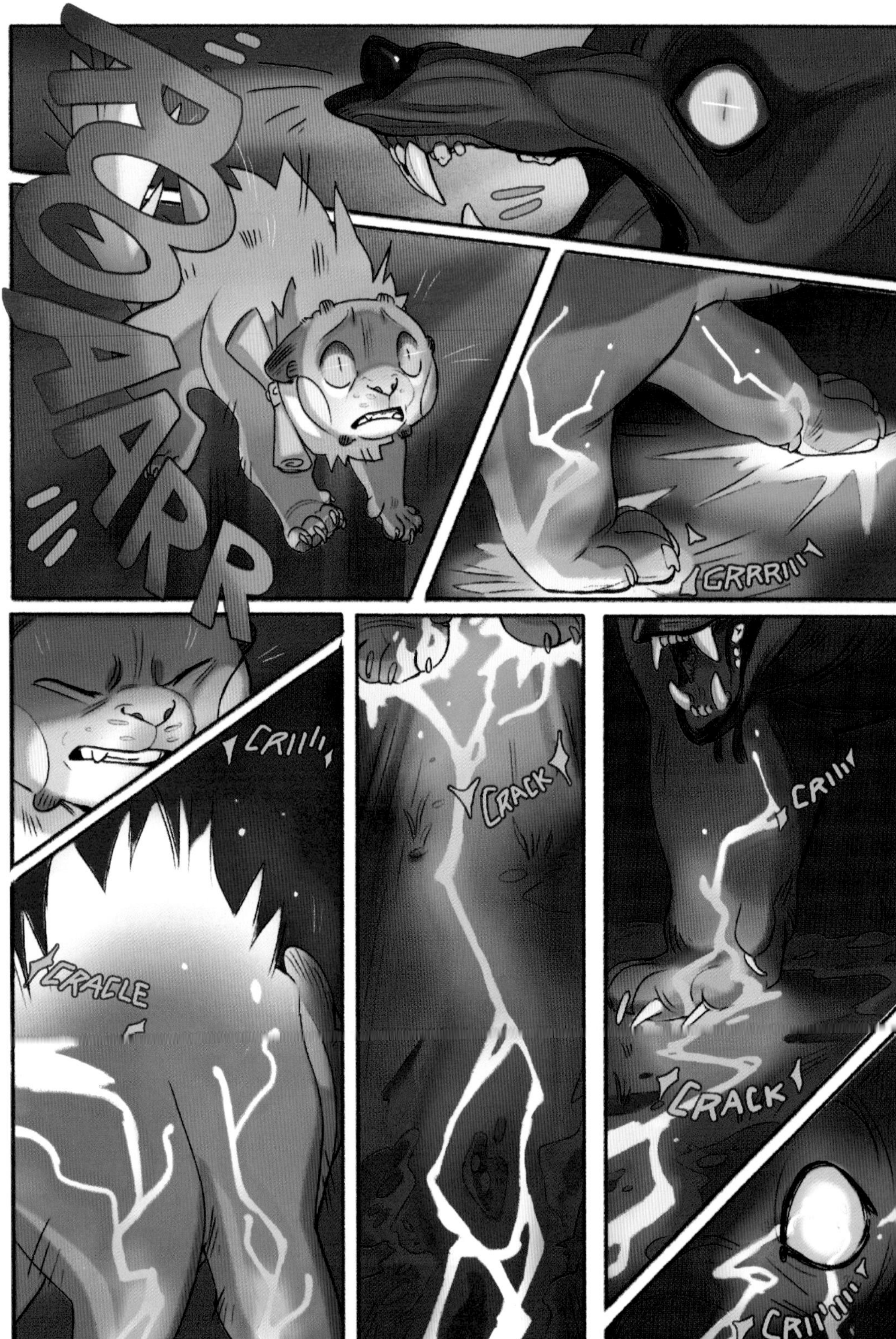

ROOOAARRR
GRRRR
CRII
CRACK
CRACLE
CRII
CRACK
CRII

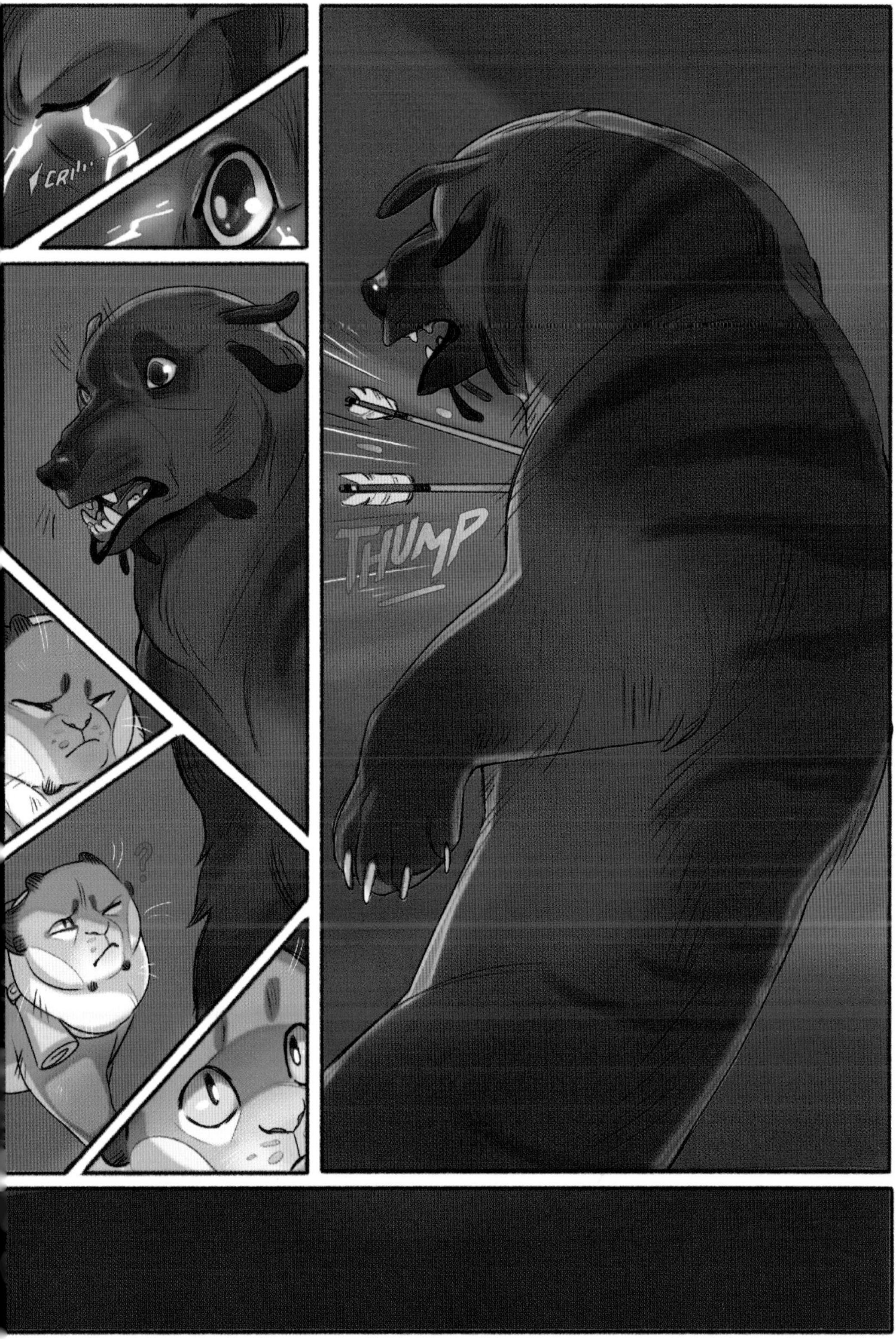
CRI...
THUMP

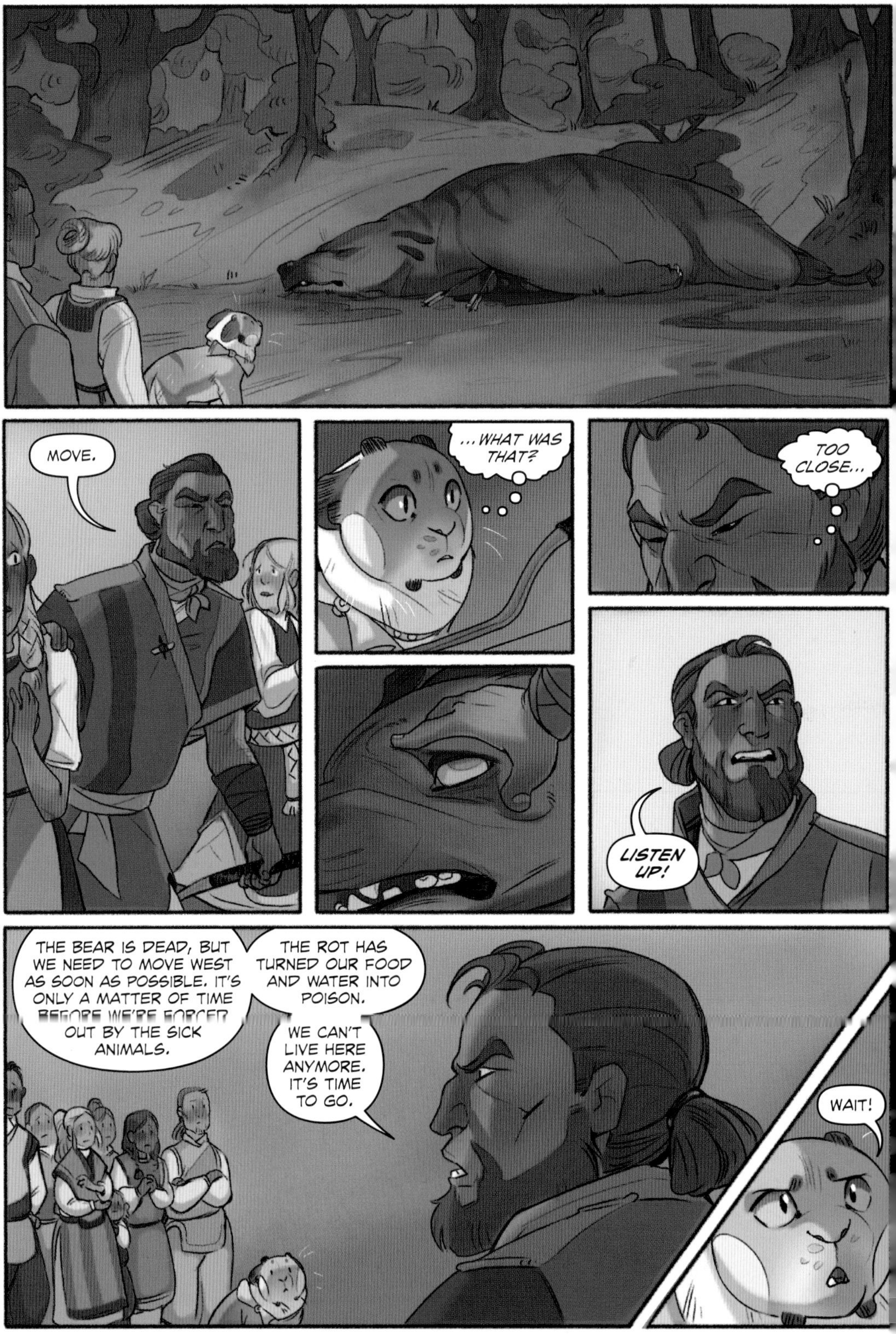
MOVE.
...WHAT WAS THAT?
TOO CLOSE...
LISTEN UP!
THE BEAR IS DEAD, BUT WE NEED TO MOVE WEST AS SOON AS POSSIBLE. IT'S ONLY A MATTER OF TIME BEFORE WE'RE FORCED OUT BY THE SICK ANIMALS.
THE ROT HAS TURNED OUR FOOD AND WATER INTO POISON.
WE CAN'T LIVE HERE ANYMORE. IT'S TIME TO GO.
WAIT!

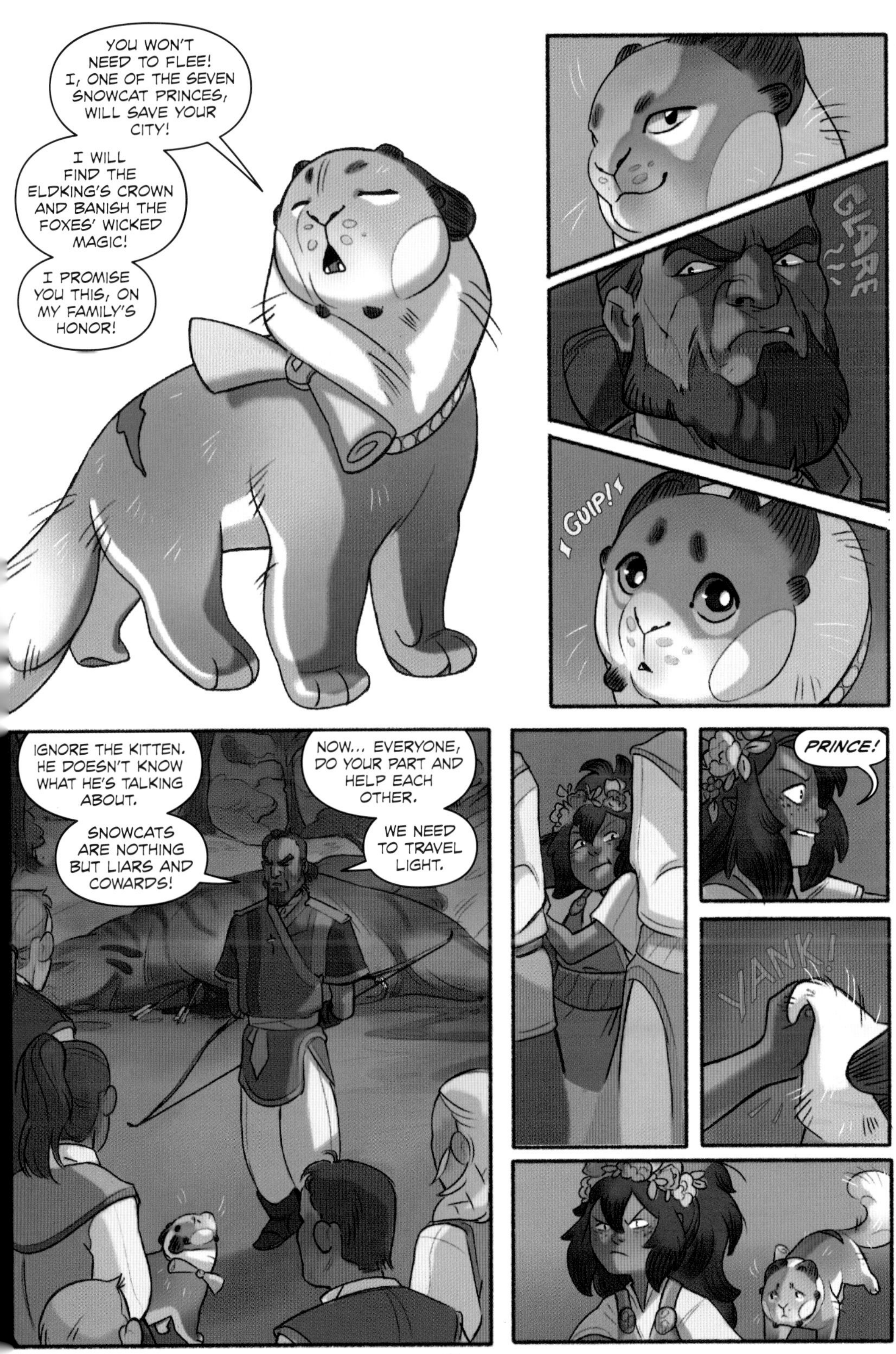
YOU WON'T NEED TO FLEE! I, ONE OF THE SEVEN SNOWCAT PRINCES, WILL SAVE YOUR CITY!
I WILL FIND THE ELDKING'S CROWN AND BANISH THE FOXES' WICKED MAGIC!
I PROMISE YOU THIS, ON MY FAMILY'S HONOR!
GLARE
GULP!
IGNORE THE KITTEN. HE DOESN'T KNOW WHAT HE'S TALKING ABOUT.
SNOWCATS ARE NOTHING BUT LIARS AND COWARDS!
NOW... EVERYONE, DO YOUR PART AND HELP EACH OTHER.
WE NEED TO TRAVEL LIGHT.
PRINCE!
YANK!

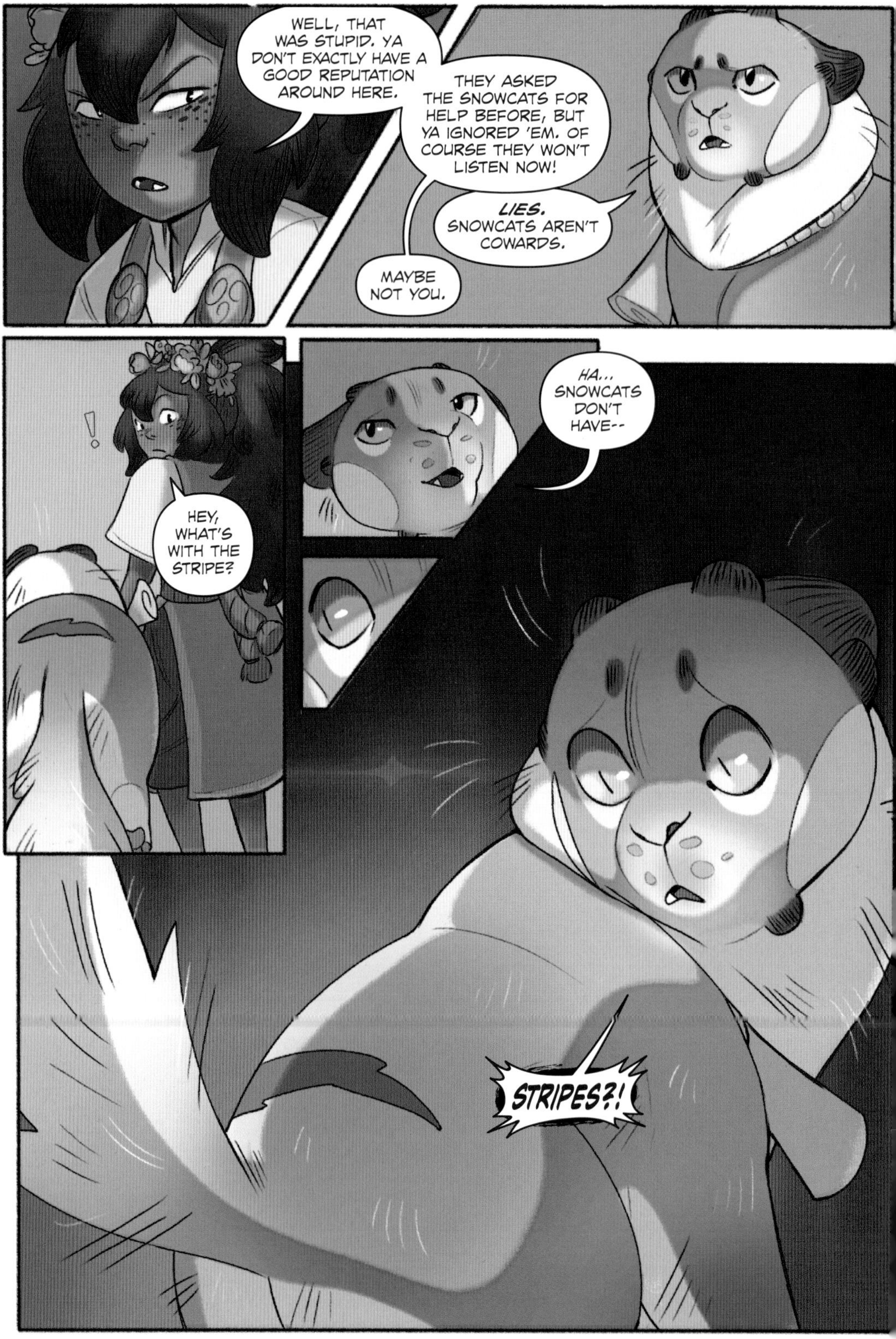

WELL, THAT WAS STUPID. YA DON'T EXACTLY HAVE A GOOD REPUTATION AROUND HERE.
THEY ASKED THE SNOWCATS FOR HELP BEFORE, BUT YA IGNORED 'EM. OF COURSE THEY WON'T LISTEN NOW!
LIES. SNOWCATS AREN'T COWARDS.
MAYBE NOT YOU.
!
HEY, WHAT'S WITH THE STRIPE?
HA... SNOWCATS DON'T HAVE--
STRIPES?!

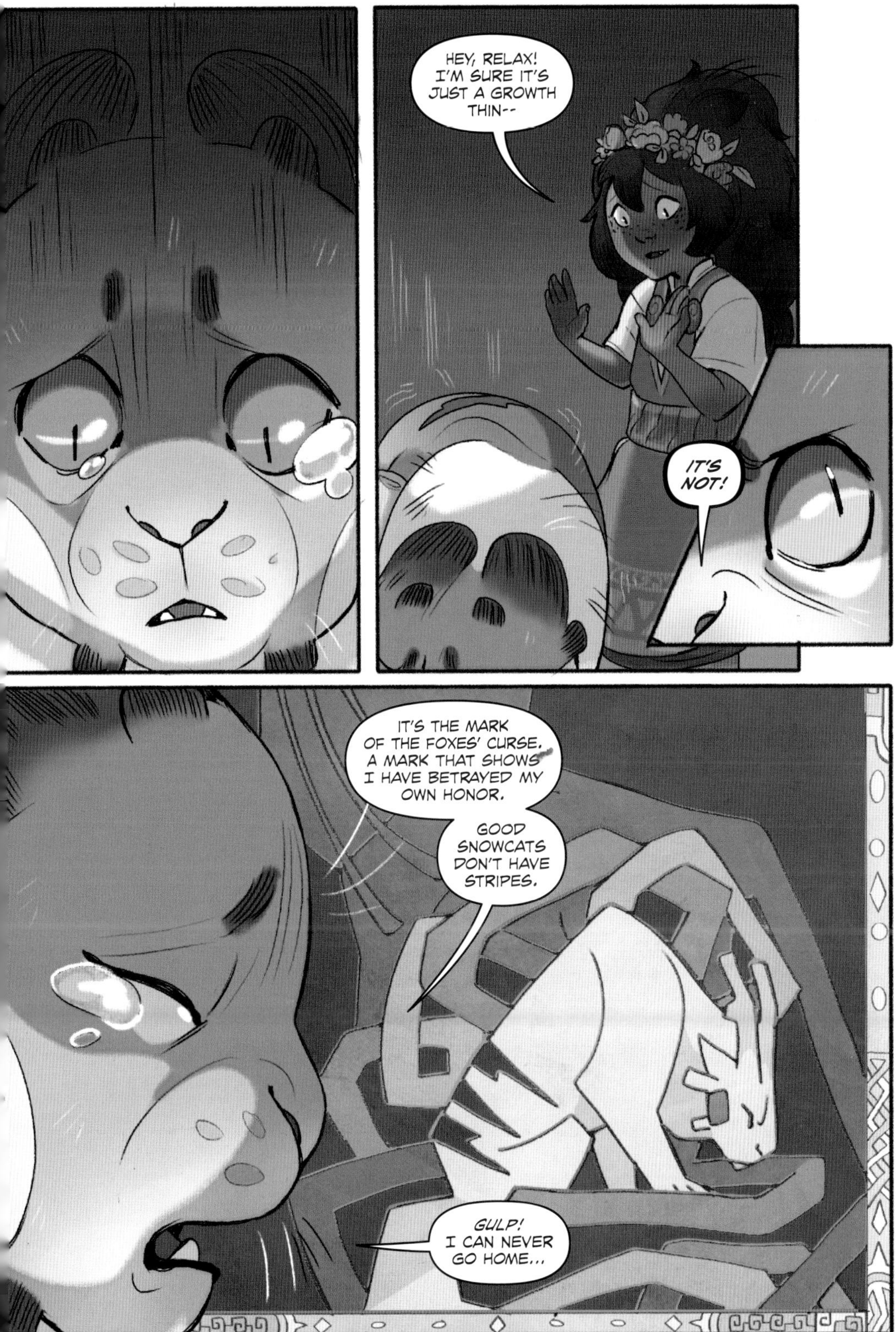
HEY, RELAX! I'M SURE IT'S JUST A GROWTH THIN--
IT'S NOT!
IT'S THE MARK OF THE FOXES' CURSE. A MARK THAT SHOWS I HAVE BETRAYED MY OWN HONOR.
GOOD SNOWCATS DON'T HAVE STRIPES.
GULP! I CAN NEVER GO HOME...

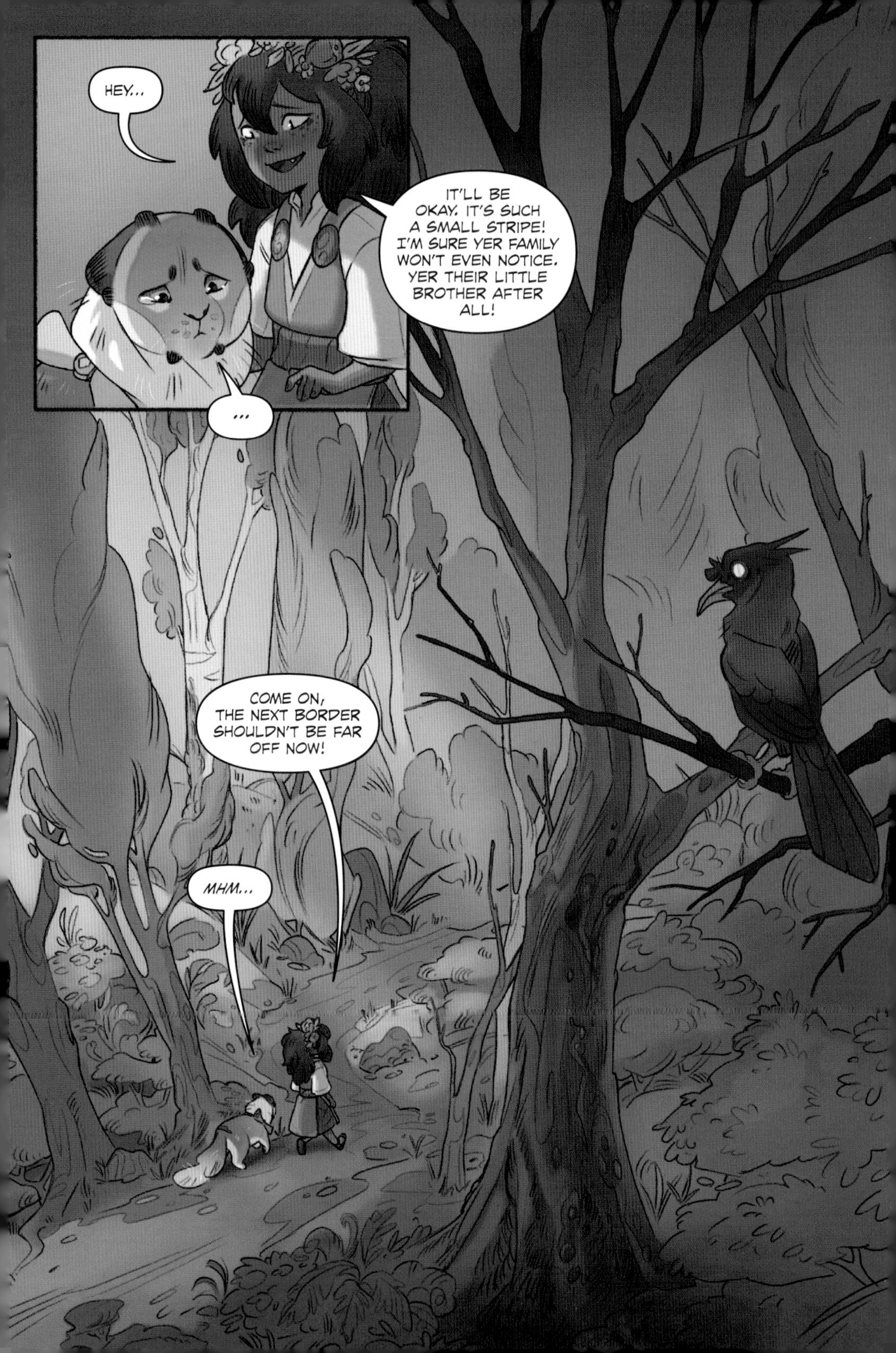
HEY...
IT'LL BE OKAY. IT'S SUCH A SMALL STRIPE! I'M SURE YER FAMILY WON'T EVEN NOTICE. YER THEIR LITTLE BROTHER AFTER ALL!
...
COME ON, THE NEXT BORDER SHOULDN'T BE FAR OFF NOW!
MHM...

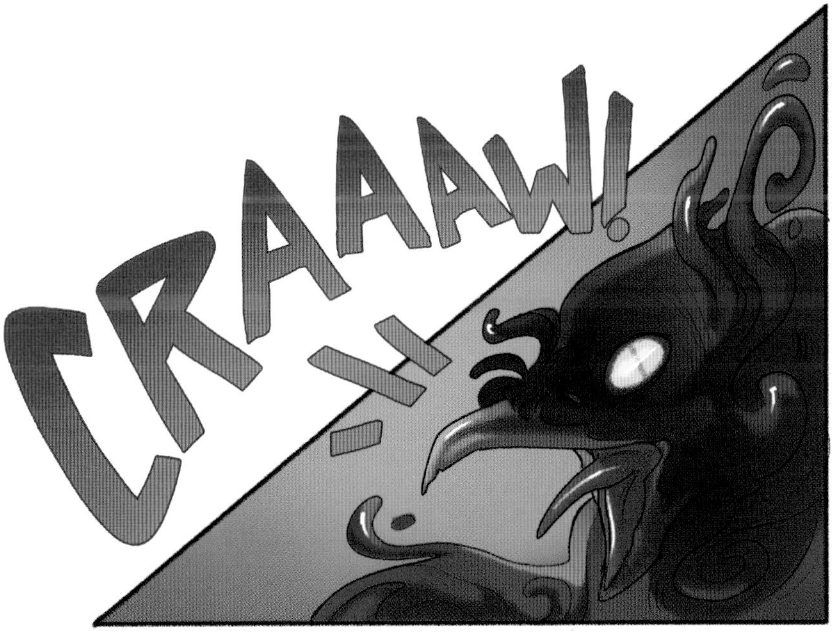
CRAAAW!

Chapter 4
THE LOST PRINCES

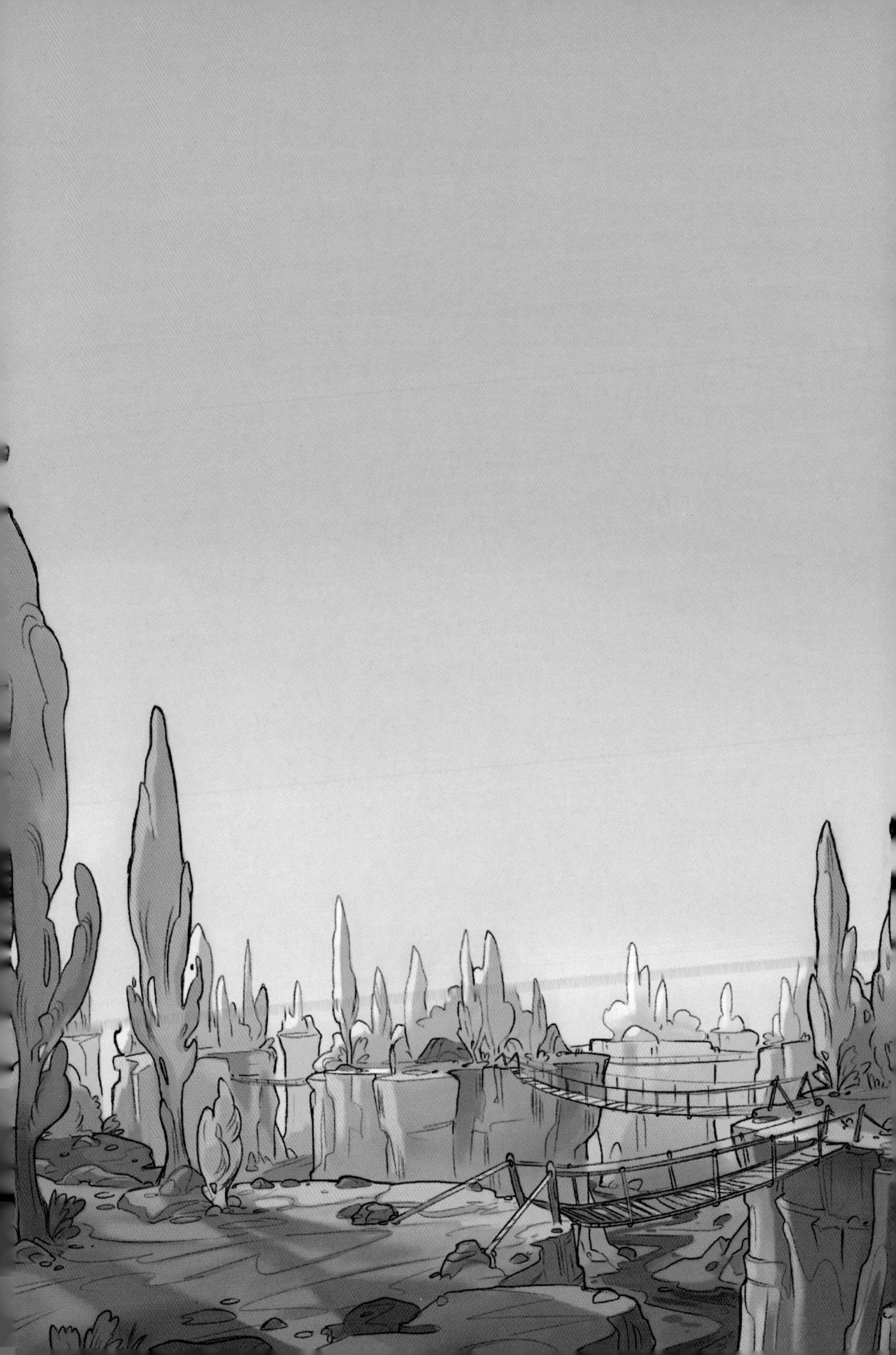

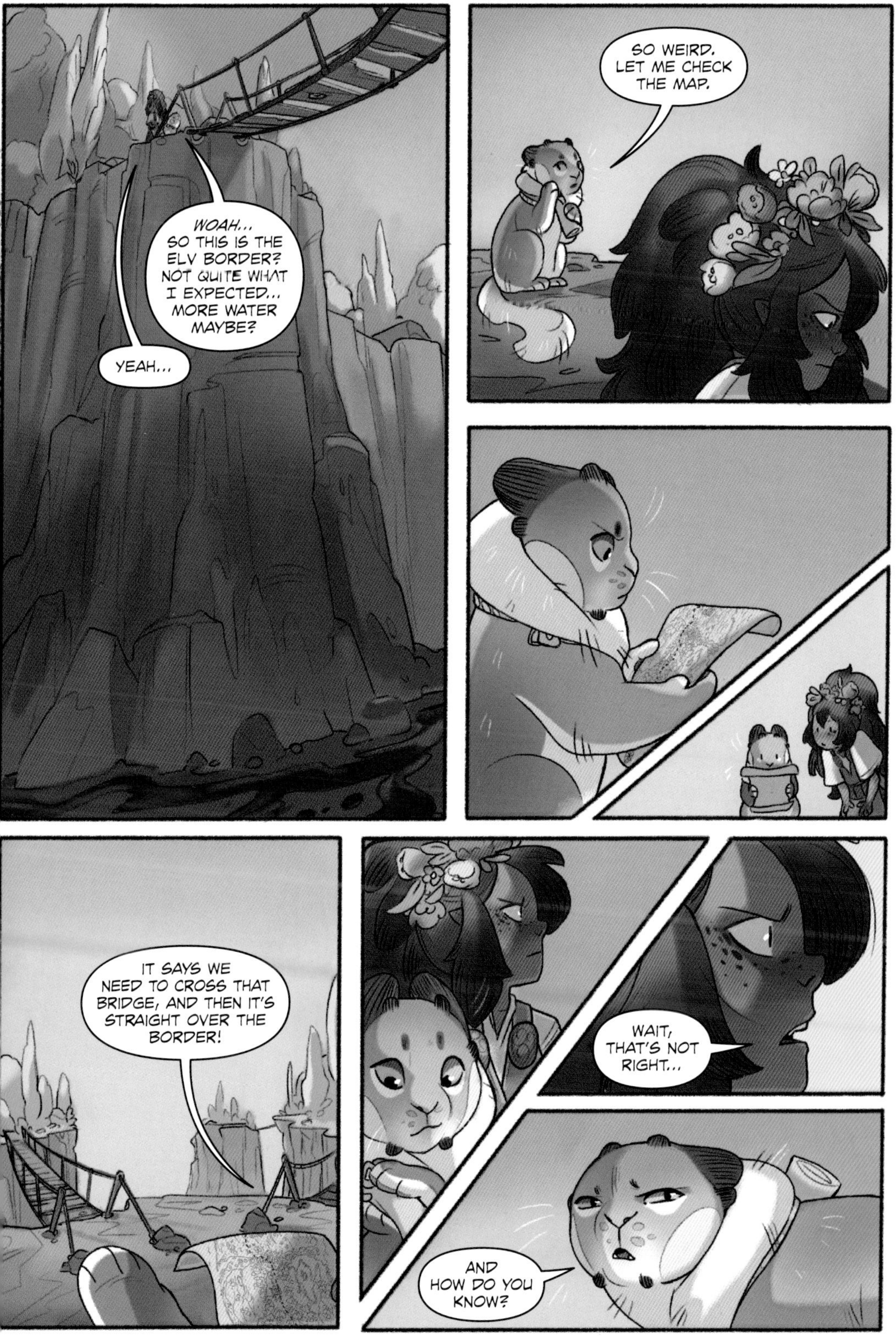
WOAH... SO THIS IS THE ELV BORDER? NOT QUITE WHAT I EXPECTED... MORE WATER MAYBE?
YEAH...
SO WEIRD. LET ME CHECK THE MAP.
IT SAYS WE NEED TO CROSS THAT BRIDGE, AND THEN IT'S STRAIGHT OVER THE BORDER!
WAIT, THAT'S NOT RIGHT...
AND HOW DO YOU KNOW?

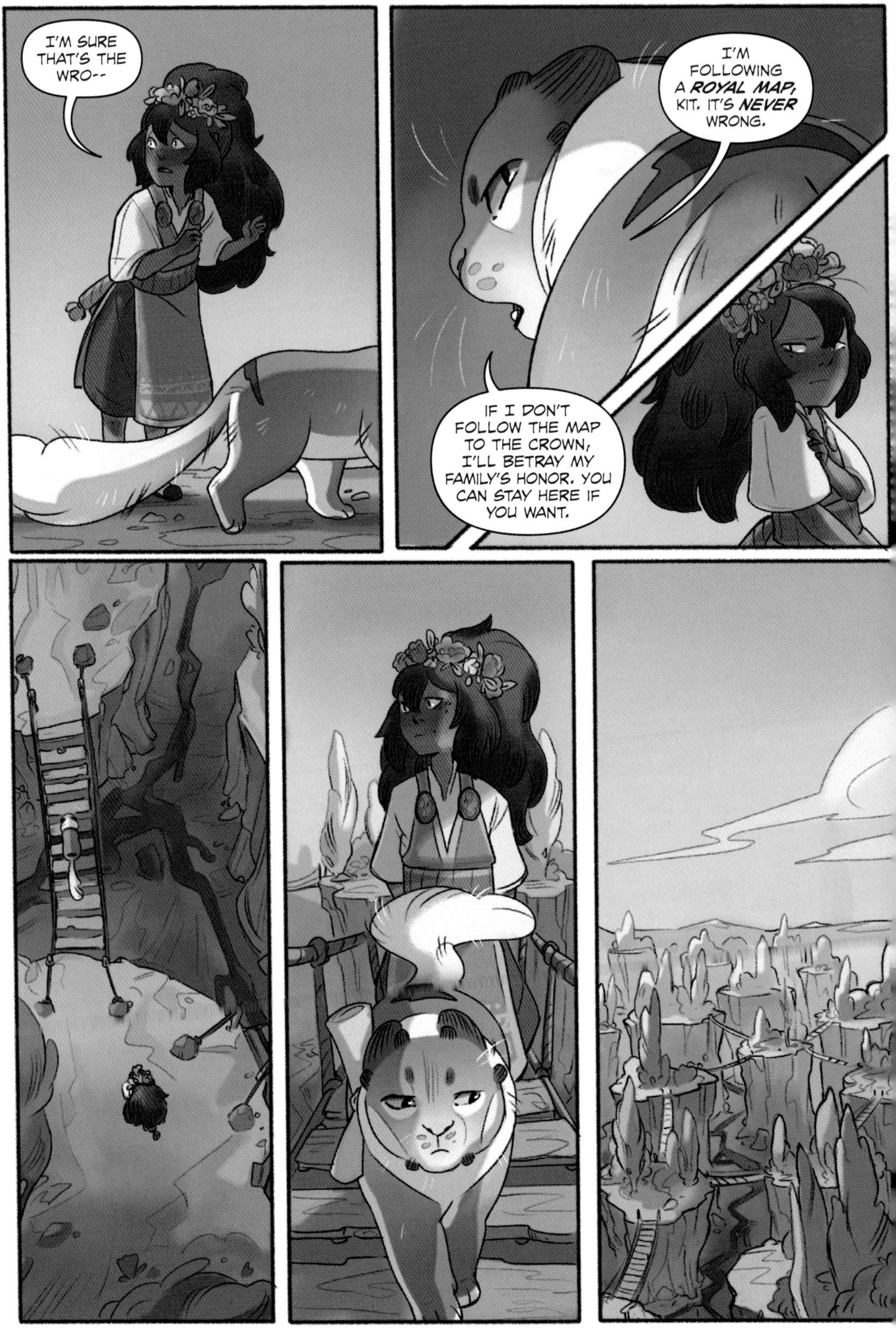
I'M SURE THAT'S THE WRO--
I'M FOLLOWING A **ROYAL MAP,** KIT. IT'S **NEVER** WRONG.
IF I DON'T FOLLOW THE MAP TO THE CROWN, I'LL BETRAY MY FAMILY'S HONOR. YOU CAN STAY HERE IF YOU WANT.

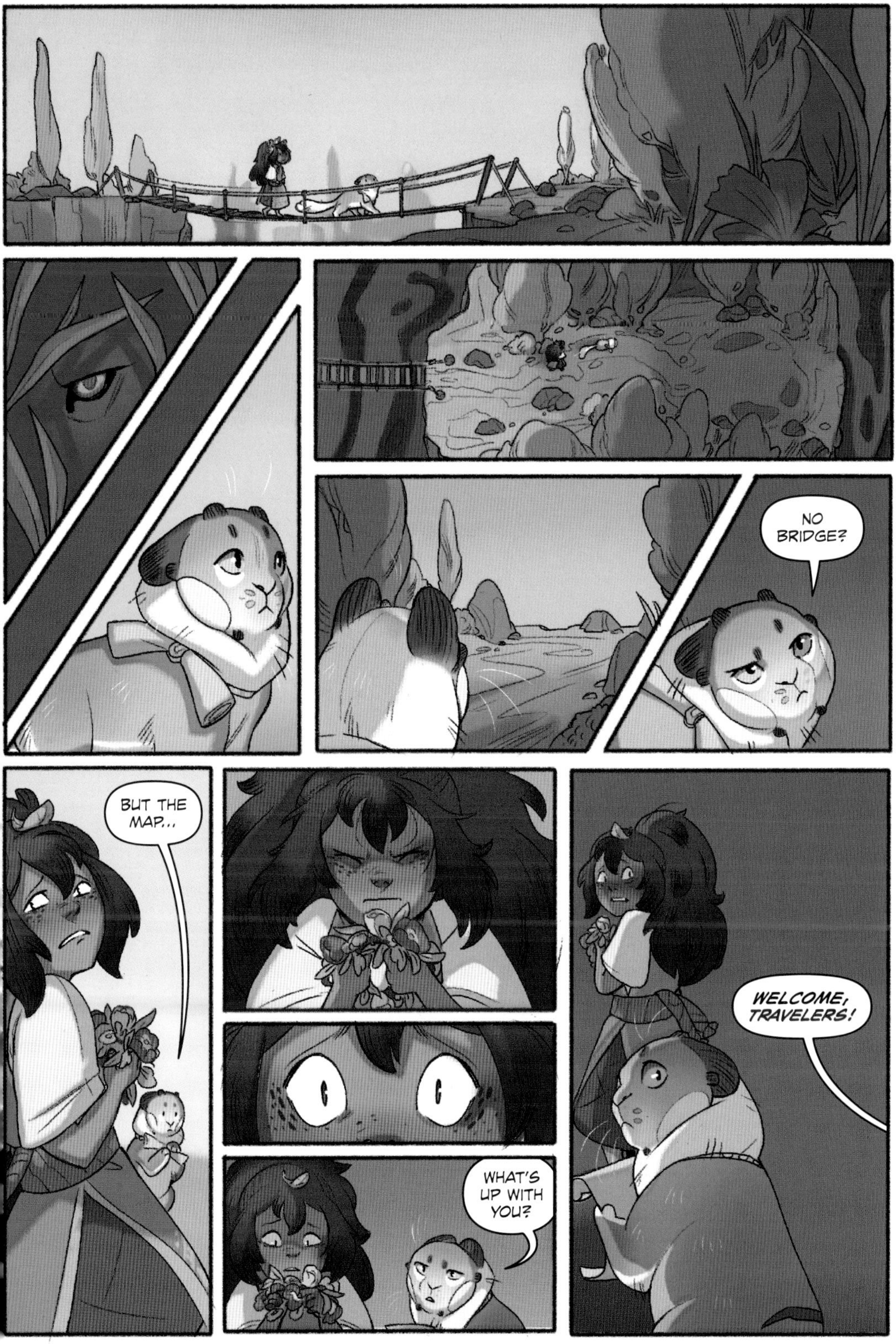
NO BRIDGE?
BUT THE MAP...
WHAT'S UP WITH YOU?
WELCOME, TRAVELERS!

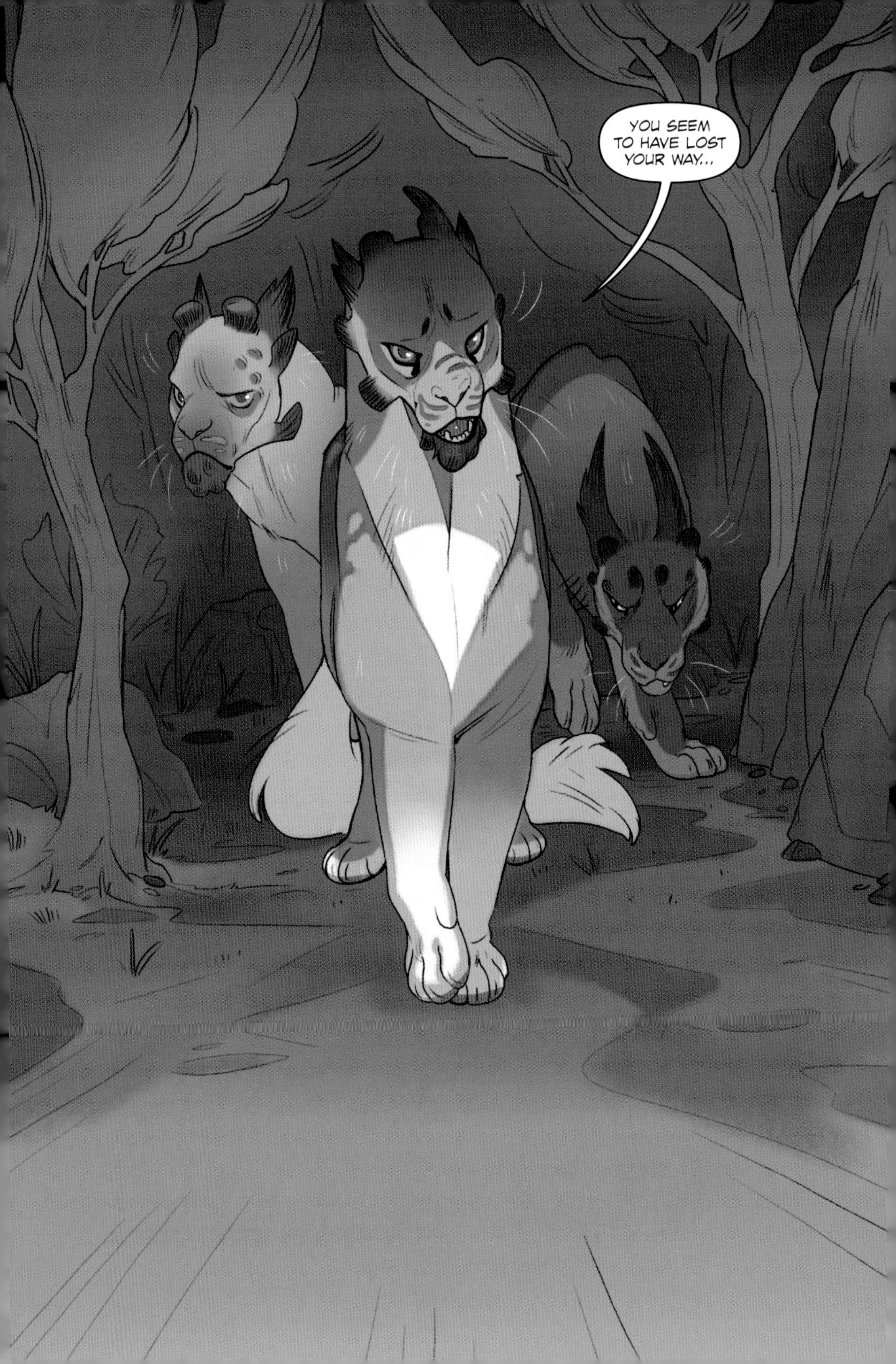
YOU SEEM TO HAVE LOST YOUR WAY...

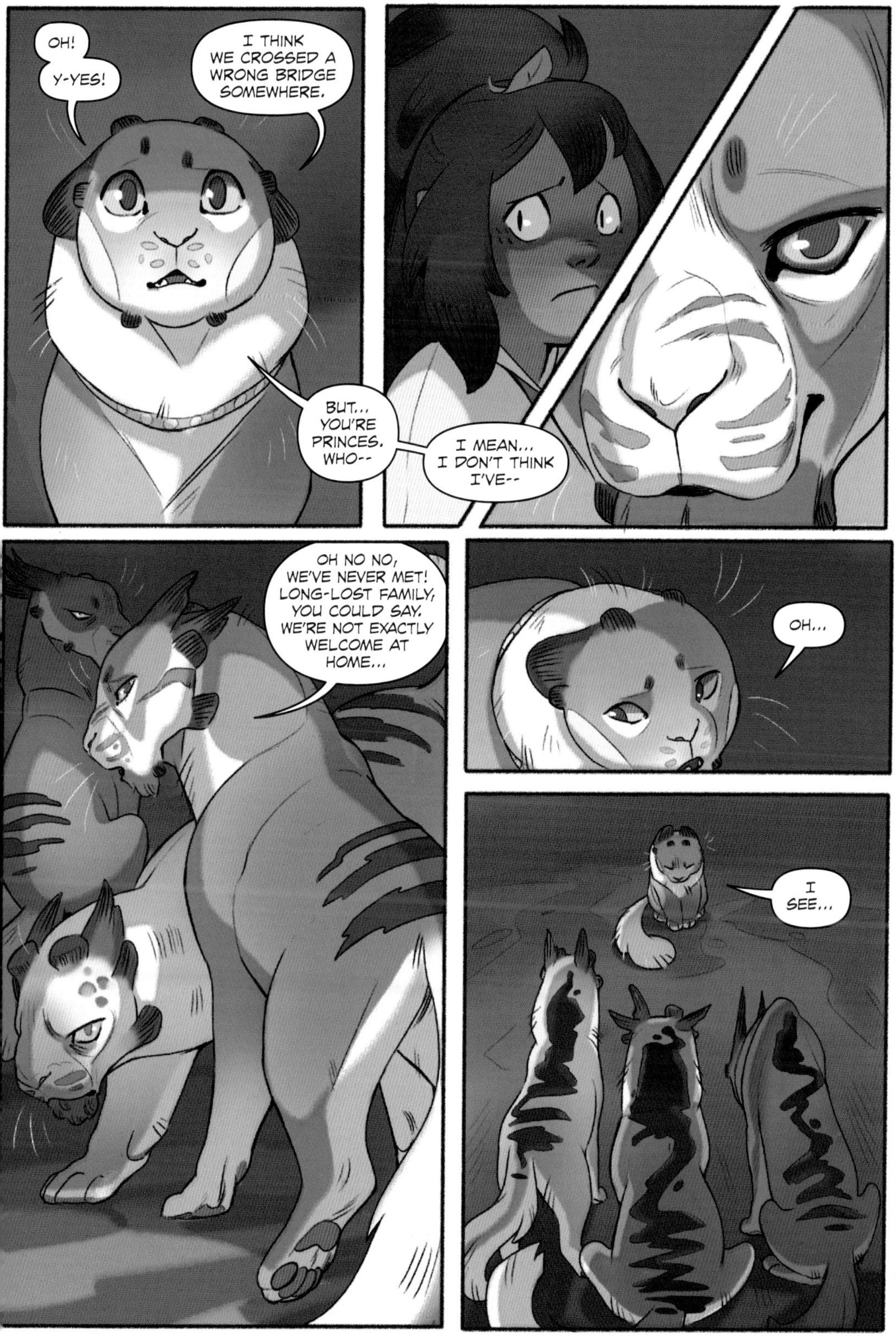
OH!
Y-YES!
I THINK WE CROSSED A WRONG BRIDGE SOMEWHERE.
BUT... YOU'RE PRINCES. WHO--
I MEAN... I DON'T THINK I'VE--
OH NO NO, WE'VE NEVER MET! LONG-LOST FAMILY, YOU COULD SAY. WE'RE NOT EXACTLY WELCOME AT HOME...
OH...
I SEE...

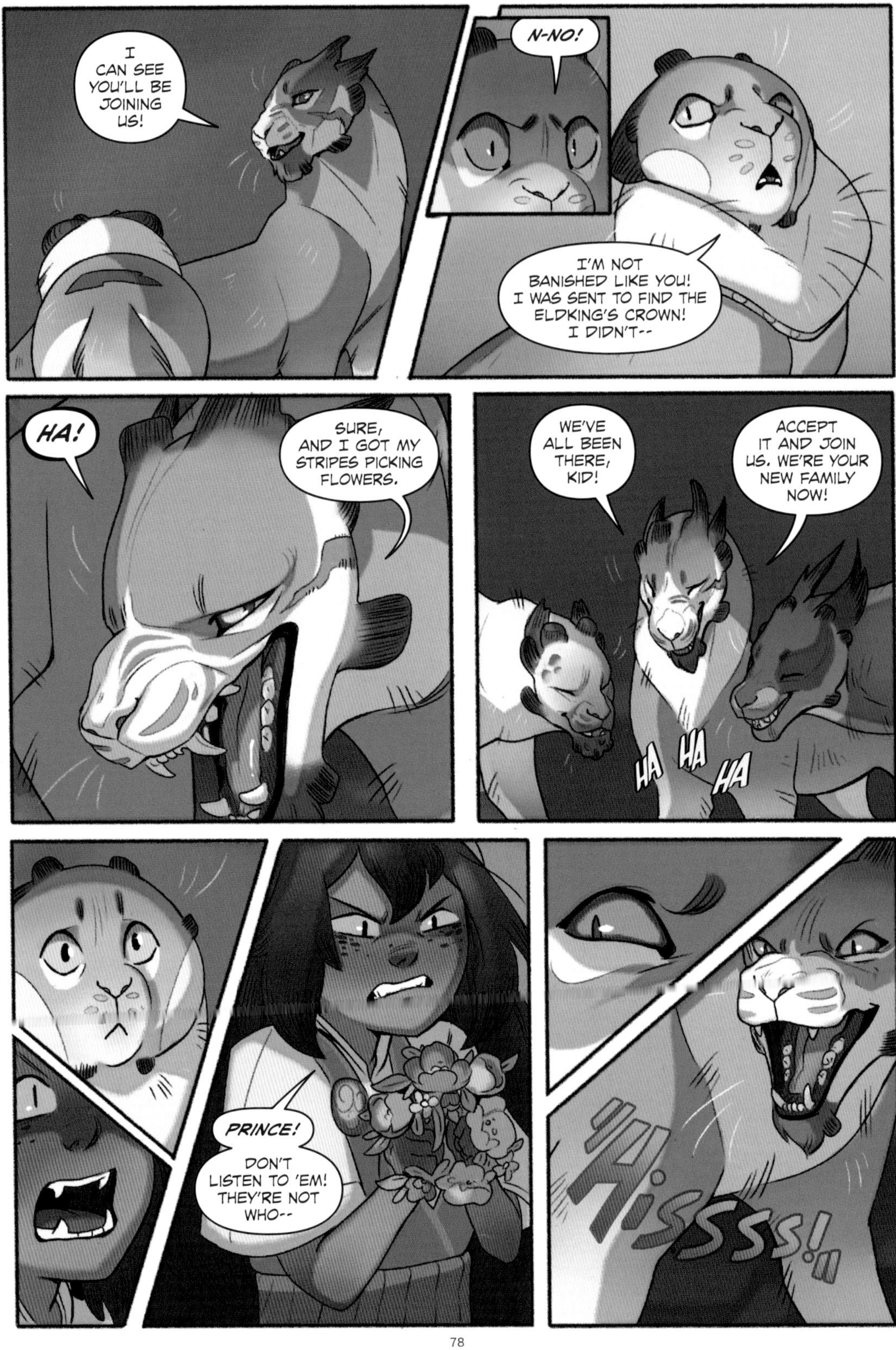
I CAN SEE YOU'LL BE JOINING US!
N-NO!
I'M NOT BANISHED LIKE YOU! I WAS SENT TO FIND THE ELDKING'S CROWN! I DIDN'T--
HA!
SURE, AND I GOT MY STRIPES PICKING FLOWERS.
WE'VE ALL BEEN THERE, KID!
ACCEPT IT AND JOIN US. WE'RE YOUR NEW FAMILY NOW!
HA HA HA
PRINCE!
DON'T LISTEN TO 'EM! THEY'RE NOT WHO--
HISSSS!!

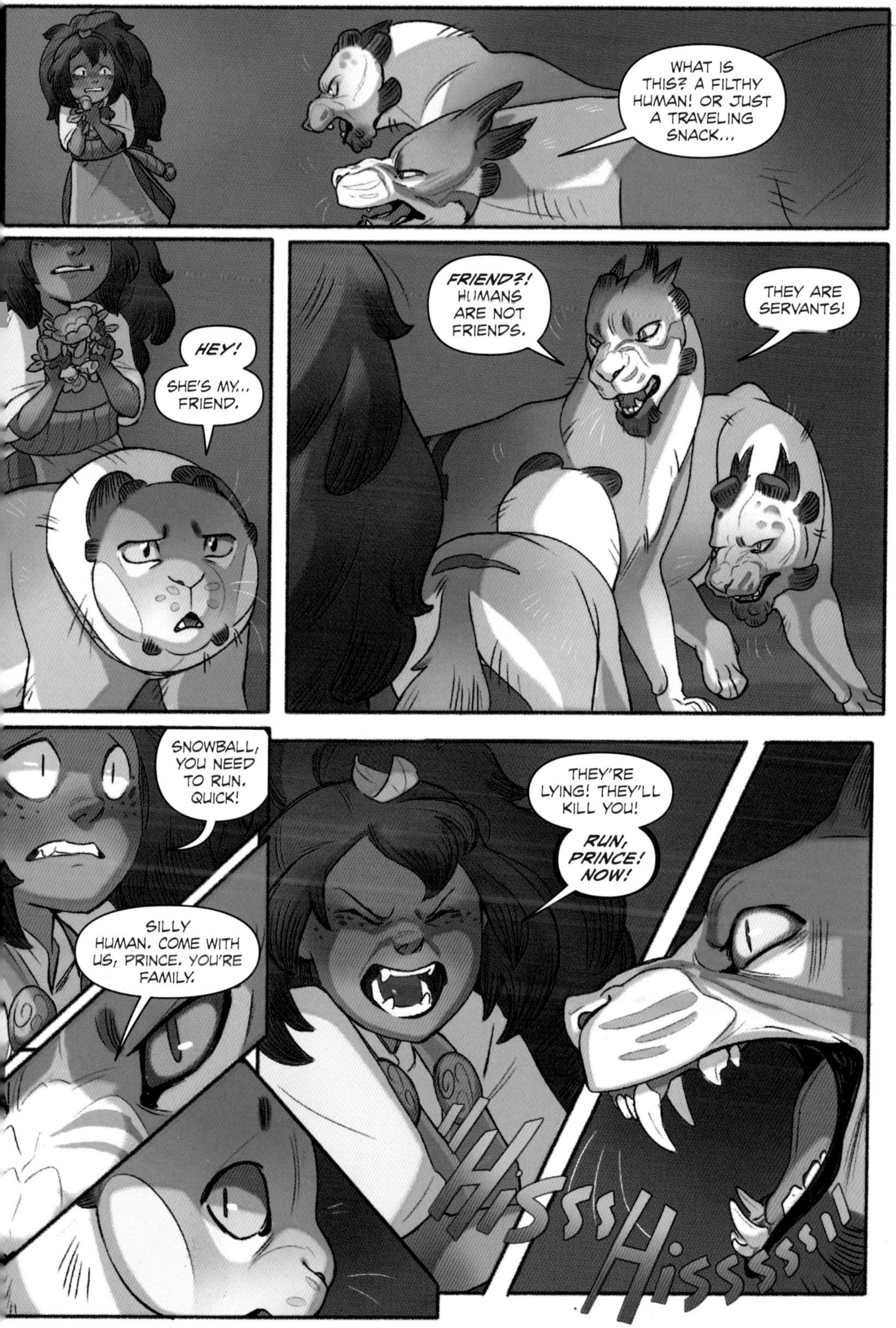
WHAT IS THIS? A FILTHY HUMAN! OR JUST A TRAVELING SNACK...
HEY!
SHE'S MY... FRIEND.
FRIEND?! HUMANS ARE NOT FRIENDS.
THEY ARE SERVANTS!
SNOWBALL, YOU NEED TO RUN. QUICK!
SILLY HUMAN. COME WITH US, PRINCE. YOU'RE FAMILY.
THEY'RE LYING! THEY'LL KILL YOU!
RUN, PRINCE! NOW!
HISSS
HISSSSS!!

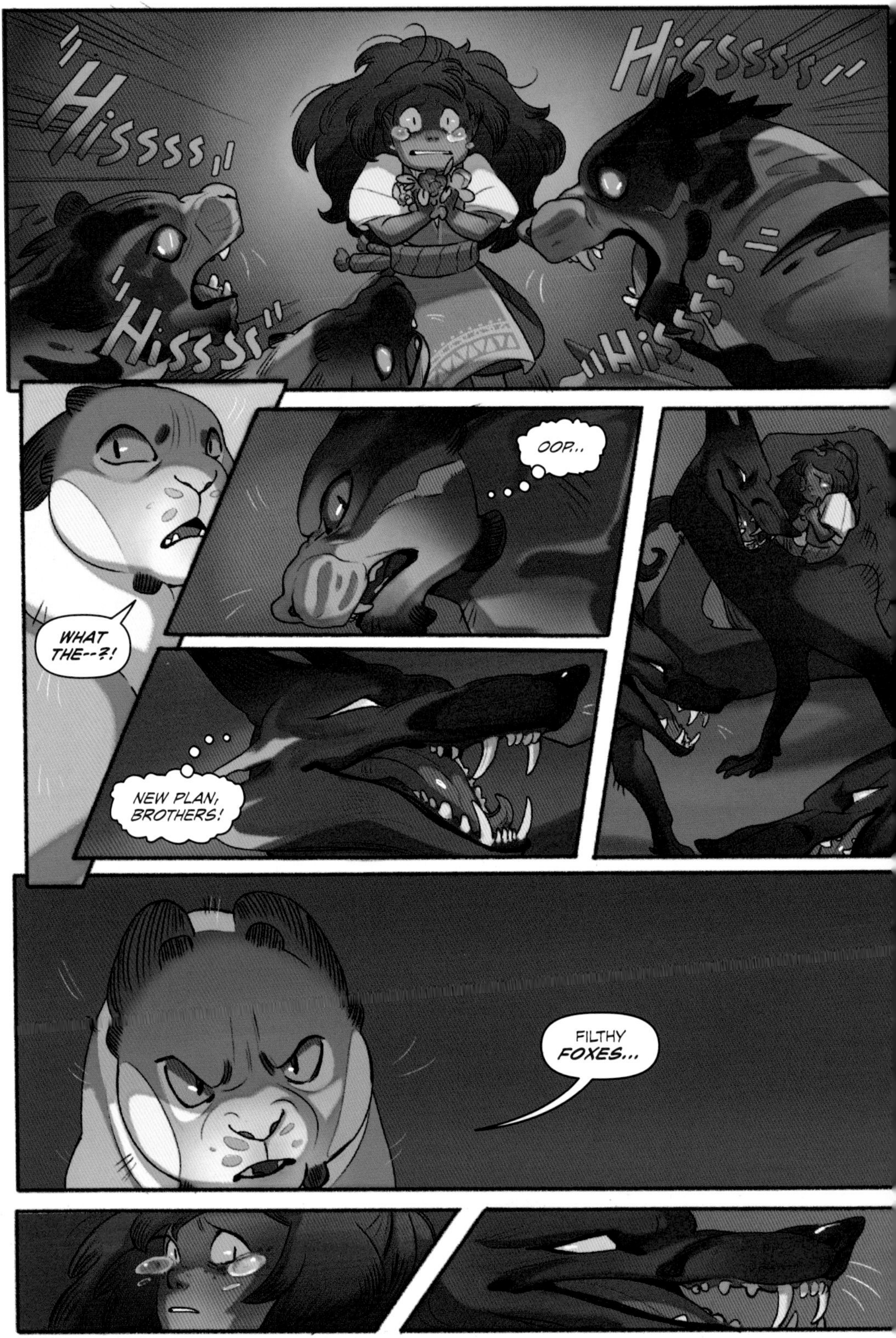
HISSSS!
HISSSSS!
HISSSS!
HISSSS!
WHAT THE--?!
OOP...
NEW PLAN, BROTHERS!
FILTHY FOXES...

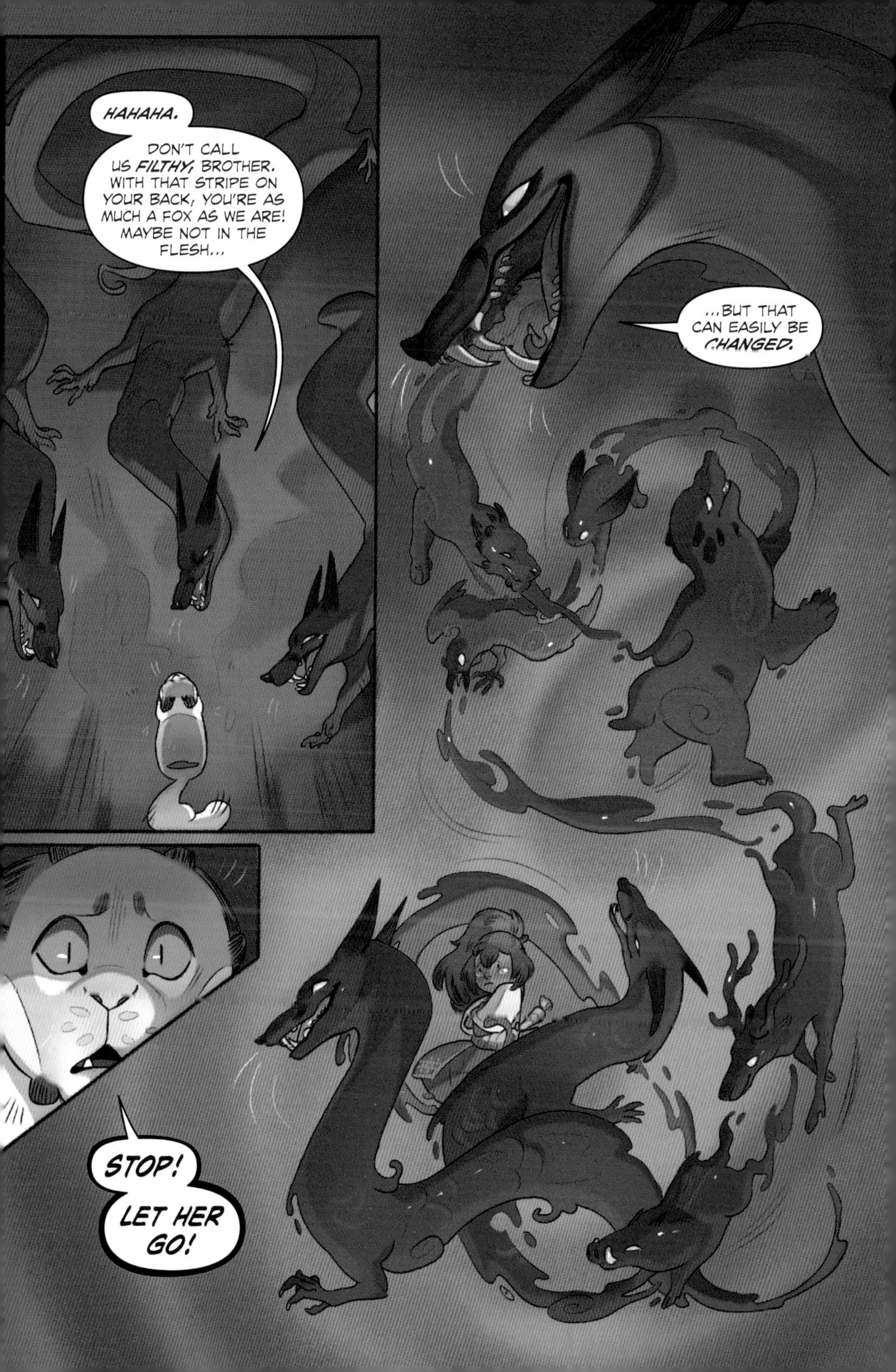
HAHAHA.
DON'T CALL US FILTHY, BROTHER. WITH THAT STRIPE ON YOUR BACK, YOU'RE AS MUCH A FOX AS WE ARE! MAYBE NOT IN THE FLESH...
...BUT THAT CAN EASILY BE CHANGED.
STOP! LET HER GO!

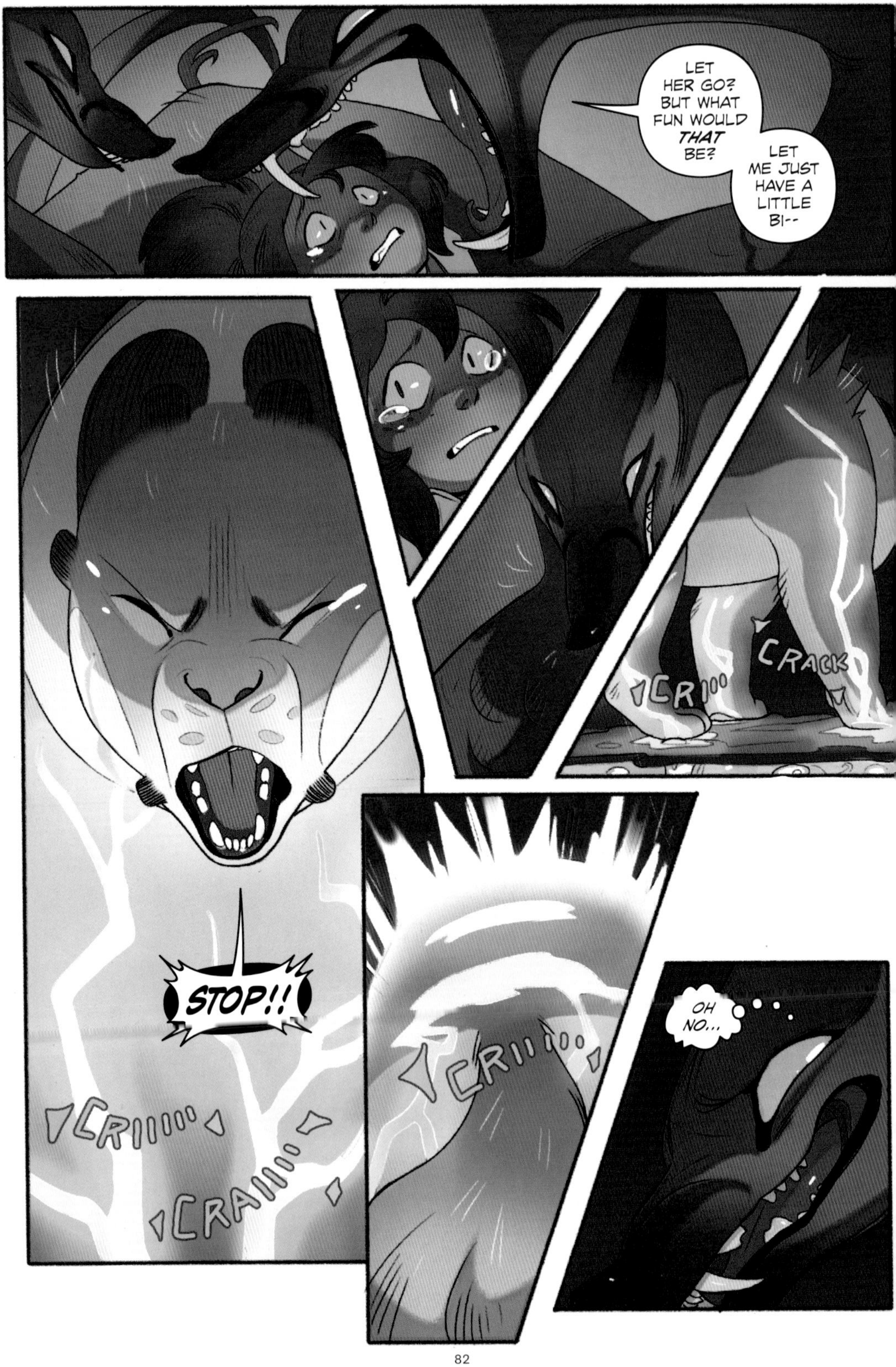
LET HER GO? BUT WHAT FUN WOULD *THAT* BE?
LET ME JUST HAVE A LITTLE BI--
CRACK
CRI
STOP!!
CRIIIII
CRAIIII
CRIIII
OH NO...

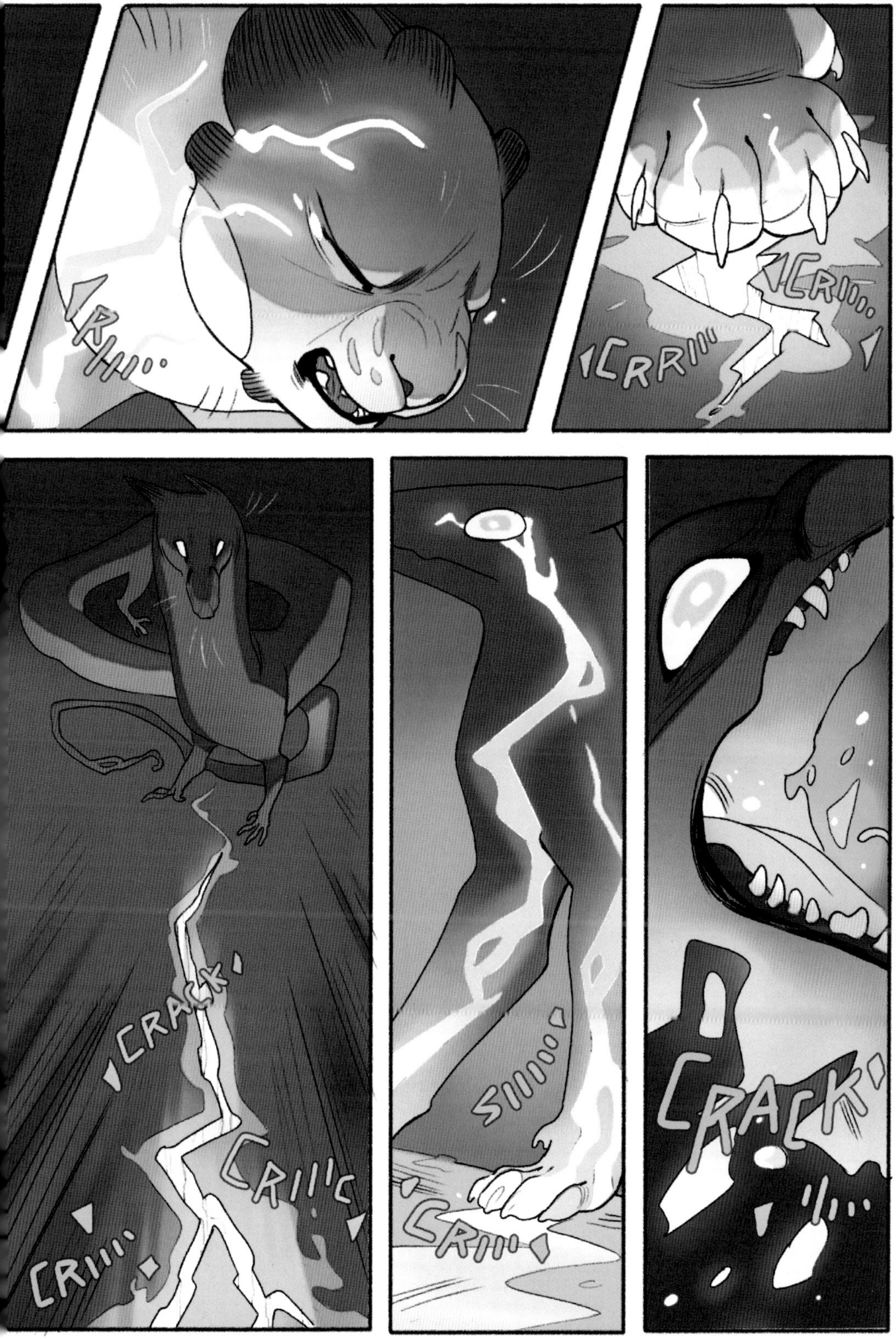
RIIII..
CRII..
CRRI''
CRACK
CRI''C
CRIIII
SIIIIII
CRII''
CRACK

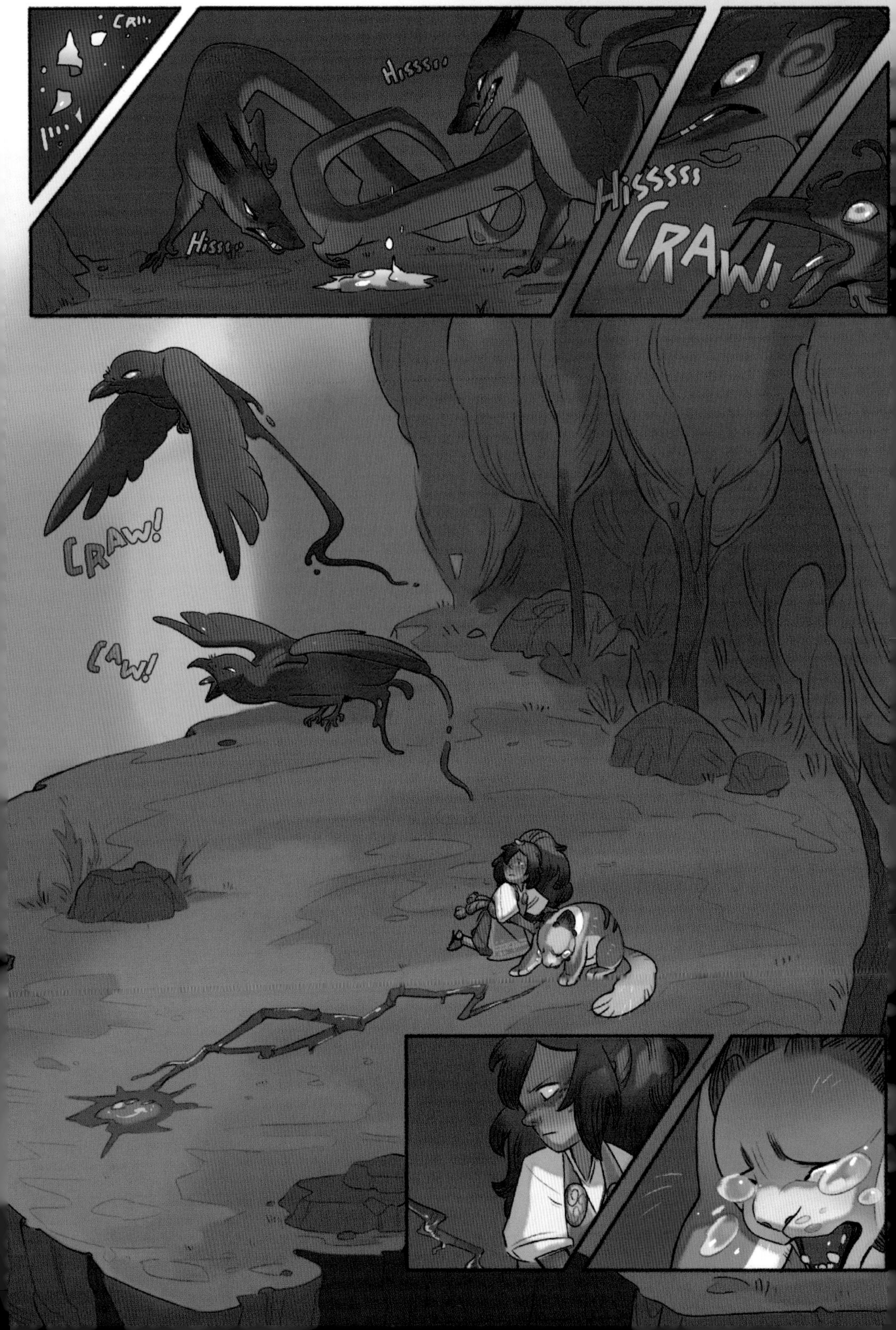
CRII
HISSSS
HISSS
HISSSSS
CRAW!
CRAW!
CAW!

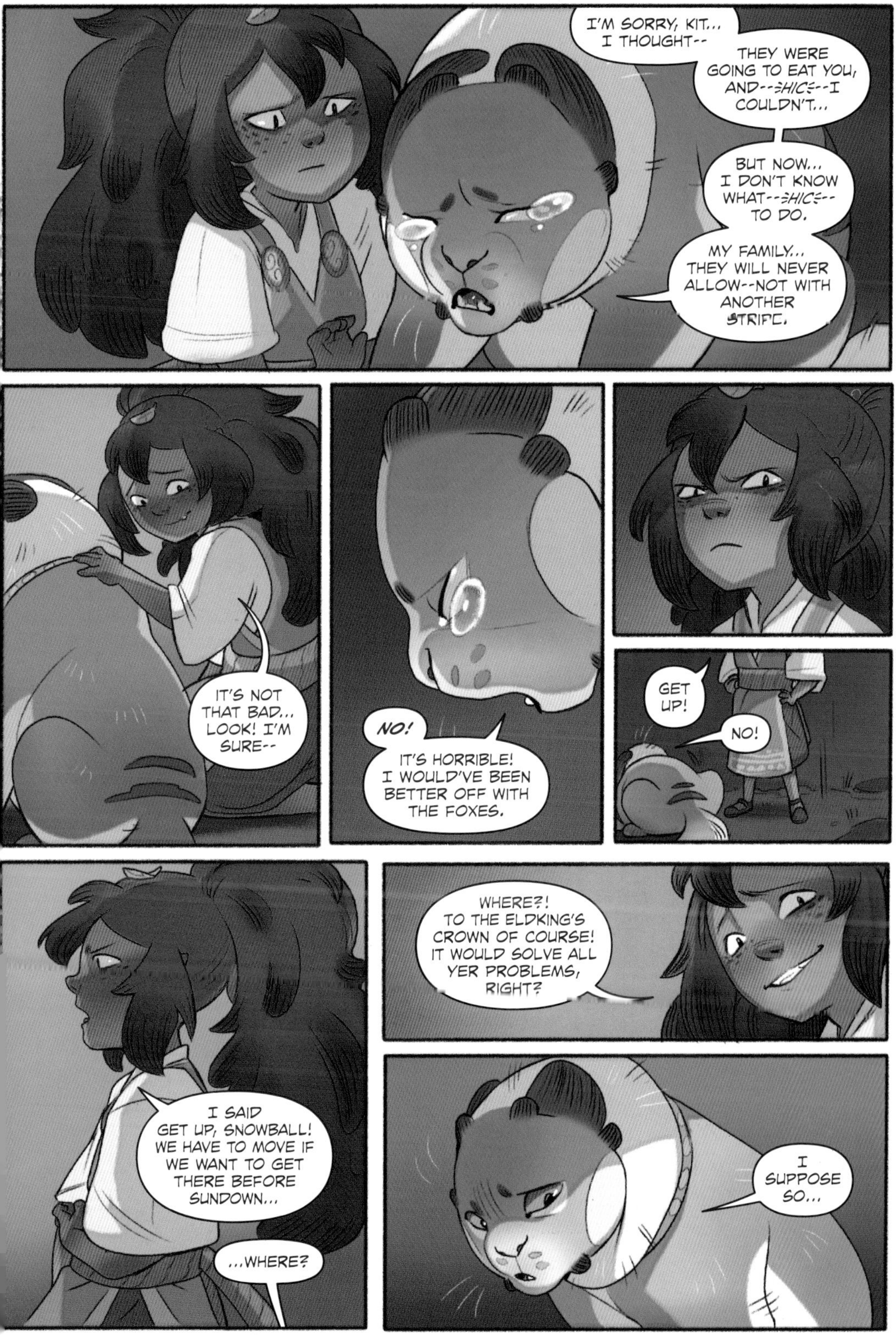
I'M SORRY, KIT... I THOUGHT--
THEY WERE GOING TO EAT YOU, AND--*HIC*--I COULDN'T...
BUT NOW... I DON'T KNOW WHAT--*HIC*-- TO DO.
MY FAMILY... THEY WILL NEVER ALLOW--NOT WITH ANOTHER STRIPE.
IT'S NOT THAT BAD... LOOK! I'M SURE--
NO!
IT'S HORRIBLE! I WOULD'VE BEEN BETTER OFF WITH THE FOXES.
GET UP!
NO!
I SAID GET UP, SNOWBALL! WE HAVE TO MOVE IF WE WANT TO GET THERE BEFORE SUNDOWN...
...WHERE?
WHERE?! TO THE ELDKING'S CROWN OF COURSE! IT WOULD SOLVE ALL YER PROBLEMS, RIGHT?
I SUPPOSE SO...

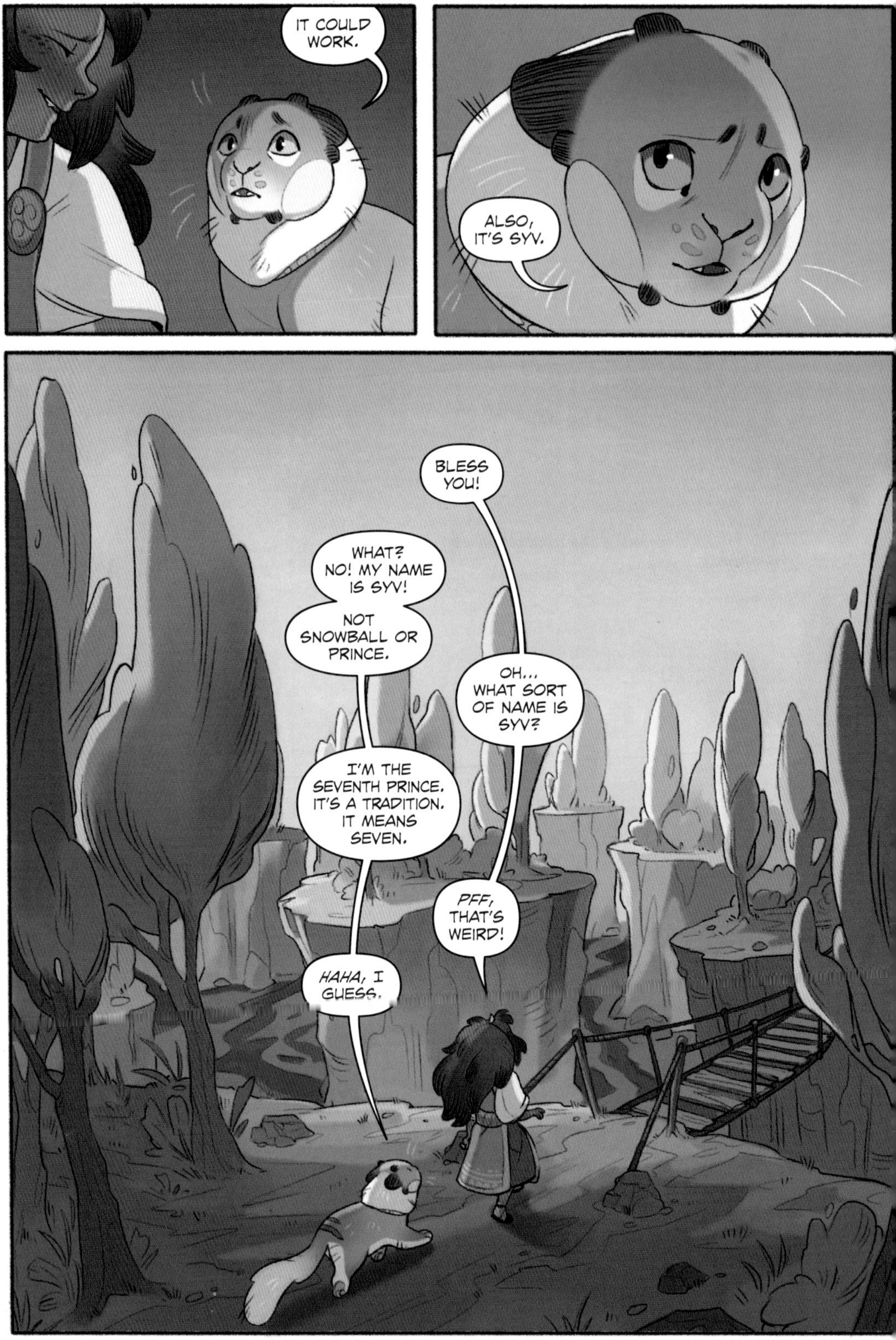
IT COULD WORK.
ALSO, IT'S SYV.
BLESS YOU!
WHAT? NO! MY NAME IS SYV!
NOT SNOWBALL OR PRINCE.
OH... WHAT SORT OF NAME IS SYV?
I'M THE SEVENTH PRINCE. IT'S A TRADITION. IT MEANS SEVEN.
PFF, THAT'S WEIRD!
HAHA, I GUESS.

Chapter 5
TEMPLE OF THORNS

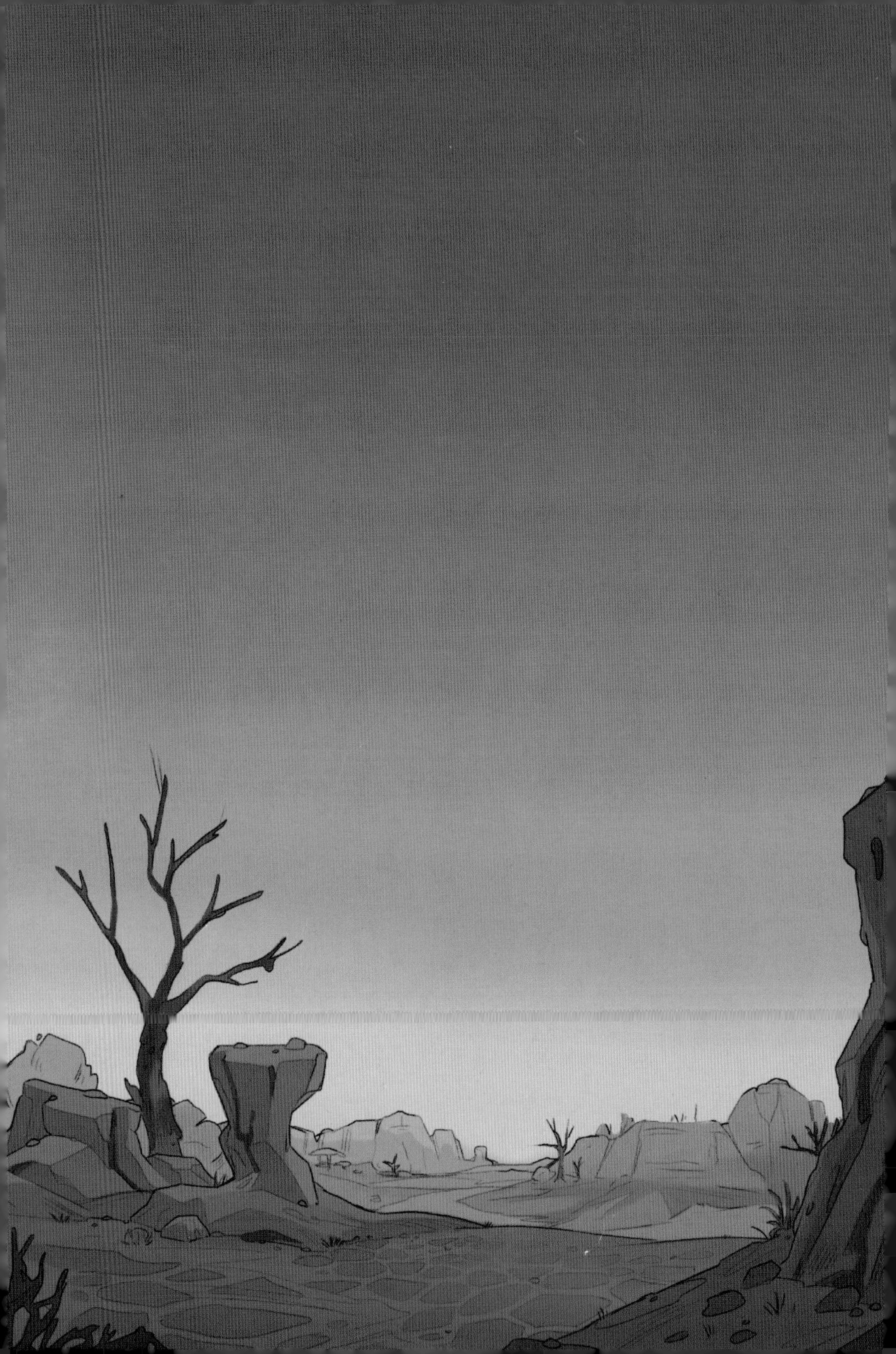

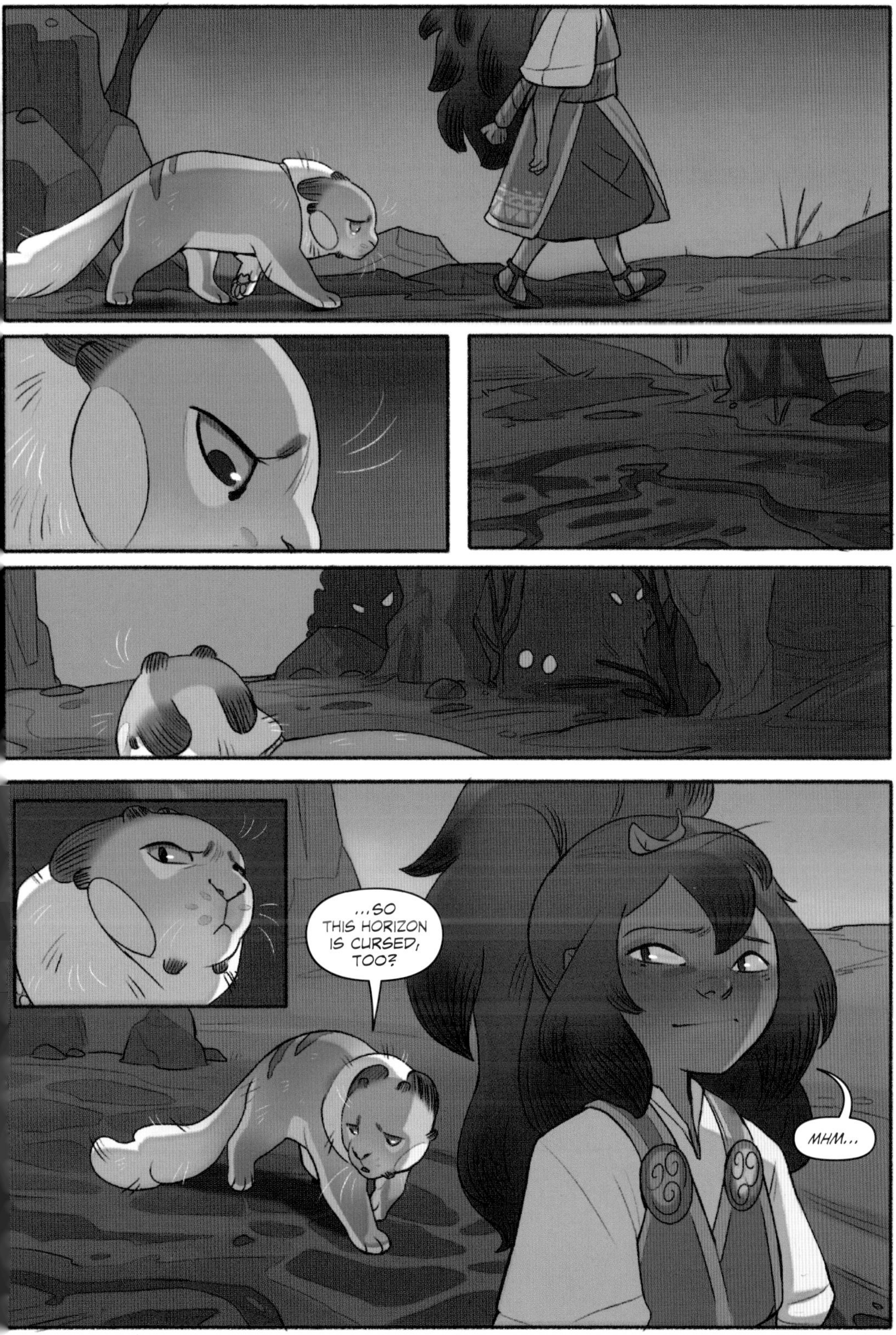
...SO THIS HORIZON IS CURSED, TOO?
MHM...

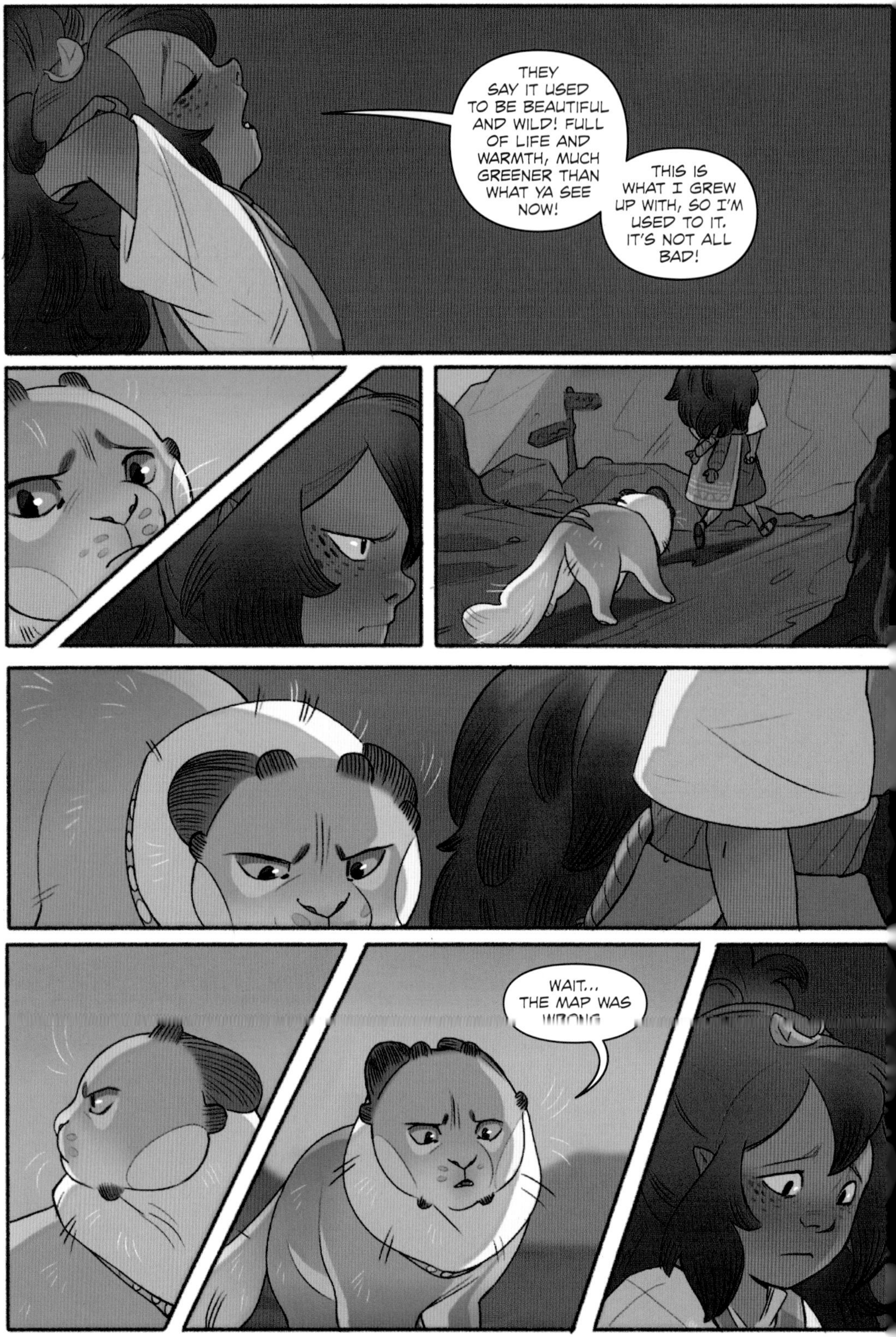
THEY SAY IT USED TO BE BEAUTIFUL AND WILD! FULL OF LIFE AND WARMTH, MUCH GREENER THAN WHAT YA SEE NOW!
THIS IS WHAT I GREW UP WITH, SO I'M USED TO IT. IT'S NOT ALL BAD!
WAIT... THE MAP WAS

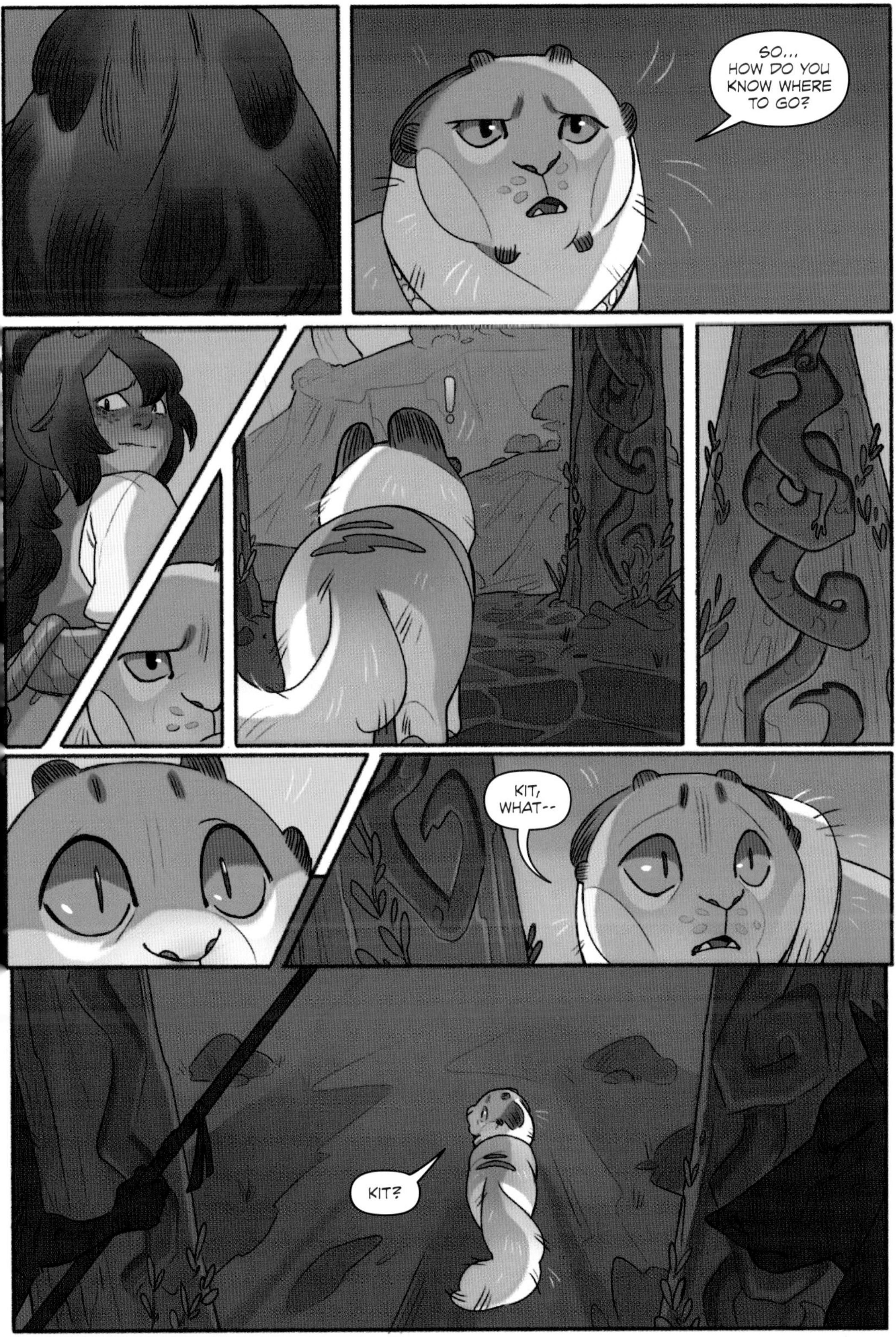
SO... HOW DO YOU KNOW WHERE TO GO?
!
KIT, WHAT--
KIT?

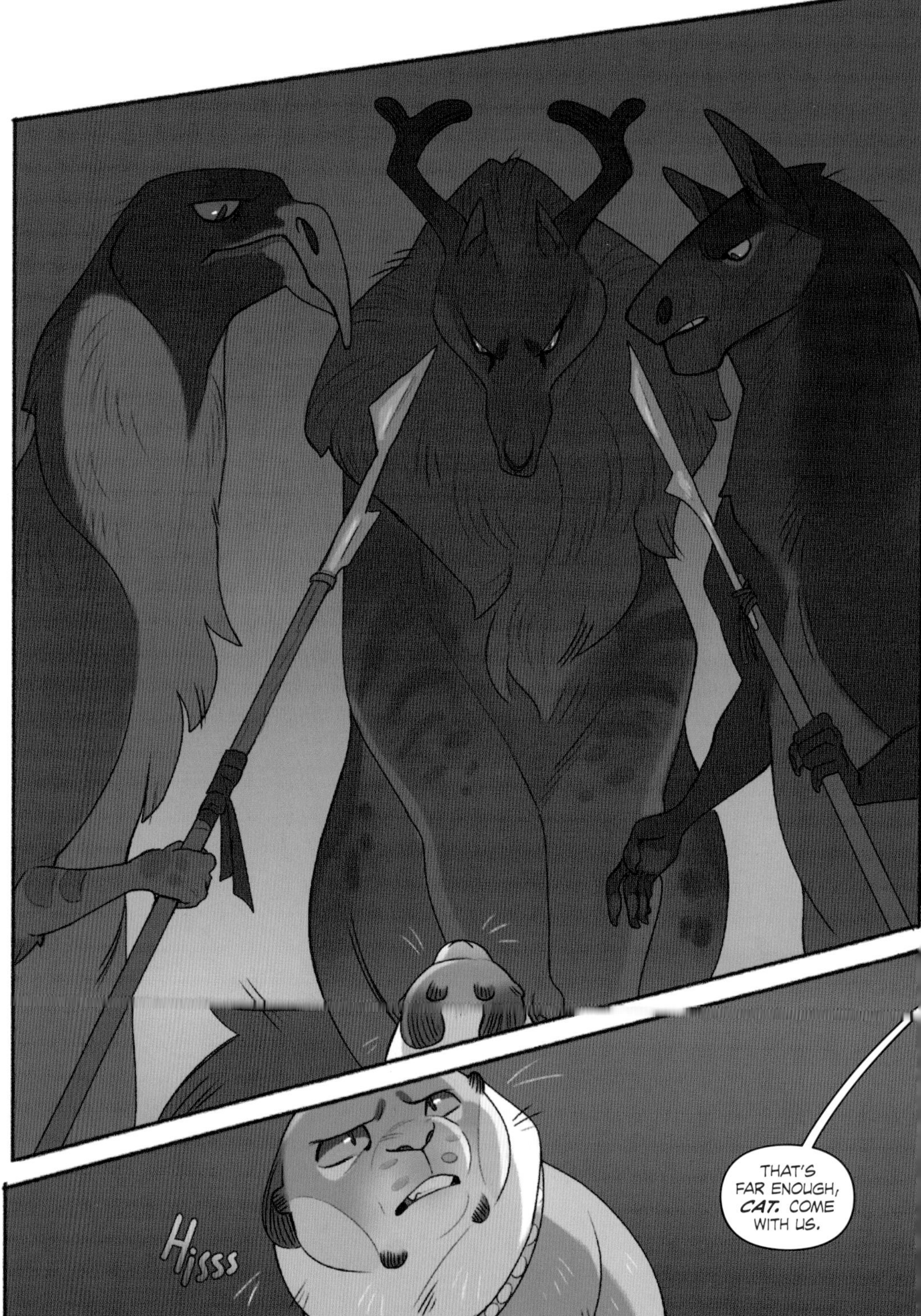
Hisss
THAT'S FAR ENOUGH, *CAT.* COME WITH US.

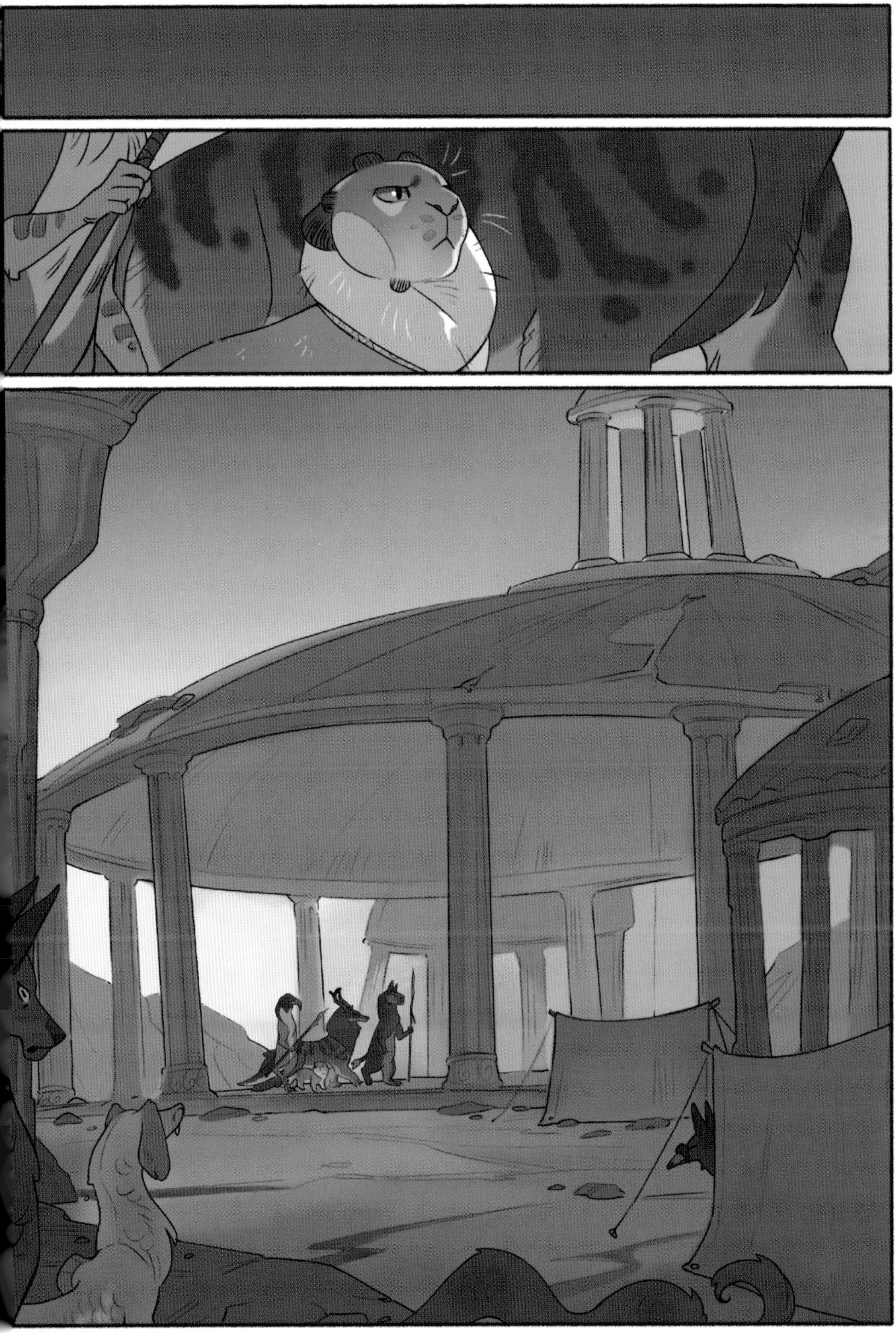

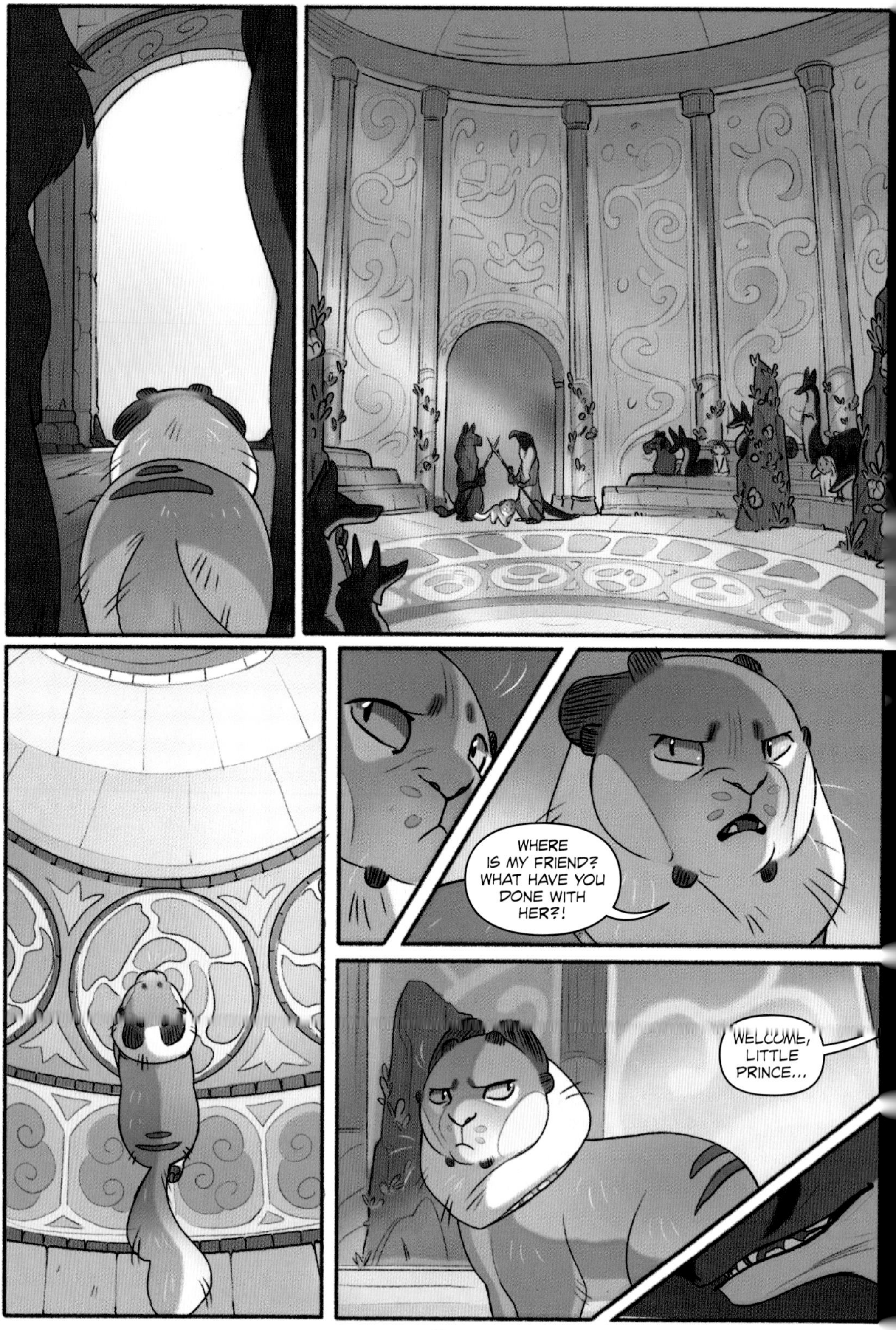
WHERE IS MY FRIEND? WHAT HAVE YOU DONE WITH HER?!
WELCOME, LITTLE PRINCE...

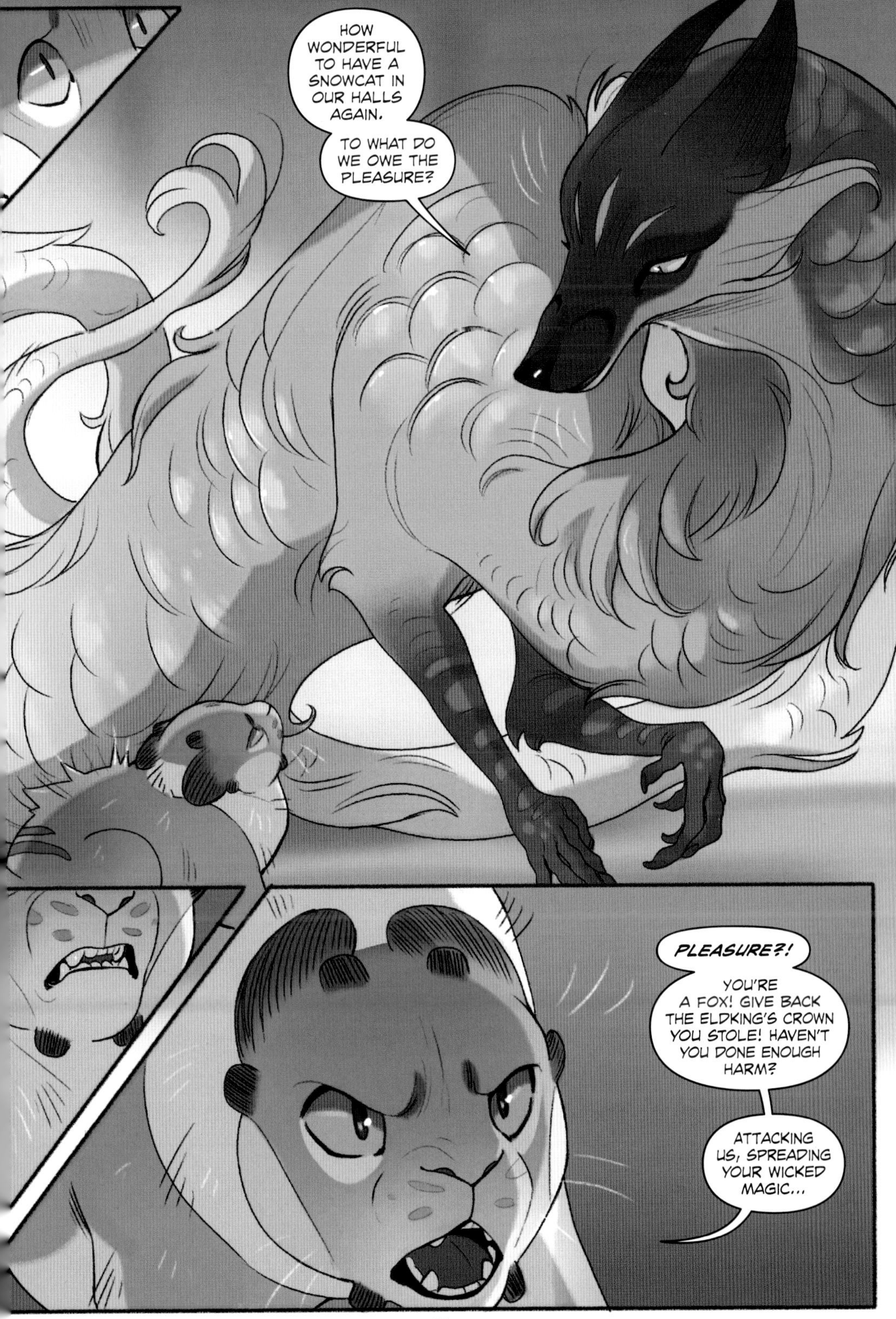
HOW WONDERFUL TO HAVE A SNOWCAT IN OUR HALLS AGAIN.
TO WHAT DO WE OWE THE PLEASURE?
PLEASURE?!
YOU'RE A FOX! GIVE BACK THE ELDKING'S CROWN YOU STOLE! HAVEN'T YOU DONE ENOUGH HARM?
ATTACKING US, SPREADING YOUR WICKED MAGIC...

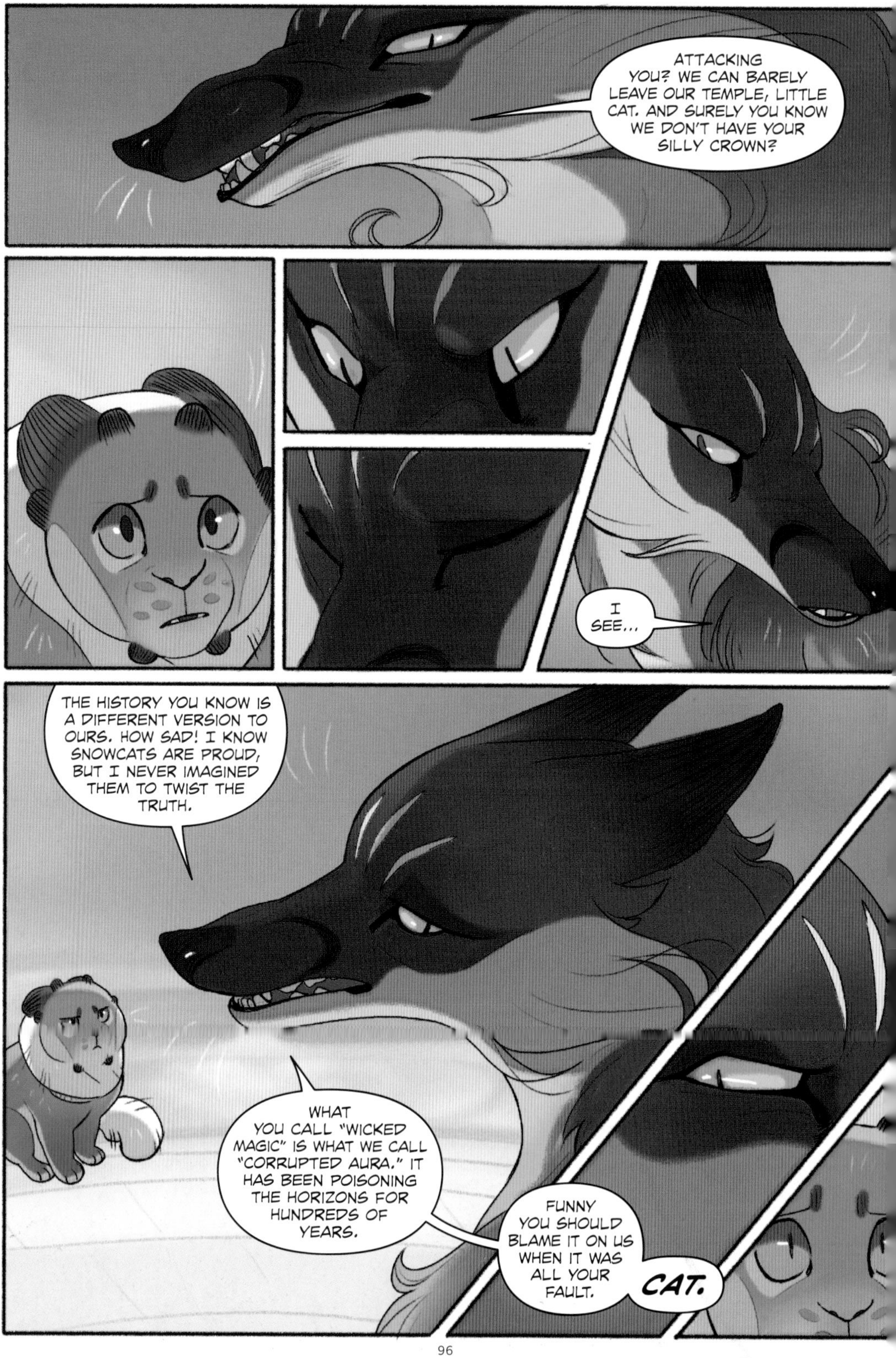
ATTACKING YOU? WE CAN BARELY LEAVE OUR TEMPLE, LITTLE CAT. AND SURELY YOU KNOW WE DON'T HAVE YOUR SILLY CROWN?
I SEE...
THE HISTORY YOU KNOW IS A DIFFERENT VERSION TO OURS. HOW SAD! I KNOW SNOWCATS ARE PROUD, BUT I NEVER IMAGINED THEM TO TWIST THE TRUTH.
WHAT YOU CALL "WICKED MAGIC" IS WHAT WE CALL "CORRUPTED AURA." IT HAS BEEN POISONING THE HORIZONS FOR HUNDREDS OF YEARS.
FUNNY YOU SHOULD BLAME IT ON US WHEN IT WAS ALL YOUR FAULT.
CAT.

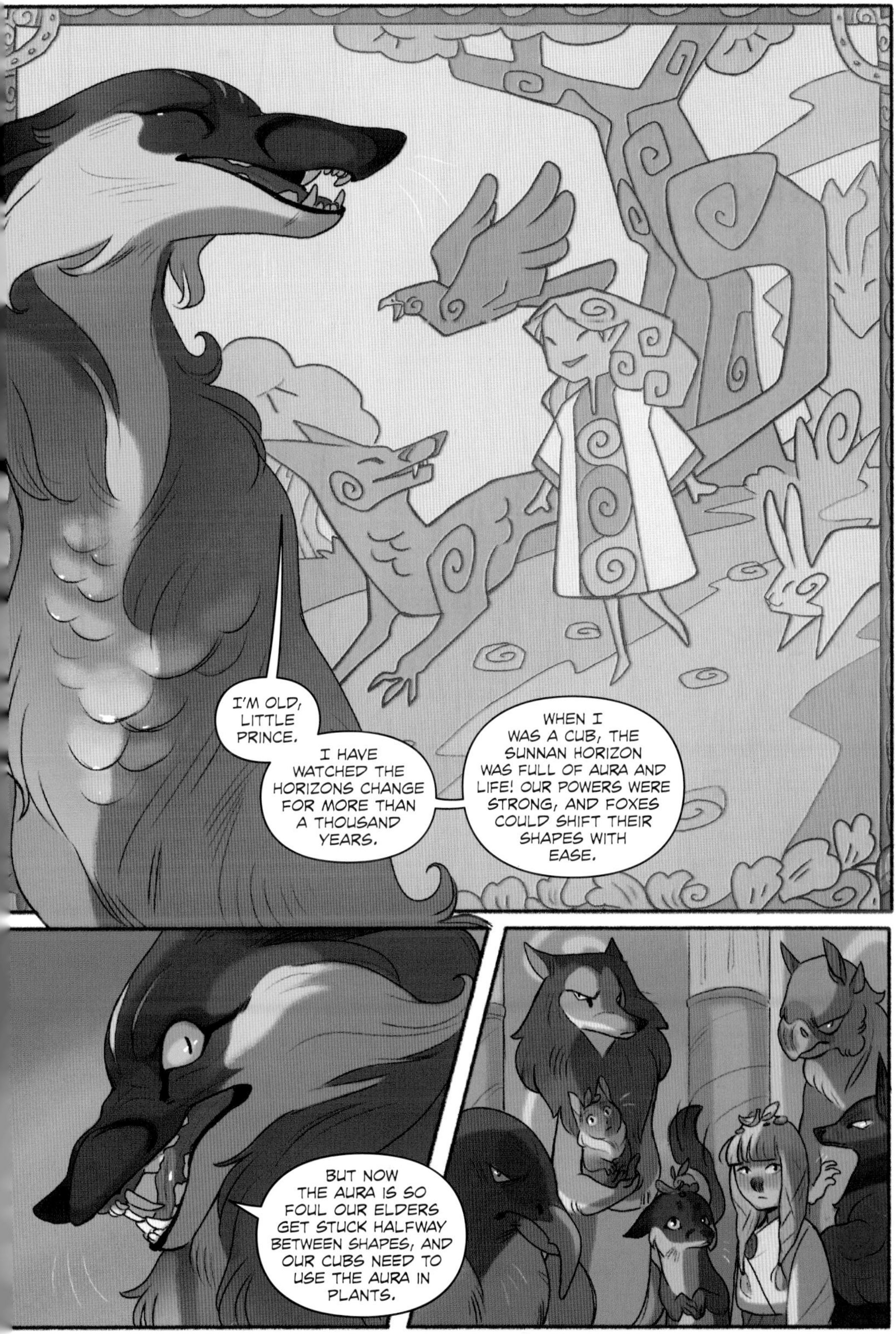
I'M OLD, LITTLE PRINCE.
I HAVE WATCHED THE HORIZONS CHANGE FOR MORE THAN A THOUSAND YEARS.
WHEN I WAS A CUB, THE SUNNAN HORIZON WAS FULL OF AURA AND LIFE! OUR POWERS WERE STRONG, AND FOXES COULD SHIFT THEIR SHAPES WITH EASE.
BUT NOW THE AURA IS SO FOUL OUR ELDERS GET STUCK HALFWAY BETWEEN SHAPES, AND OUR CUBS NEED TO USE THE AURA IN PLANTS.

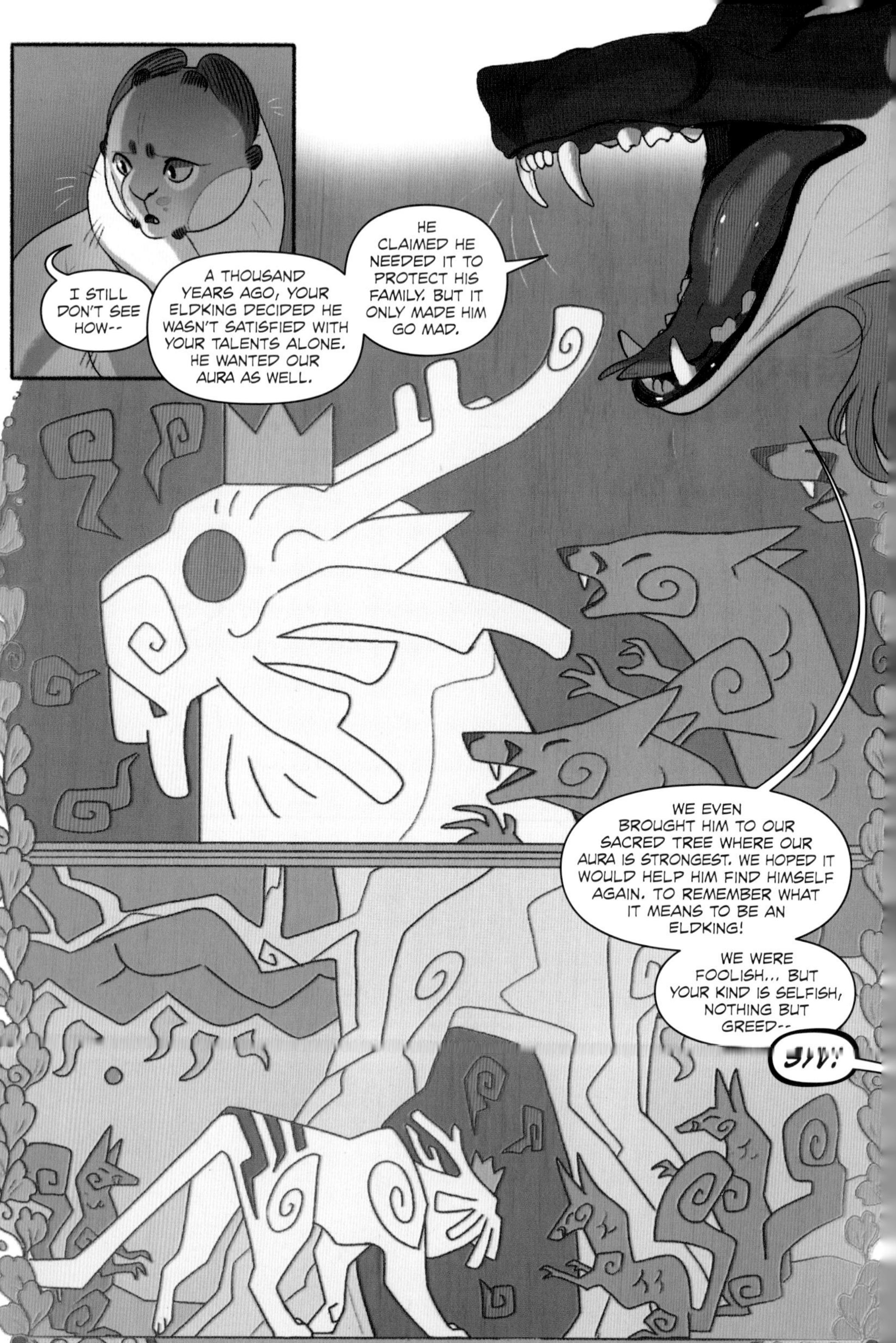

I STILL DON'T SEE HOW--
A THOUSAND YEARS AGO, YOUR ELDKING DECIDED HE WASN'T SATISFIED WITH YOUR TALENTS ALONE. HE WANTED OUR AURA AS WELL.
HE CLAIMED HE NEEDED IT TO PROTECT HIS FAMILY. BUT IT ONLY MADE HIM GO MAD.
WE EVEN BROUGHT HIM TO OUR SACRED TREE WHERE OUR AURA IS STRONGEST. WE HOPED IT WOULD HELP HIM FIND HIMSELF AGAIN. TO REMEMBER WHAT IT MEANS TO BE AN ELDKING!
WE WERE FOOLISH... BUT YOUR KIND IS SELFISH, NOTHING BUT GREED--

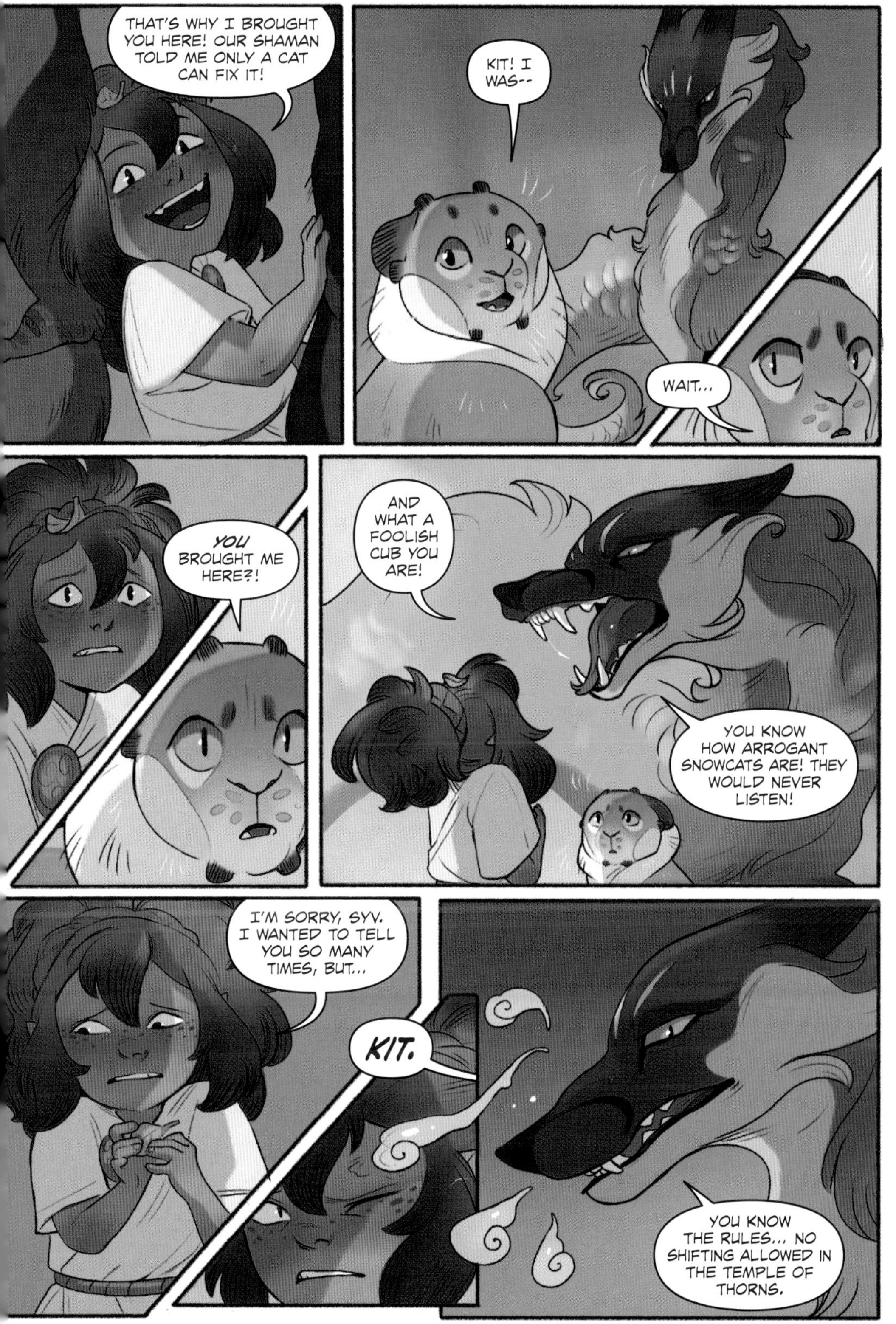
THAT'S WHY I BROUGHT YOU HERE! OUR SHAMAN TOLD ME ONLY A CAT CAN FIX IT!
KIT! I WAS--
WAIT...
YOU BROUGHT ME HERE?!
AND WHAT A FOOLISH CUB YOU ARE!
YOU KNOW HOW ARROGANT SNOWCATS ARE! THEY WOULD NEVER LISTEN!
I'M SORRY, SYV. I WANTED TO TELL YOU SO MANY TIMES, BUT...
KIT.
YOU KNOW THE RULES... NO SHIFTING ALLOWED IN THE TEMPLE OF THORNS.

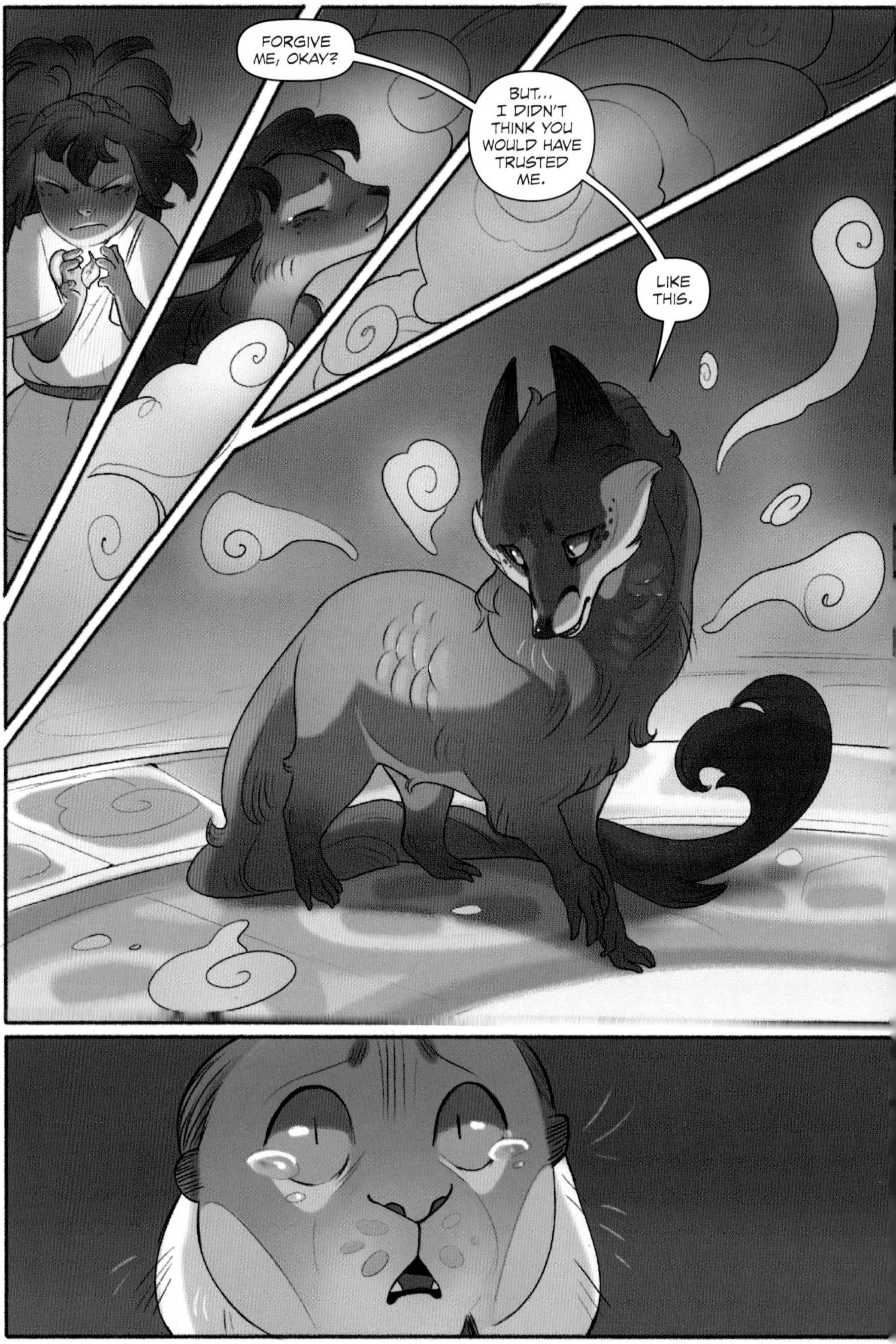
FORGIVE ME, OKAY?
BUT... I DIDN'T THINK YOU WOULD HAVE TRUSTED ME.
LIKE THIS.

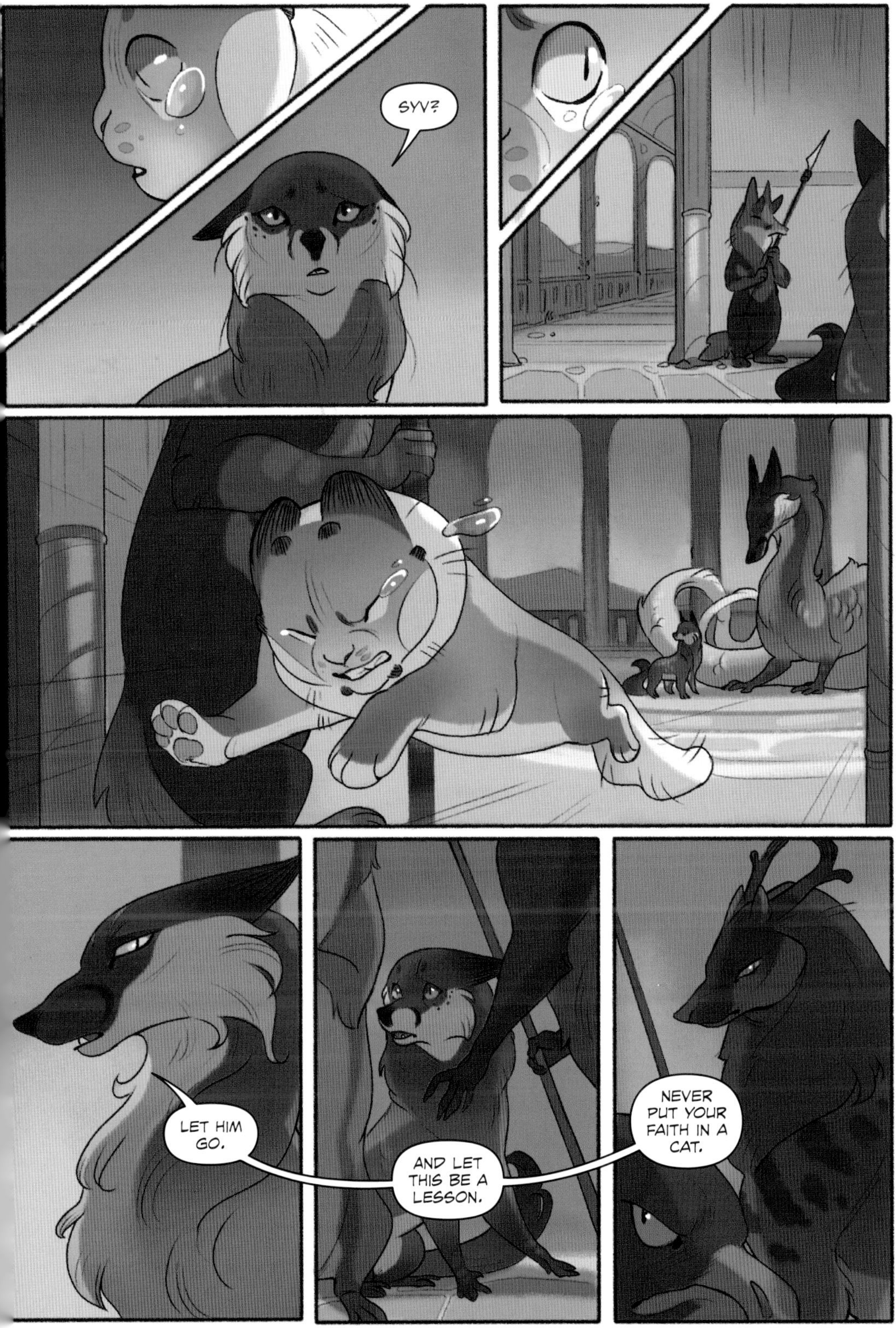
SYV?
LET HIM GO.
AND LET THIS BE A LESSON.
NEVER PUT YOUR FAITH IN A CAT.

THERE IS NO HOPE...

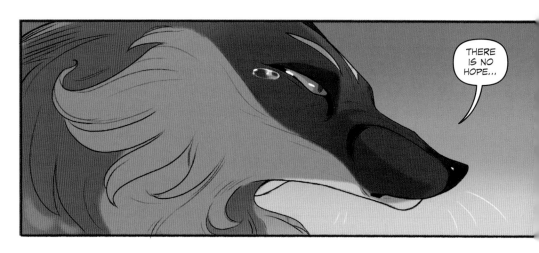

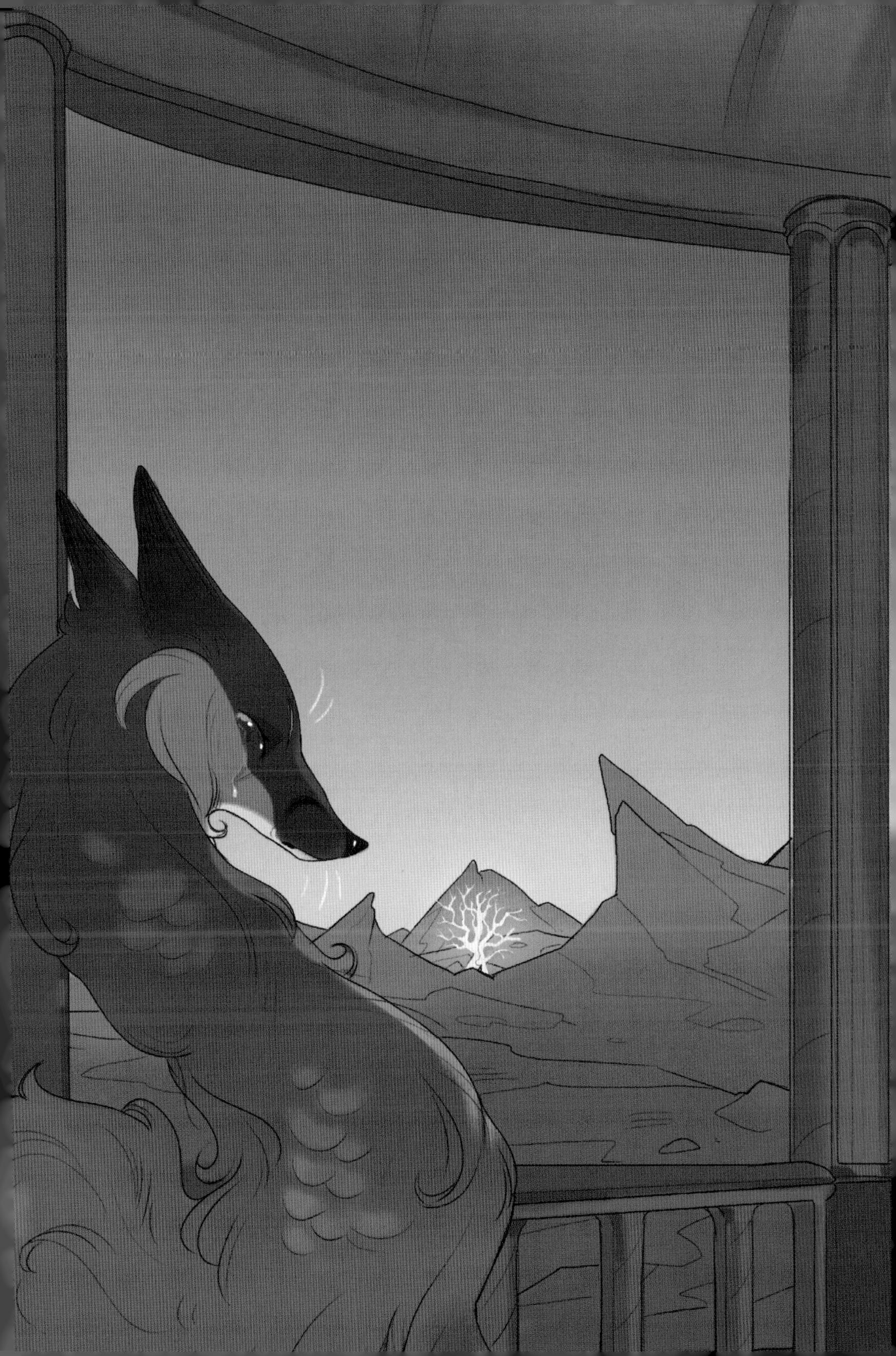

Chapter 6
THE BLACK CAT

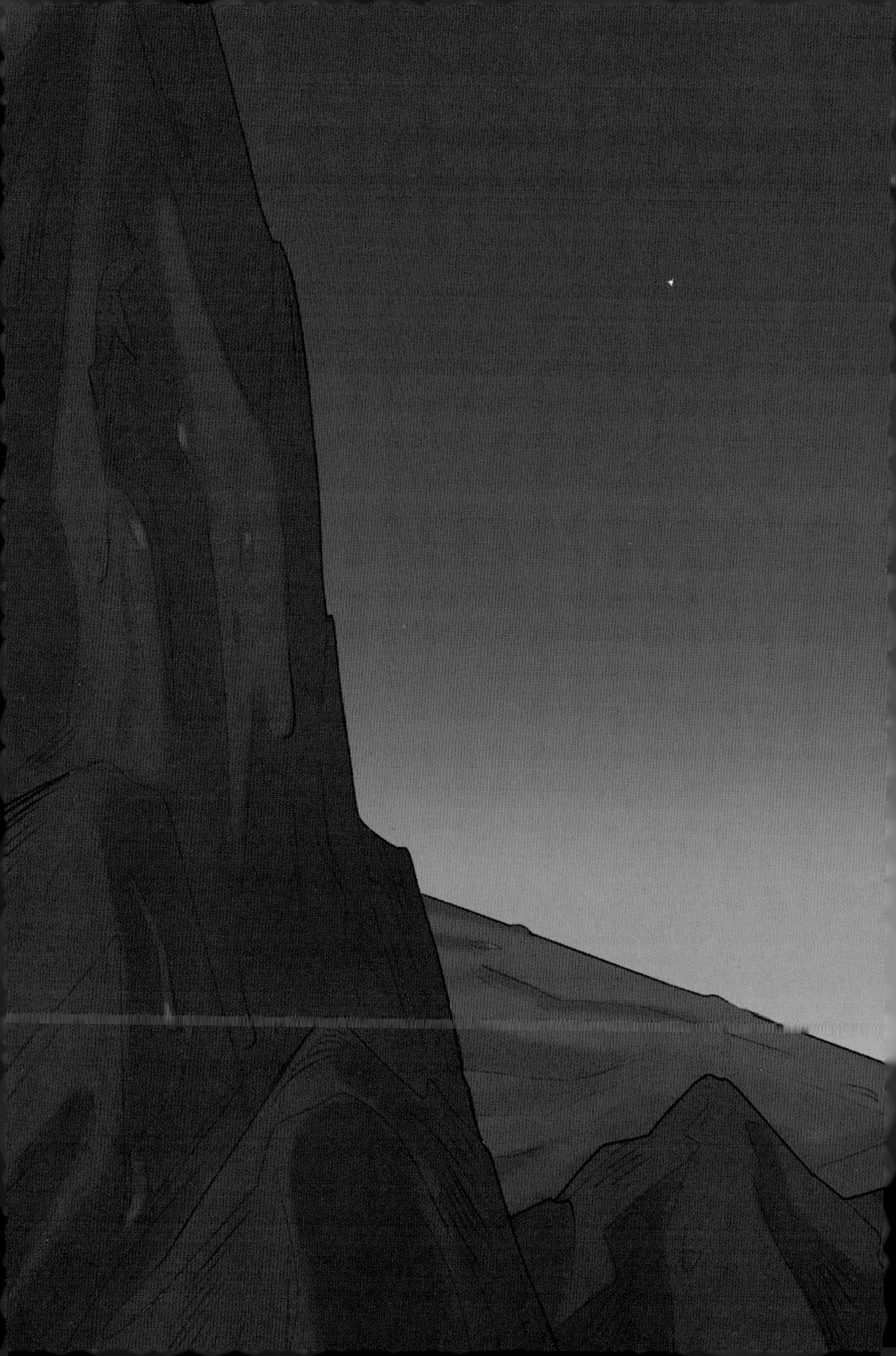

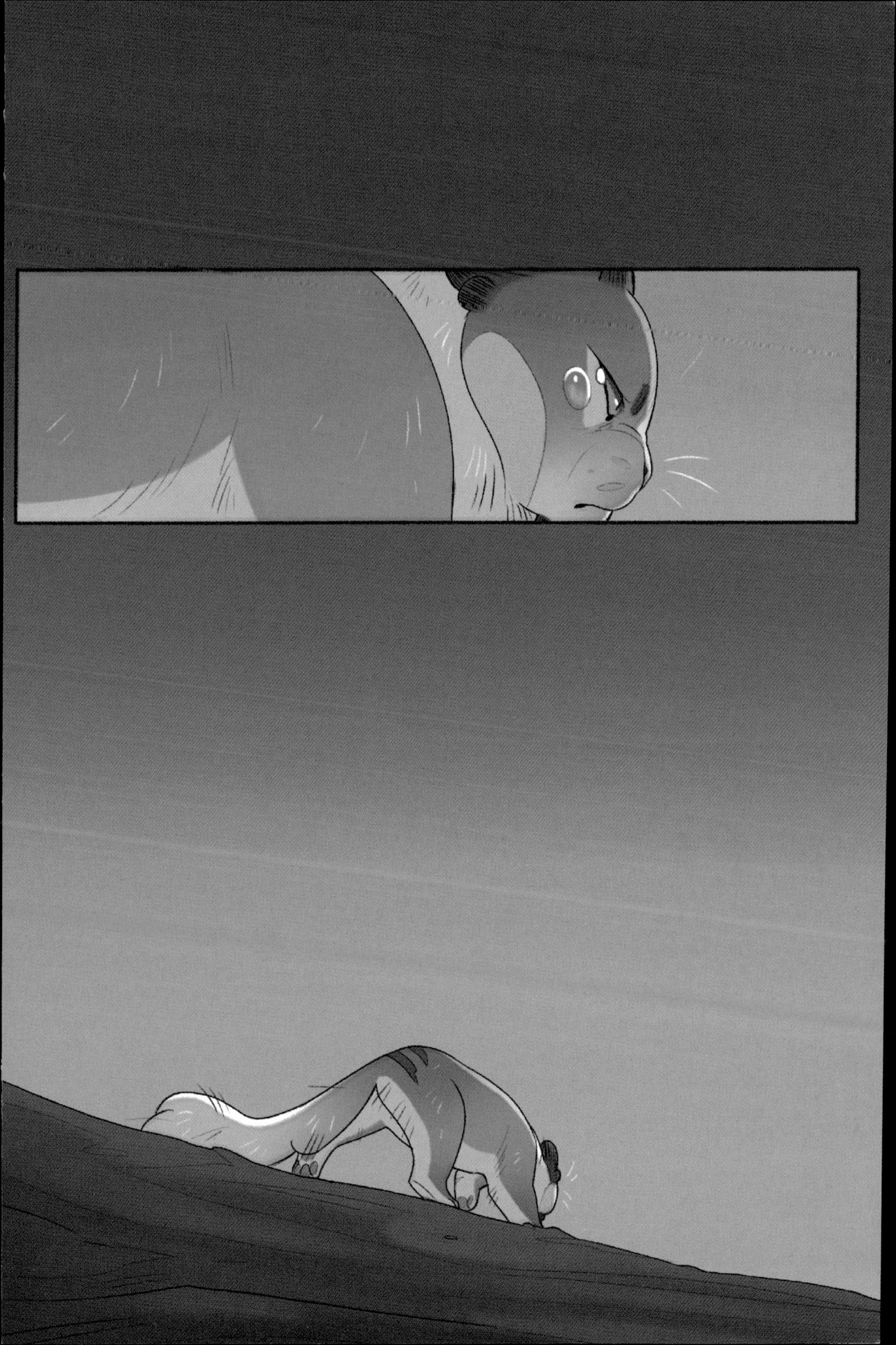

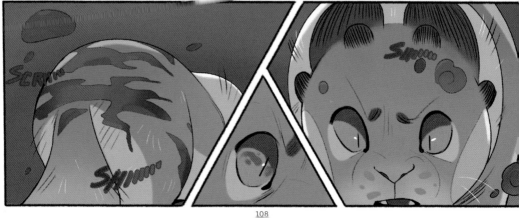

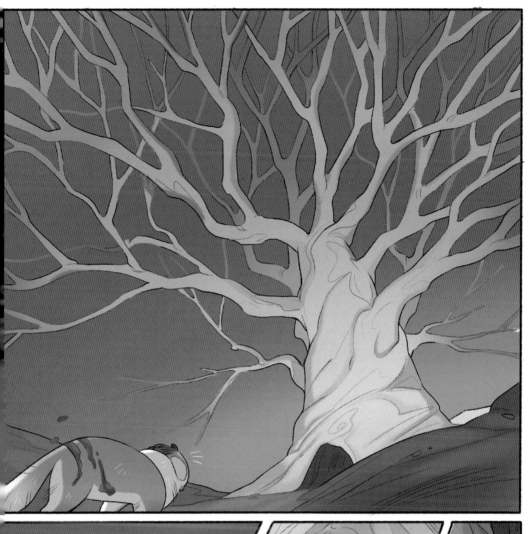

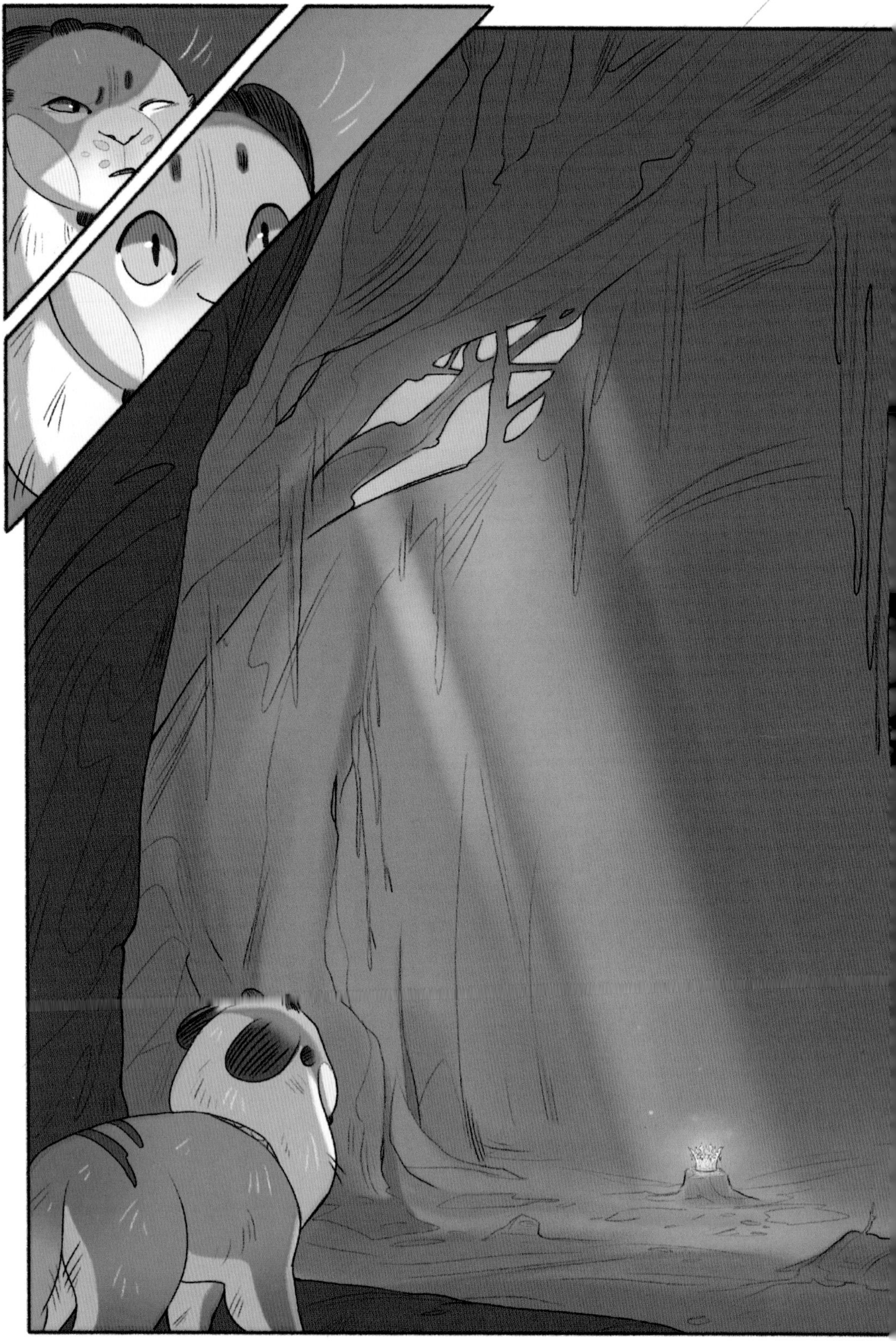

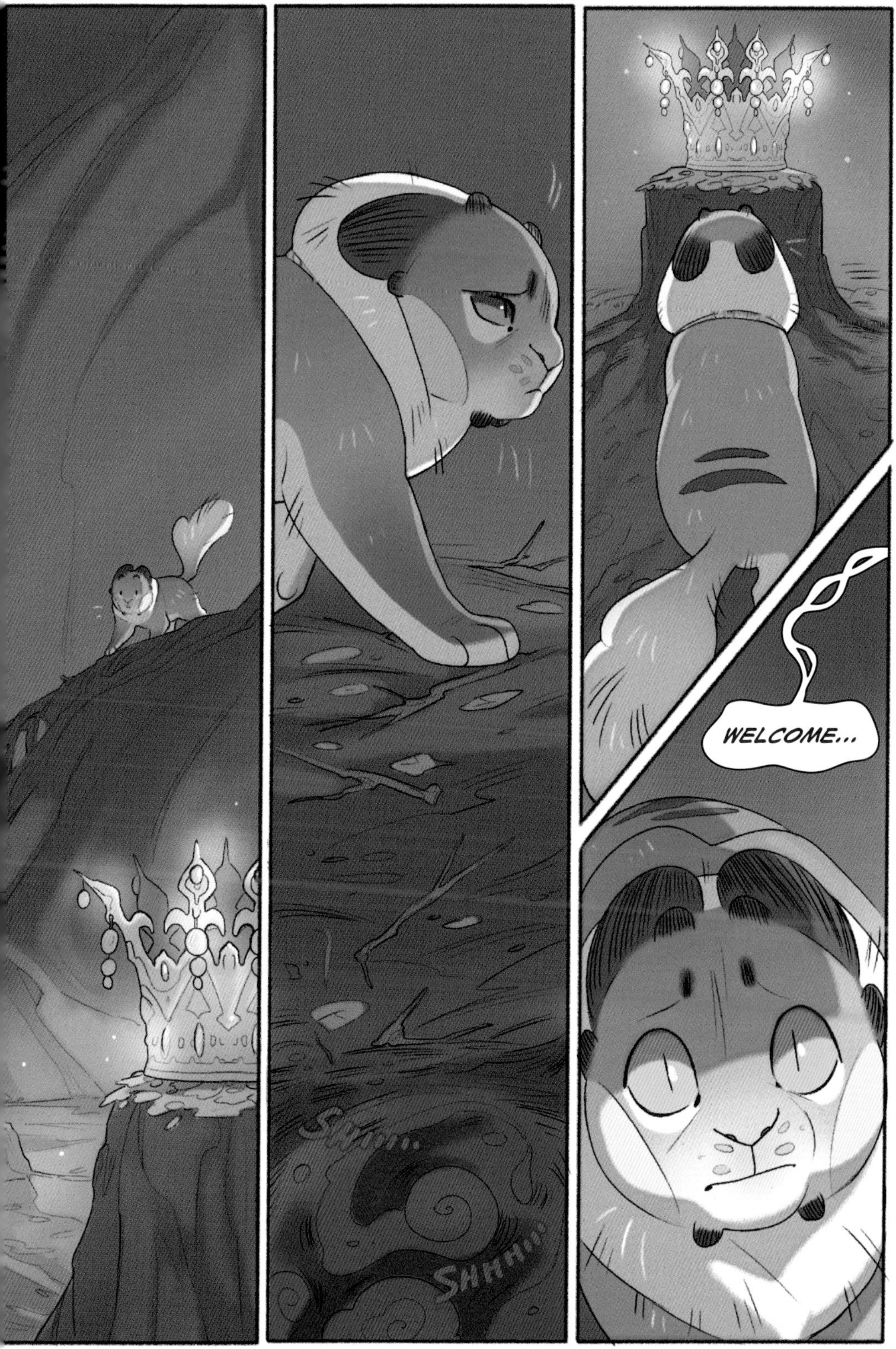
SHHH...
SHHH...
WELCOME...

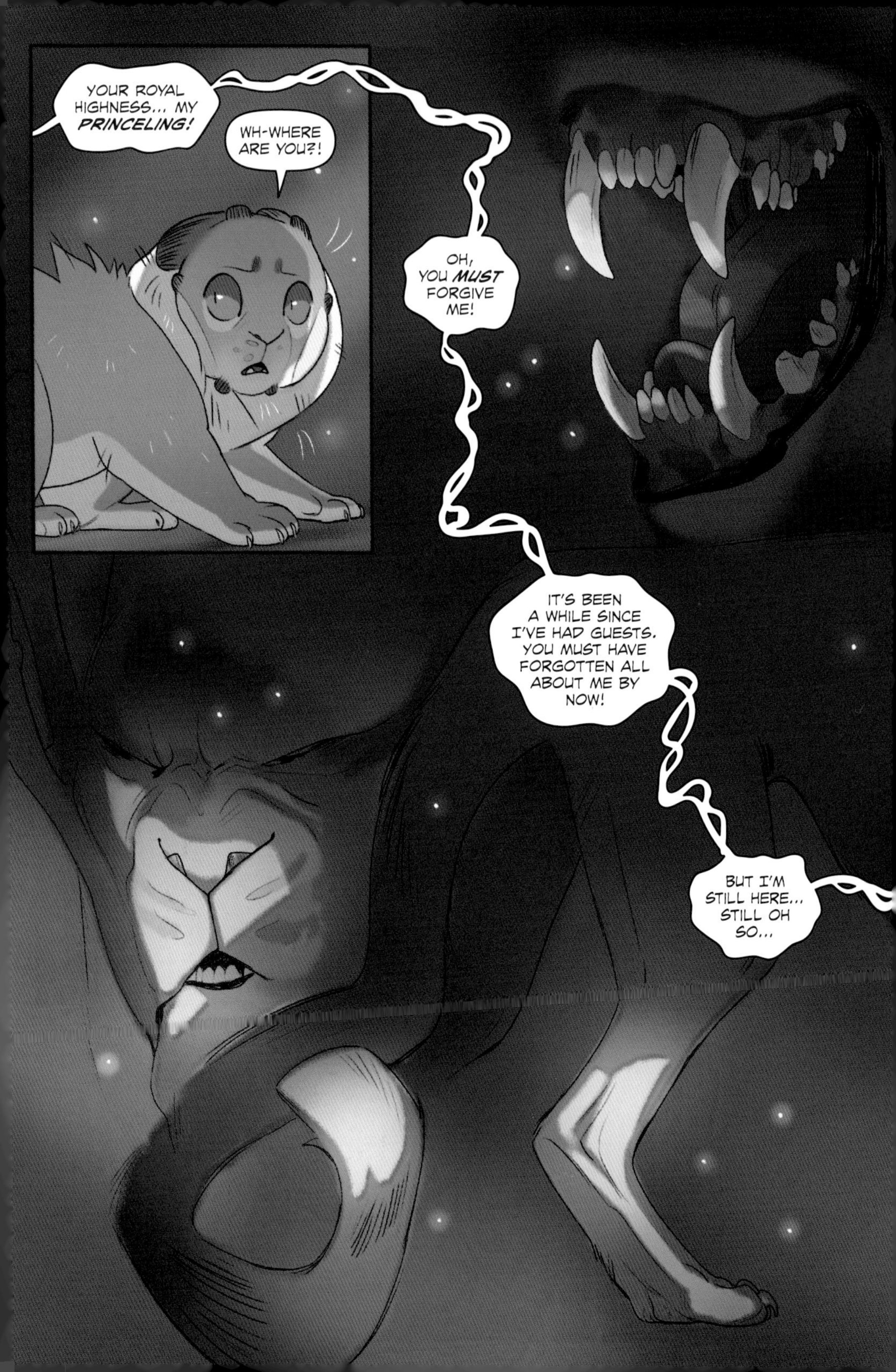
YOUR ROYAL HIGHNESS... MY *PRINCELING!*
WH-WHERE ARE YOU?!
OH, YOU ***MUST*** FORGIVE ME!
IT'S BEEN A WHILE SINCE I'VE HAD GUESTS. YOU MUST HAVE FORGOTTEN ALL ABOUT ME BY NOW!
BUT I'M STILL HERE... STILL OH SO...

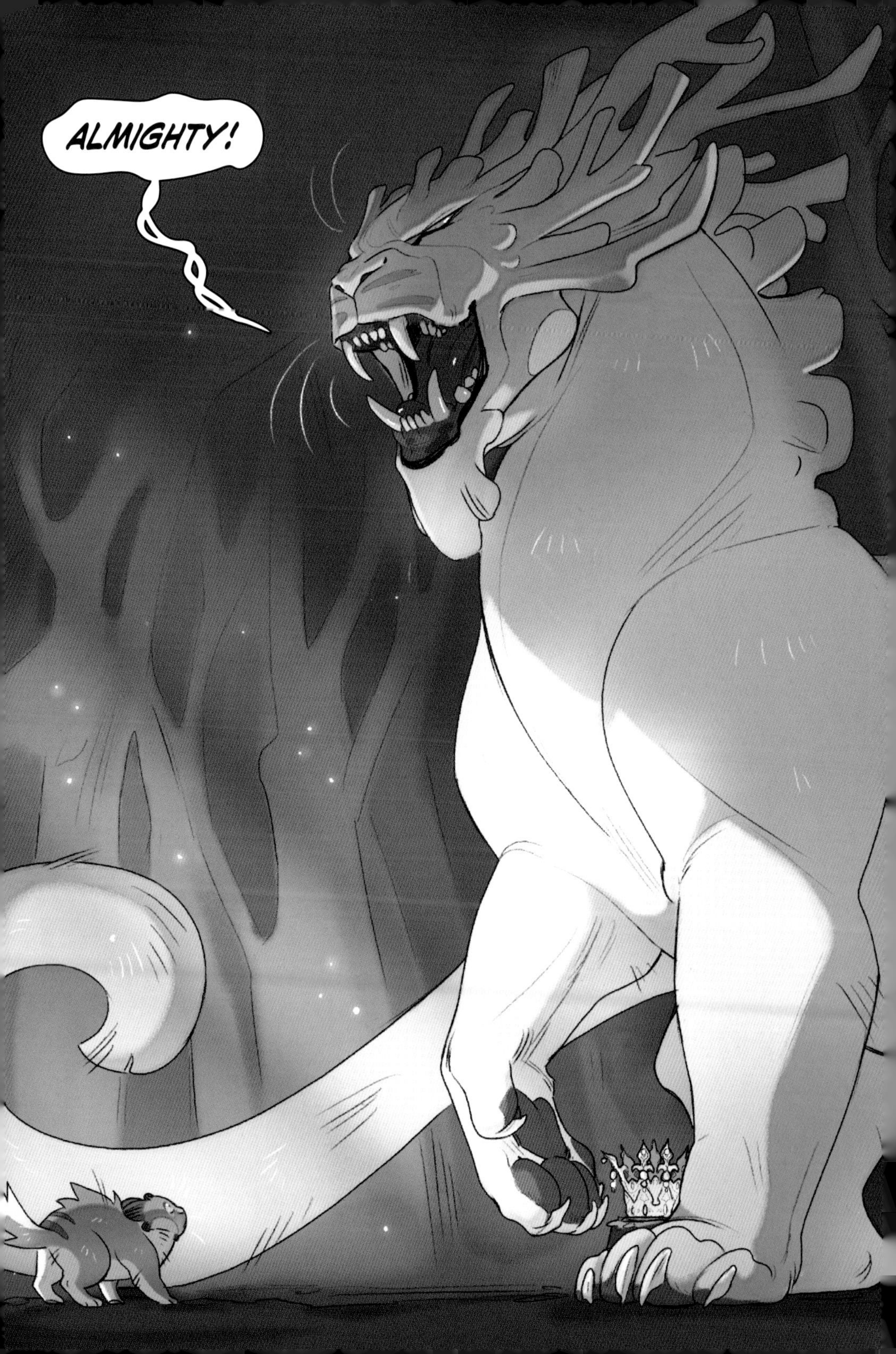
ALMIGHTY!

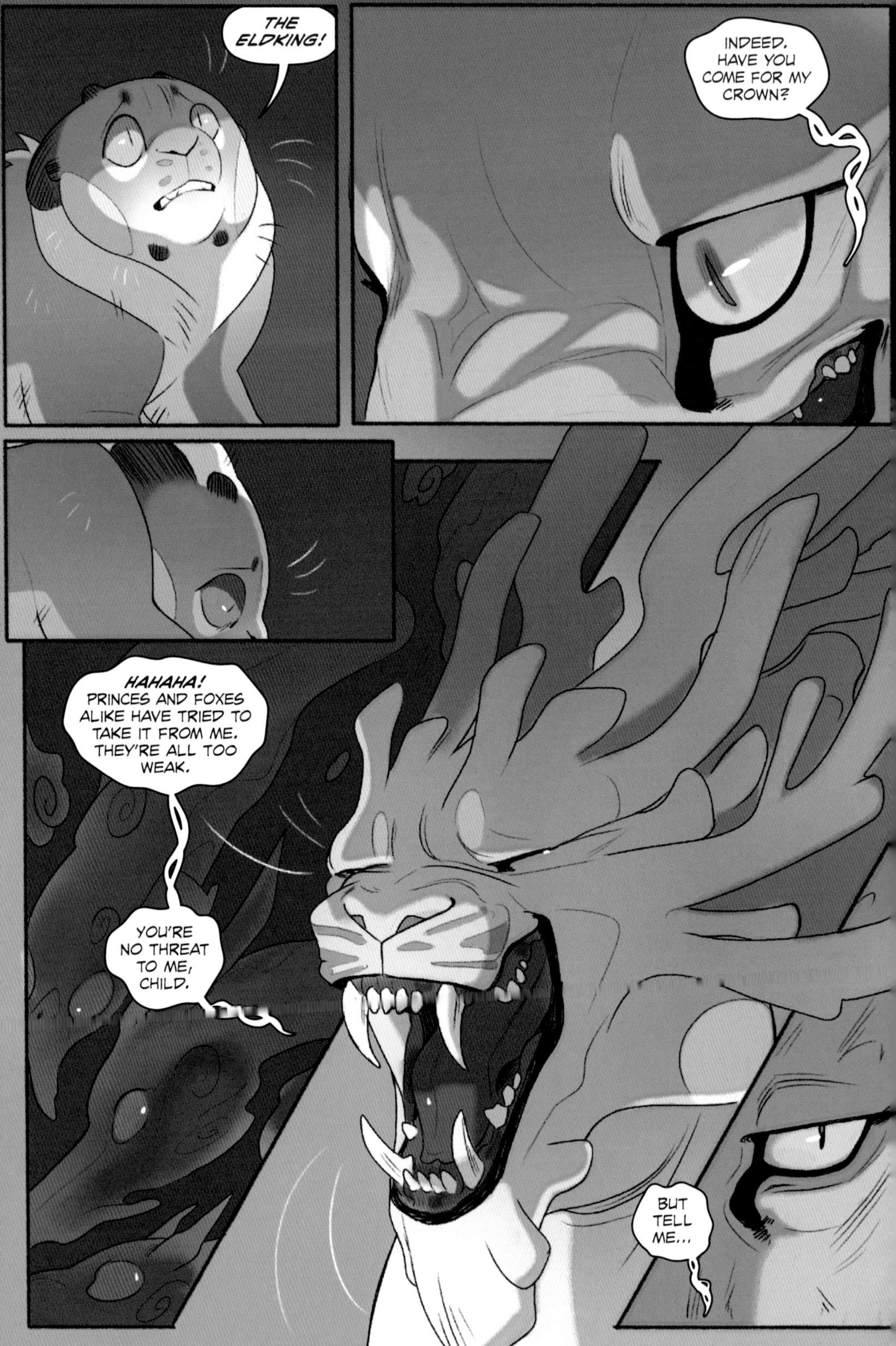
THE ELDKING!
INDEED. HAVE YOU COME FOR MY CROWN?
HAHAHA! PRINCES AND FOXES ALIKE HAVE TRIED TO TAKE IT FROM ME. THEY'RE ALL TOO WEAK.
YOU'RE NO THREAT TO ME, CHILD.
BUT TELL ME...

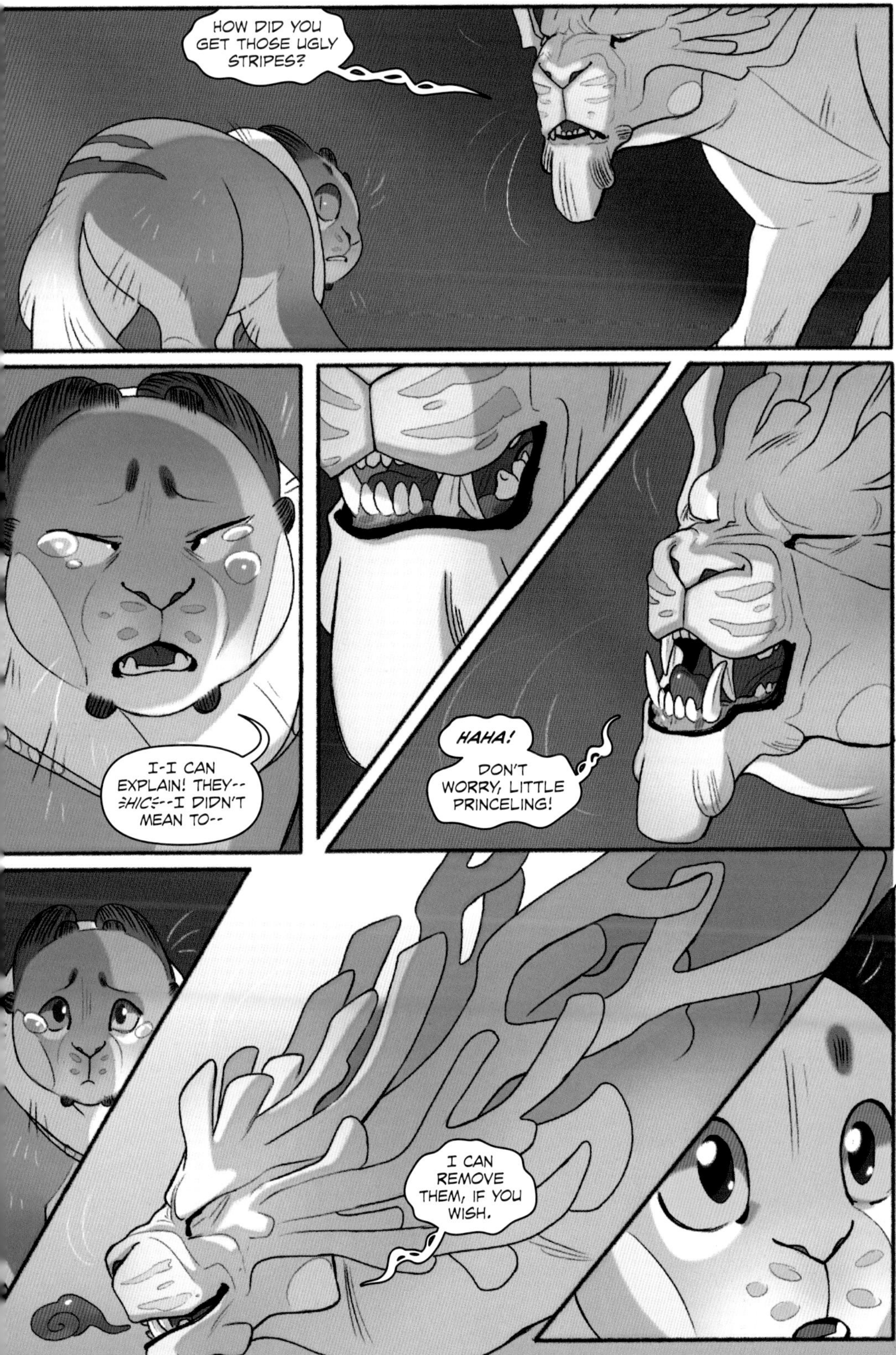
HOW DID YOU GET THOSE UGLY STRIPES?
I-I CAN EXPLAIN! THEY-- *HIC* --I DIDN'T MEAN TO--
HAHA!
DON'T WORRY, LITTLE PRINCELING!
I CAN REMOVE THEM, IF YOU WISH.

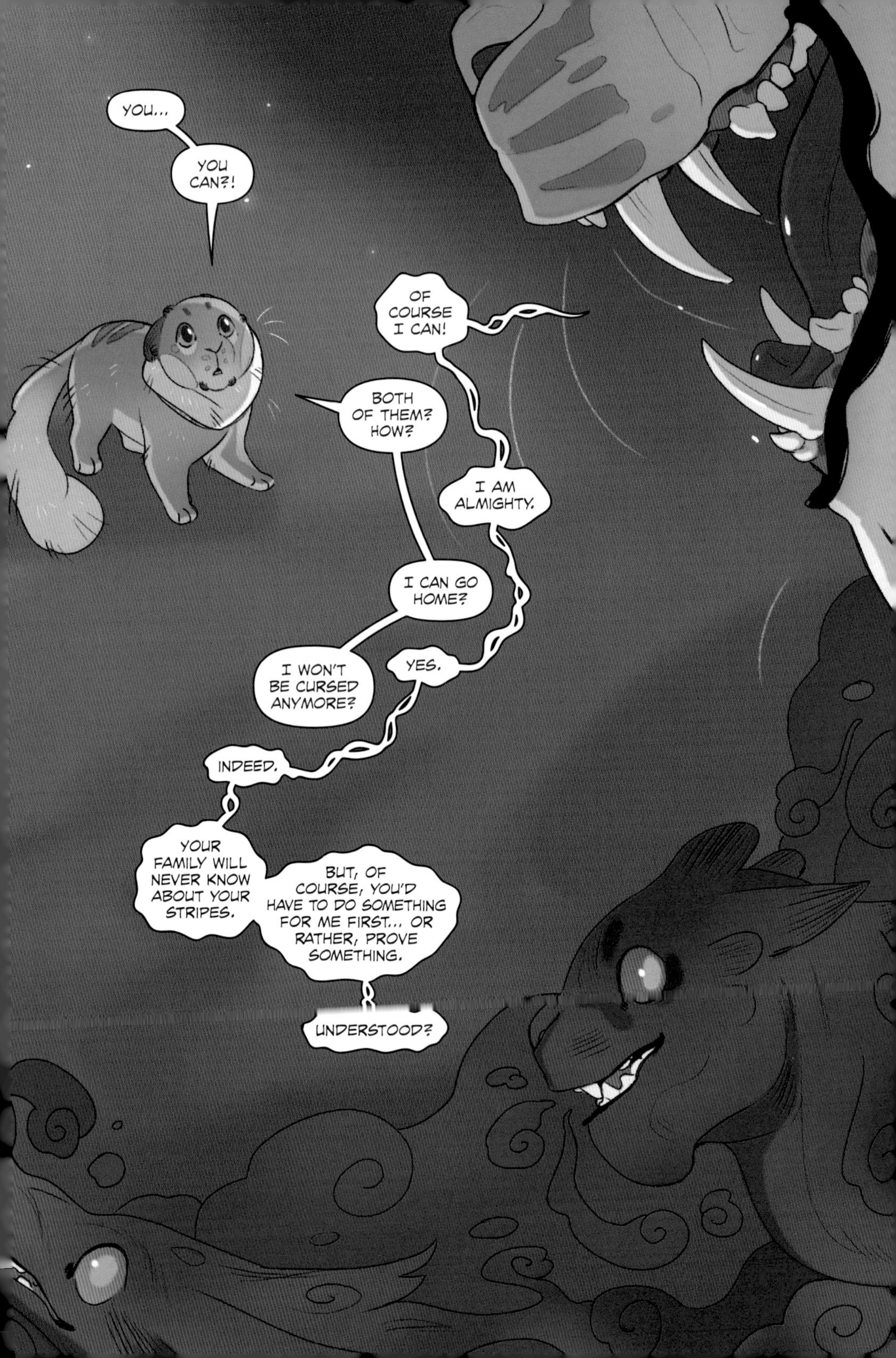
YOU...
YOU CAN?!
OF COURSE I CAN!
BOTH OF THEM? HOW?
I AM ALMIGHTY.
I CAN GO HOME?
YES.
I WON'T BE CURSED ANYMORE?
INDEED.
YOUR FAMILY WILL NEVER KNOW ABOUT YOUR STRIPES.
BUT, OF COURSE, YOU'D HAVE TO DO SOMETHING FOR ME FIRST... OR RATHER, PROVE SOMETHING.
UNDERSTOOD?

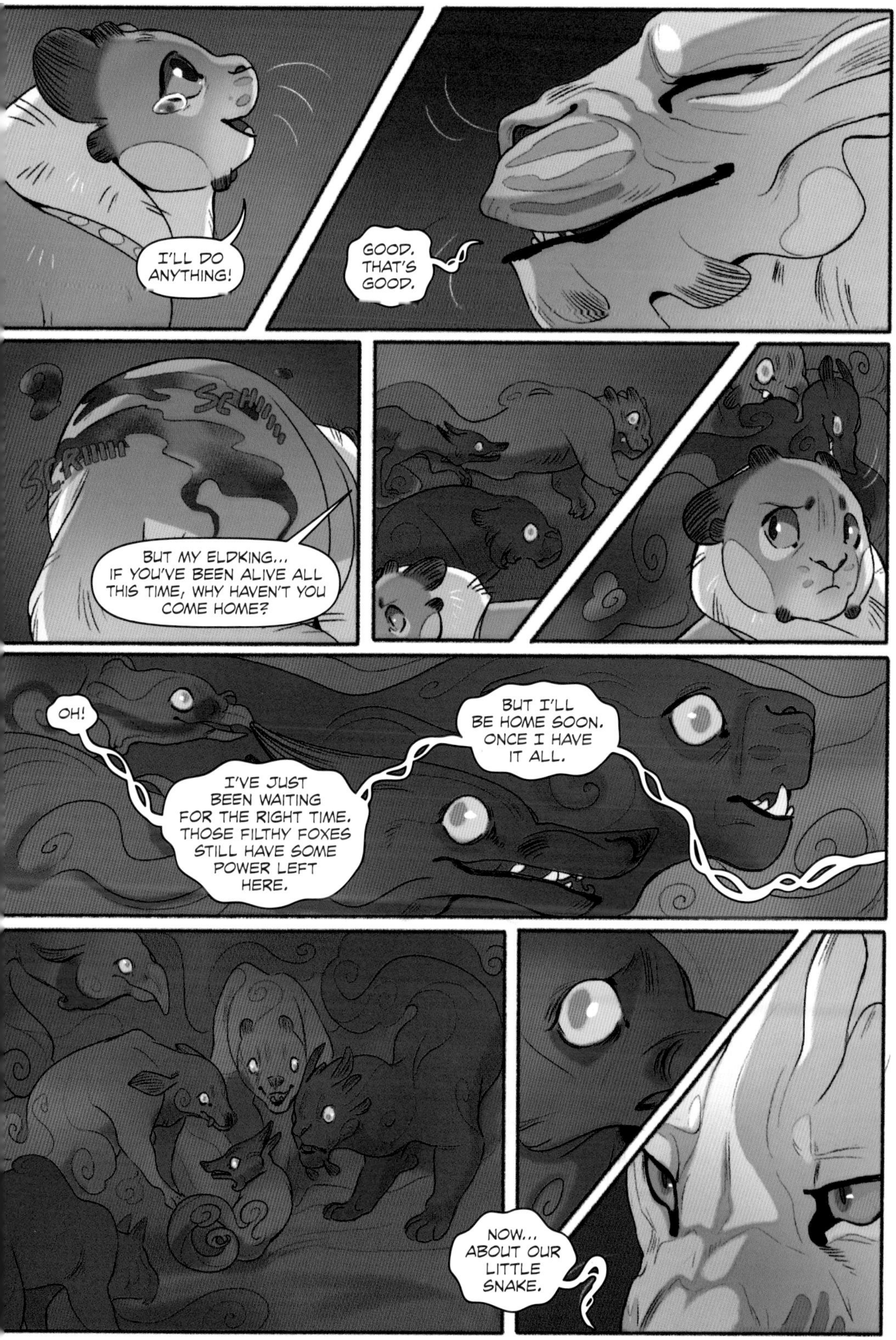
I'LL DO ANYTHING!
GOOD. THAT'S GOOD.
BUT MY ELDKING... IF YOU'VE BEEN ALIVE ALL THIS TIME, WHY HAVEN'T YOU COME HOME?
OH!
I'VE JUST BEEN WAITING FOR THE RIGHT TIME. THOSE FILTHY FOXES STILL HAVE SOME POWER LEFT HERE.
BUT I'LL BE HOME SOON. ONCE I HAVE IT ALL.
NOW... ABOUT OUR LITTLE SNAKE.

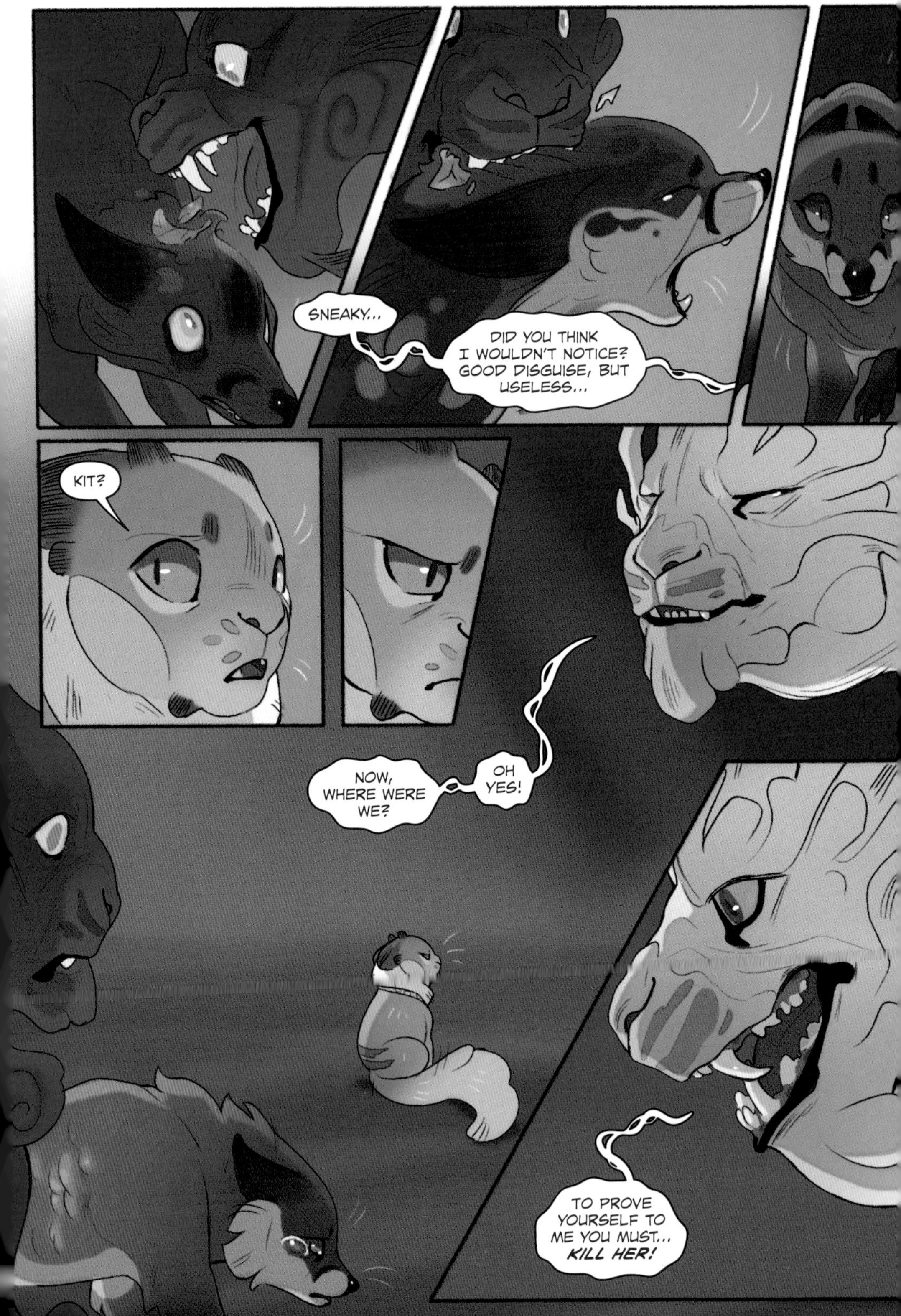
SNEAKY...
DID YOU THINK I WOULDN'T NOTICE? GOOD DISGUISE, BUT USELESS...
KIT?
NOW, WHERE WERE WE?
OH YES!
TO PROVE YOURSELF TO ME YOU MUST... **KILL HER!**

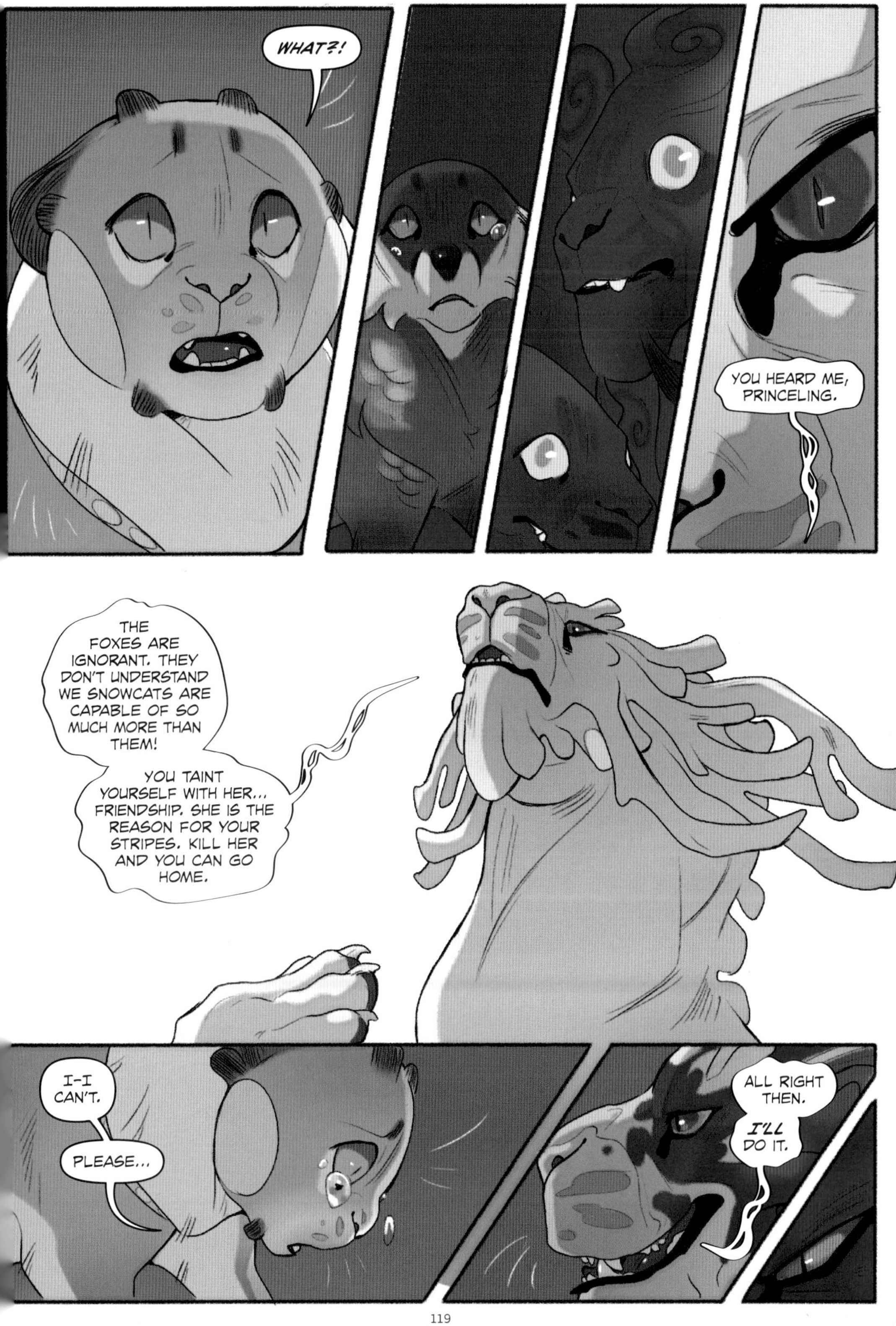

WHAT?!
YOU HEARD ME, PRINCELING.
THE FOXES ARE IGNORANT. THEY DON'T UNDERSTAND WE SNOWCATS ARE CAPABLE OF SO MUCH MORE THAN THEM!
YOU TAINT YOURSELF WITH HER... FRIENDSHIP. SHE IS THE REASON FOR YOUR STRIPES. KILL HER AND YOU CAN GO HOME.
I-I CAN'T.
PLEASE...
ALL RIGHT THEN.
I'LL DO IT.

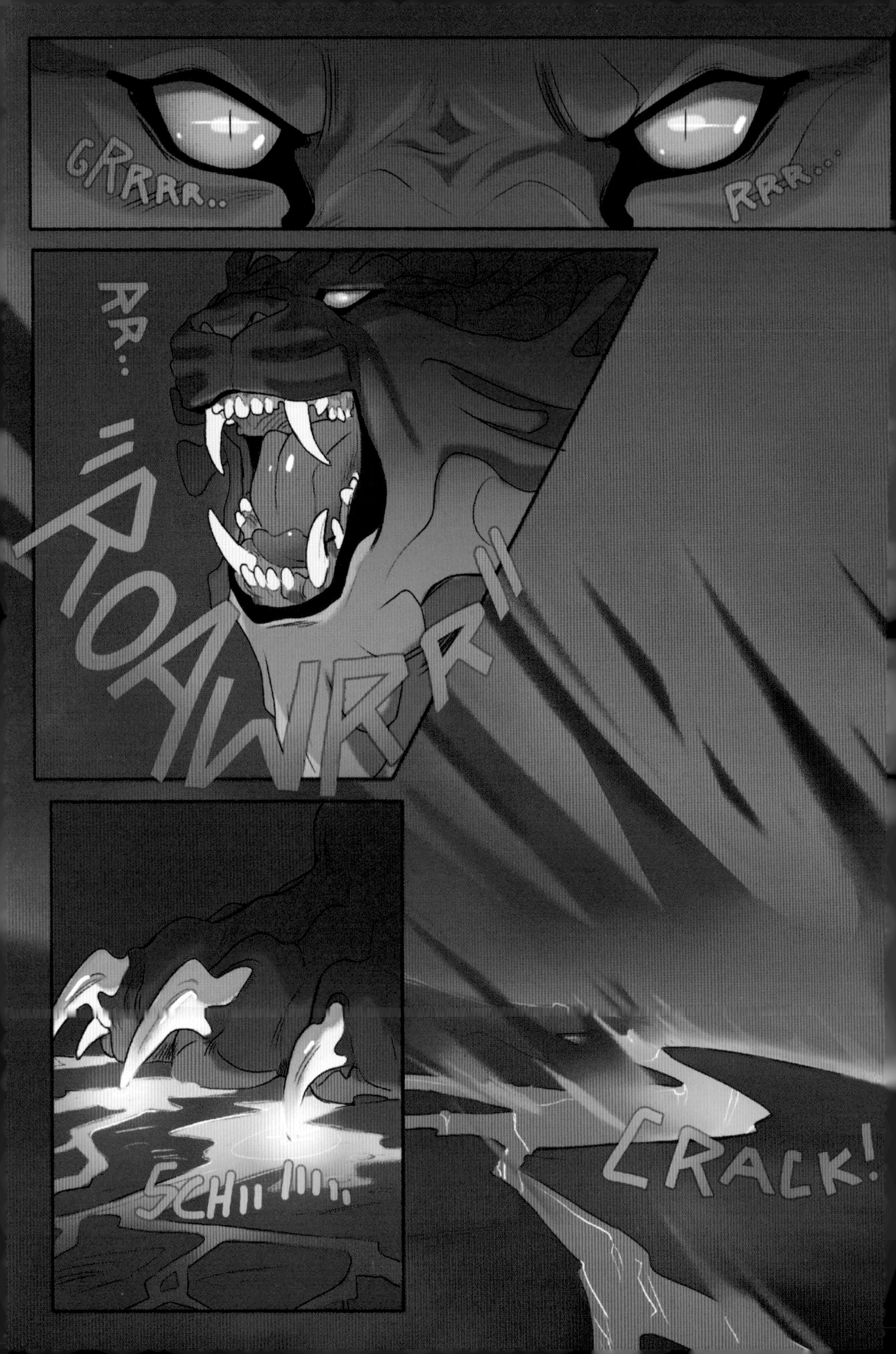
GRRRR..
RRR...
RR..
ROAWRR
SCH
CRACK!

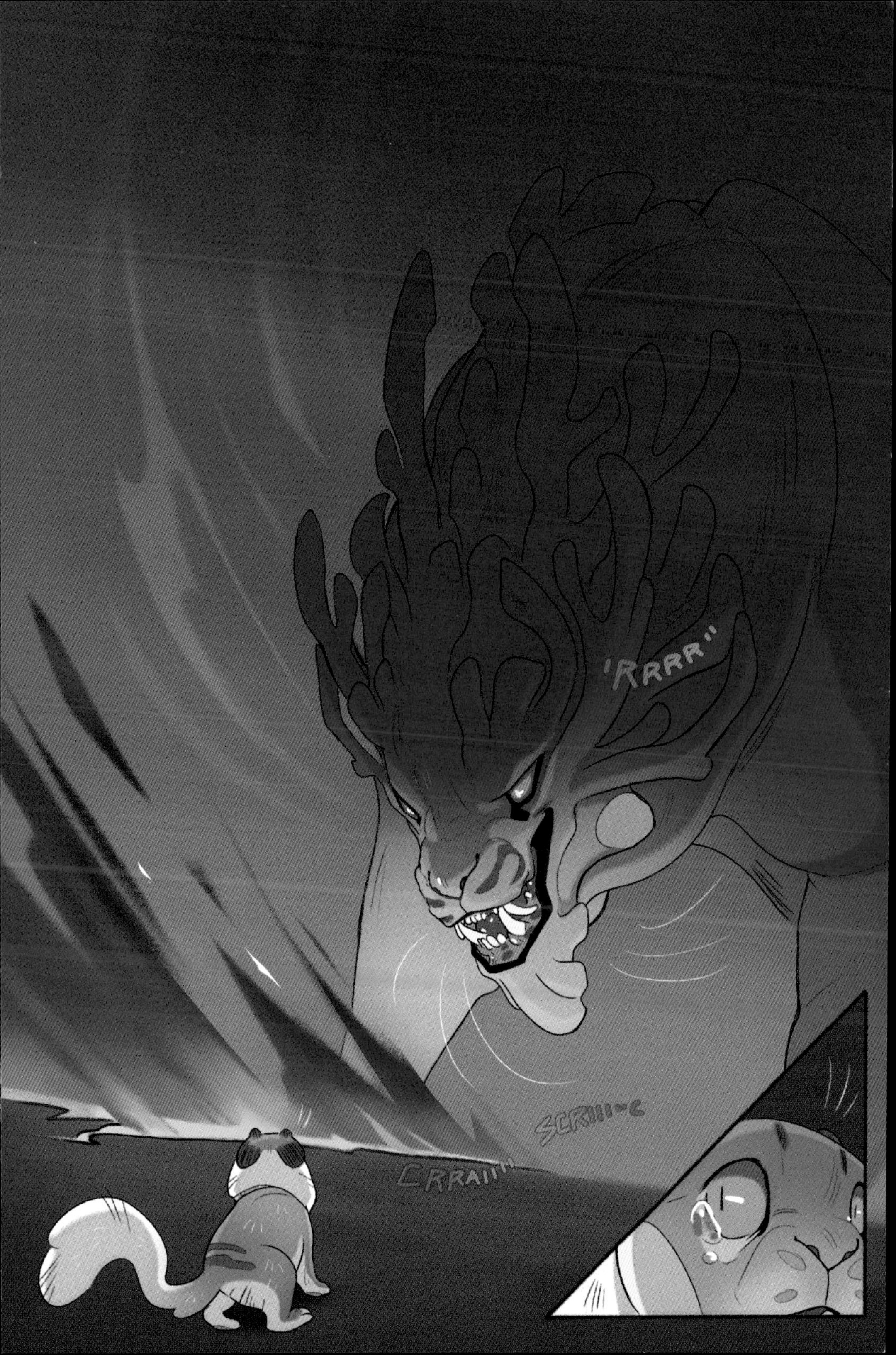
RRRR
CRRAI

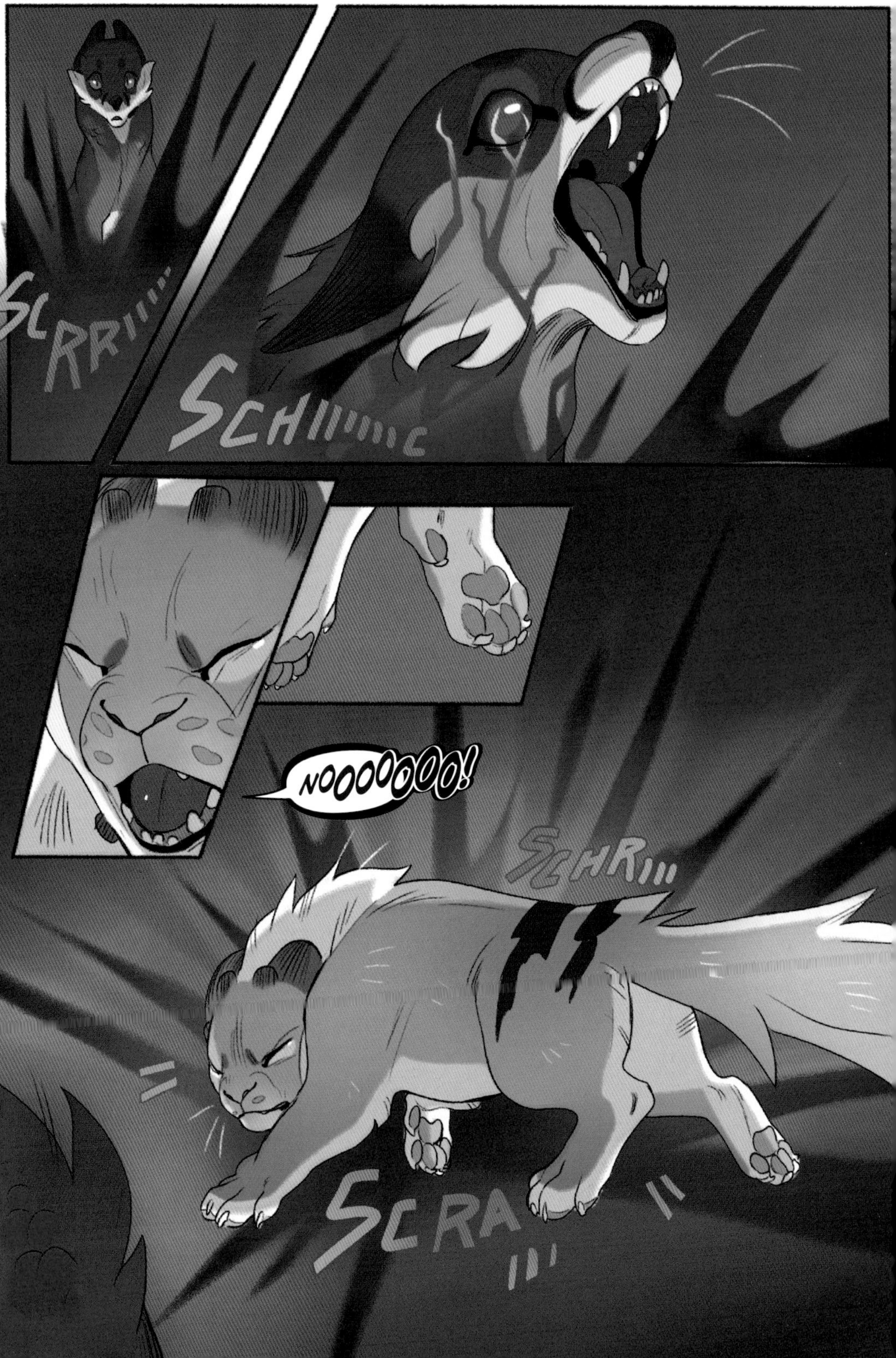
SCRRI'''
SCHI'''''NG
NOOOOOOO!
SCHRI''
SCRA''

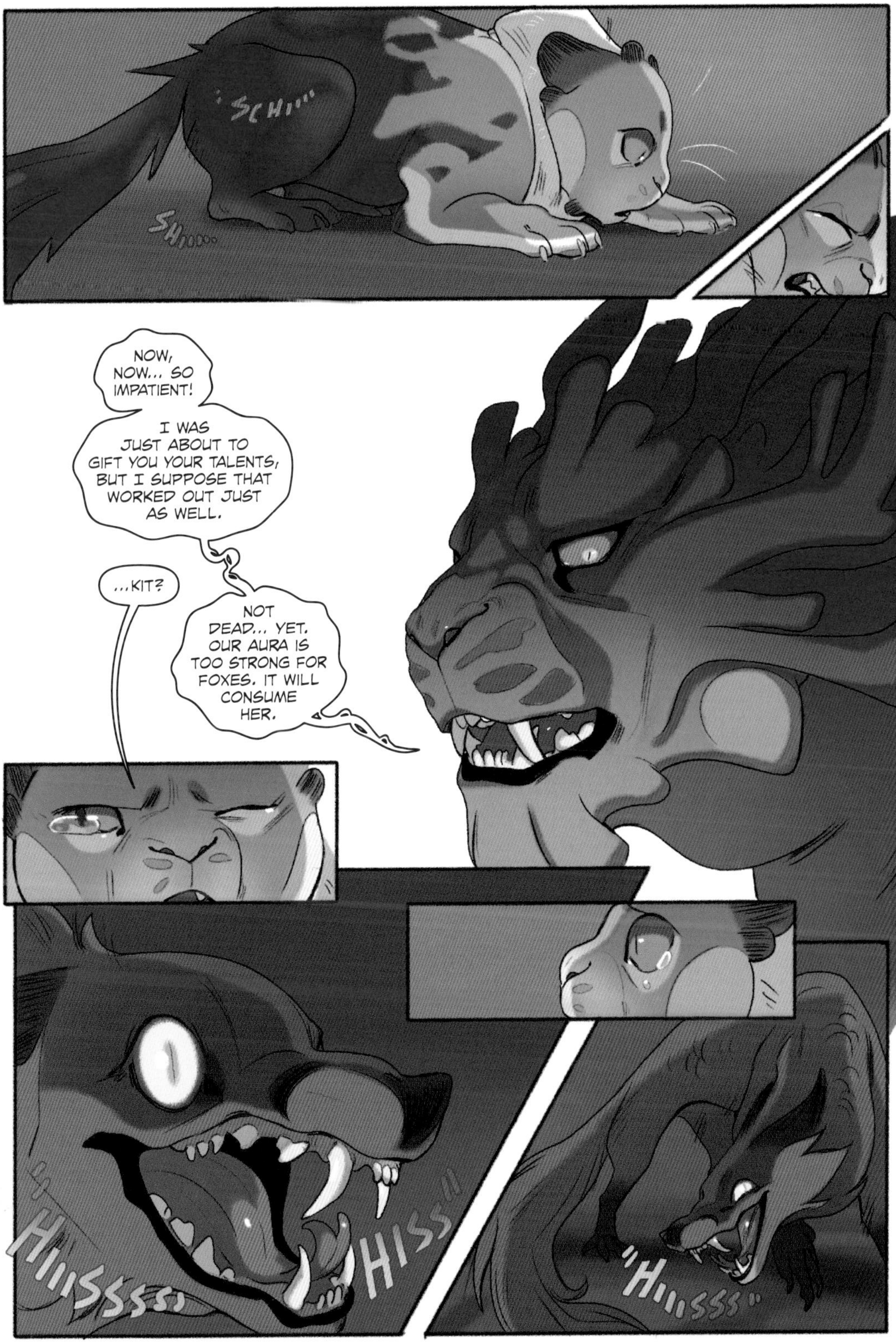
SCHI
SHIIOOO
NOW, NOW... SO IMPATIENT!
I WAS JUST ABOUT TO GIFT YOU YOUR TALENTS, BUT I SUPPOSE THAT WORKED OUT JUST AS WELL.
...KIT?
NOT DEAD... YET. OUR AURA IS TOO STRONG FOR FOXES. IT WILL CONSUME HER.
HIISSSS
HISS
HIISSS

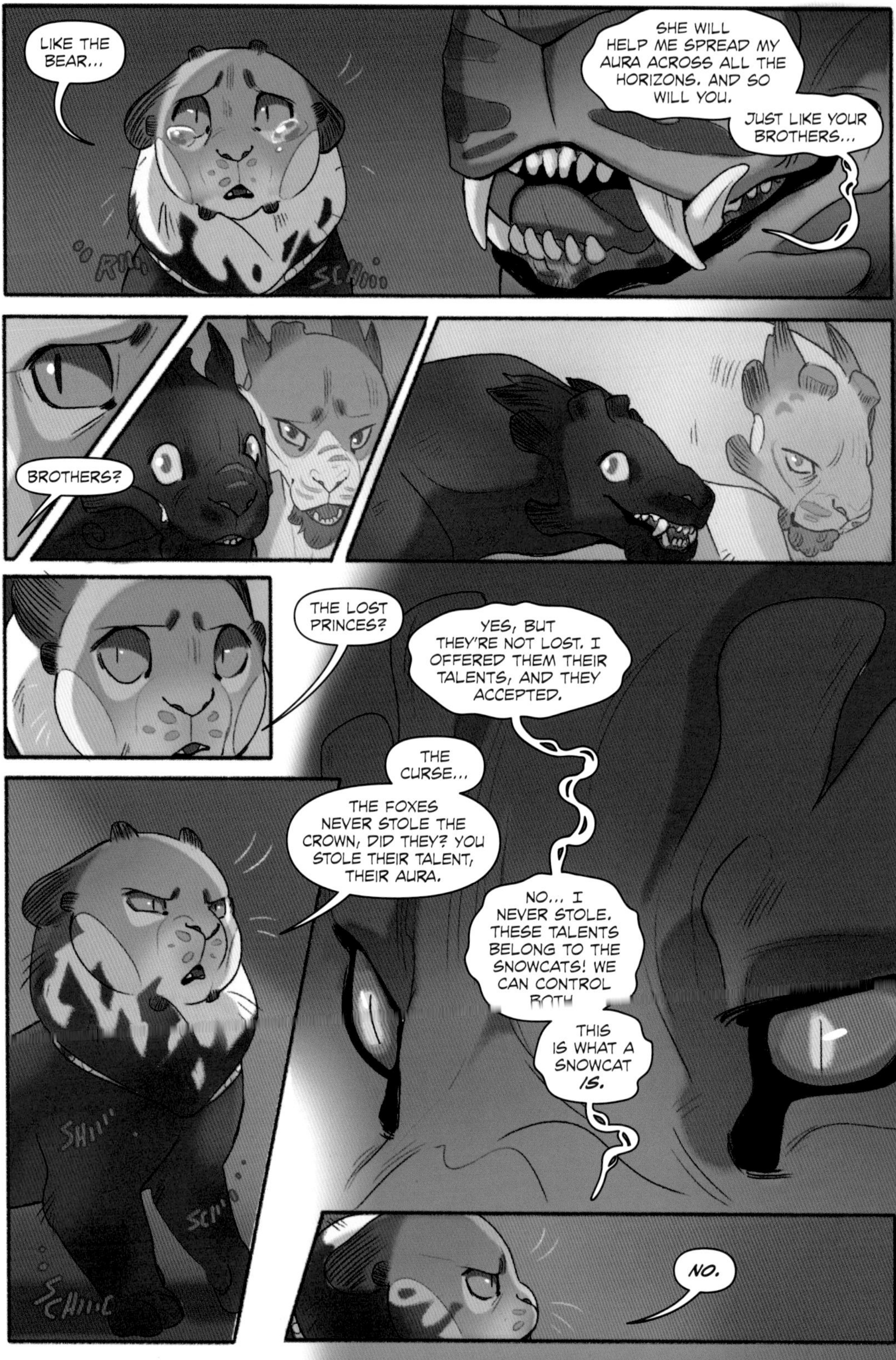

LIKE THE BEAR...
SHE WILL HELP ME SPREAD MY AURA ACROSS ALL THE HORIZONS. AND SO WILL YOU.
JUST LIKE YOUR BROTHERS...
BROTHERS?
THE LOST PRINCES?
YES, BUT THEY'RE NOT LOST. I OFFERED THEM THEIR TALENTS, AND THEY ACCEPTED.
THE CURSE...
THE FOXES NEVER STOLE THE CROWN, DID THEY? YOU STOLE THEIR TALENT, THEIR AURA.
NO... I NEVER STOLE. THESE TALENTS BELONG TO THE SNOWCATS! WE CAN CONTROL BOTH.
THIS IS WHAT A SNOWCAT *IS*.
NO.

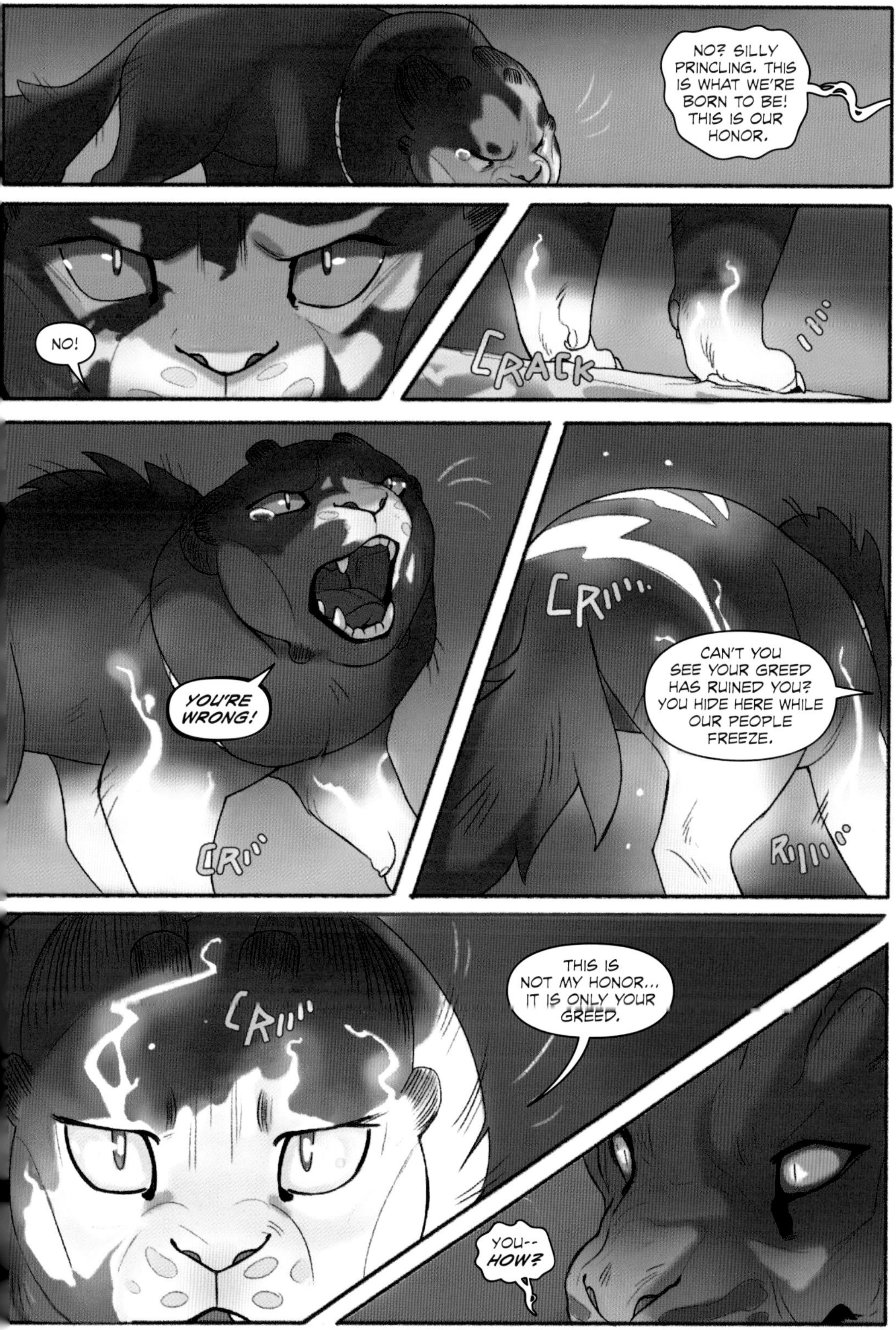
NO? SILLY PRINCLING. THIS IS WHAT WE'RE BORN TO BE! THIS IS OUR HONOR.
NO!
CRACK
YOU'RE WRONG!
CRI
CRI
CAN'T YOU SEE YOUR GREED HAS RUINED YOU? YOU HIDE HERE WHILE OUR PEOPLE FREEZE.
RIII
CRI
THIS IS NOT MY HONOR... IT IS ONLY YOUR GREED.
YOU-- HOW?

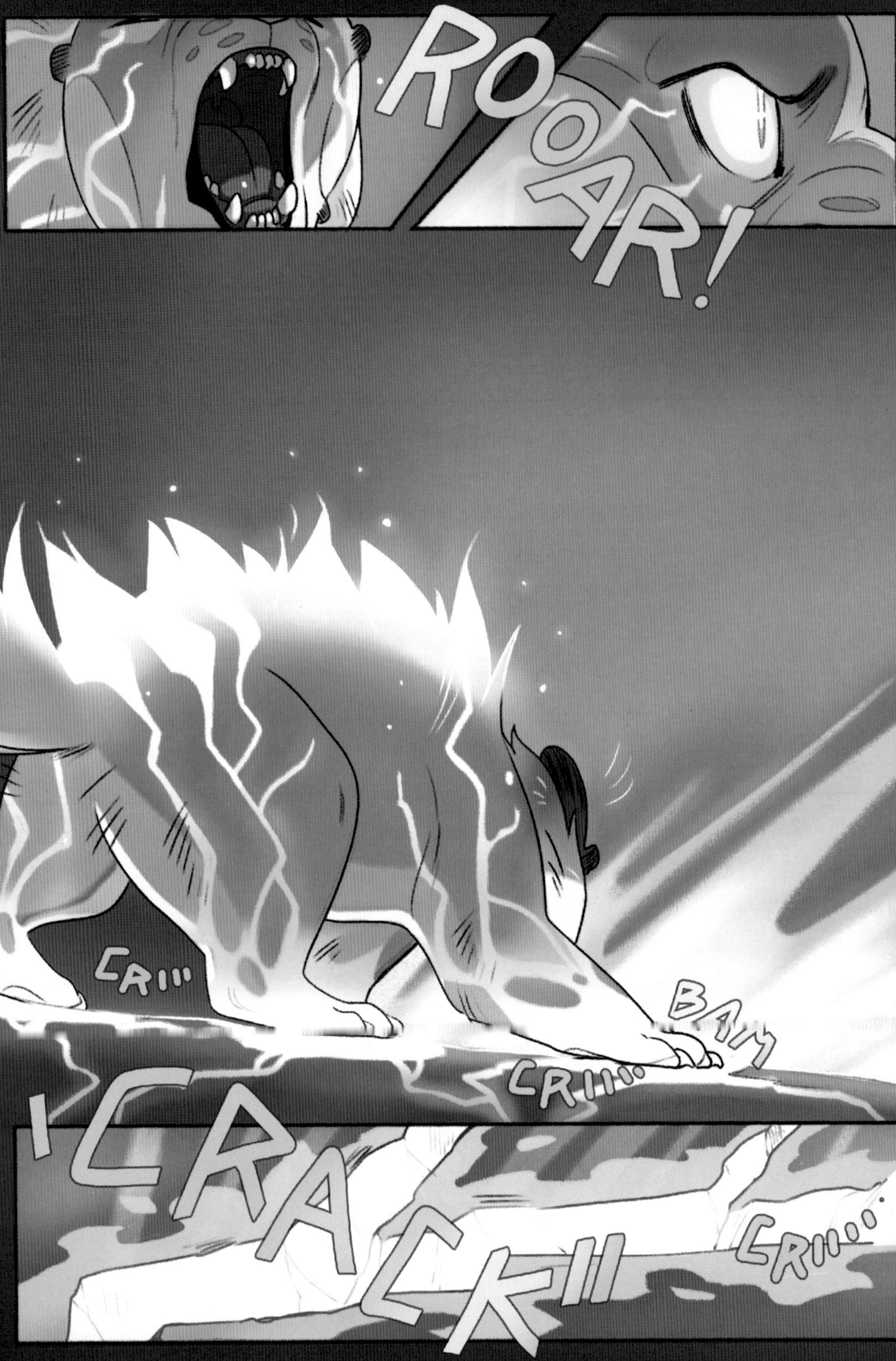
ROOAR!
CRI''
BAM
CRI'''
CRACK''
CRI''''

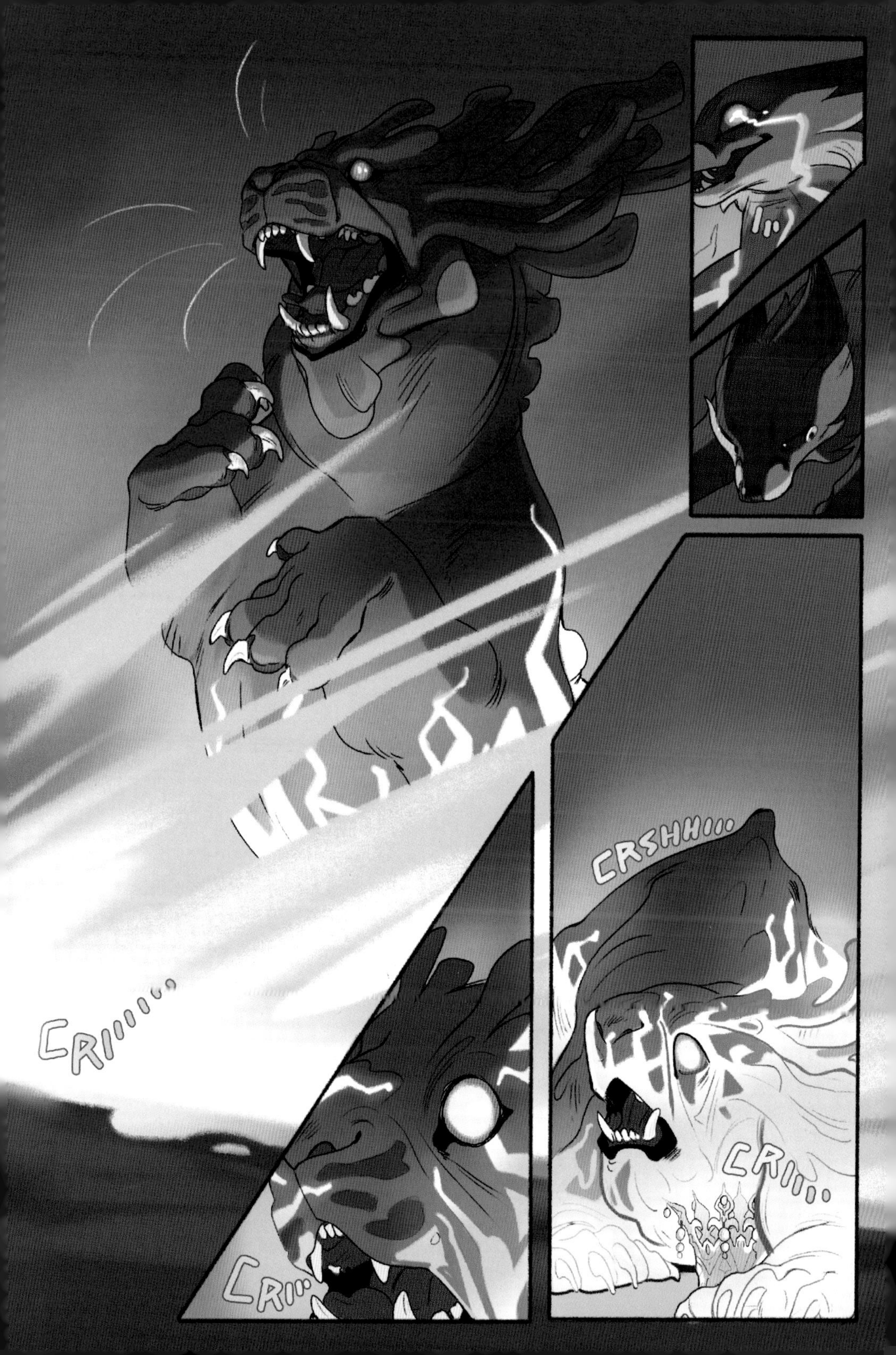
CRI''''''
CRSHH'''
CRI'''
CRI''

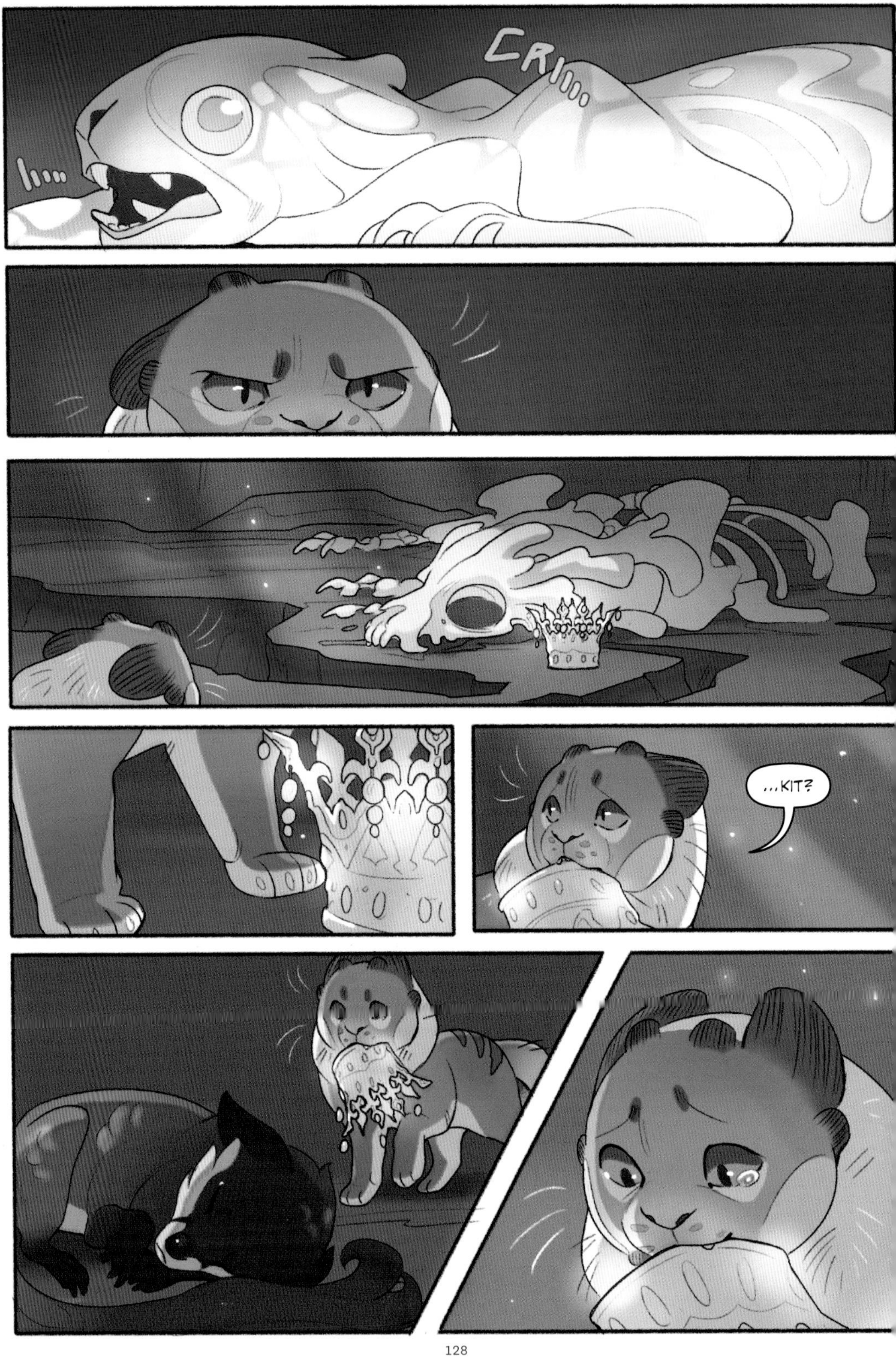
CRI...
I...
...KIT?

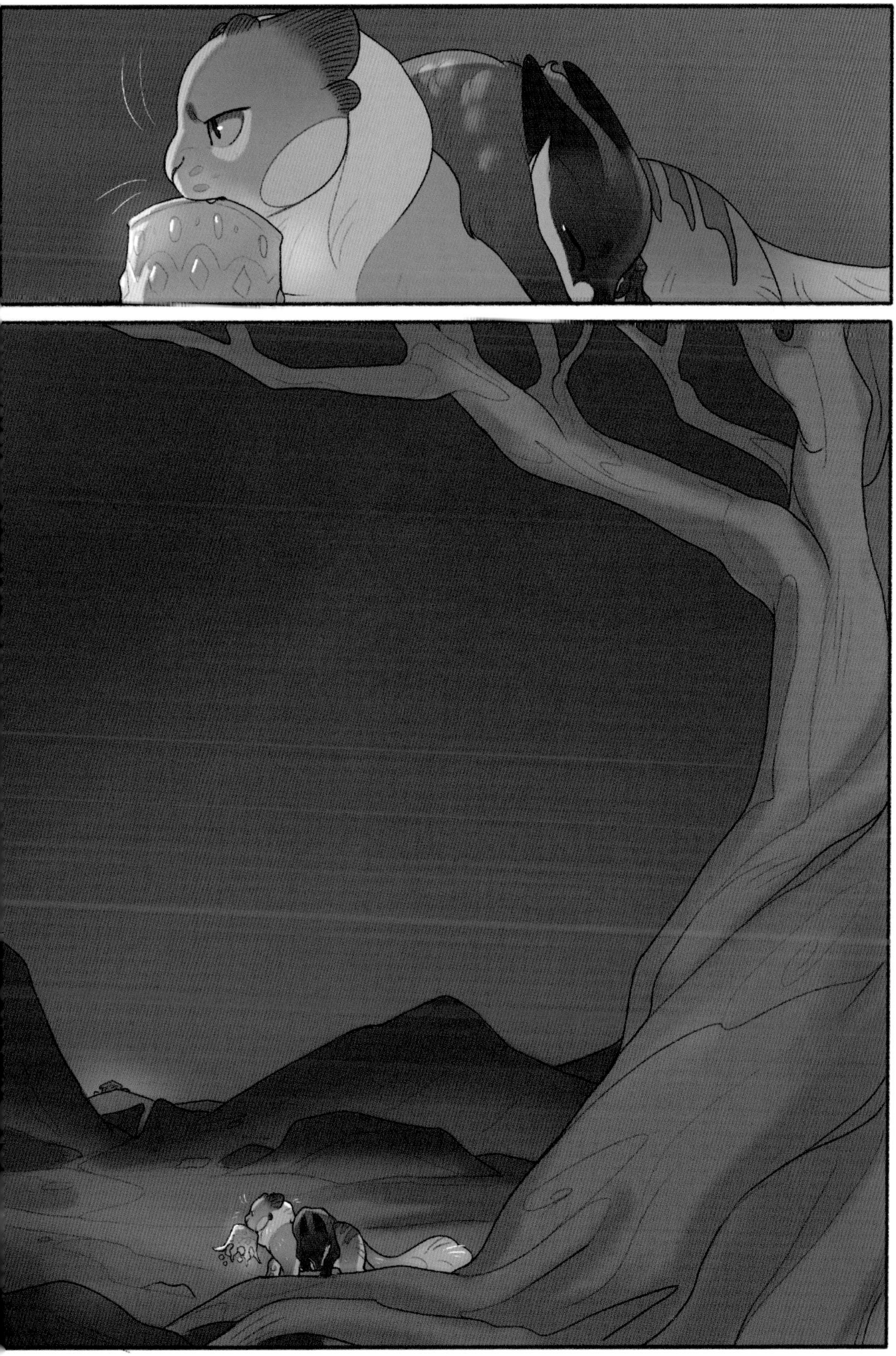

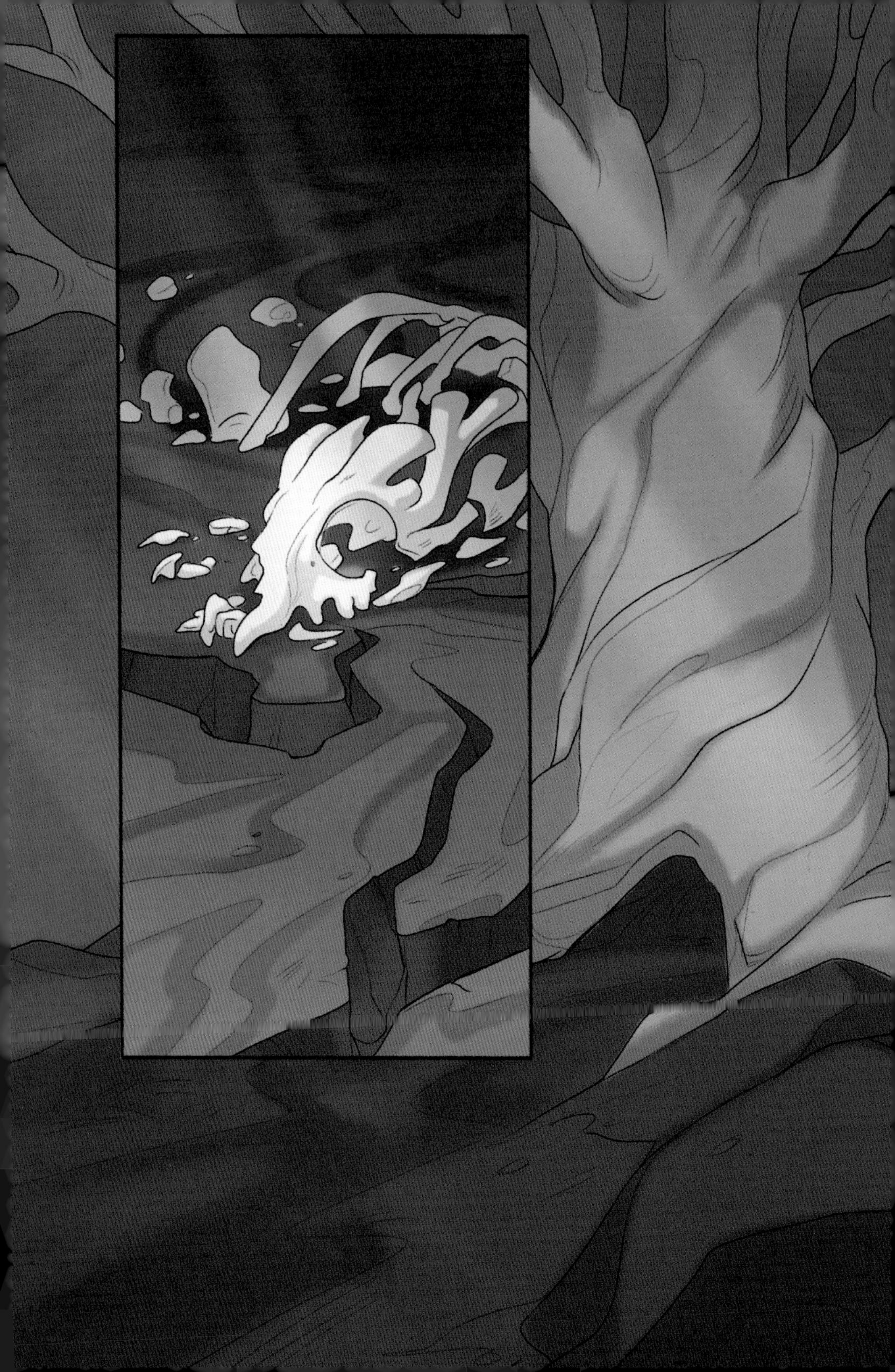

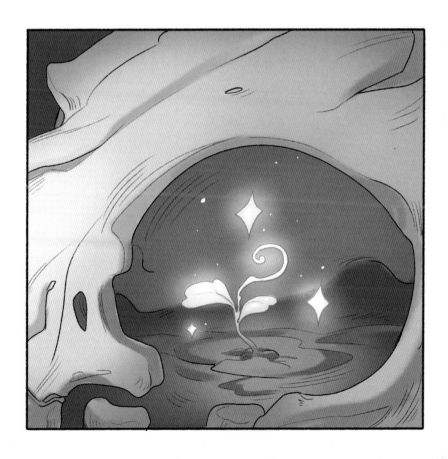

Chapter 7
HALLS OF GOLD

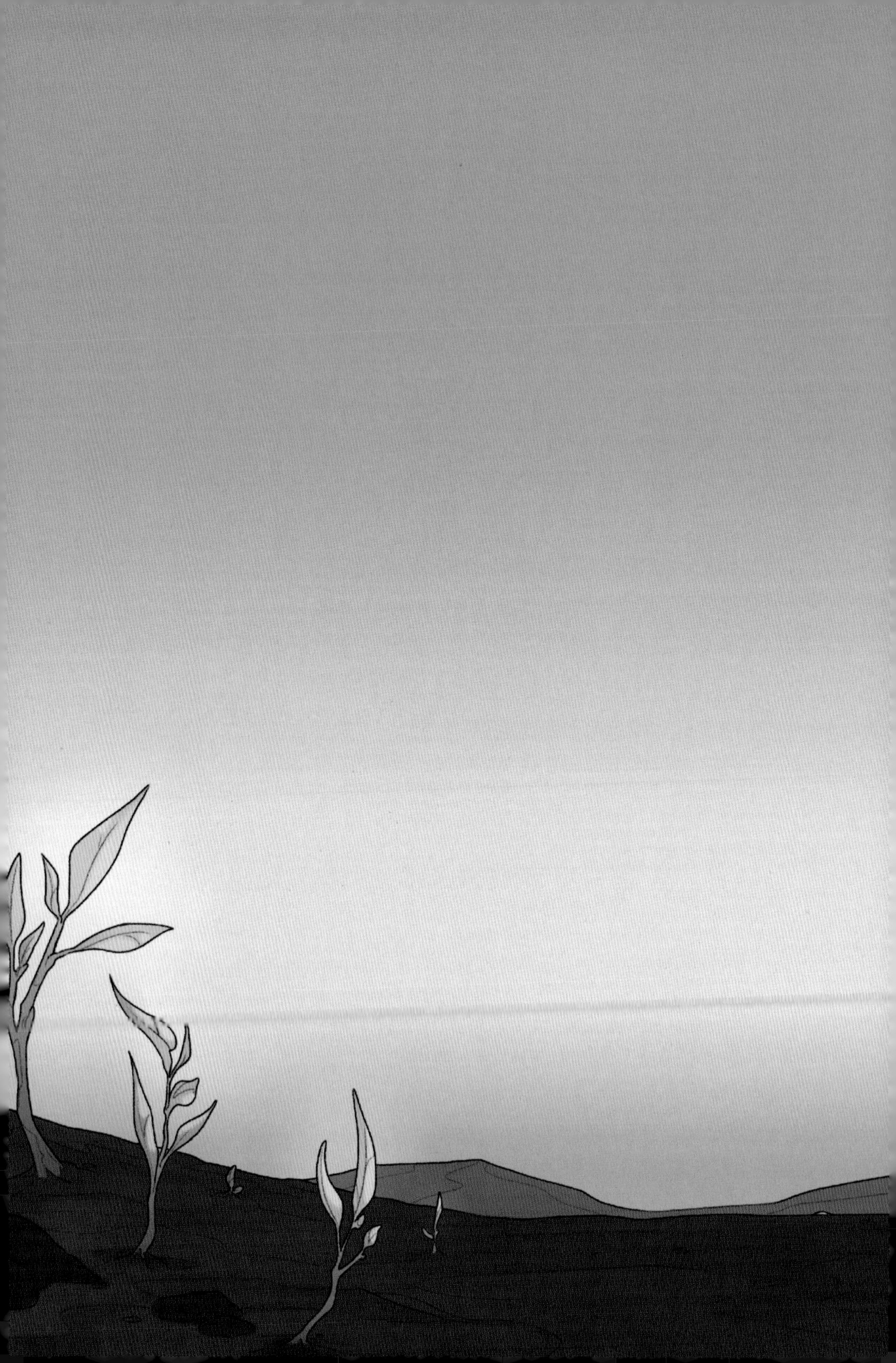

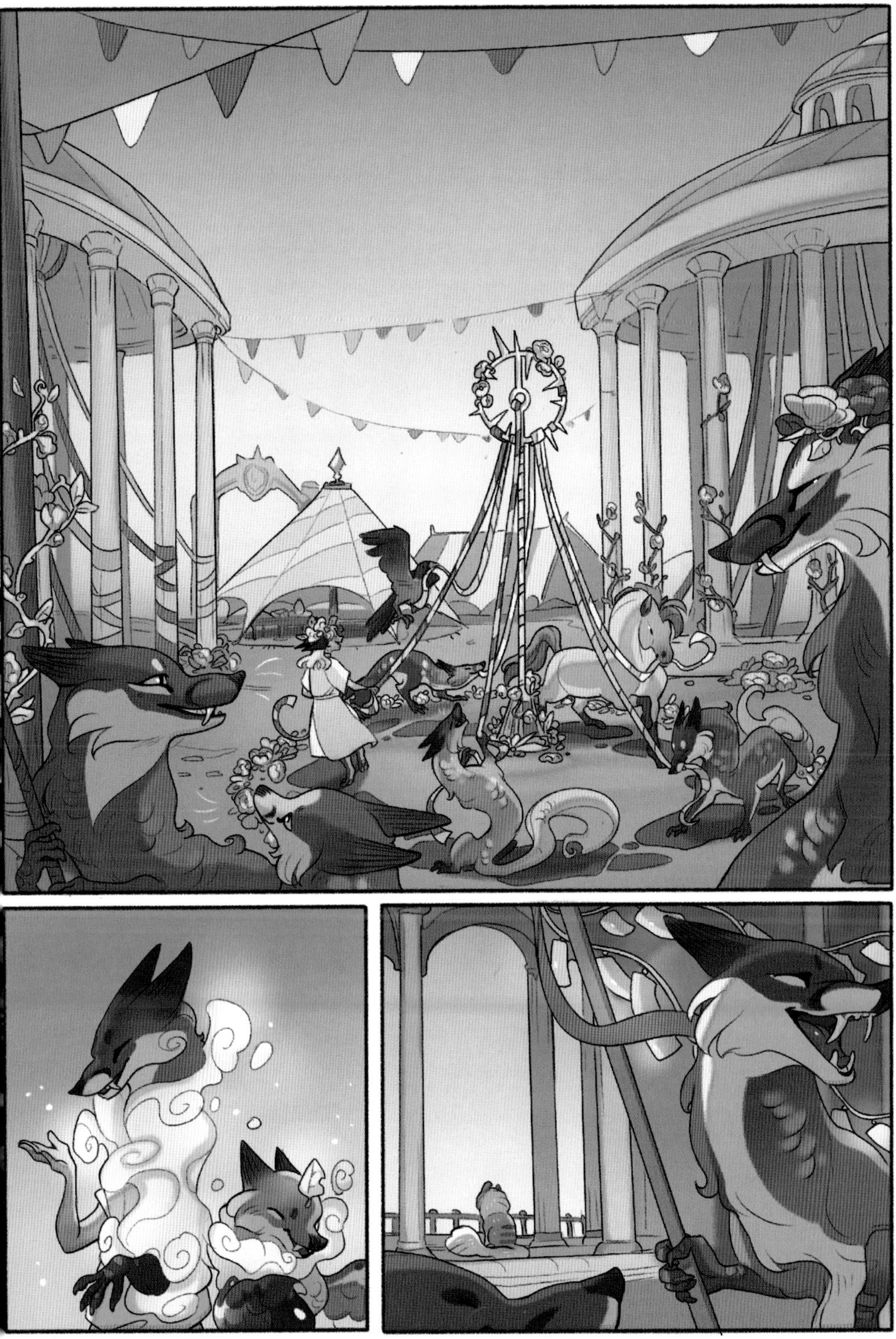

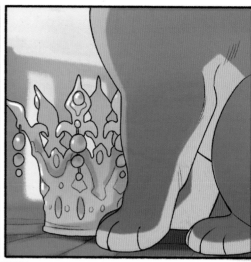

YOU KNOW...

THAT CROWN NEVER HELD ANY POWER.

ONLY THE GREEDY HEART OF THE ELDKING.

YOU DON'T NEED TO GO HOME, SYV. YOUR BROTHERS CAN RULE THE NORPAN HORIZON.

AND NOW THAT THE CURSE IS BROKEN, YOUR PEOPLE WILL THRIVE!

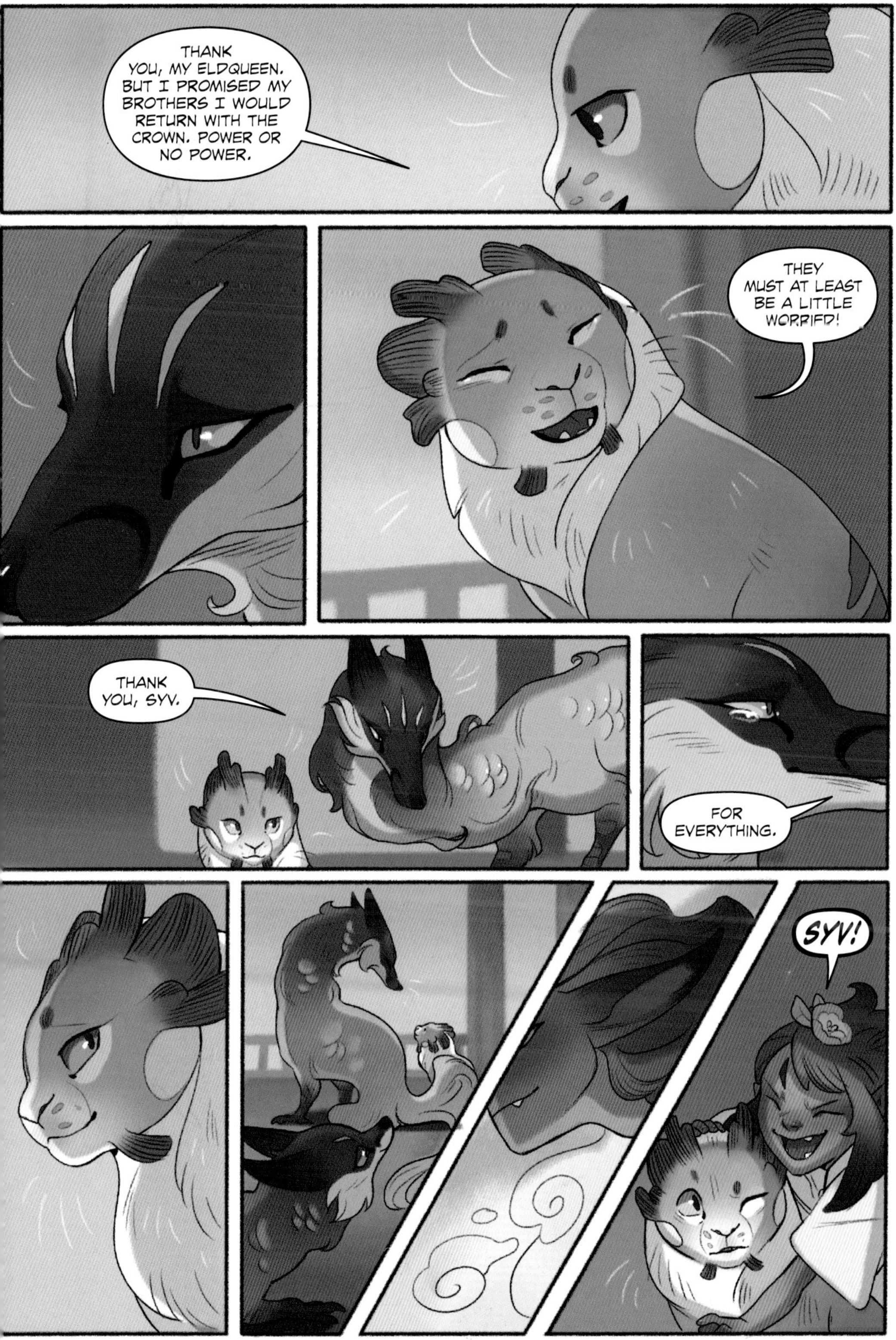
THANK YOU, MY ELDQUEEN. BUT I PROMISED MY BROTHERS I WOULD RETURN WITH THE CROWN. POWER OR NO POWER.
THEY MUST AT LEAST BE A LITTLE WORRIED!
THANK YOU, SYV.
FOR EVERYTHING.
SYV!

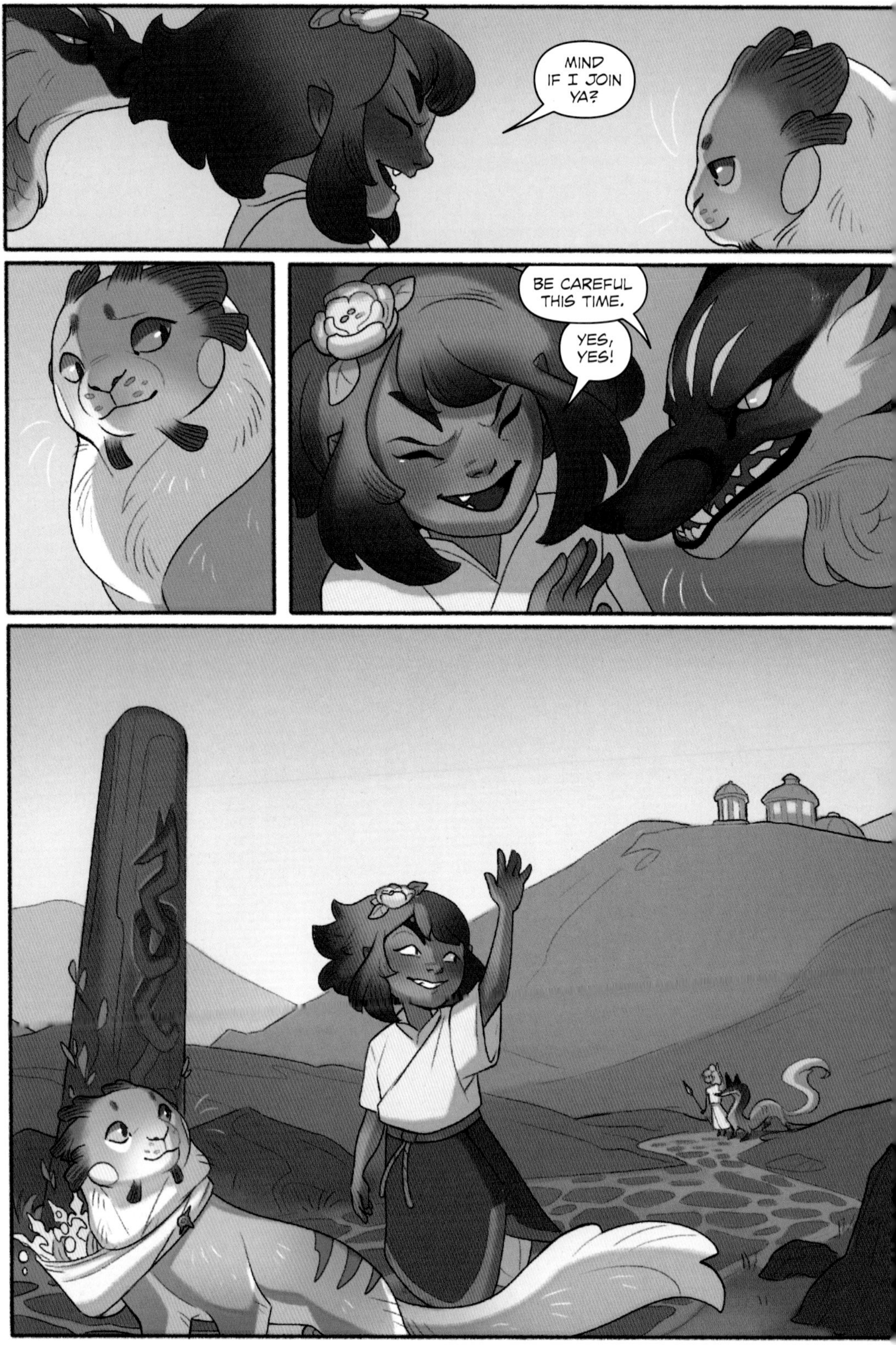
MIND IF I JOIN YA?
BE CAREFUL THIS TIME.
YES, YES!

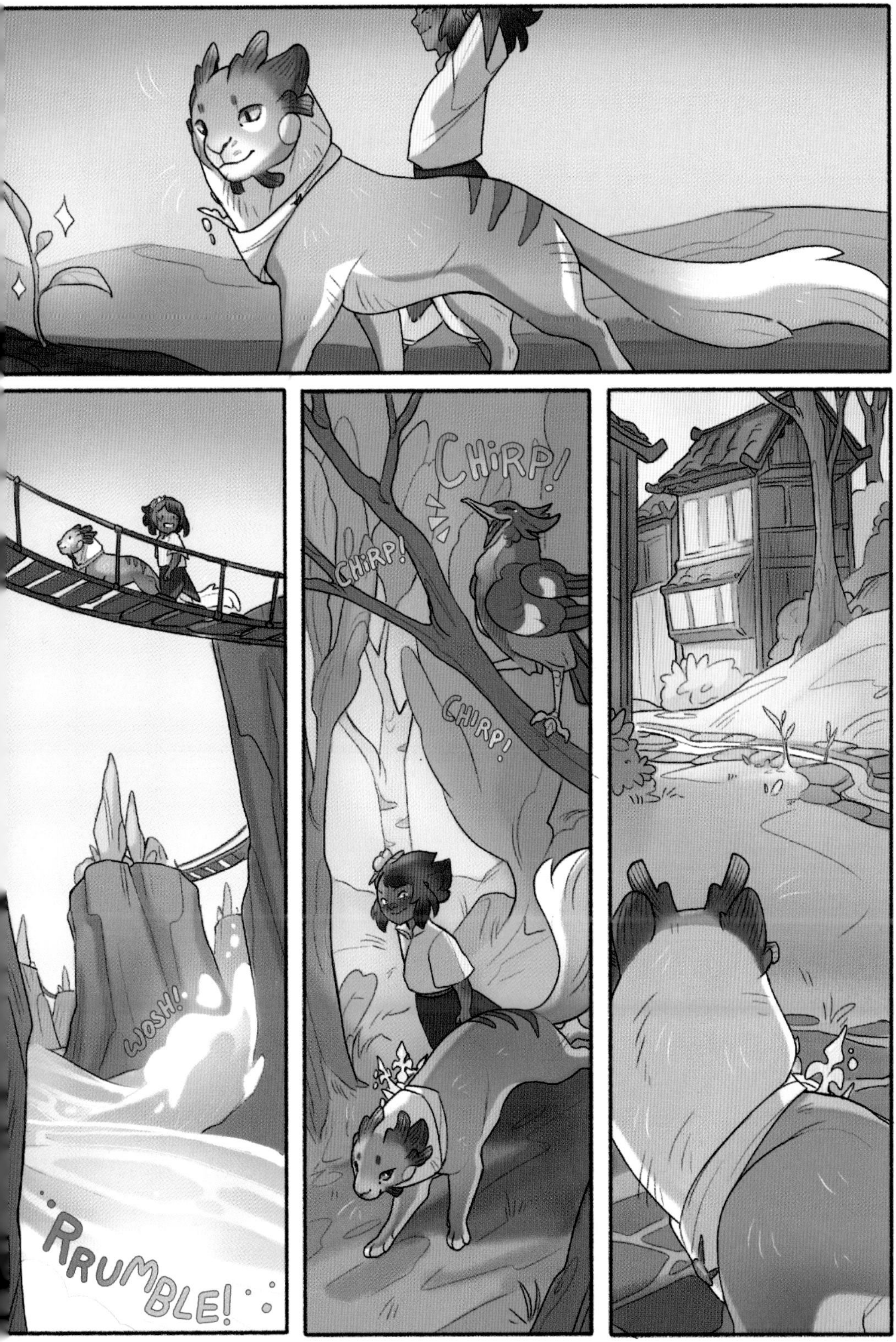
WOSH!
RRUMBLE!
CHIRP!
CHIRP!
CHIRP!

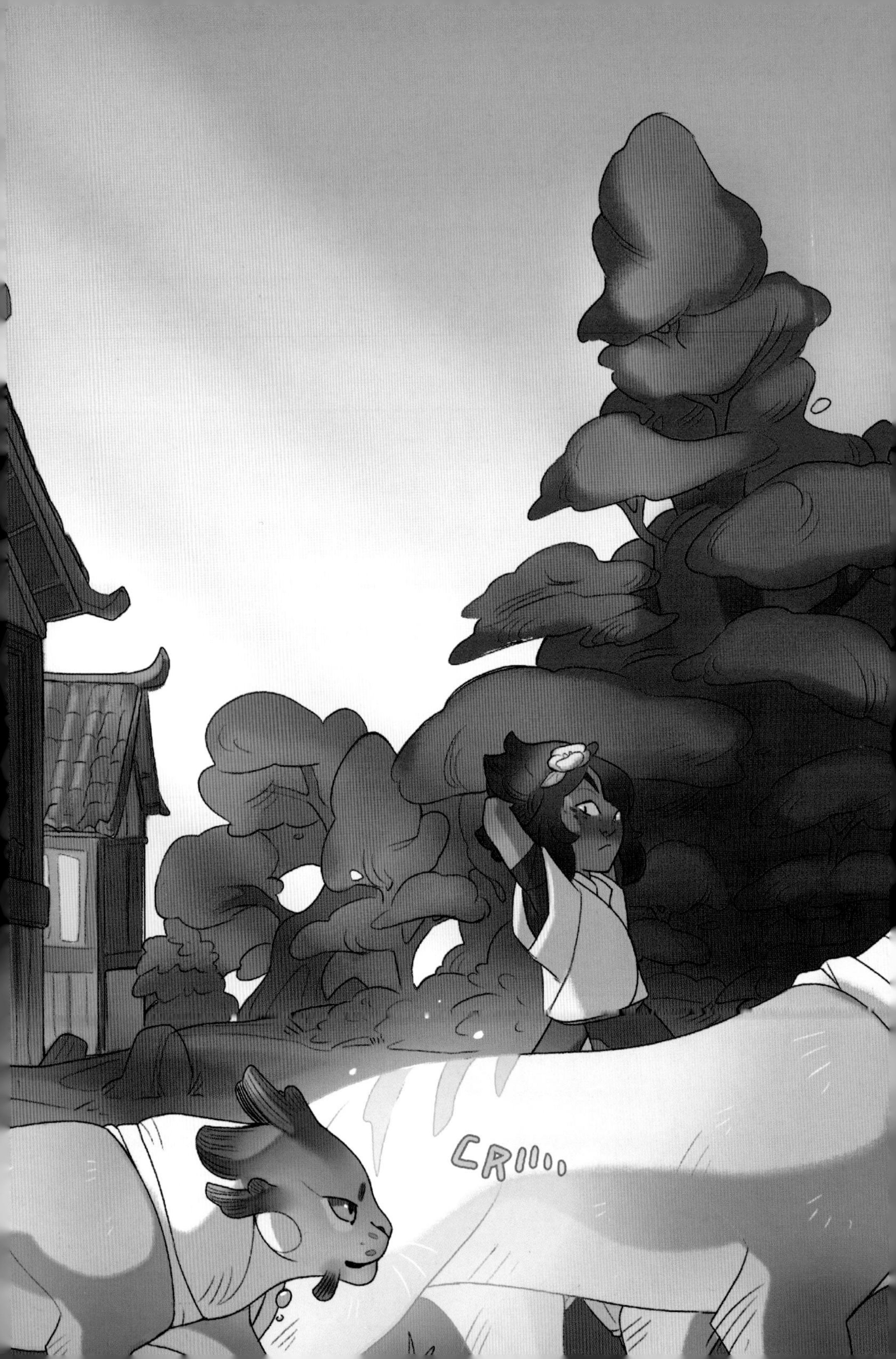
CRIIIII

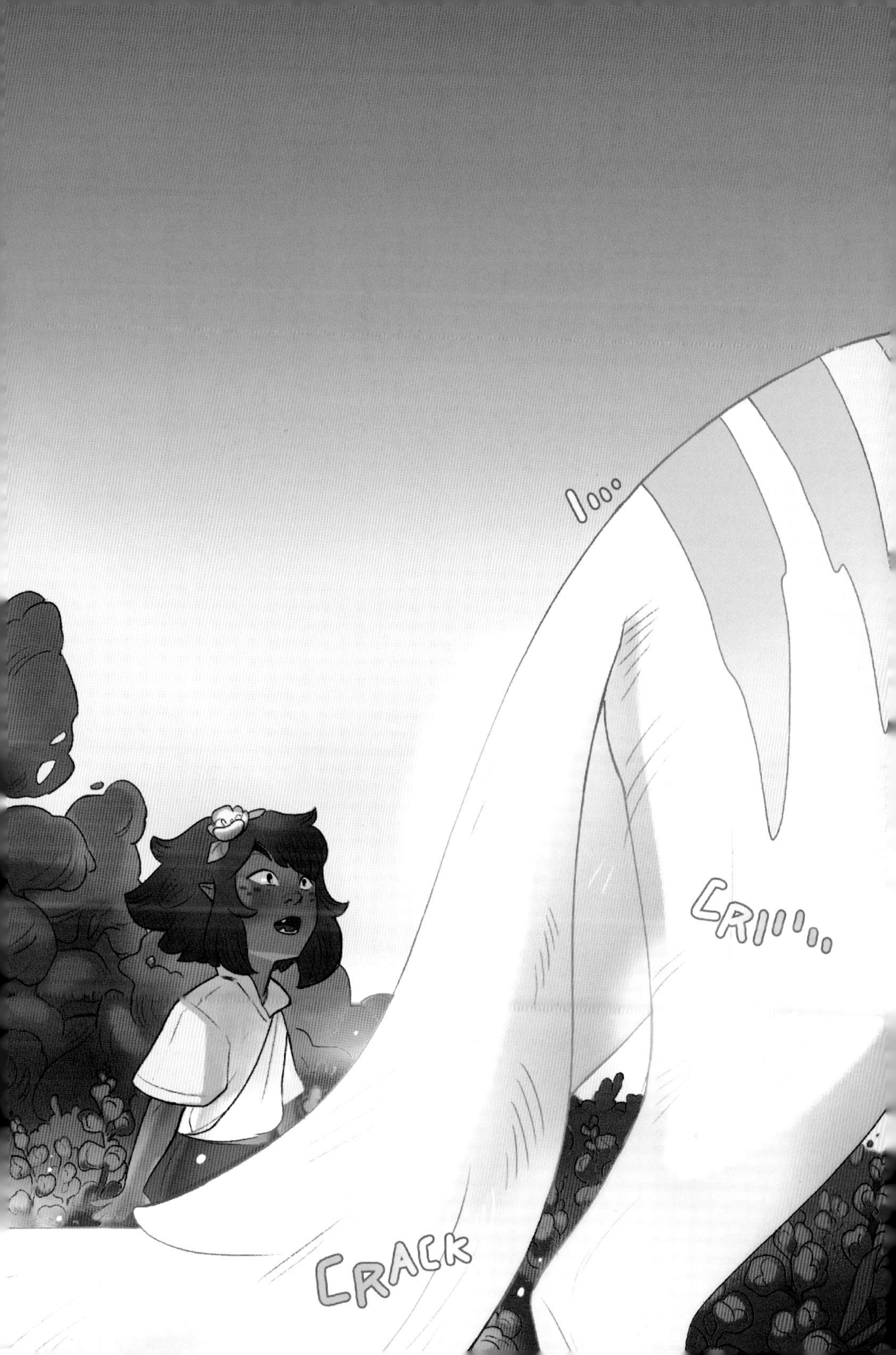
Iooo
CRIIIIII
CRACK

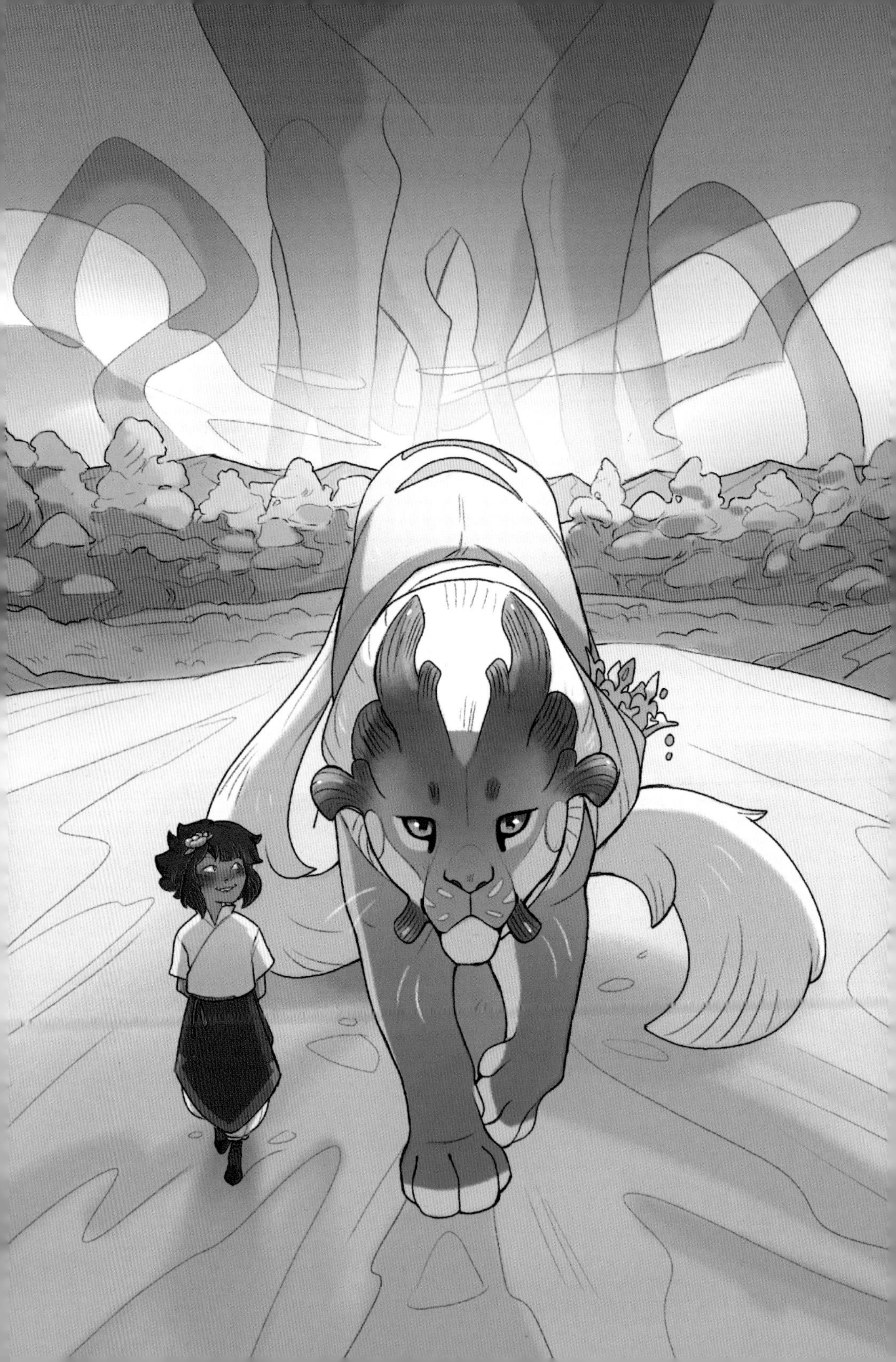

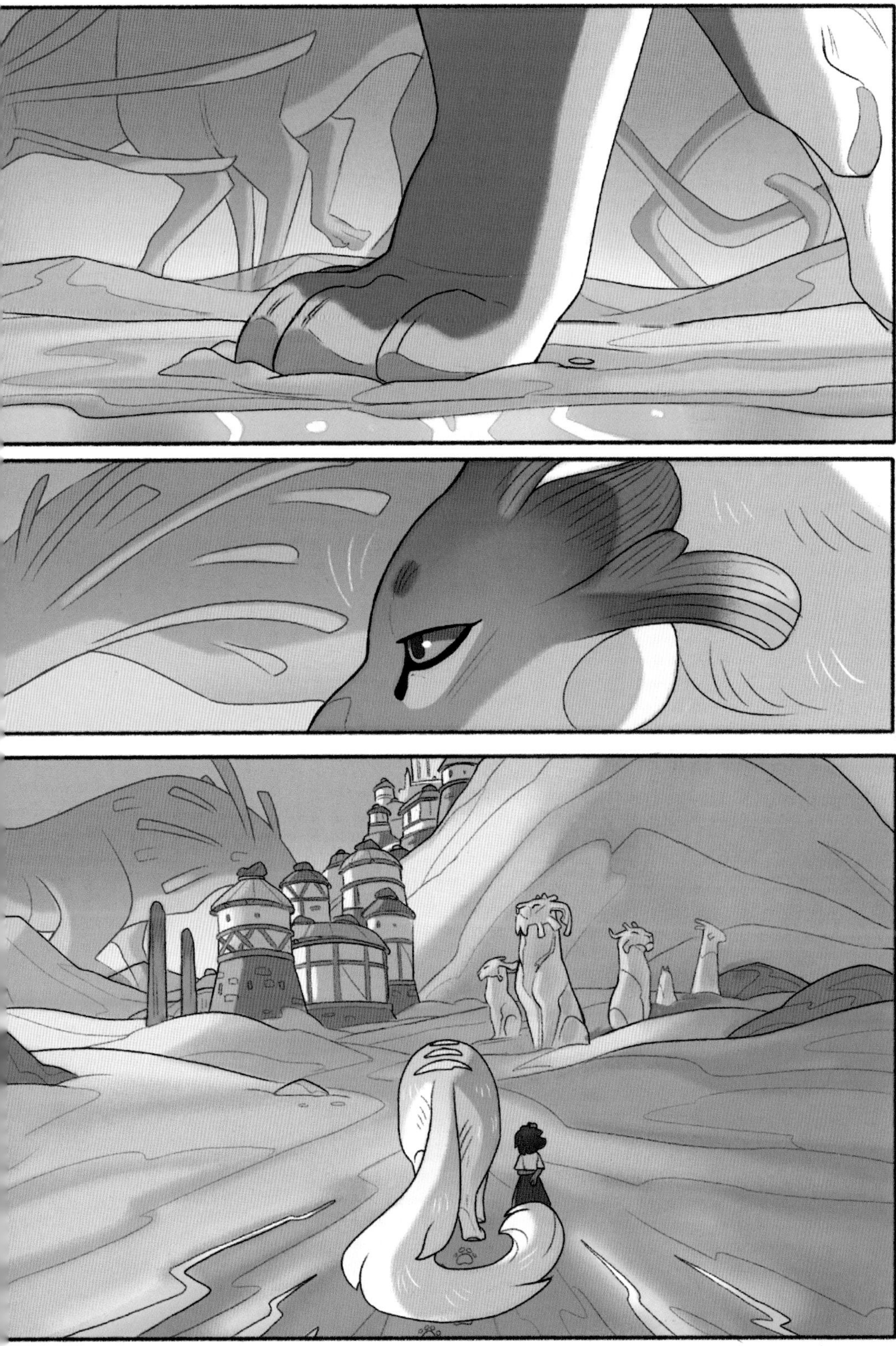

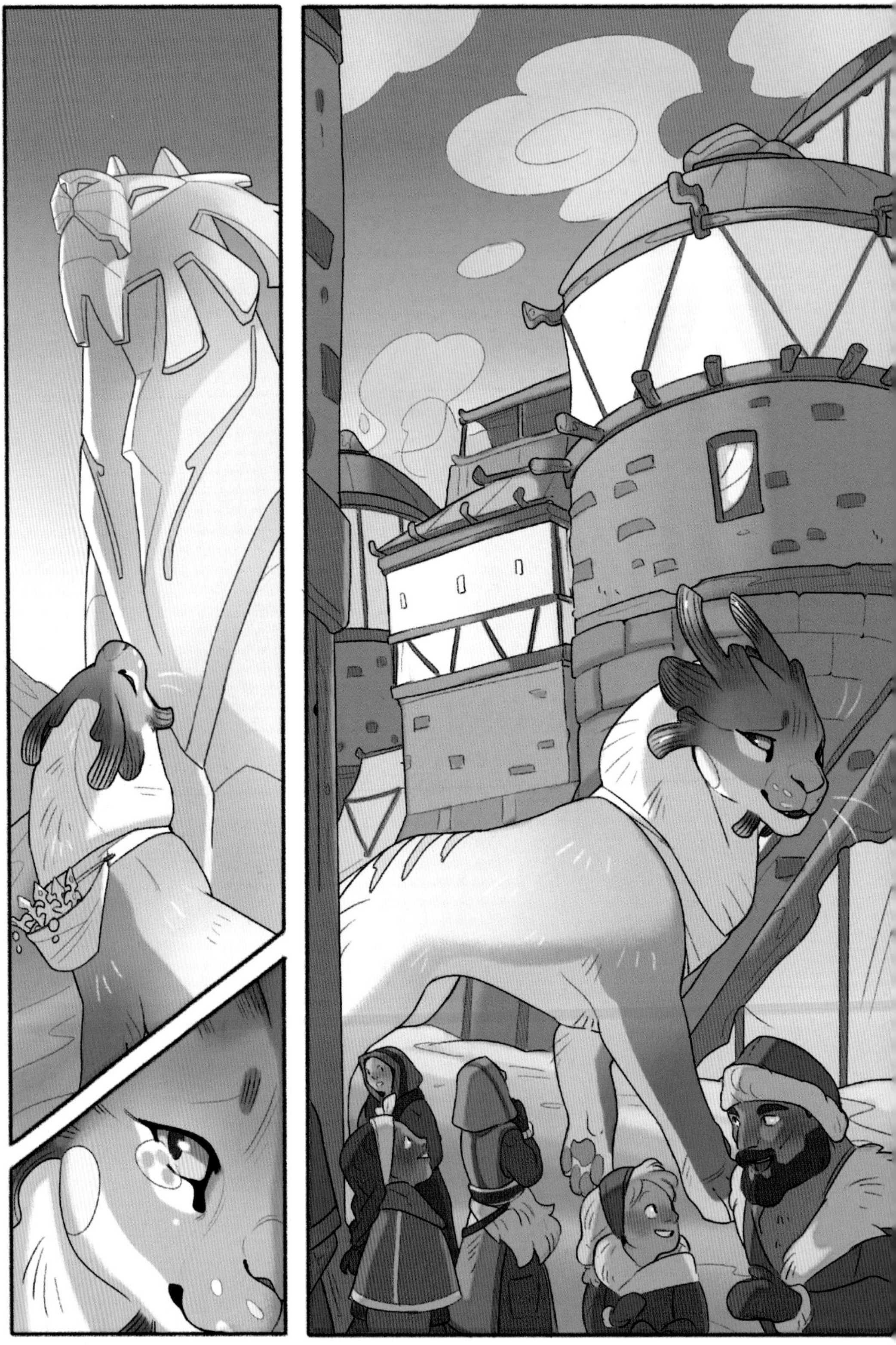

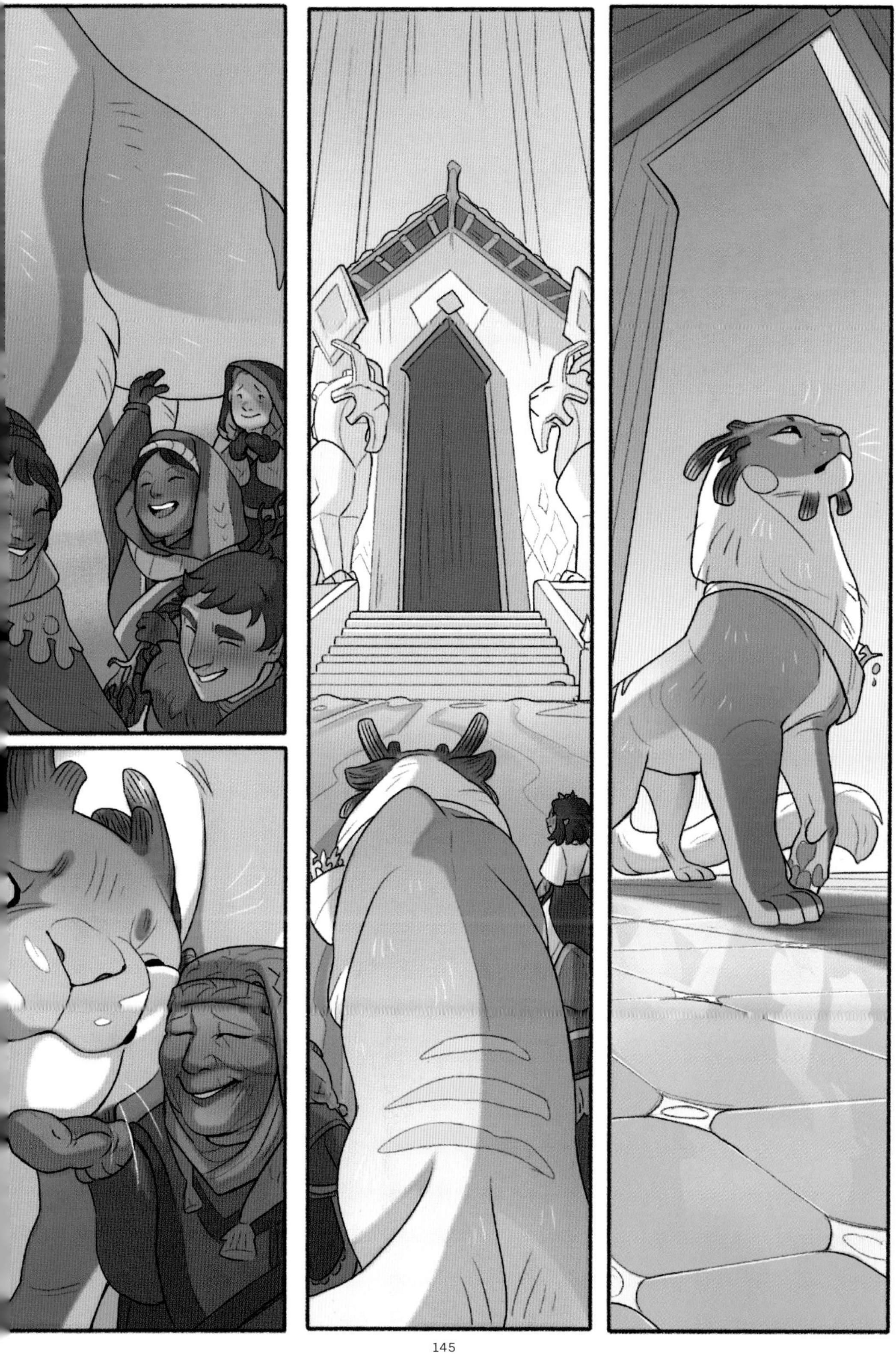

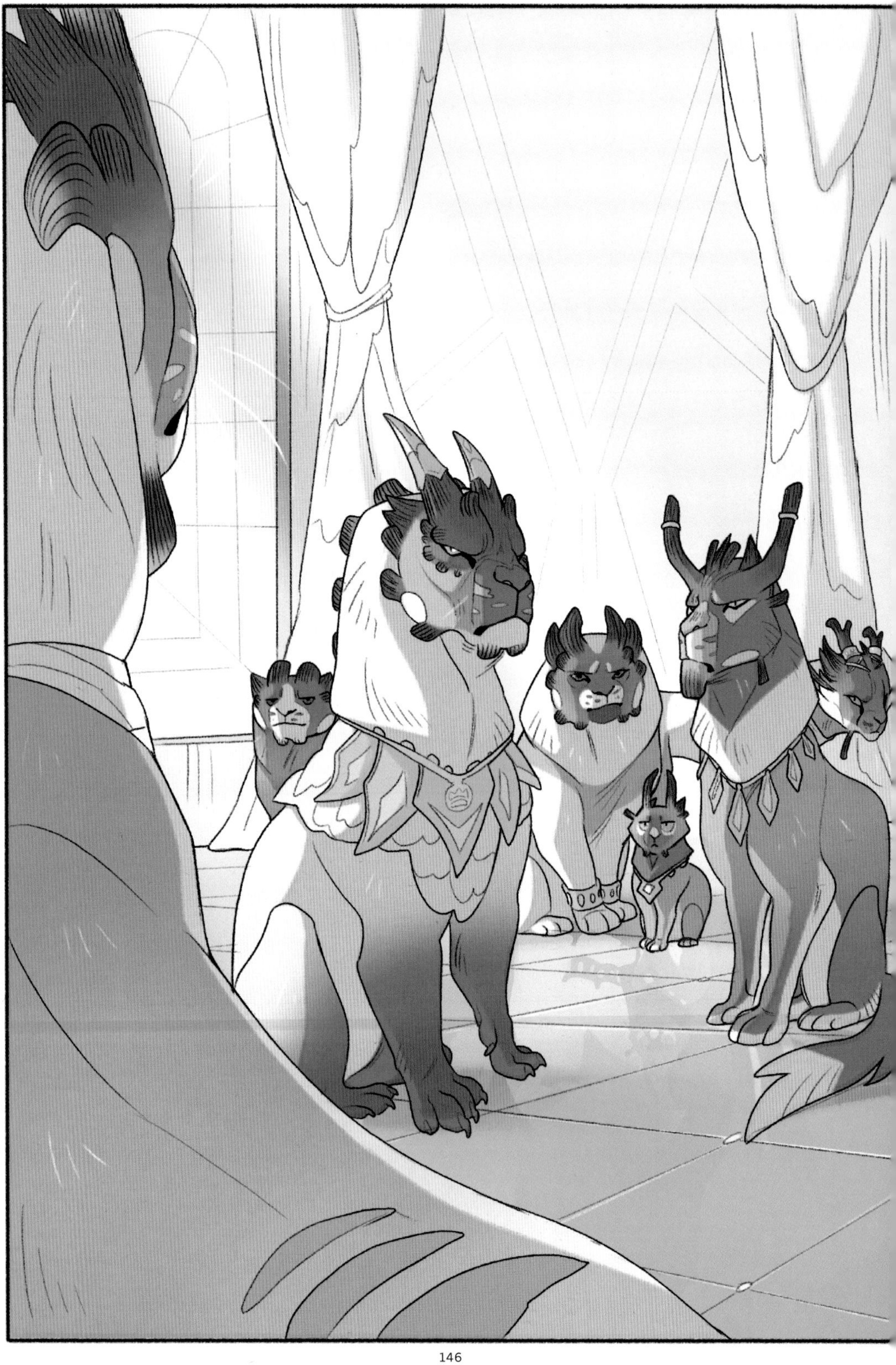

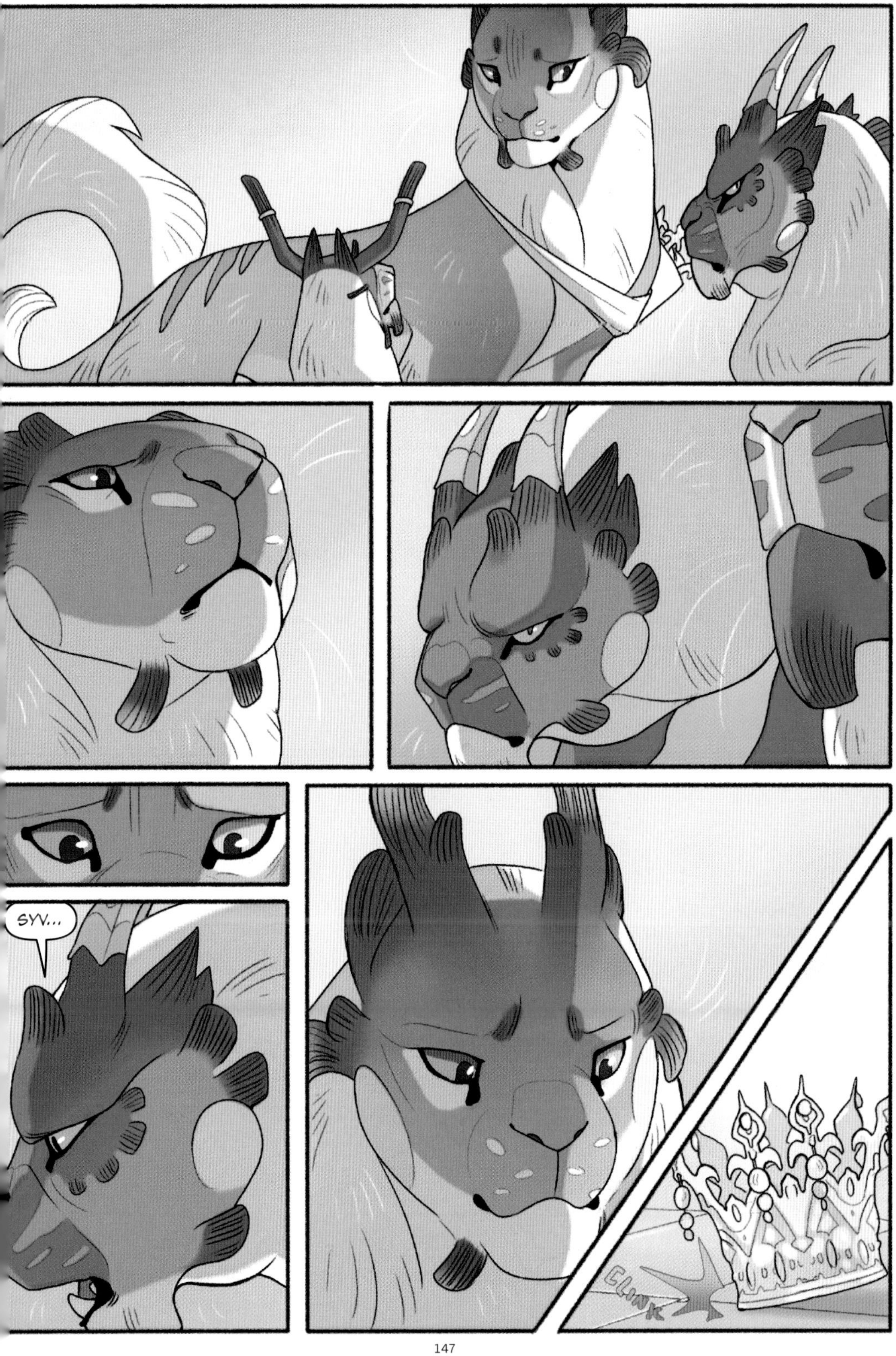
SYV...
CLINK

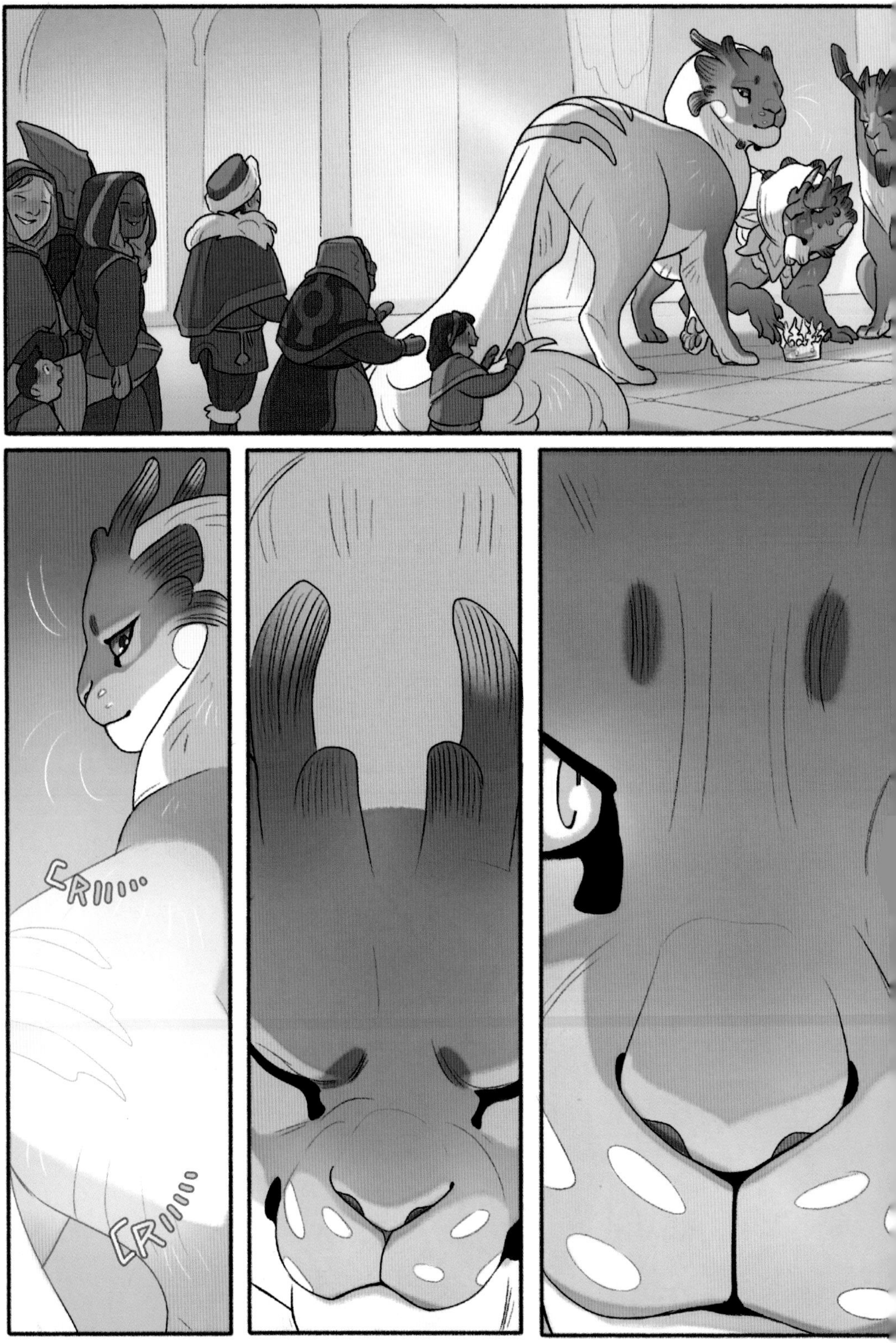
CRIIooo
CRIIooo

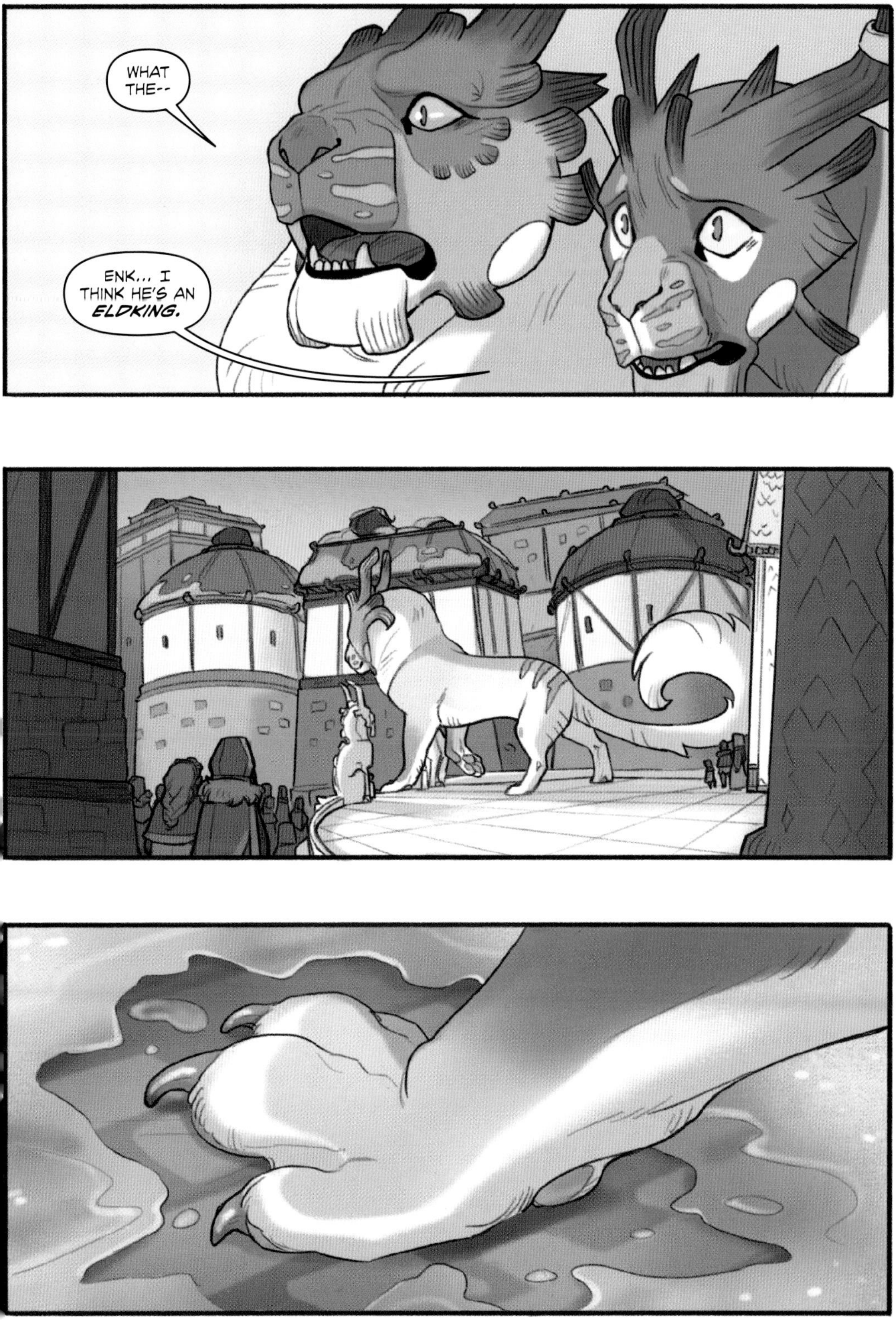
WHAT THE--
ENK... I THINK HE'S AN ***ELDKING.***

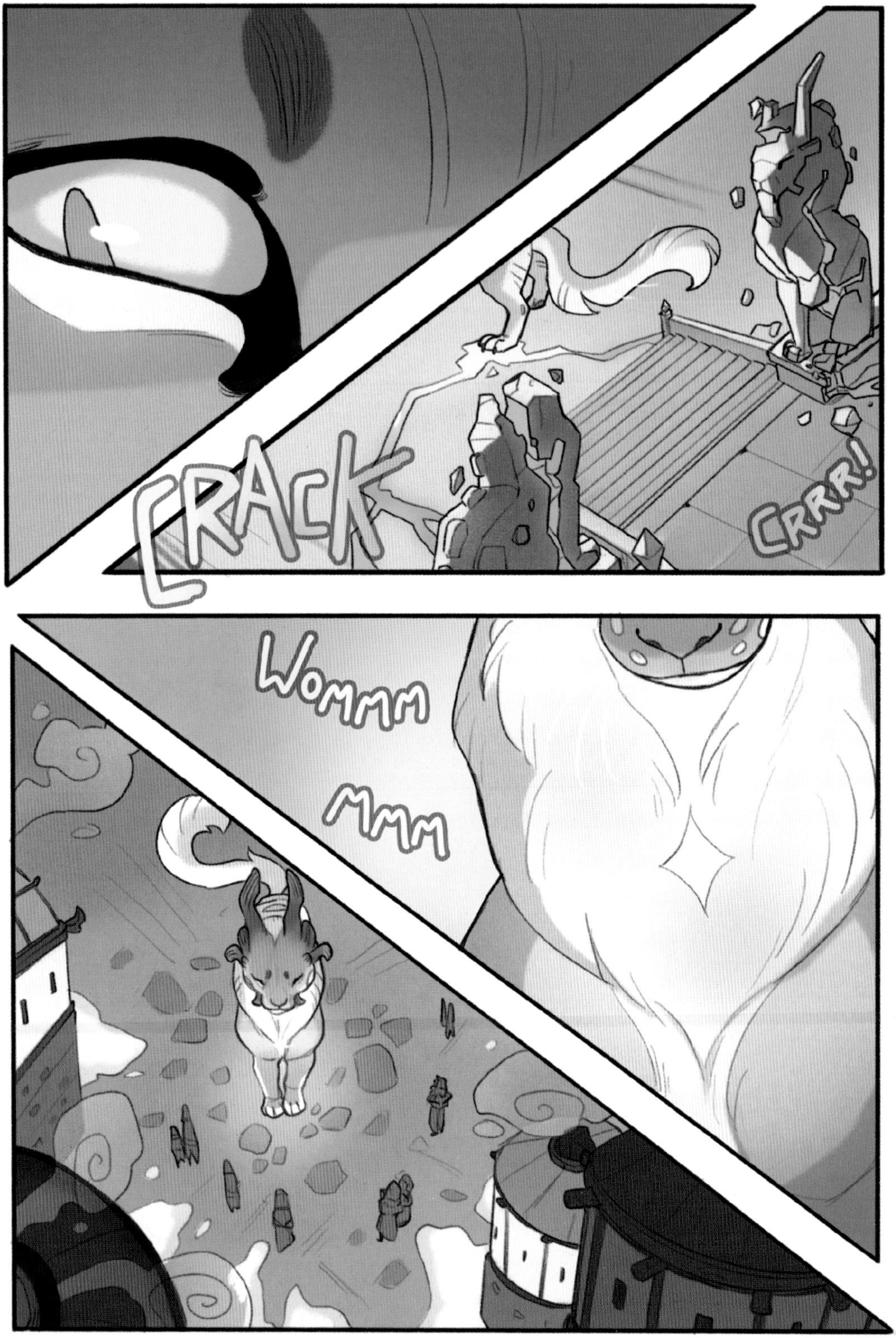
CRACK
CRRR!
Wommm
mmm

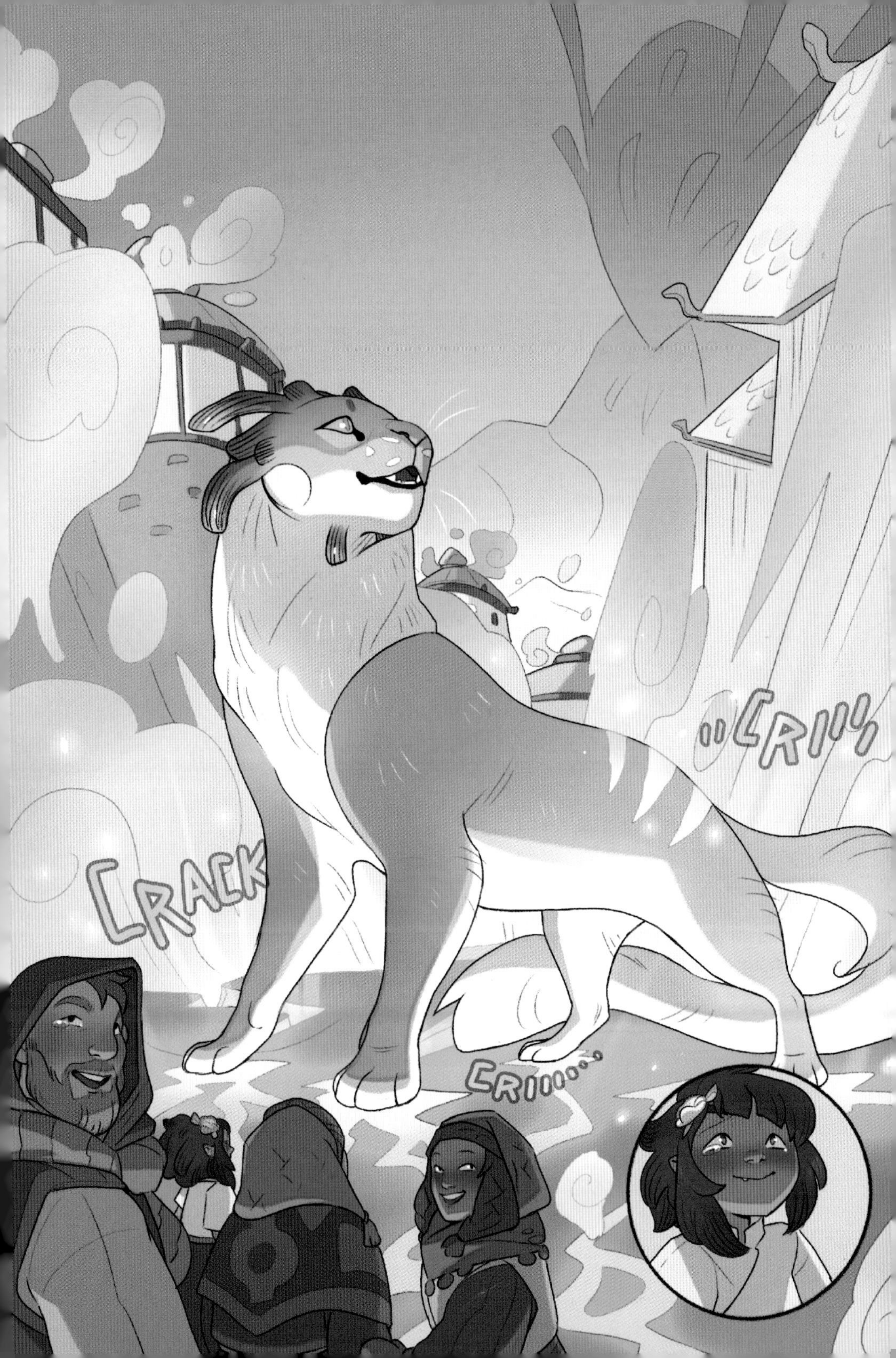
CRI
CRACK
CRIIIII

MANY YEARS LATER...

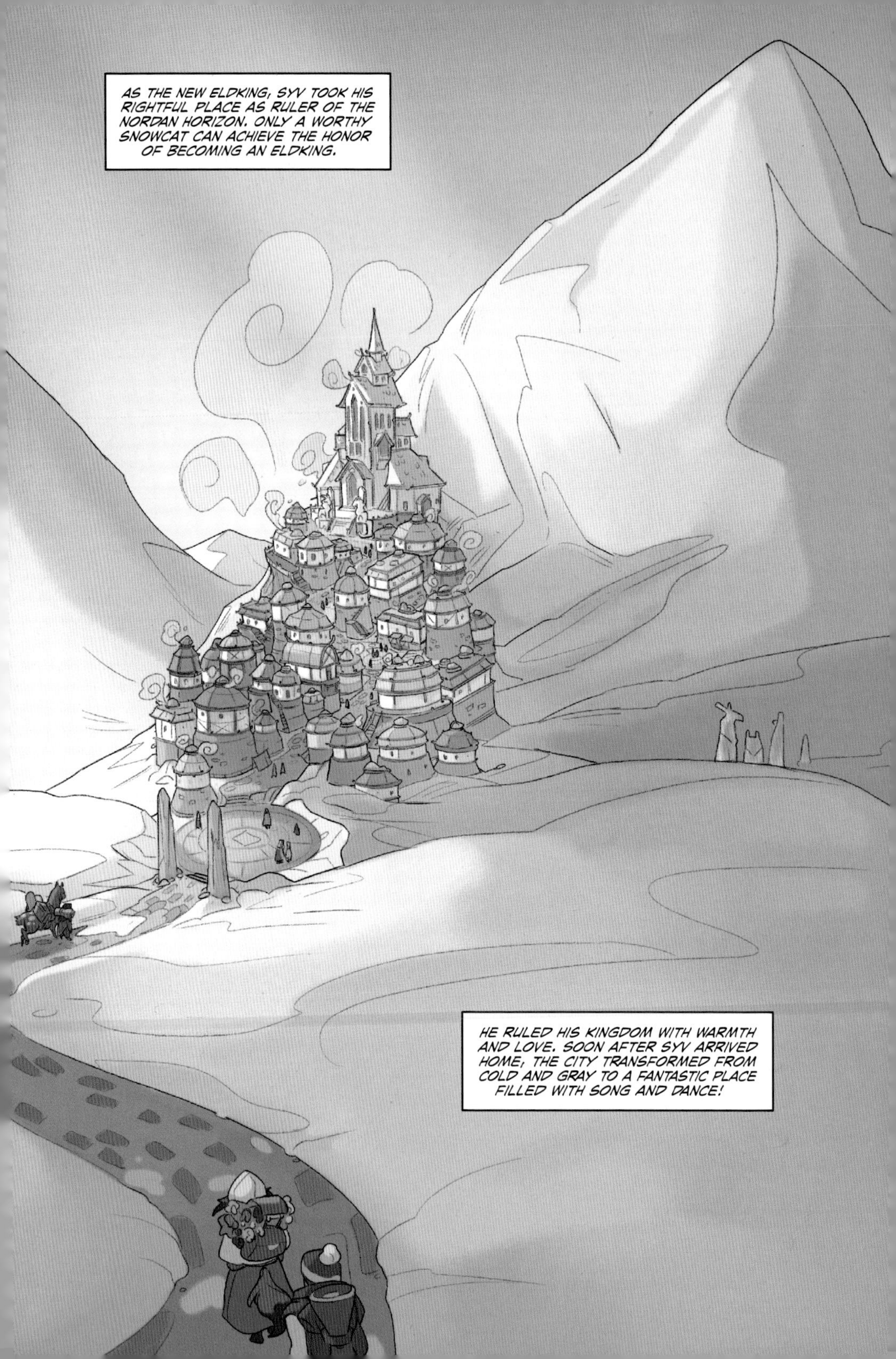
AS THE NEW ELDKING, SYV TOOK HIS RIGHTFUL PLACE AS RULER OF THE NORDAN HORIZON. ONLY A WORTHY SNOWCAT CAN ACHIEVE THE HONOR OF BECOMING AN ELDKING.
HE RULED HIS KINGDOM WITH WARMTH AND LOVE. SOON AFTER SYV ARRIVED HOME, THE CITY TRANSFORMED FROM COLD AND GRAY TO A FANTASTIC PLACE FILLED WITH SONG AND DANCE!

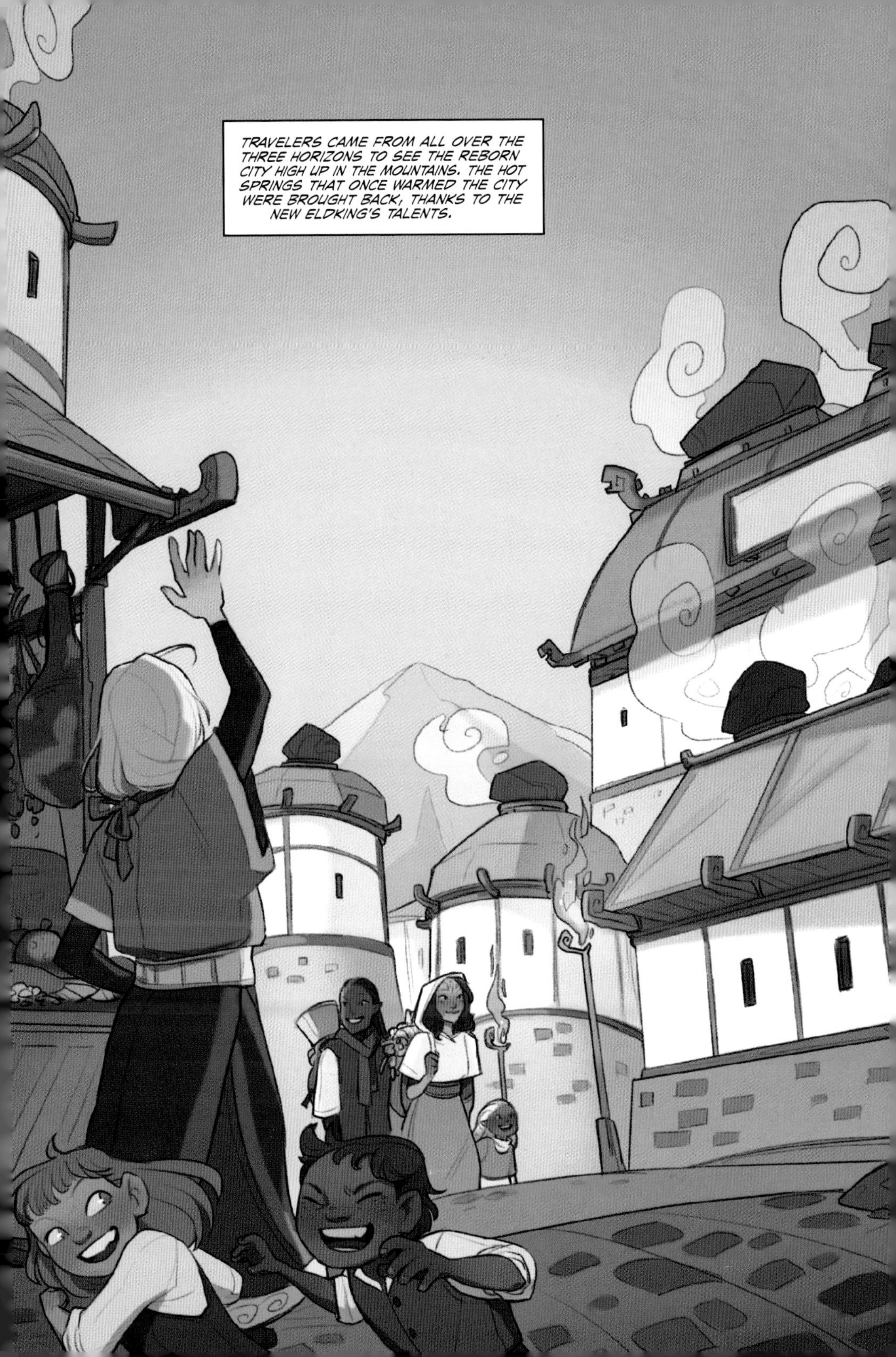
TRAVELERS CAME FROM ALL OVER THE THREE HORIZONS TO SEE THE REBORN CITY HIGH UP IN THE MOUNTAINS. THE HOT SPRINGS THAT ONCE WARMED THE CITY WERE BROUGHT BACK, THANKS TO THE NEW ELDKING'S TALENTS.

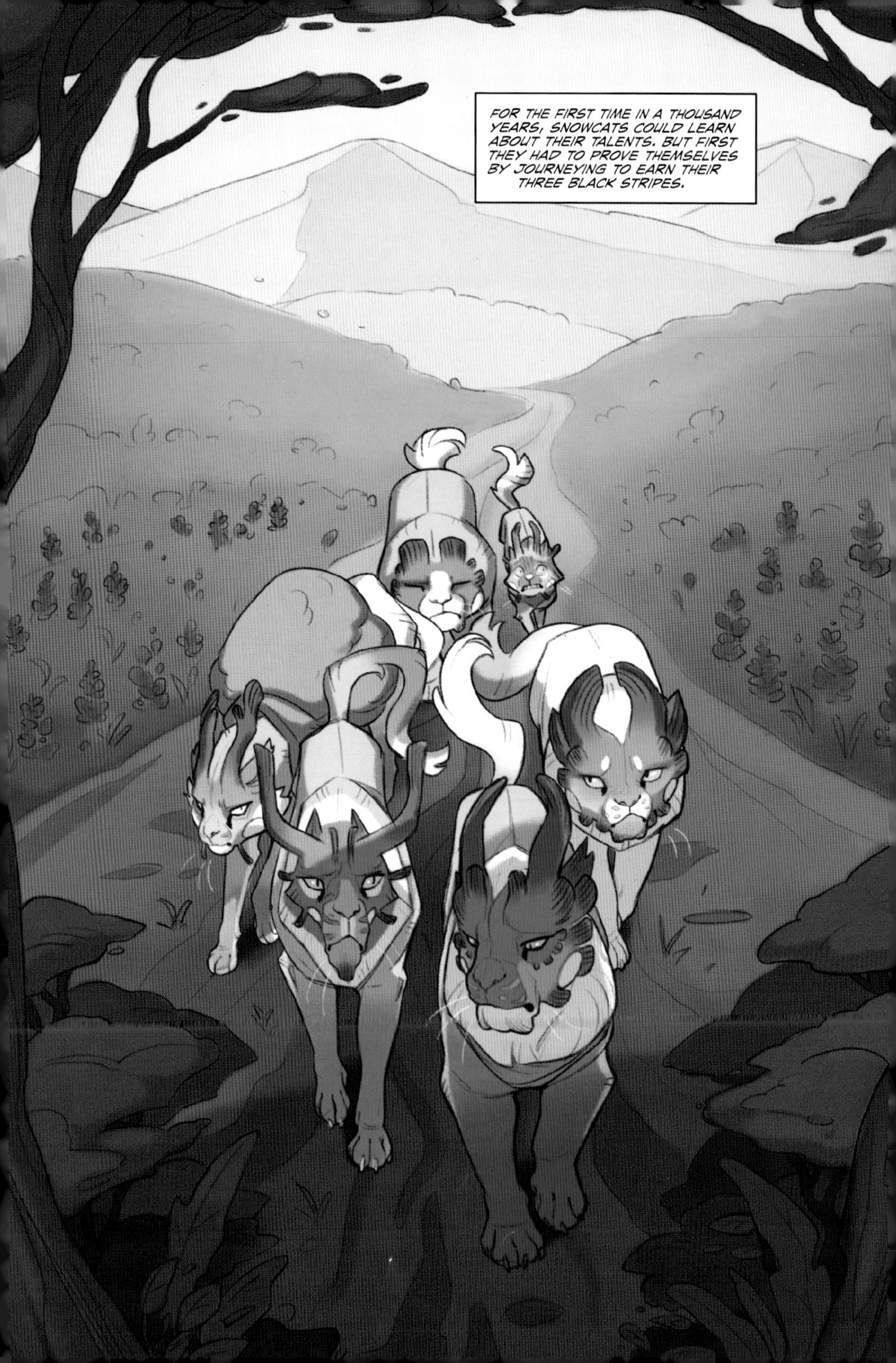
FOR THE FIRST TIME IN A THOUSAND YEARS, SNOWCATS COULD LEARN ABOUT THEIR TALENTS. BUT FIRST THEY HAD TO PROVE THEMSELVES BY JOURNEYING TO EARN THEIR THREE BLACK STRIPES.

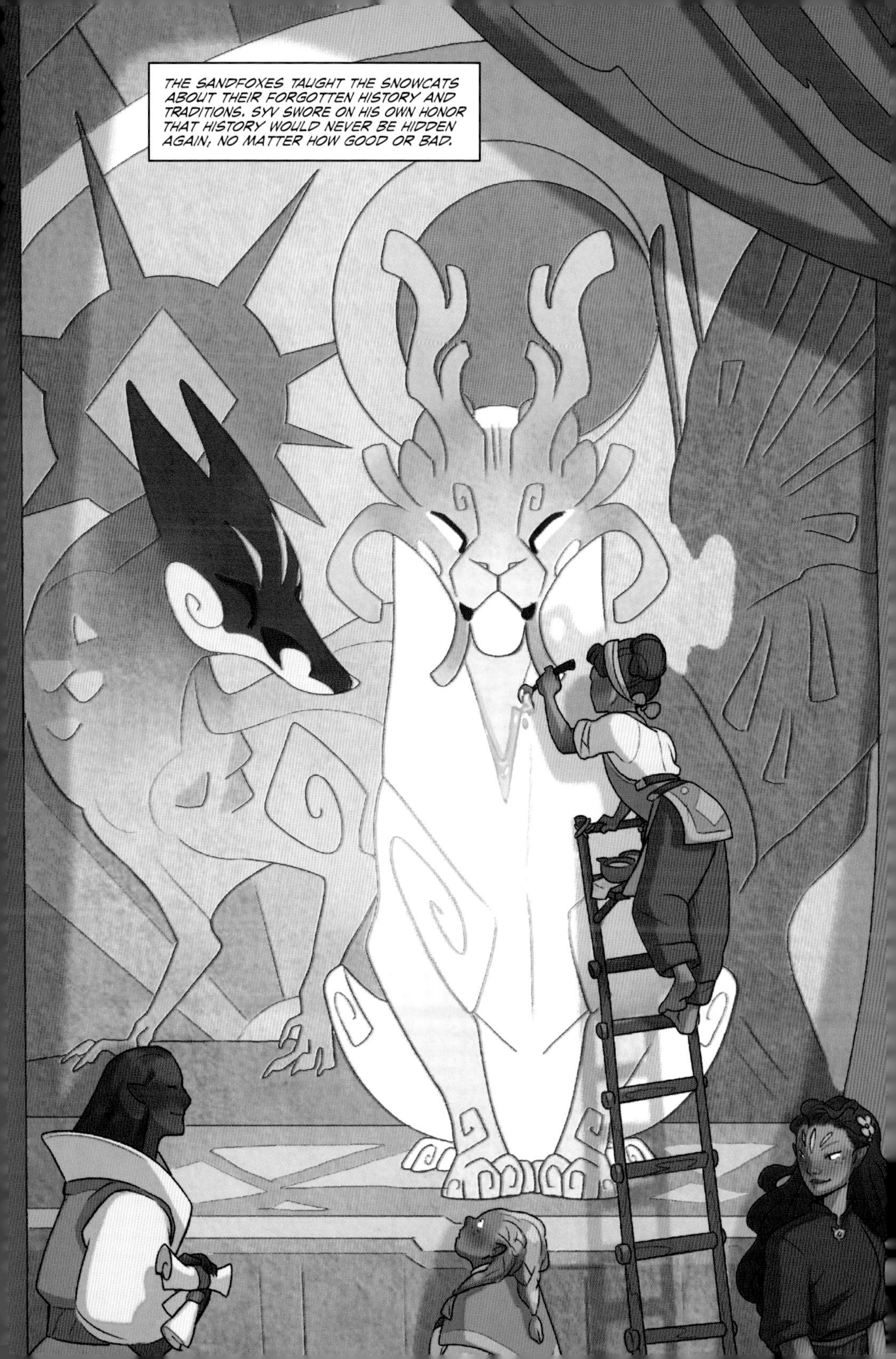
THE SANDFOXES TAUGHT THE SNOWCATS ABOUT THEIR FORGOTTEN HISTORY AND TRADITIONS. SYV SWORE ON HIS OWN HONOR THAT HISTORY WOULD NEVER BE HIDDEN AGAIN, NO MATTER HOW GOOD OR BAD.

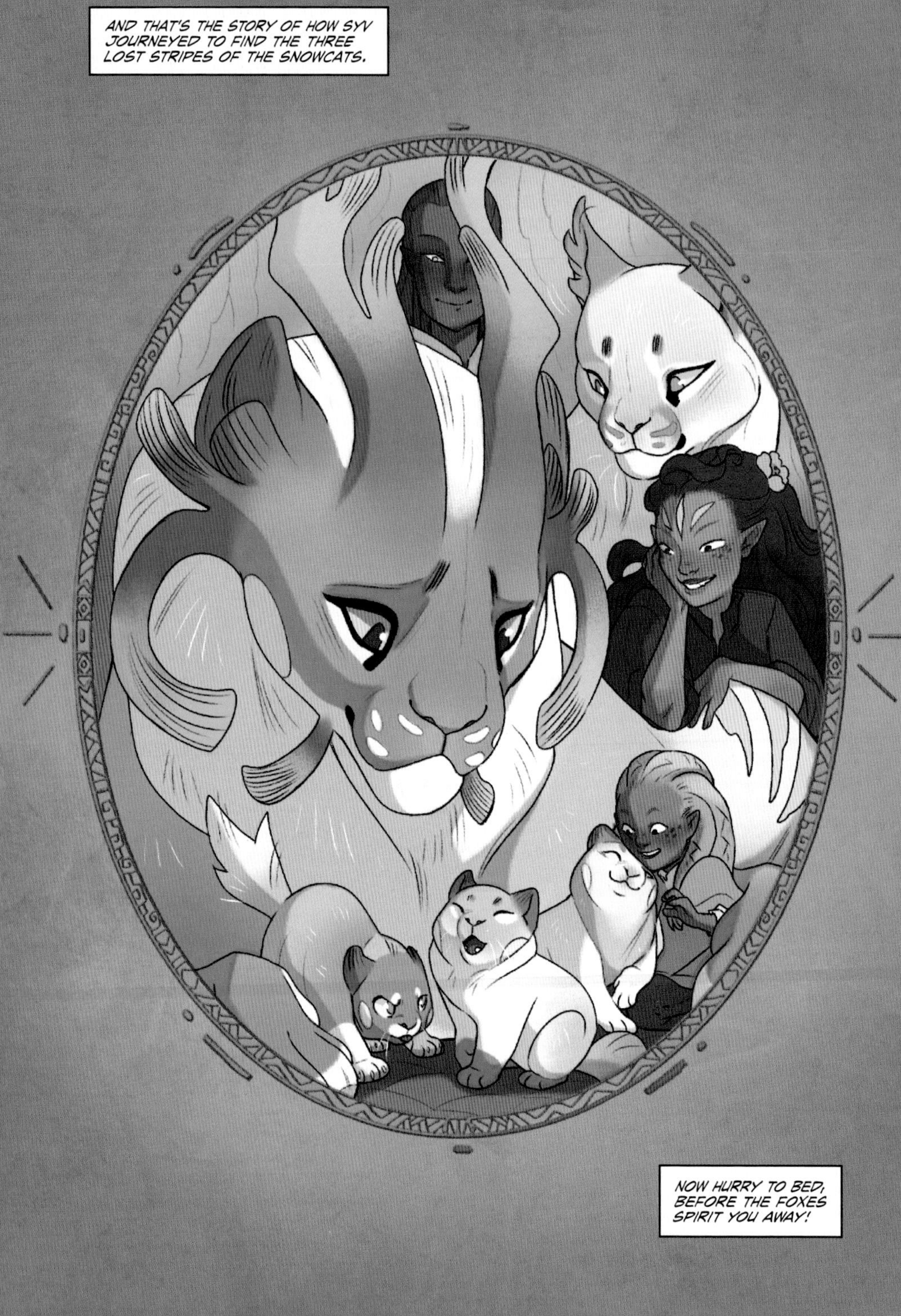
AND THAT'S THE STORY OF HOW SYV JOURNEYED TO FIND THE THREE LOST STRIPES OF THE SNOWCATS.
NOW HURRY TO BED, BEFORE THE FOXES SPIRIT YOU AWAY!

BONUS MATERIAL

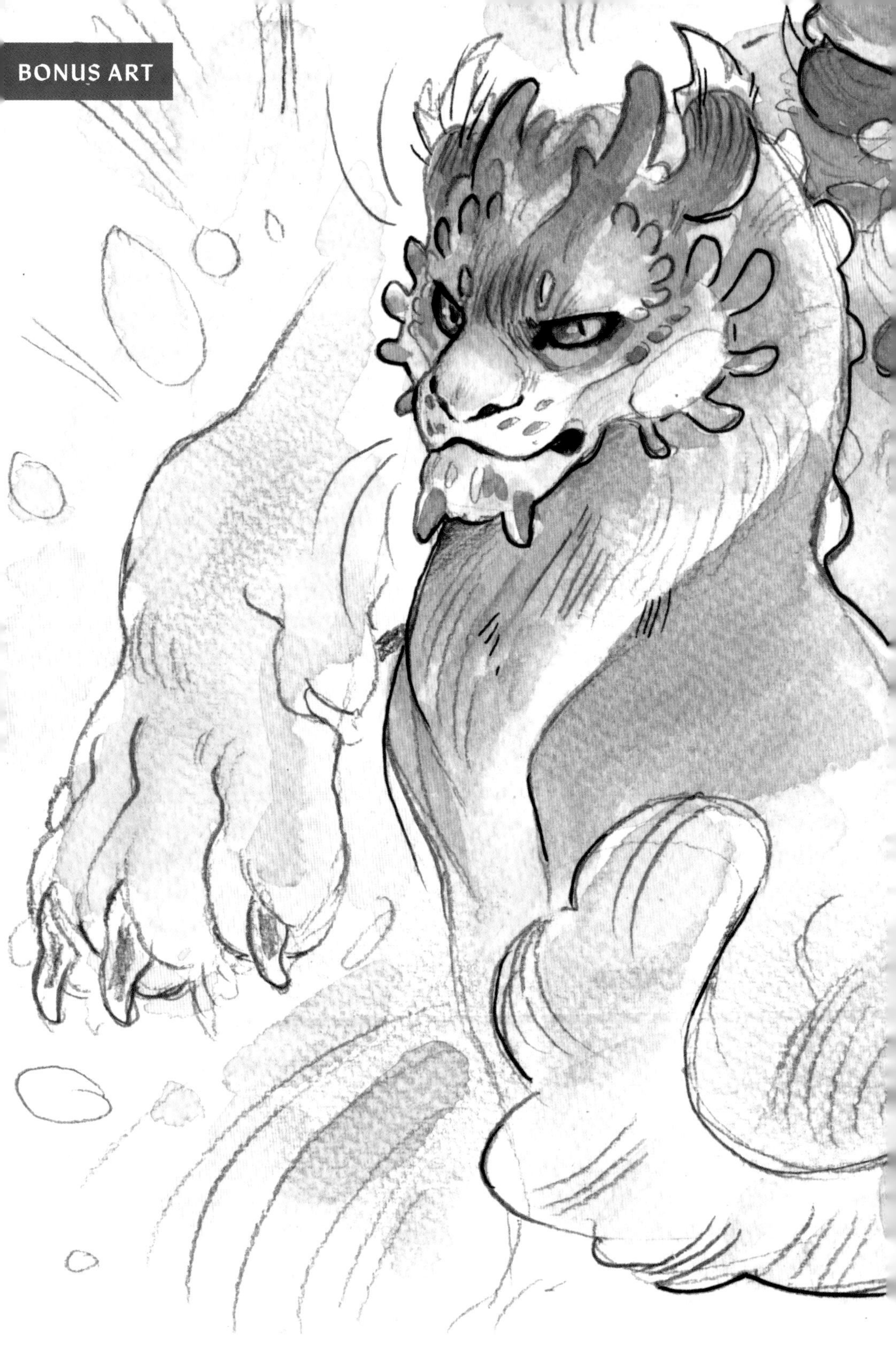

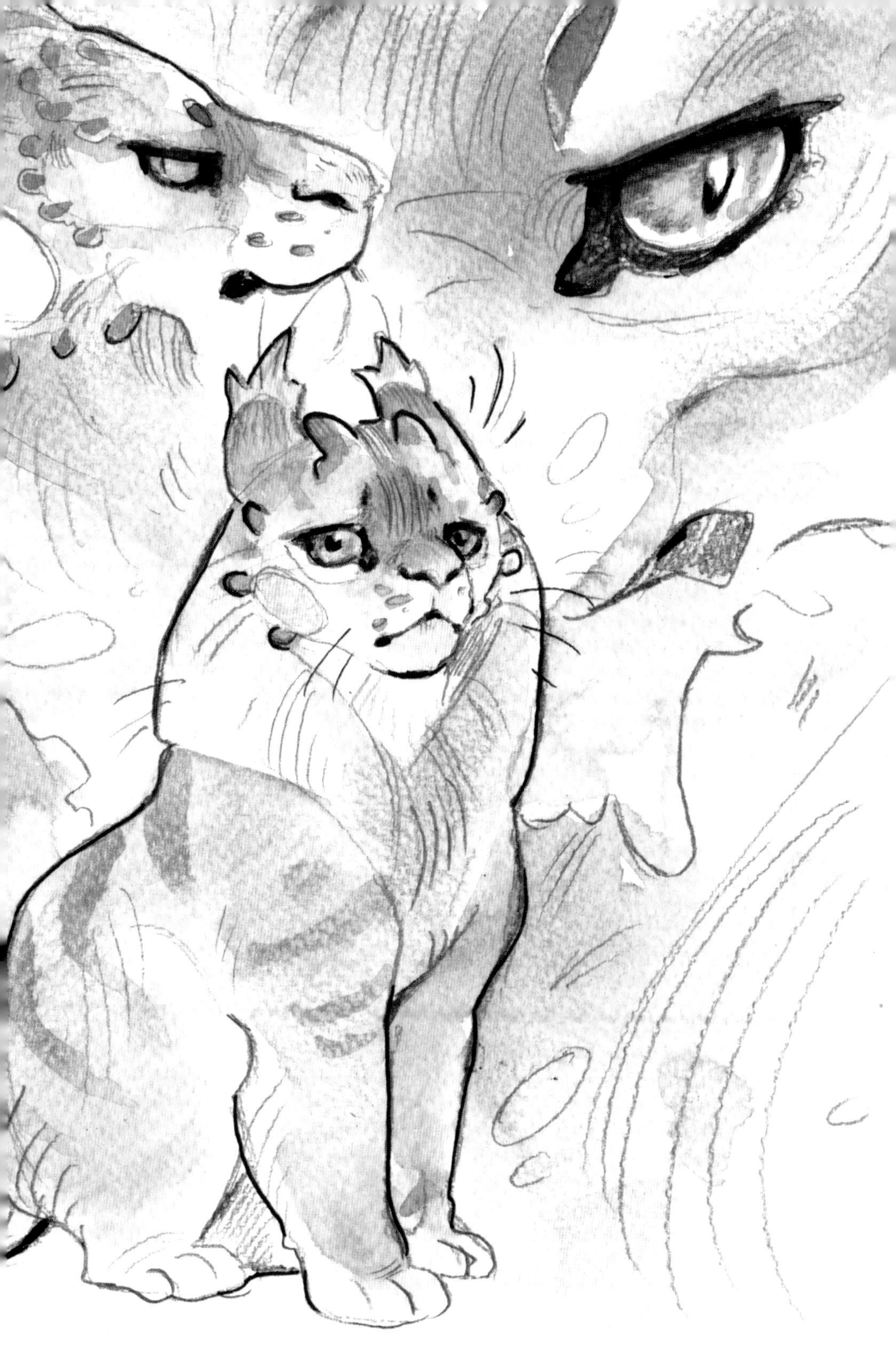

EARLY CHARACTER DESIGNS: SYV

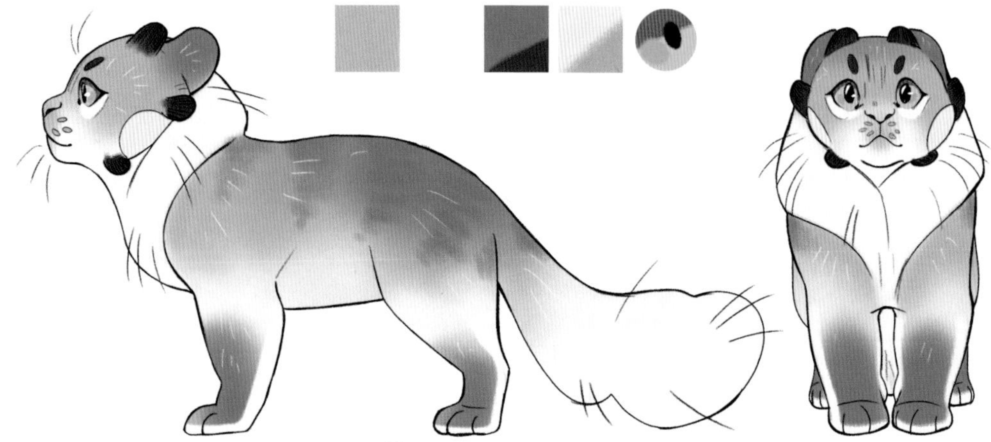

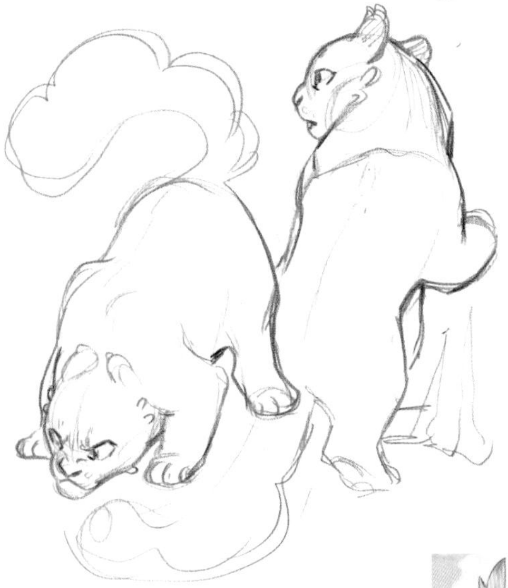

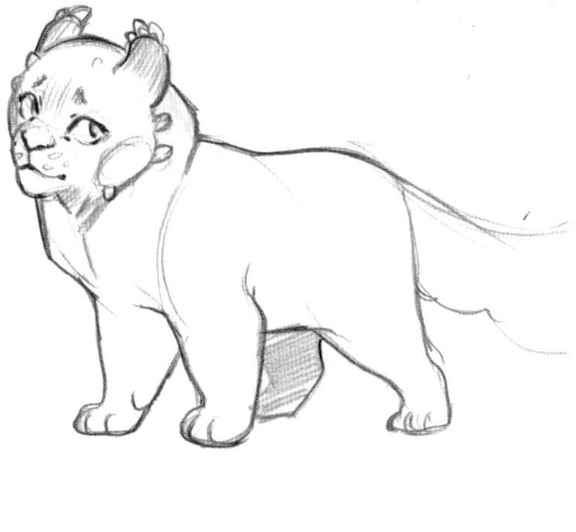

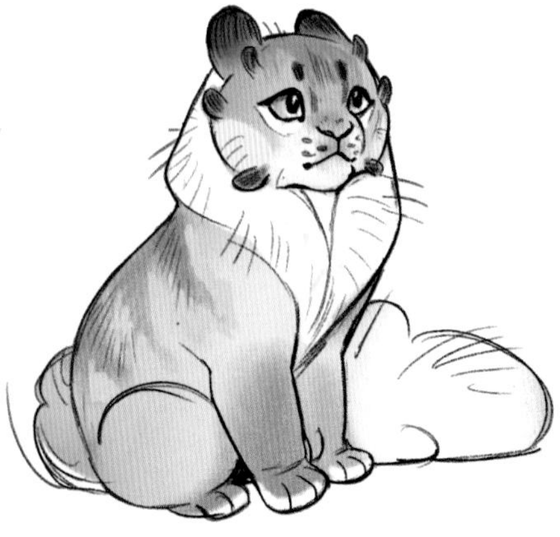

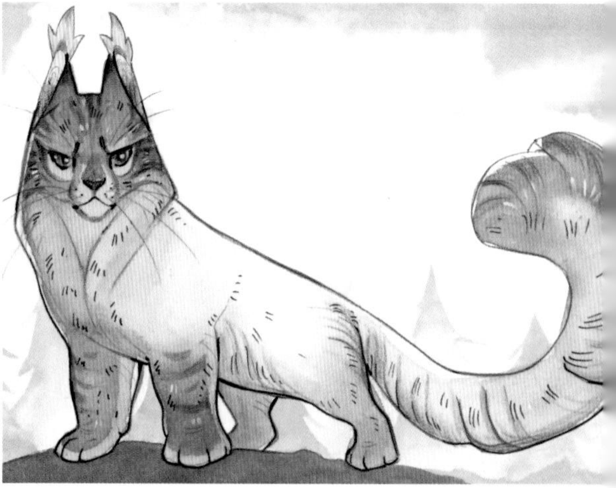

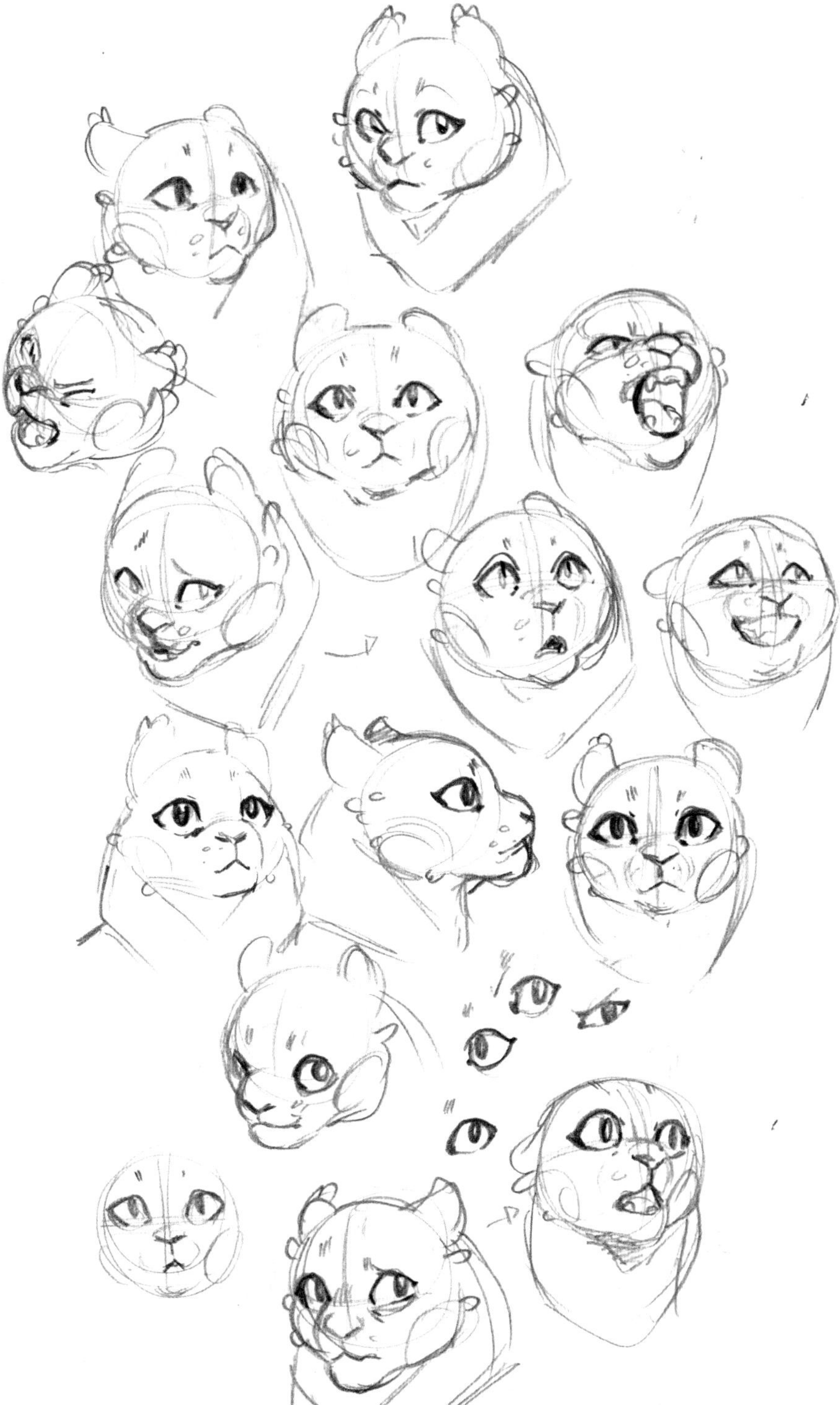

EARLY CHARACTER DESIGNS: KIT

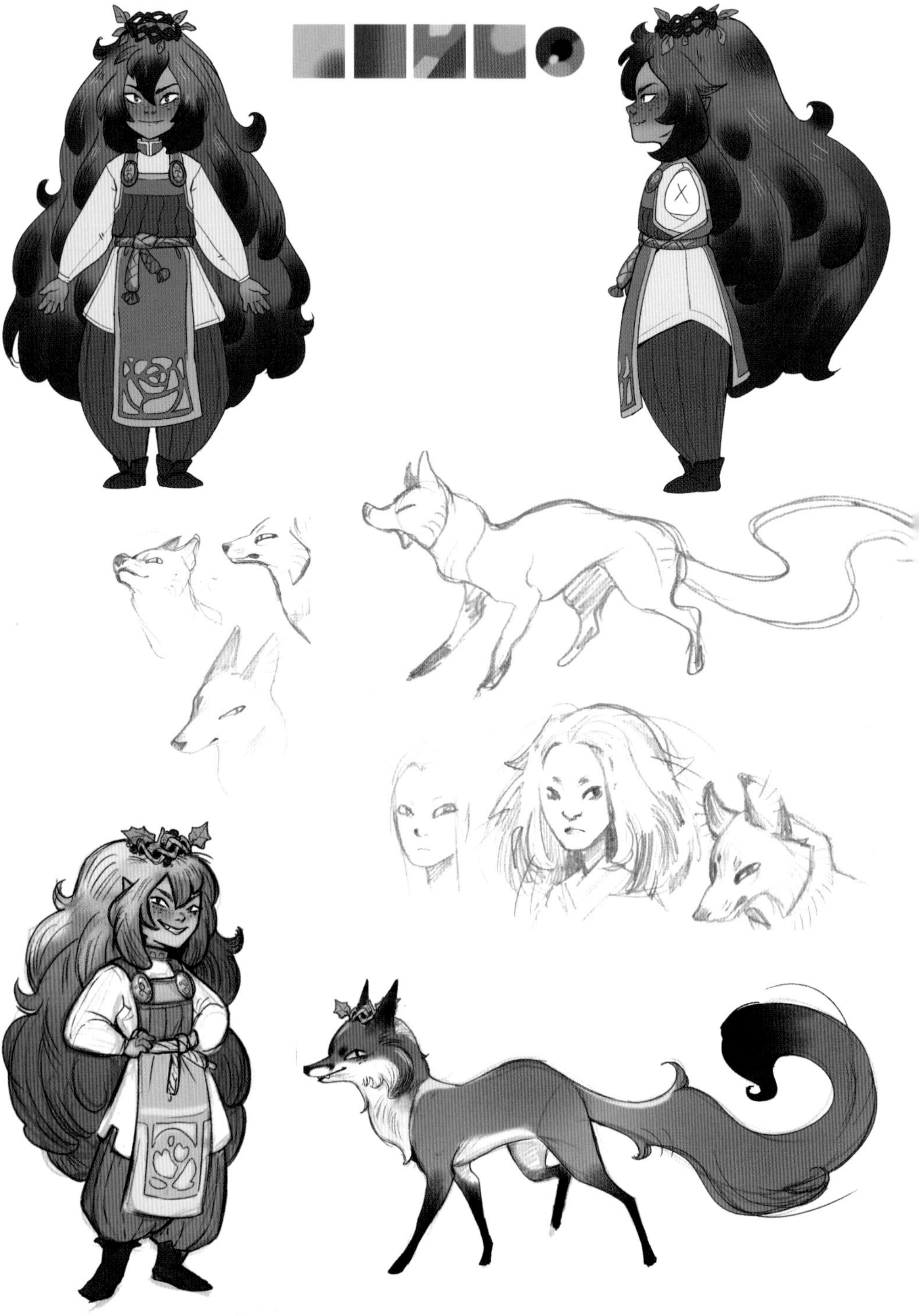

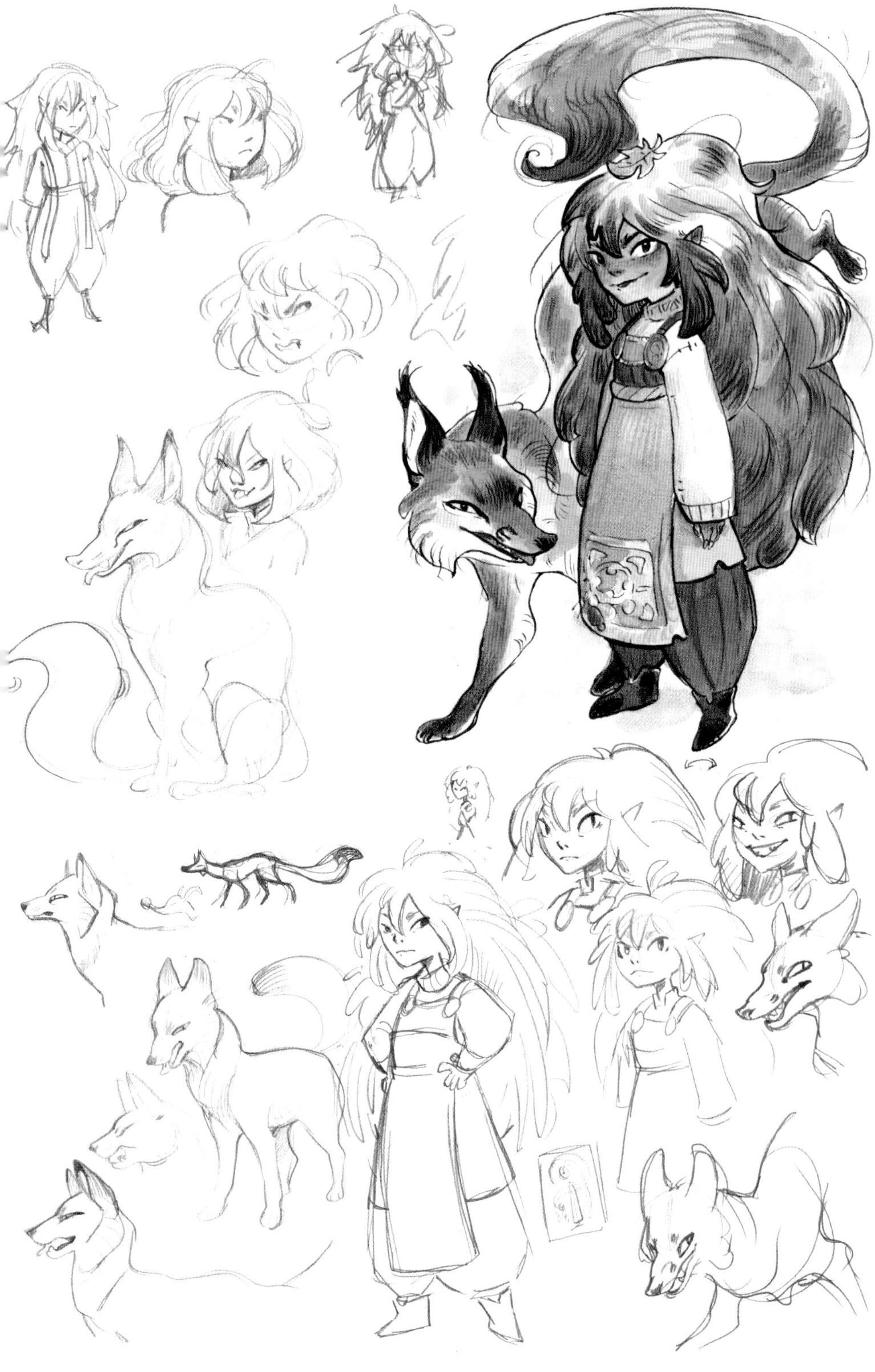

the SNOWCAT

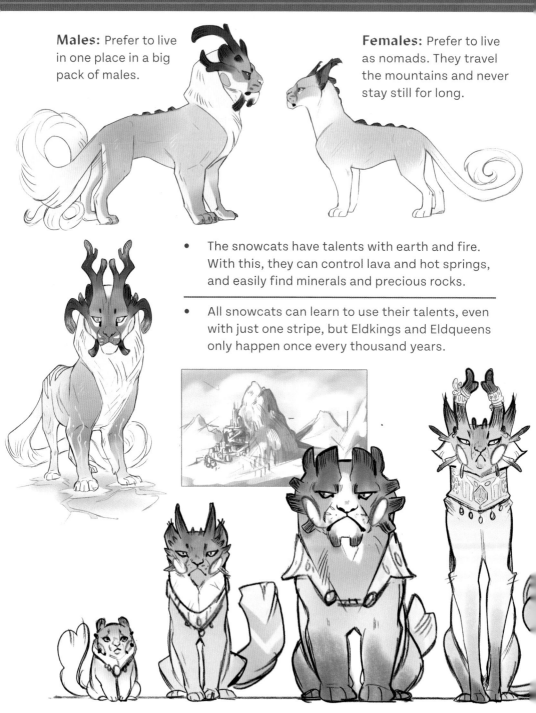

Males: Prefer to live in one place in a big pack of males.

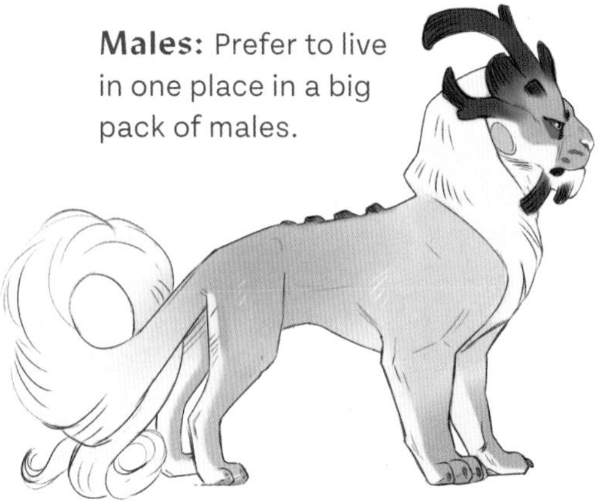

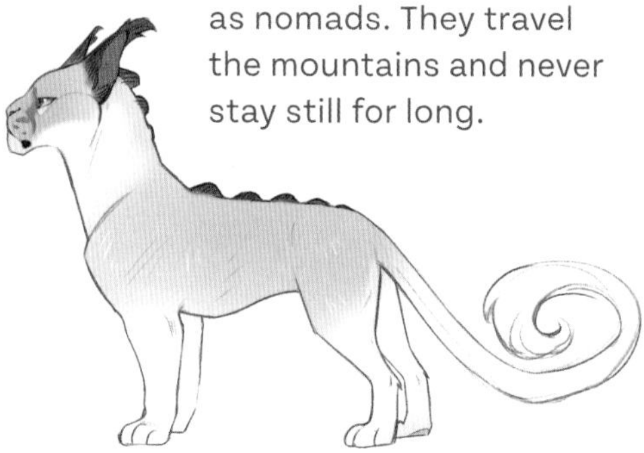

Females: Prefer to live as nomads. They travel the mountains and never stay still for long.

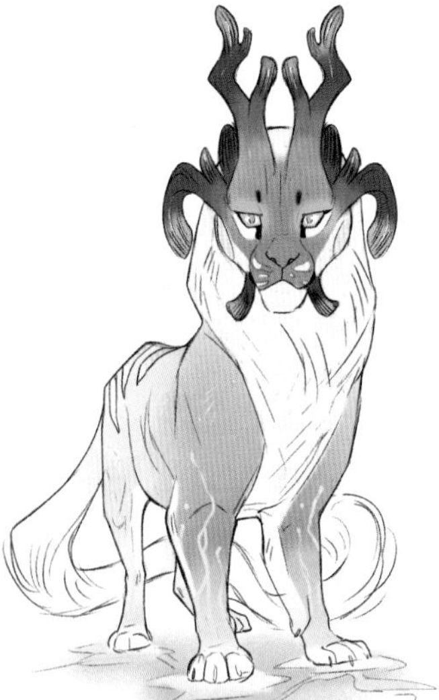

- The snowcats have talents with earth and fire. With this, they can control lava and hot springs, and easily find minerals and precious rocks.

- All snowcats can learn to use their talents, even with just one stripe, but Eldkings and Eldqueens only happen once every thousand years.

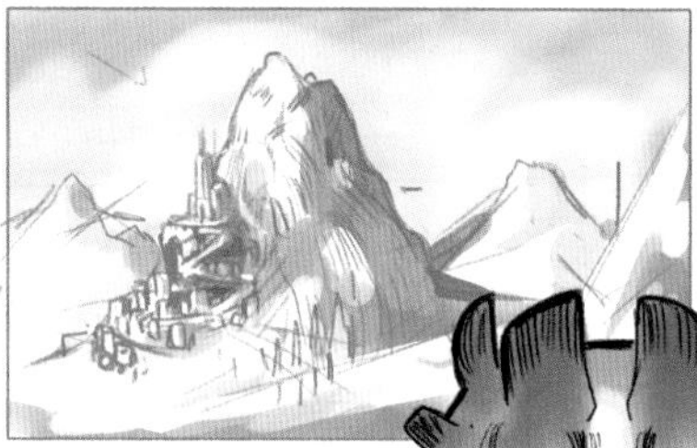

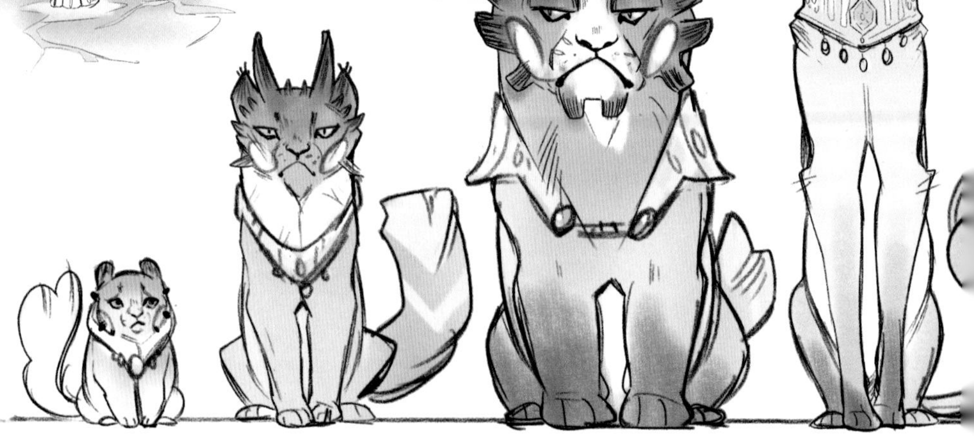

Syv: 15 **Set: 21** **Femt: 27** **Fir: 32**

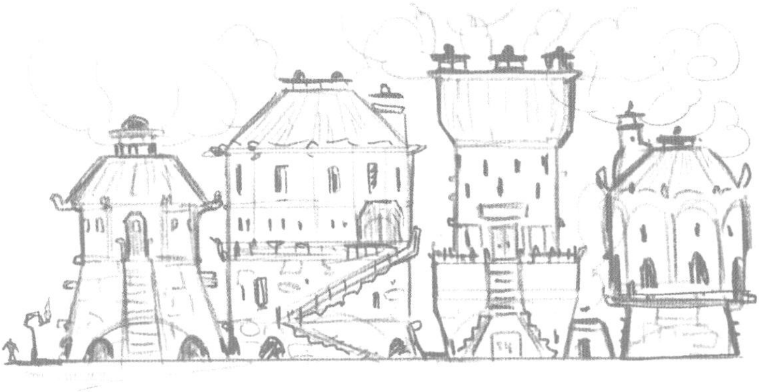

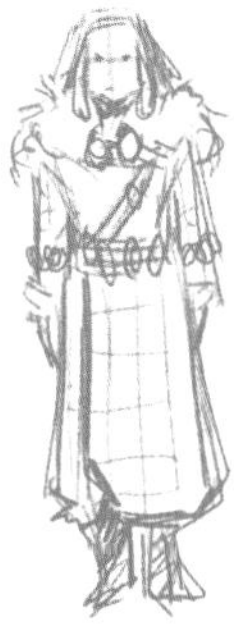

- The age gap between the brothers is very big! The female cats only come to mate every ten years or so. They are also not blood related. Any male snowcat that stays with the male pack is considered a prince. All females are considered princesses.

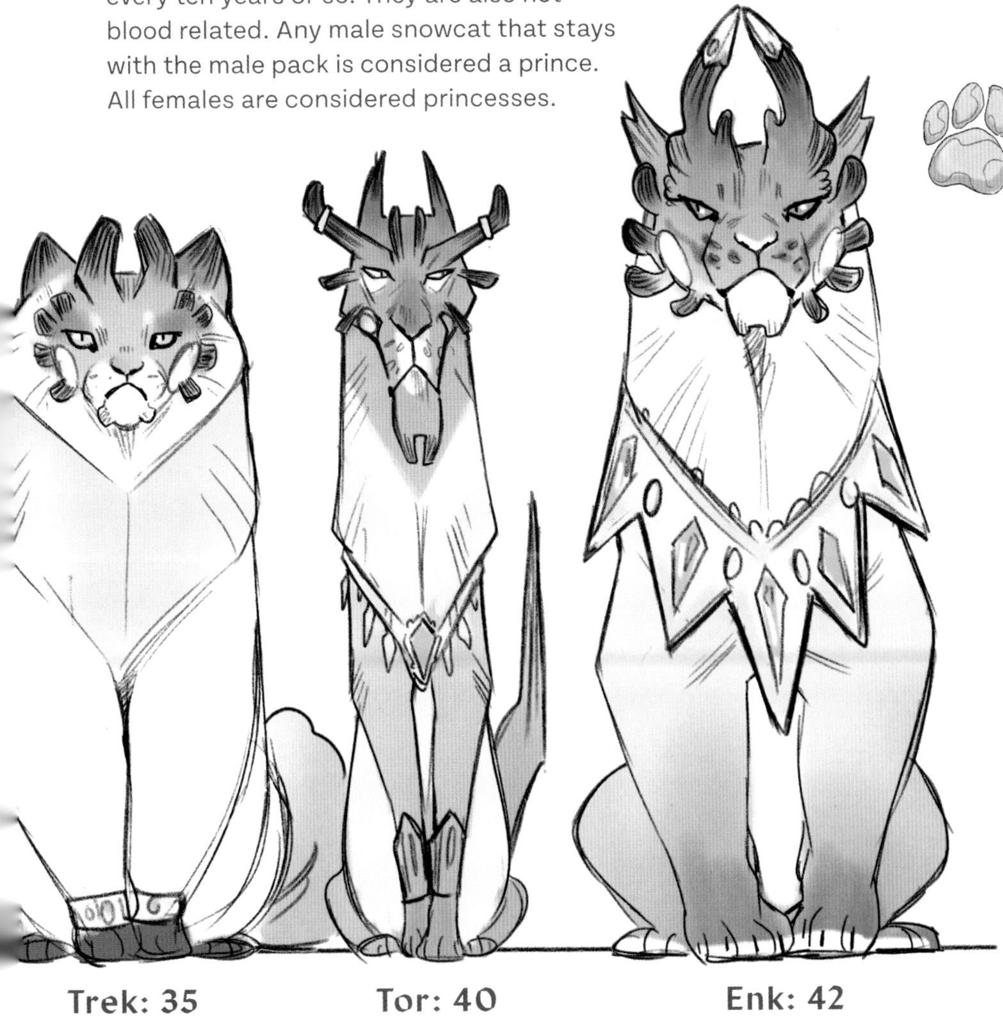

Trek: 35 **Tor: 40** **Enk: 42**

the SANDFOX

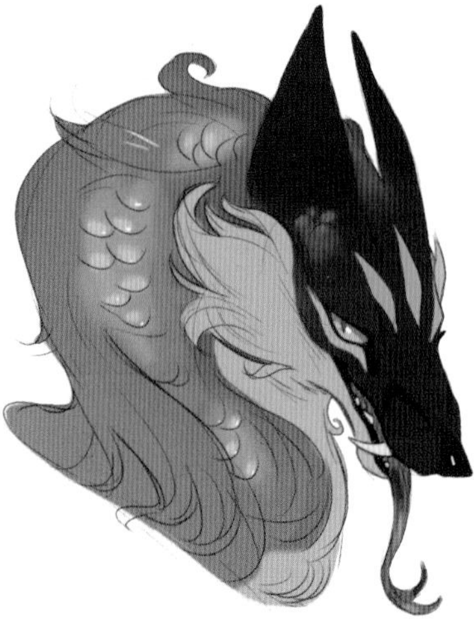

- The foxes have talents with wind and water. They can control wind and weathers, as well as change their shape into other animals and objects. They can also fly, if they're strong enough!

- Like the snowcats, the sandfoxes need to prove themselves with three stripes on their forehead. Eldqueens and Eldkings only happen once in a thousand years.

- They have a much more natural connection to their talents and can normally use them without a stripe. But using aura from plants usually makes it easier and makes the fox a little stronger.

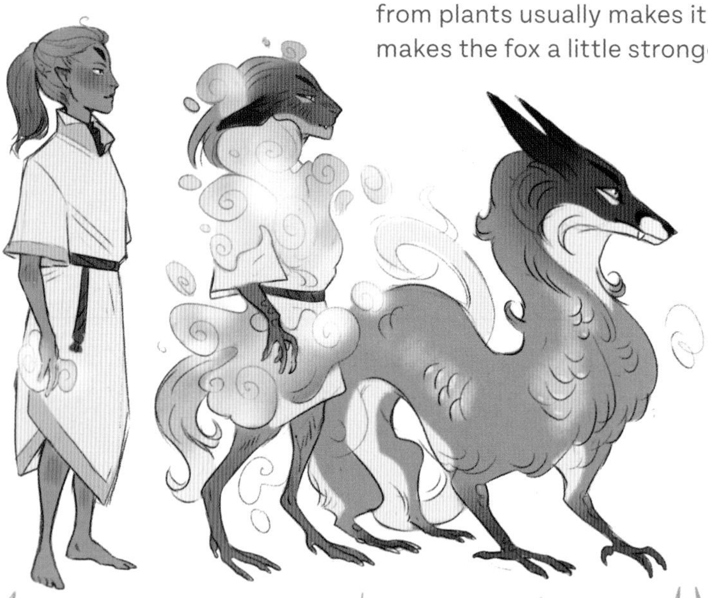

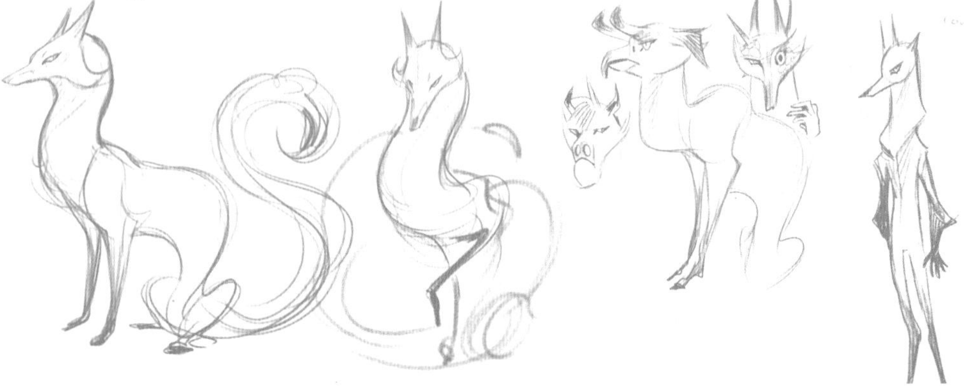

Aura is the very energy of the earth and what all living things need to survive. In the story of *The Snowcat Prince*, we learn about corrupt aura. The old Eldking was so greedy he poisoned his own talents by wanting more. When his body couldn't contain any more, including the foxes' aura, it spilled into the earth, corrupting everything it touched.

When the corrupt aura spilled into the earth, it also corrupted the creatures. Their fur grows dull and their eyes glow yellow and pink.

Adding clean aura will cleanse the corrupt aura and cancel the poison. The old Eldking's aura was based in his own talents, so only a snowcat could stop him.

Mad

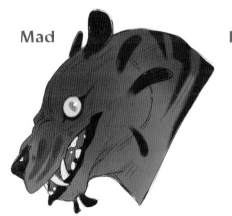

Healthy

BONUS ART

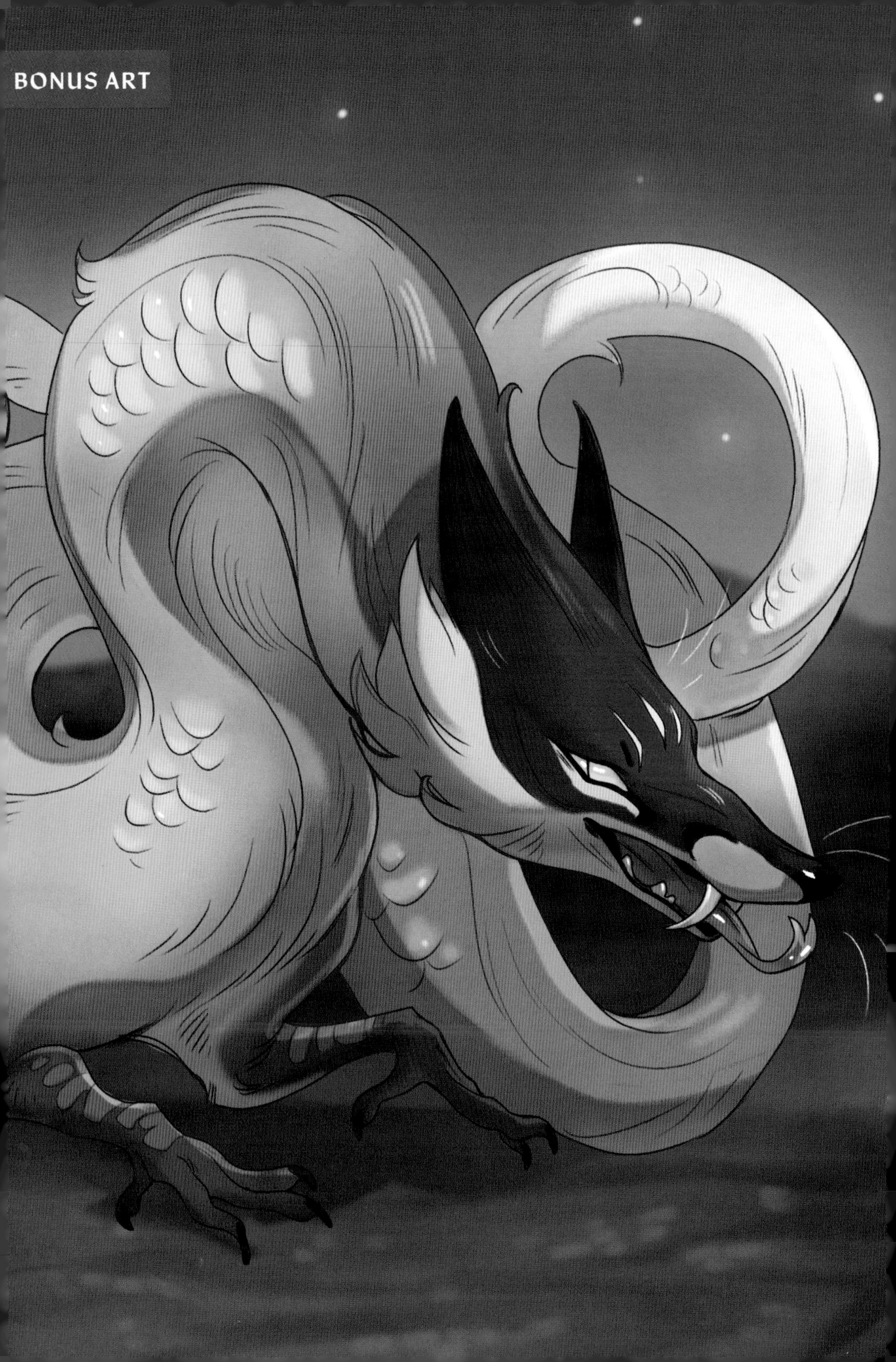

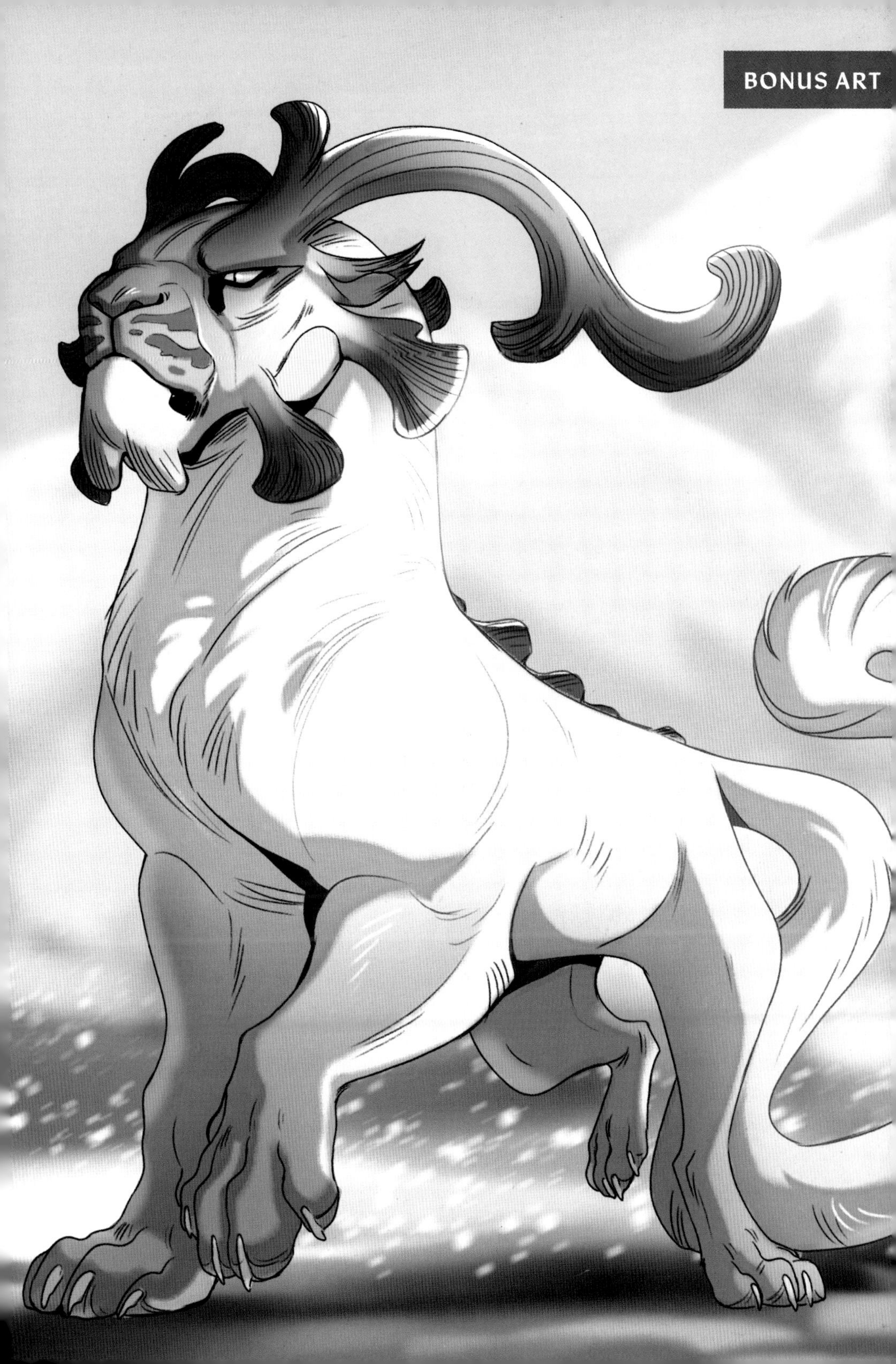

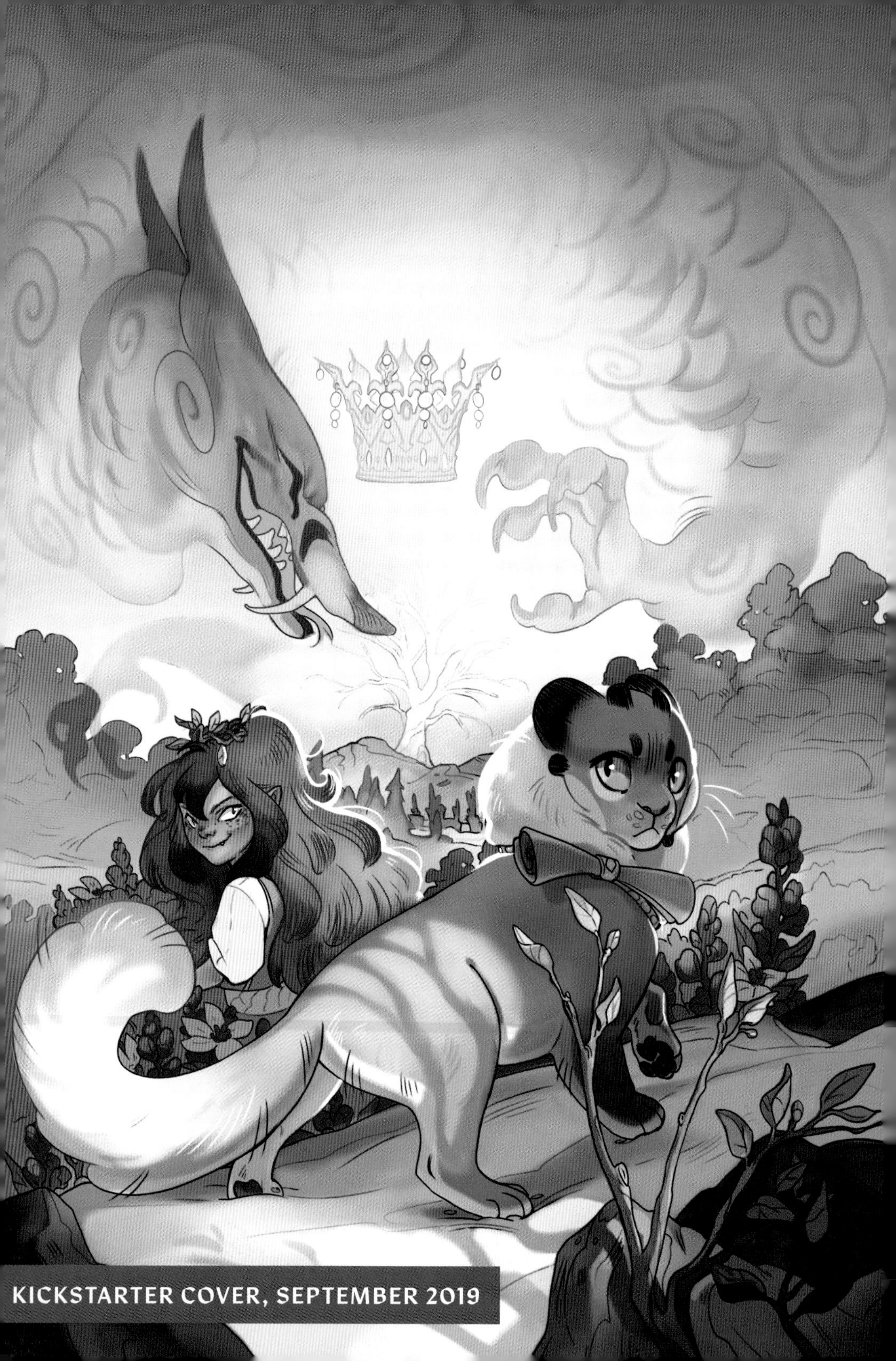

KICKSTARTER COVER, SEPTEMBER 2019

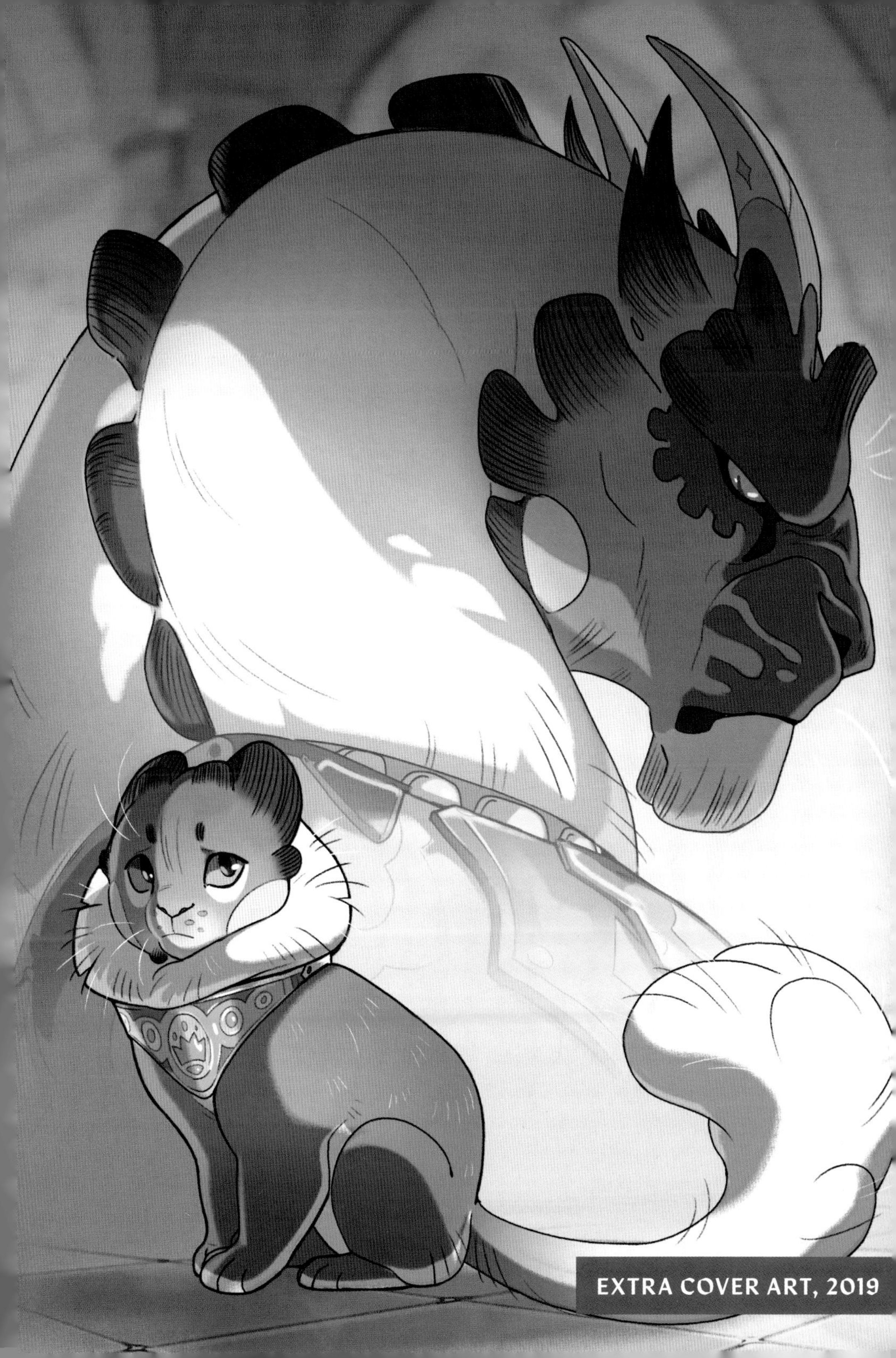

EXTRA COVER ART, 2019

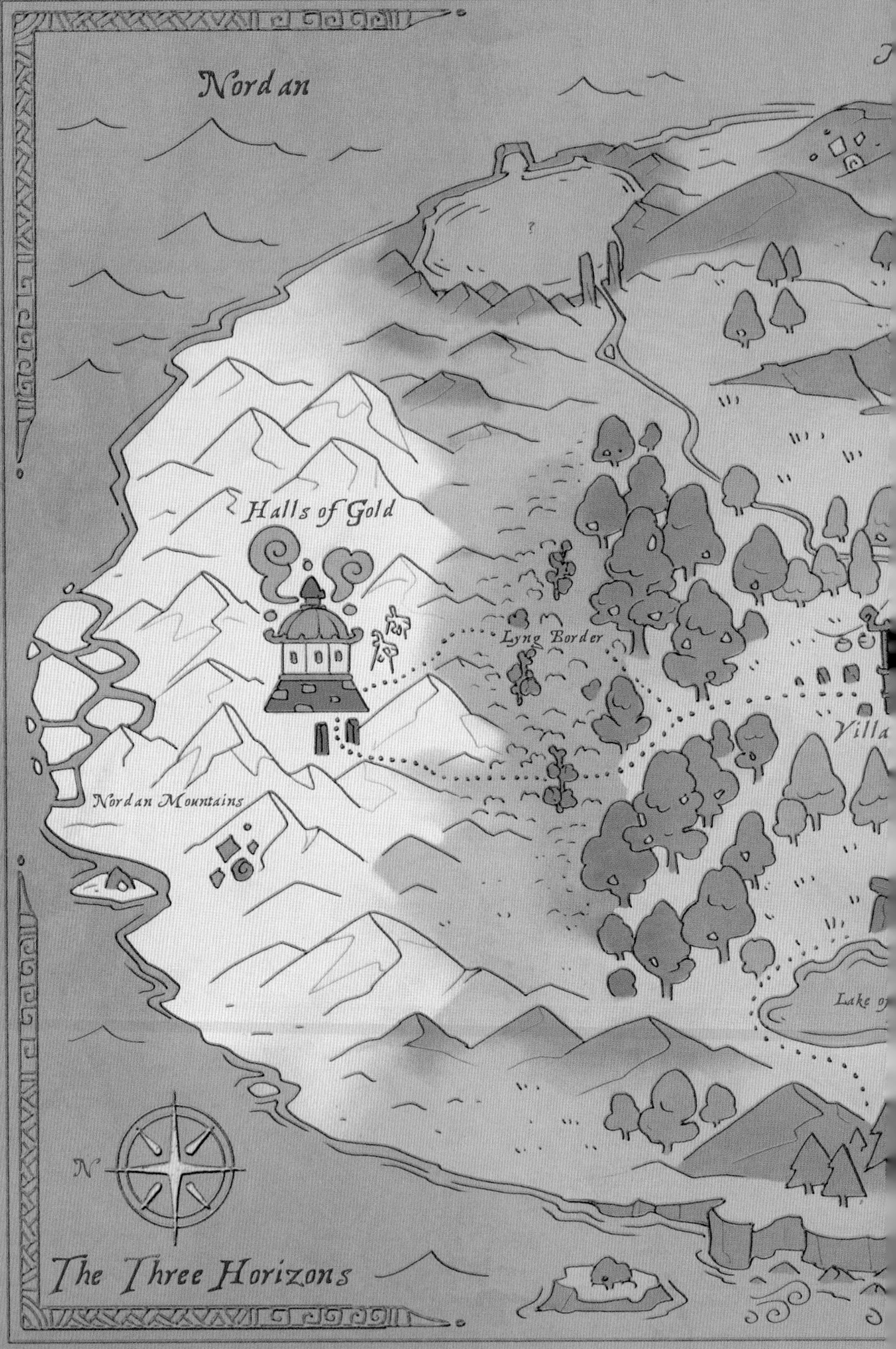
Nordan
Halls of Gold
Lyng Border
Nordan Mountains
N
The Three Horizons

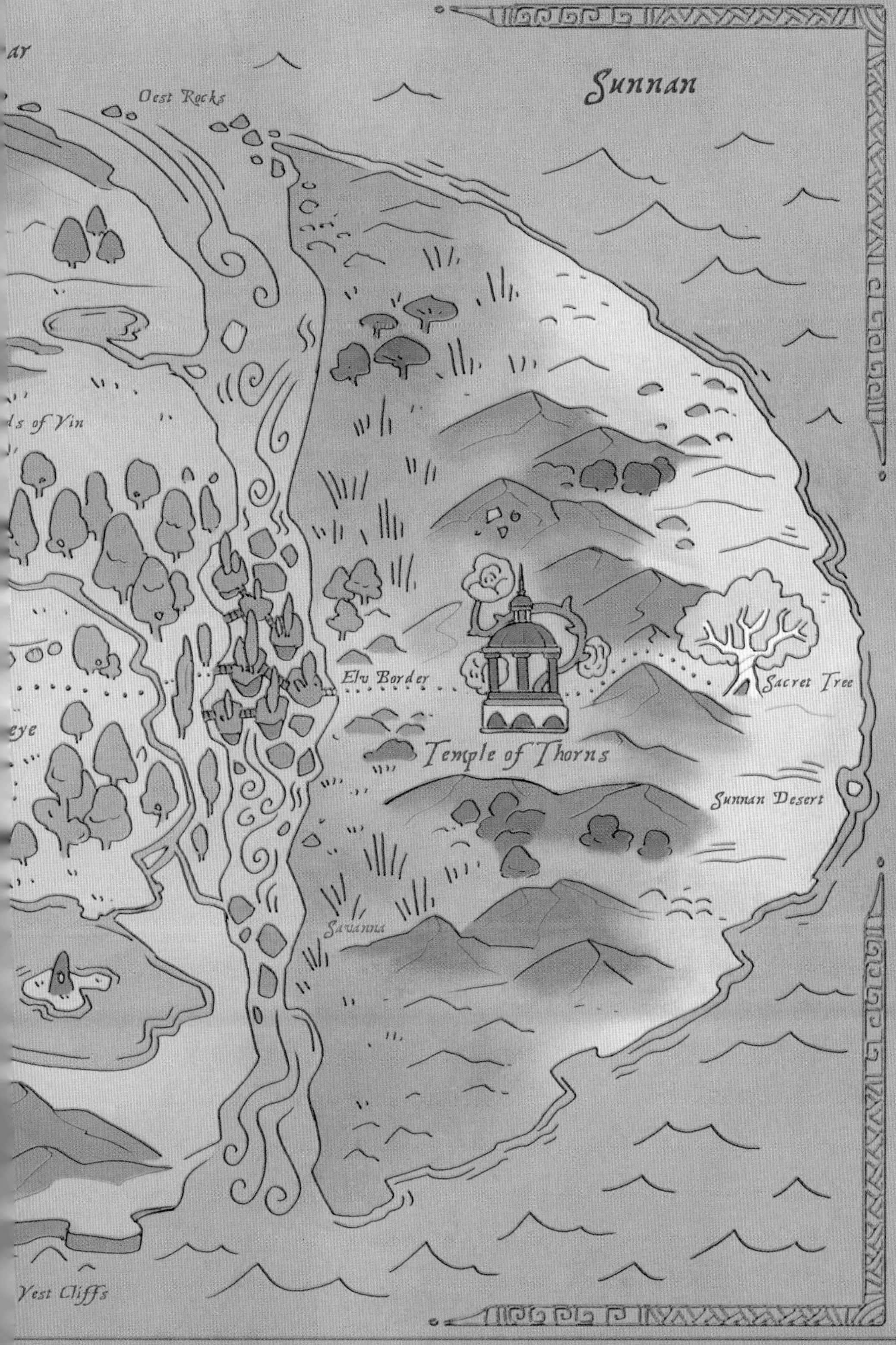

ar
Oest Rocks
Sunnan
ds of Vin
Elv Border
Sacret Tree
eye
Temple of Thorns
Sunnan Desert
Savanna
Vest Cliffs

ABOUT the AUTHOR

Dina Norlund is an artist who likes to dabble in all things creative. Everything from painting, storytelling, sculptures, crafting, or designing, she has probably tried it all at one point. Surprisingly she has managed to focus on one thing for long enough to write, illustrate, and finish a comic project or two. Growing up in the lush forests of Norway, she takes a lot of inspiration from the culture and folklore when writing and illustrating her stories. Currently she spends her days wandering around the forests with her cat, daydreaming about her next magical adventure.